*

THE GOLDEN LIBRARY
NO. 28

THE BRIDE

*

By the same Author

*

ROYAL FLUSH
THE PROUD SERVANT
THE STRANGER PRINCE
MRS. OLIVER CROMWELL
STILL SHE WISHED FOR COMPANY
MADAME FEARS THE DARK
KNOCK FOUR TIMES
NONE SO PRETTY

*

Chatto & Windus

LOUISE HOLLANDINA, PRINCESS PALATINE

*From the painting by Hanneman in the Fürstenhaus
at Herrenhausen*

THE BRIDE

THE STORY OF
LOUISE AND MONTROSE

Margaret Irwin

LONDON
CHATTO & WINDUS
1941

FIRST PUBLISHED : JULY 6, 1939
SECOND IMPRESSION : JANUARY, 1940
THIRD PRINTING : APRIL, 1940
FIRST ISSUED IN THE GOLDEN LIBRARY
MAY, 1941

To

J. R. MONSELL, and to the two others who helped me most in this book, JEAN and PETER KILPATRICK, since they enabled me to go so closely over the ground of the Scottish scene, and of the family history of Sir John Hurry and Neil Macleod.

I should like also to thank Madame Grootenhuis for showing me so much in Holland, and William Roughead, to whose uncomfortably exciting legal histories of famous Scots Trials I owe the grisly figure of the Edinburgh warlock, Major Weir.

THE BRIDE: the story of Louise and Montrose is one of
Margaret Irwin's series of seventeenth-century historical
novels of which the others previously published are:

ROYAL FLUSH: The story of Minette
THE PROUD SERVANT: The story of Montrose
THE STRANGER PRINCE: The story of Rupert of the Rhine

Also by the same Author

STILL SHE WISHED FOR COMPANY
THESE MORTALS
KNOCK FOUR TIMES
FIRE DOWN BELOW
NONE SO PRETTY
MADAME FEARS THE DARK

Foreword

THE BRIDE is one of four books about certain people in the seventeenth century whose lives were linked together. When I began *Royal Flush* I meant it to be a very short book, taking about three months to write. That was nine years ago, and only now, in finishing *The Bride*, have I accomplished what I then began. For Montrose was mentioned in *Royal Flush*, and I grew so much interested in him that his story had to be the theme of my next book, *The Proud Servant*. There followed *The Stranger Prince*, Rupert of the Rhine, who had already met Minette in *Royal Flush* and Montrose in *The Proud Servant*.

Rupert's artist sister, the Princess Louise, who came into *Royal Flush* and *The Stranger Prince*, was betrothed to Montrose (as her sister Sophia of Hanover tells us in her own Memoirs) four years after the death of his wife, Magdalen. I could not bring another woman after Magdalen into *The Proud Servant*, so left it to this book, *The Bride*, to tell the story of that betrothal of Louise and Montrose. It also tells what happened afterwards to many of the people in the three other books, to Rupert, to his mother Elizabeth of Bohemia and his sister Sophia of Hanover, to Charles II, to Minette's husband, Monsieur, to that supreme soldier of fortune, Colonel Sir John Hurry, and others.

All the characters in the four books are historical, and the quotations from letters and documents, except where someone destroys a letter as soon as written, in which case it is necessarily invention! People's own words are used a good deal, especially Sophia's and Hyde's, for they spoke so copiously and characteristically for themselves in their letters, journals and histories that for the most part they had only to do the same when they spoke in this book. Montrose's own words, too, have been used to a great extent, particularly at the end of this book.

Contents

BOOK I

'BEYOND SEAS'

A

I

A FAT man sat writing sadly in a cold room; his purple fingers stiff and clumsy, his swollen feet swathed in flannel, damp-chill in spite of their wrappings, itching to be nearer the fire, yet shrinking from the inevitable torture that the tingling warmth would bring to his poor man's gout.

He wrote 'The Hague. Thursday, at 3 o'clock of the afternoon' at the top of his paper. Though Sir Edward Hyde was an English lawyer, and Chancellor of the Exchequer, without an Exchequer, he was singularly unbusinesslike in the dating of his letters, and since he could not remember what day of the month it was, it was not worth while to put 'January 1649.'

He wrote: 'My Lord; The Prince of Wales has given me a private command to wait upon Your Lordship in any place and at any time you please to appoint. You may believe me very glad of this employment, and to have the opportunity of kissing the hands of a person who has acted so glorious a part in the world.'

Here he blew on his fingers, tried to twiddle his toes, and uttered a sharp groan at the twinge that followed, shivered at the draught from the high closed window, got up to fling another faggot on the fire, which was puffing out more ashes and smoke than heat under the gusts of wind down the chimney, but counted what were left in the basket and reflected he had better not; opened a cupboard instead and brought out a jug of thin ale and a large silver cup which he filled and drank; then decided that the ale was getting flat and he had better finish it off, so filled the cup again and carried it over to his writing-table, then drank, then sighed, then drank again, then thought that if he sold the cup he would be able to buy at least one more cask of tolerably good wine, then remembered that the cup had been a school prize and that his mother had been prouder of him for bringing it home to Dinton than when he began to make a name for himself as a rising young bencher of the Middle Temple.

3

It had been a long time since he had thought of his father's parsonage at Dinton, the cottages there snug as mice burrowing down into the hollow, even the garden walls cosily thatched against the weather; they and the squat little church tower, and the barns built like fortresses of solid stone with slits for windows, had all stayed the same for the past three hundred years or so, and would stay the same for another three hundred years. He might have gone down and seen it again and again in those last few years at the Middle Temple, and he had only done it once. Now that it was impossible, now that he dared not set foot in England and had no notion when he ever could again, he found himself longing with an agonized passion of homesickness, such as he had not felt since his schooldays, that he could go jogging once again down that long Salisbury road over the downs, turn his nag in through the rectory gates, and roll his aching body between the smooth lavender-scented sheets of his own goosefeather bed behind the blue dimity curtains in the little west room; and there he would hear his mother come slowly, carefully up the stairs with a mug of warm ale brewed by herself between her sturdy hands, and the soft white froth of a roasted apple spread like lamb's wool all over the top of it.

So entirely had he become again that tired, happy, home-returning schoolboy, that the tears filled his eyes; he could no longer bear to think of Dinton, or that King Charles was prisoner in England and his son Charles the Prince of Wales an exile here like Hyde himself, as were most of Hyde's friends who had not been killed in the Civil War. Now that war was over, few had cared to remain in England at the cost of compounding with Cromwell's party.

Hyde himself preferred to remain here in such desperate poverty that he and four of his friends now joined together to share their single meal a day, and even the price of that had been owing for months to their kind-hearted hostess. As long as he had bread and books he had all he really wanted, so he said, not quite truthfully. But it was true enough that no money could make him even wish to forsake his loyalty, and that that shrewd brain of his told him even more positively than his heart that his discomfort in these miserable conditions was nothing to what his wretchedness would be if he bettered them at the expense of his conscience.

There is a point at which logic becomes inspiration, and Hyde reached it when he wrote to a weaker friend: 'Think, think! think how little it will mean to you to die the richer by a thousand pounds!'

'To *die* the richer'—there he showed the foresight not merely of the thinker but the seer.

But that was no reason why he should not in all honour and peace of conscience consider what chance there was, or that he could make, to leave this pestilent, squabbling, slandering, mischief-making company of poverty-ridden exiles in this cold northern, perpetually windswept town of The Hague, built up by the positively inhuman industry of its inhabitants, ant-like, beaver-like, out of the very sea.

What a country! Where not even a stone happened of itself; the very soil was sand, and the gravel for the garden paths was nothing but sea-shells, brought from the sea-shore two miles away in carts or barges—always barges, pushing slow and blunt-nosed along the canals, silent and endless as the procession of a dream. A country of wind and water, water all round him, water beneath the house, water in canals above the level of the road, and nothing but a few low sand-dunes in constant need of repair between the whole flat low land and the sea.

No wonder his bones were racked and rotted with rheumatism; no wonder he was sick with longing for the sight of a hill, for the rolling chalk downs round Salisbury and the dimpled valleys purple with cool shadow in the high summer, and the rich red-brown of English earth. A hide of land was the old measurement of terrain in England; never had he been so proud of the origin of his name as now when he had no chance of owning a hide of English land— an outcast, a wanderer, he told himself pitifully, then brisked up, drank again, remembered the many dispossessed landowners who were growing maudlin in exile, and his bracing contempt for them, and thought that though he could not return to England he might yet contrive to go on a mission to some warm and pleasant, natural-growing country such as Spain.

Big oranges, such as the artist fellows here loved to paint on dishes of blue and white porcelain with a curling strip of their ruddy-tawny peel dangling down over the edge of the table, red wine in tall glasses, women with dark eyes gleaming behind their mantillas, now ousted his homesick vision of England for an instant, but were even more quickly dismissed.

The place he had got to think of now was some convenient rendezvous with the Marquis of Montrose.

So, picking up the cup and finding it empty, and cursing it and setting it down, he wrote:

'I shall very greedily wait your summons and attend you accordingly. Only, give me leave to inform Your Lordship, that there is now so great jealousy of a treaty betwixt the Prince of Wales and Your Lordship, and your countrymen are so scattered over all the neighbouring towns'—('these damned Scots' I had all but written, but no I can't say that to him, and he the proudest Scot of the lot)—'that it will not be possible for Your Lordship to be in these parts without discovery; and in this conjuncture the *highest secrecy is absolutely necessary.*'

He scribbled down the names of possible meeting-places, but some-one was coming up the stair, the firm, clanking tread of a boot was coming along the passage (how long was it since he himself had been able to walk as freely as that?) and so he hastened to sign himself, before the interruption of a visitor, as 'Your Lordship's most humble most obedient servant, EDWARD HYDE.'

The door opened, a very tall man bent his head under the lintel, and stood there an instant looking at the dim room, the dull fire, the empty jug, and the little fat man so busily writing. The bleak wind from outside seemed to have blown into the small room, ruffling its dismal yet self-satisfied air; Hyde felt agitated, defensive, as he flung down his pen, heaved himself gingerly on to his feet again, and bowed low to the Lord High Admiral of the Royal British fleet; then squared his shoulders truculently, facing up at that great height as at something beyond his ken.

He saw the dark lean face of a man who had passed his twenty-ninth birthday only a month ago, but who looked as though he had lived through more than twenty-nine, and more winters than summers; a man of great strength and power and still greater courage, who had never sought his own ends, but who in all things expected and took his own way. It was a face that women used to call as beautiful as an angel, but that men were beginning to call saturnine and grim, for it had been scarred deep, not only by resolve and fixed purpose, but by savage anger and pride, and by his remorse for these and for the evil results they had had.

To Hyde, after years of shared struggle and endeavour in the same cause, this Prince was still 'a strange creature'; just as his name with most Englishmen was still Rupert of the Rhine, though he had fought far longer and harder for his uncle King Charles I in England than for his dead father's principality in Germany. Even now that the English Civil War had been over for two and a half years, and he had been summarily dismissed from the country by command of his uncle, yet Rupert had since refused all the honours and wealth offered him as Field-Marshal of France, in order to take over a few leaky, ill-equipped, undermanned ships that had mutinied from the English Parliament; and in the last four months he had built them up, without help or naval advice, and above all without money, into a fleet in the service of an imprisoned King and an exiled Prince of Wales.

Oh, it was admirable, amazing, incredible to any who had not seen it done, and so Hyde freely admitted, in writing, to all his important friends; and that was what gave him this uncomfortable sense of indignation whenever he met him—that Rupert never appreciated (or even perhaps never cared) how much Hyde now appreciated him.

Here he was writing letter after letter to Lord Ormonde in Ireland, with whom Rupert and his ships were to join forces, telling him of 'the extraordinary arts' employed by treacherous and jealous friends as well as foes 'to bring this fleet to nothing,' so that the crews melted away almost as fast as they were got together. That was why it had been decided on all sides, in spite of the prejudices of the 'true English' courtiers, that Prince Rupert of the Rhine was 'the fittest person to undertake so shaken a design,' for no other would or could attempt it.

And Hyde had publicly admitted how the very existence of the fleet, let alone its preservation, was all due to the unwearied industry and dexterity with which Rupert put all things in order when he took charge. 'Seriously,' he had written, very seriously, his plump cheeks puffing out with the effort of his commendation (which never came as easily to him as criticism), 'he has expressed better temper and discretion in it than you can imagine.' *There* was praise for a hot-headed young half-foreigner whose violent temper only a few years ago had offended half the English Court and the King, his uncle, most bitterly of all.

But just because the Prince stood six foot four in his stockings and had the strength of a tiger, would he ever see the value of Hyde's friendship, of his tremendous and balanced intellect—did he indeed ever see him as anything but a fussy, pursy little man?

This appalling question did just flash into the back of the Chancellor's mind but was instantly expelled, for there are some things that no human being can recognize in himself, and though a man may know himself to be a villain, no man has ever yet known himself to be fussy and pursy, even in the eyes of an abrupt and casual young man.

"Your Highness—" he began in polite greeting, but Rupert did not wait for that, though he swung in a hasty "Sit and spare your feet, man," in the same breath that he asked if there had been any fresh report from England. 'From England' meant 'of King Charles,' who had given himself up to the Scots Covenanters, had been sold by them to Cromwell's English army, and had been since then their prisoner.

No, Hyde had had no news since they had heard that the King had been removed from Carisbrooke Castle in the Isle of Wight to Hurst Castle on the mainland, 'a gloomier prison and unhealthy— the guard changed all the time for sick leave. And they say he is being far more closely guarded there.'

There might be good, or rather bad, reason for that, as Rupert knew better than Hyde. He had had a message from King Charles at the end of this autumn, of such urgent secrecy that the King dared not trust it to paper: not even Hyde nor any of the Privy Council were to be told of it, nor yet his own son Charles the Prince of Wales, unless Rupert thought fit—a proof of such complete trust in his nephew as might well have won the war for him, had he only given it earlier.

His message to Rupert had asked him to send a ship to wait off the coast of the Isle of Wight on a certain night when the King had planned an escape from his prison. Rupert could not go himself, for the ship was bound to be searched and examined, and his presence on board so near his uncle's prison would rouse suspicion. So he had sent the wisest of his captains, who actually managed to stay five or six days on the excuse that he lay to all that time while waiting for a wind, but at last was allowed to stay no longer and had to come away.

What had happened inside the Castle of Carisbrooke that night late in November when King Charles should have escaped? His attempt must have been discovered, since he had been moved to the closer guard of Hurst Castle. And a horrible further fear now haunted Rupert—was the whole plot of the escape a plot of the enemy's, a 'draw,' arranged through an agent provocateur, that Charles himself might wind the noose tighter about his throat?

He still dared not speak of his fears and conjectures, he said only as he marched restlessly up and down, "I don't like this calm in the news. *Something* should have happened by now," then plunged into

what he himself had been doing. His ships were still at Helvoetsluys; he had hurried from there first to Rotterdam, where he had
paused for the night to arrange the sale of one of his ships to help fit
out the rest. "Those brass guns on the *Roebuck* will fetch as high a
price as all the tackling of her sails and anchors put together."

"But Your Highness has no first-rate ships, and the *Roebuck* is
your finest of the second-rate."

"She *was*."

"That collier you captured from the Yarmouth roads with £800
on board——"

"A month ago, and all the bills of the previous months to pay.
How far do you think £800 goes among three ships of the second
rating, four frigates, and a couple of pinnaces?"

"I am not accusing Your Highness of extravagance," began
Hyde stiffly.

"Nor I you of bad mathematics. I am wondering how pirates
make it pay—I can't. So I have to sell the *Roebuck*. I have got a
Dutch merchant coming here, willing to buy, but these Dutch are
slow as death; if I wait to finish the bargain I'll find the whole fleet
melted away by the time I get back to Helvoetsluys."

"Is Your Highness still having trouble——?"

"There's not enough pay nor food for them, and though their
fleet's left, the Parliament agents are at 'em night and day bribing
them to desert or mutiny or damage their own ships. They've
rotted in harbour all the winter, and if I don't get 'em to sea quickly
and over to Ireland, why, then there'll be none left to get there. So
will you finish this deal for me, in two days if you can?"

"I, Your Highness? But I know nothing of the rigging of
ships."

"You'll learn," said Rupert simply. "I knew nothing of it
myself four months ago."

"You learned to con your own flagship in less than a week, I've
heard. You must have pity on us born landlubbers."

"Born landlubbers be damned! If they've got to have a bowlegged old trooper like me for admiral, surely the Chancellor of the Exchequer can be ship's chandler?"

"Well, well," observed Hyde more indulgently, "I suppose even a statesman may 'suffer a sea change.'"

"He *must*—now the royal cause is all at sea."

Hyde chuckled, but discreetly. Even in making a mild joke, His Highness' expression was not encouraging; it was, in fact, at this moment intent to the point of ferocity. He was staring at the table, at Montrose's letter. From where he stood he could not read a word of it, but no doubt he recognized the handwriting, for he shot out:

"When is Montrose coming here?"

"He is not. We daren't risk it. The Hague is full of his enemies."

"You might trust him to look after himself."

"The danger is to the cause as much as himself. Since the Scots lords are here who have changed sides and fought for the King last summer——"

"——they are to be valued more, I suppose, than those who have always fought for him, instead of against him. Is that what you are telling him?"

Hyde's round eyes and ruffled air made him look like an owl.

"On the contrary, I am writing on behalf of the Prince of Wales to entreat his help. As I've told Prince Charles myself, Montrose is the clearest spirit of all his servants. And he is very impatient to be up and doing."

"He can't do much if you tell him to go on kicking his heels at Brussels," muttered Rupert, but before Hyde's indignation could swell up to bursting-point he went on, "He has been writing to me. He hopes to raise Scotland again for the King, and this time in conjunction with Ormonde and myself in Ireland, with my ships to bring over fresh troops from there. It might be done—what do you think?"

The question, flung suddenly over his shoulder as Rupert walked restlessly up and down, surprised and mollified Hyde into a most polite answer. "To me, the only prospect that has any light or pleasure in it is that of Ireland, and Your Highness' fleet." He paused, but as Rupert did not even bow his acknowledgments he transferred his compliments to Rupert's ally. "Ormonde is the best Lord Lieutenant we could have in Ireland—if he can unite the country for the King and combine with Scotland——"

"It needs close co-operation—not easy to work out at a distance——" Rupert flung himself into a chair which squawked out a sharp creak in protest.

"Is *all* your furniture broken?" he demanded as he sprang up again and pulled out the leg which had cracked in its socket.

"It soon will be, sir, if that is how you treat it."

"I? I'm treating it like a doctor."

To Hyde's amazement he had begun to mend it with a splinter of broken wood for splicing, the rusty nail he had extracted, and the heavy bronze paperweight on the writing-table for hammer, sitting on the edge of the table and working with remarkable neatness and quickness as he talked.

"Young Charles hopes to go to Ireland with me later. It might be a good plan."

"To have the Prince of Wales with you would certainly help the scheme. Your Highness, I beg you not to trouble with that chair——"

"No trouble. It's all but done. It's something to have got him away from his mother in Paris. That woman has the morals of Machiavelli without the brains."

The Chancellor's eyes looked as if they would pop out of his head at Rupert's opinion of Queen Henrietta Maria. For an instant he seemed about to share it, but swerved to matters less dangerous. "Prince Charles' friends here do him no good. They are rotting under the continued disaster, the enforced idleness that they, and he, have to bear."

"Charles bears that last pretty well," said Rupert with a chuckle, giving his final blow to the chair and running his hand over the joint to make sure that it was sound.

"As all his friends bear it. They are always hopeful of the future, not to say certain. They drink to it in company with every whore and blackguard in The Hague, they bet on it, roar out tipsy songs in honour of it, keep despair at bay by deafening it—but they can't banish it. Misfortune is not ennobling in itself, and it is a very hard thing for people who have nothing to do, to keep from doing something they ought not to do."

Rupert smiled at the portentous utterance.

"So you want me to take the Prince to Ireland to keep him out of mischief. At eighteen that is found anywhere and is not serious."

"It is serious, sir, when it might endanger the succession. A young woman of no character is already claiming here that when her bastard by Prince Charles is born it will be his legitimate heir."

"Shall I kidnap her, then, instead of him and drop her over-board?" He swung the chair round in his hand to the floor and tried sitting on it, but this time more carefully. "This plan of Montrose," he said, "I must see him about it before we sail. Since he can't come here, I shall go to him."

"Your Highness, I beg of you, consider. If you do this, you give everything away to his enemies, you show them that he is in our councils, you frighten them away just as they are coming round entirely to our side. Lauderdale and Lanark——"

"That red swine and his shadow! Look how they bungled their campaign in Scotland last summer. *Their* service won't help us."

"Their money and influence in Scotland will. We can use it to help Montrose himself if we go about it carefully. I shall go into the whole matter with him with entire frankness——"

"Letters, letters, letters," muttered Rupert, glancing dubiously at the papers that littered the table, as though in disbelief of their ever being read.

"*No*, sir. *I* am going to him in person to Sevenbergen or some such place that will be free of the other Scots. This letter I am writing even now is to the Lord Montrose to ask him to appoint whatever time and place he thinks fit."

"But your foot, man, you've not got it into a boot for over a year!"

"Nor had a boot to get it into," Hyde answered with a wry smile; "but Harry Jermyn's sent me the price of a pair from Paris, and if I get them large enough to fit Gargantua's foot, or Lauderdale's head, I shall manage well enough on a quiet old nag."

That rigid mouth of the Prince, shutting his face into its stern lines, relaxed into a friendly and admiring grin. The sympathy aroused by gout in the ungouty is usually small enough, yet Rupert could not but recognize an indomitable spirit in this stout little man with feet swaddled like babies and as tender. God! What a hideous infirmity to be unable to ride and stride at large over the springy earth!

He exaggerated, for Hyde had never much cared about riding and striding even in those days when he had come home for the holidays; even then those firm fat fingers, with the bulging round forehead hanging over them as they wrote, had been his best minister. A table, pen and paper, and the light on his left-hand side, that was Hyde's field of action, but Rupert, not recognizing that it lay before him, started up from it, pushed back his chair and swung round to the high window that ran all along the top of the wall, and there looked out over low gabled roofs and flat fields beyond them, to a huge moving sky that swept forward like an advancing army of grey banners.

Seagulls were tumbling against those torn clouds like scraps of blown paper; a scrubby thornbush was tossing and stretching before the bitter wind; the windmills, three, four, five, were turning full tilt; and the straight line of water in the near canal, instead of showing a stripe of clear mirror, was dark and ruffled like broken iron. Here was the breeze he had been longing for these past weeks, an easterly gale to take his ships westward through the English Channel to Ireland.

If he did, he would miss seeing Montrose. But how much would that really affect matters? Hyde here was a sound fellow for all his pomposity, he'd see to it that Montrose had a fair field.

He burst out laughing. "Look at that hat!" he exclaimed, oblivious of the fact that only he could have looked at anything out of that window, which was placed above the height of an ordinary man. A high-crowned steeple hat, blowing along the path below in leaps and sudden pauses for reflection, was giving great sport to two or three little boys who were chasing it with whoops and yells of excitement. Its stout owner, a gentleman of some consequence, for he walked attended by a couple of servants who were now chasing the boys who were chasing the hat, was being blown along in its wake like a ship in full sail, his voluminous cloak bellying out in front of him and masses of shaggy red hair flying past his face like a tattered tawny flag.

Rupert's laugh broke sharply into a curse; he flung round from the window, saying, "Lauderdale's in the street. If he's coming here, I'm off. Hyde, I'll come with you to Sevenbergen. It's a risk to leave the fleet for even that much time, but it may be a worse risk not to meet Montrose—the mere sight of that swine below has told me so. Come, shall we go together, or shall I be your ambassador and leave the price of those boots to pay for a keg of wine?"

He had noticed the empty cup. Hyde knew he would. There was nothing escaped him. Not that there was anything to be ashamed of in a cup emptied of thin ale. Because the Prince had shown an inhuman abstinence ever since he had taken over the fleet, that was no reason why he should make everyone else feel like a sot.

Rupert would have quite agreed. His chaff of Hyde had been intended in all good humour, but he had not allowed either for Hyde's touchy sense of his moral integrity or for his own increasingly sardonic countenance. A joke was apt to sound grim from him these latter years.

"If Your Highness imagines—" began Hyde slowly, in a voice so stuffed with injury that it was scarcely audible—and then in sudden irritable inconsequence, "Do I get any pleasure here, is it self-indulgence to stay in this poor lodging? Once I could hear you'd got your ships safely to Ireland I'd get out of this crowd."

"Devil you would! And where would you get to?"

Hyde did not like to say 'Spain,' for that plan was not nearly far enough matured. He hurled out petulantly, "I never lived any part of my life with less satisfaction to myself!"

"And which of us is getting satisfaction I'd like to know? Come, man, all authors go gloomy over their cups and think they're the only ones that suffered in the war. At least you'll be able to write your book about it."

"Which reminds me—I have already asked you to——"

"Well, you can't again, for there's the door banging below, and Lauderdale's upon us. Shall I go with you or without you to Montrose?"

"Not a word of that, I beg—don't say his name even—it may have the most disastrous consequences—Your Highness, *remember*——" was all that Hyde could finish in agonized entreaty as the door rattled open, and since the street door below had not yet shut, the Earl of Lauderdale most literally blew into the room.

II

EVEN the gust of air that blew in the Earl of Lauderdale was different from the sea-wind that had seemed to usher in the Prince. The exhalations of his recent dinner attended this man with the gross face and matted red hair. He breathed stuffed pork and brandy as strongly as he did fulsomeness to Rupert and friendliness to Hyde and eloquence directed mainly at the image he always held before him of himself.

For the Earl of Lauderdale had a reputation to keep up both as a wag and a scholar; in compensation for his uncouth looks and messy habits he felt that he resembled his late Sovereign, King James VI of Scotland and I of England, who had also been uncouth and messy and ate and drank far too much and none too pleasantly, but was a glutton for learning as well as dainties, could wield a pretty pen on any and every subject from tobacco-smoking to witch-craft, and theology to classic fable, and talked as much and with as shrewd and pawky a wit as Lauderdale fancied in himself.

He was only approaching his middle thirties, but debauchery, richly mixed with pedantry and assurance, had made him a much older man. He believed himself, not quite truly, to be as much at his ease in a foreign Court as in the warm ale-breathing reek of the 'Black Bull' in his little town of Lauder, not far from Edinburgh, where he liked to drop in from the seclusion of his castle, cloistered in deep woods, for the casual company of the farmers and travelling merchants who sat spellbound by the learned allusions, the gusto and coarseness of the great lord's conversation.

Lauderdale and his kinsman Lord Lanark were here at The Hague in the same position, on the face of it, as all the Royalist exiles, for they had been banished from Scotland by the Marquis of Argyll, who was Chief Elder of the Kirk and head of the Scottish Government. They had held by him all through the war and fought against the King and Montrose, the King's Lieutenant in

Scotland; but once Argyll was firmly settled in power, they had found his tyranny and that of the Kirk more than they had bargained for. So they called themselves the Moderates as opposed to the extreme Covenanters, and last summer had joined in a rising of both Scots and English, whose main object was to free the King. Cromwell's army had at once squashed it, and all the leaders who had been captured were either shot out of hand by a firing-squad or were now in the Tower awaiting trial for high treason, Lanark's elder brother the Duke of Hamilton among them.

To hear Lauderdale talk, one would have thought this belated loyalty of his in the last few months had been the breath of his nostrils from babyhood; but then loyalty seemed a habit with him, and a complicated one, for he was also passionately loyal to the Solemn League and Covenant ordained by the Kirk—and there were those who said that he had by no means forgone his loyalty to the Chief Elder of that Kirk, the Marquis of Argyll, and that for all he was at present under sentence by him, he had a very good understanding with him and even kept up a secret correspondence.

His punishment, they said, had been mainly a gesture of Argyll's to impress Cromwell, for there was a close alliance between the two dictators. Cromwell had come up to Scotland last autumn after crushing the rising; he had stayed in Edinburgh, dined constantly with Argyll, and held long private conclaves with him in Moray House. Cromwell had pronounced the Lords of the Covenant to be 'Christians and men of honour'; the ministers were not so polite about Cromwell, they disliked his capacity for weeping on all occasions ('And still he sat and still he grat') and called him 'a great liar and a greeting devil.' Lauderdale had heard of this last and told it with delight at The Hague; you couldn't deceive a Scots minister, he said, bubbling and blowing his laughter.

He was bubbling now, but more solemnly and confusedly, slightly taken aback at finding Prince Rupert here, but determined not to show it. He had already given his opinion of the Prince, and it was a high one; report said that the Prince's opinion of Lauderdale was not so high, but Lauderdale was not going to make himself uncomfortable by enquiring what it was. Prince Rupert had more influence over his young cousin, Charles the Prince of Wales, than any other man—that was the thing to remember; and what was more, he had built up a sound working fleet, which Lauderdale had already tried to commandeer for Scotland, until the sailors expressed their strong desire to throw him and his Covenant overboard together—but Lauderdale was not the man to remind himself of that.

"Your Highness! this is chance indeed! 'Think of the Devil' I had all but said, calling to mind Your Highness' most famous nickname and most justly earned towards your enemies, for I had been thinking of you this moment, coming here, big with news as I am, news that concerns us all, glorious news, if we prepare to meet it rightly."

"Let me be your midwife, my lord, and deliver your news."

But Lauderdale was not to be hurried, even by Prince Rupert. He laid a finger to his bulbous nose and demanded archly, "What does Virgil say?"

Rupert had no notion what Virgil said.

"'Inconsulti abeunt sedemque odere Sibyllae,'" replied Lauderdale, noting with satisfaction that, though Hyde at once recognized the tag, it was lost on Rupert, a mere illiterate soldier of fortune for all he was a prince, who had refused to learn Greek or any more Latin than what he might find useful in international parleys.

"'They go off,'" he translated, "'without waiting for counsel, hating the abode of the Sibyl.' Let that not be said of us. In this case the Sibyl is Caledonia, my unhappy country, Scotland. Finding you here together, the mailed fist with the arm of the law, I must snatch my chance to ensure that my country shall not be delivered into the hands of her unnatural enemies. I have heard a lying rumour—for I am sure both the Prince here and the Chancellor will give it the lie—that the Prince of Wales, led away by his youth and mistaken counsel, has entered into negotiations with that traitor, that monster of cruelty, that devourer of his own country, the Marquis of Montrose."

He stopped out of breath and drew his sleeve across his forehead like a ploughboy mopping his face. Hyde was ruffling his feathers, preparing a properly legal retort to the charge that should combine caution with rebuke, when Rupert struck in coolly:

"What's your news?"

It was Lauderdale's turn to ruffle now, but under the Prince's eye he abandoned the attempt to return to his charge, and gave out as reluctantly as a traveller handing his purse to a highwayman: "The Parliament have signed a treaty with His Most Sacred Majesty, King Charles. Both the Houses are agreed, and they are bringing him to London. The city is preparing an array for him."

Hyde's judicial bearing was actually shaken into a yap of excitement. He covered it by asking Lauderdale his authority, which proved to be a responsible Dutch merchant come direct from London. But it was plain that Hyde had swallowed the good news whole, as starving men do with their first dainty for weeks; he repeated, "A treaty! Both Houses! And the City preparing an array! *Now* we shall see!"

He turned, glowing and rubbing his hands, to Prince Rupert, then checked, amazed by the expression on the young man's face.

A Frenchman had said that Rupert in his black moods could look like a soul in hell. And now, on hearing this good news of his beloved uncle, there was such concentrated pain and ferocity in his face as made Hyde shrink from him. Rupert saw him do so, and pulled himself together.

"What sort of an array?" he asked.

"Why, what array could it be but a loyal triumph?" Hyde replied.

Rupert could not explain to himself the fear that had fallen on him at sound of the apparently simple words; nor why, when he

had pictured the London crowds mustered in the streets to see King
Charles go by, he had imagined them, not as a cheering mob, but
all standing in a deathly silence.

He did not dismiss that queer cold fancy from his mind, for he
had learned that such fancies had generally some origin in reason,
and was now seeking it.

"What use is a treaty with Parliament?" he said.

This was too much for Hyde. "Is Your Highness mad? The
King has made peace with his Parliament with whom he has been at
war and who hold him prisoner, and you say, 'What use is a treaty?'
Is it of no use that he is now in agreement with the representatives
of his people—that the people themselves are preparing a loyal
triumph for him?"

"None whatever," replied Rupert imperturbably. "The Parliament does not represent the people. If it did, there would be some
Royalists in it, and no Royalist has been allowed in Parliament for
years. But it makes no odds, for the people, whether inside or
outside Parliament, do not count any longer. The King is not
the Parliament's prisoner, but Cromwell's. If Parliament show
itself friendlier to the King than Cromwell approves, so much the
worse for it—and for the King."

Lauderdale was goggling at him like an over-fed spaniel.

"Cromwell," he said, "has betrayed the Church of God, even
the most holy and Solemn League and Covenant and the Kirk of
Scotland which the Parliament promised us should be made the
Church of England. Only for that, for the sake of God's holy
Kirk, did we ever ally ourselves to the English Parliament—but
Cromwell took promises for piecrusts, the lying, cheating grazier—
brewer—a sweating tradesman—so rich in the possession of dirt
that he passes himself off as a country gentleman——"

The words fell thickly out of his loose mouth, the abuse dropped
to a bar-and-brothel quality unusual on behalf of a holy cause.

"Ah well," said Rupert, "you can't have it both ways—church as
well as cash. You got your pay when you sold the King to the

English army two years ago. How much did you pocket out of it yourself? I hear your friend Argyll got £30,000."

Hyde heard the short contemptuous voice hurling the words like stones from a sling across the table. Now it was all up. Now there would be no more hope of attaching Lauderdale and the rest of the Moderate Covenanters to their side.

Montrose himself, whom all these Covenanters hated with the venom of a defeated enemy since he had triumphed over their armies in Scotland, could not have done more damage. What could Hyde do now? His brain refused to work, his tongue to move; there was only one thing which might have passed it off, and that was to ply Lauderdale with brandy so fast and so deep that in the ensuing stupor he would forget all about the insult. But he had no brandy, only some thin ale—which now he remembered he had drunk. In miserable certainty he raised his eyes to the probably apoplectic nobleman, and caught him in the act of winking at the Prince.

"Ah, wouldn't Your Highness like to know?" he said. "Well, all men have their price—the thing is to put it high enough. Little Warriston now, that holy man of God, he fetched away £3000 out of the pickings—not bad for the scrubby lawyer's clerk he was a few years ago."

An astoundingly impudent rascal and hypocrite? Hyde wondered. No, it was not so simple. The man had had the ring of the fanatic in his voice when he spoke of the Kirk a minute ago, and now he was once again the gross cynic, careless even of his uncouth appearance since he was so sure of himself as the bluff man of the world. Not even Rupert's cold scorn staring him in the face could shake his confidence. One might as easily shake a hippopotamus.

"Good God!" Rupert was murmuring in a kind of awe. "And my sailors wanted to throw you overboard! I wonder what prevented it?"

"What's that?" asked Lauderdale cheerfully, for he was sometimes a little deaf when it was convenient, and had half closed his eyes with the smile still firmly printed on his mouth to prevent it from wincing. "A great work that of Your Highness in pulling the fleet together. To be soldier and sailor too—admirable; quite an Admirable Crichton, as we say at Saint Andrews—or should I say an Admiral Crichton, ha ha? I'm no sailor myself, mighty sick I got of wagging on the waves."

"You'd have got sicker of wagging in them," continued Rupert with the same quiet abstraction, unable to leave this game of seeing how many insults Lauderdale could swallow.

To Hyde's intense relief, though that proved sadly fleeting, his servant was knocking his apologetic tap on the door, edging his shock of hair round it. But his words brought the angry blood rushing back into his master's head.

"The Princess Louise is below, sir, and asking for Prince Rupert."

Lauderdale's bonhomie at once blew up to twice its former size. The Princess Louise, one of Rupert's younger sisters, was a mad, unbiddable girl, so Lauderdale had heard already from the sober Dutch citizens here; she was the wildest daughter in that huge family of King Charles' sister, the Queen of Bohemia, exiled now for so many years at The Hague—just as Rupert the Devil had been the wildest, most intractable and unaccountable of all her sons. 'And *that's* saying a deal,' they had assured Lauderdale solemnly over their pipes and mugs, 'for his brother Maurice was locked up here more than once as a boy for his roisterings, and Wilful Ned, as even his own family call him, carried off a fine French madam and married her against the Queen of France's consent, and Philip the youngest, a lad of eighteen, killed a man in the public street here for paying too much court to his mother and sister Louise, and indeed the only one that gives no trouble is the eldest, Carl, a decent body that's come into his own at last by sitting quiet and waiting for it, and so now he's gone back to his father's home at Heidelberg. Ah, he's the only one that's prospered or ever will prosper, I say.'

And Lauderdale had goggled agreement and was now goggling in double delight to get proof with his own eyes of the wildness and degradation of this royal family on the female side. The Princess Louise was an artist, she studied with the portrait-painter Gerard Honthorst, she painted pictures herself, she even sold them—that showed what like she was; and now here she was, running through the streets unattended and coming headlong up the stairs into whatever company her brother might be keeping.

For the Princess had not stayed below, she almost at once appeared behind the servant, so quietly and swiftly overtaking him that he stepped back as he finished speaking, gaping up at her; she surely must have flown up the stairs, her shabby red cloak spreading out from her slight form like a sail in the wind of her speed.

Its hood fell back, her face shone out, a delicate pointed face, brilliant in the flush of the cold air outside, a sudden face, its eager impulse now shot through with a flash of laughter at sight of the three men and their surprise. She did not look the sort of princess one would meet at a State banquet complete with full quota of jewels and feathers and fixed mechanic smile, she was more like a princess in a fairy-tale disguised as the woodcutter's daughter in that old cloak.

It was certainly not Lauderdale's instantly awakened sensuality that conceived this romantic image of her, nor Hyde's stout loyalty shocked to the core, nor Rupert's rather determined indifference to the fact that the sister he liked best should behave in a way no one else's sisters behaved; yet it hovered somewhere in the air, affecting all three of them, although her words, quickly uttered, were as practical as any message brought by a subordinate officer.

"Your pardon, gentlemen. Rupert, you must get back to Helvoetsluys on the instant. Maurice has sent a messenger. There's mutiny broken out on the ships."

"Which?"

"He said no more than that."

Rupert looked at Hyde. There was the end of his plan just now to go to Montrose.

"Then I must go," he said, "and get them to sea at once,—how, I don't know, till I get the money from Rotterdam, and even that will only pay for their rigging."

"Mother has a plan," said Louise softly. Her tone was low, not from discretion but absorption; she was looking at Lauderdale, and under her soft gaze that bullfrog bonhomie of his seemed to reach the bursting-point in the fable.

A fine spirited filly this, though too thin—he liked them fat himself. He showed plainly that he thought he had fascinated the charming though eccentric Princess, and so he had. Rupert saw what Louey was doing—little devil, she was drawing him in her mind, committing every grotesque feature of his huge shaggy head to memory, while Lauderdale wagged it and all but winked and made jovial insolent allusions to her courage in trusting so much beauty to run alone through the streets of The Hague.

"Ah, but the Dutch are not as gallant as you Scots," said Louise sweetly. "If they were, do you think my three sisters and I would have been left to sit and spin alone all this time?"

Rupert gave a harsh laugh.

"The Scots won't be as tolerant as the Dutch of your teasing," he said; "they're a nation that take things seriously."

"Especially princesses," said Lauderdale, "but I never had a chance to take one yet."

Now, thought Hyde, the Prince would surely demolish him, though indeed the Princess had brought it on herself. But there she kept it, for she laughed at Lauderdale and casually wished him good luck, said good-bye to Hyde, and went out instantly with her brother, to leave Lauderdale gloating and Hyde silently deploring the low manners and possibly morals learned in Dutch studios by modern young women. His mother had never left nor wished to leave their remote little country home at Dinton for more than thirty years. What was the world coming to?

He suddenly jerked his body out of his chair, padded hastily to the door, tore it open and called in agonized tones, "Your High-

ness—hi! hi there! Boy, stop them, have they gone——? Christ
in Heaven, how will I ever get at him!"

But the boy had caught them just as they were closing the house
door behind them.

"What in hell——?" demanded Rupert, turning and calling up
the stair, the wind tearing in after him and rattling all the furniture.

A puffy tufty face was hanging over the banister, eyebrows and
peaked beard bristling with anxious intensity.

"I beg you, sir, when once you are gone to sea to remember that
which I have asked before of you—to write down all the details
you can remember of the most important actions of the war in
England. They will be helpful, even essential, for when I shall
have leisure again to proceed in my unequal task."

"*What* task?" Rupert was already swinging round again. Hyde
could not believe he had forgotten—why, he had mentioned it
himself just now!

"My History of the Great Rebellion," he roared furiously, and
the wind called back derisively, "Tu whoop—ooo!"

The door slammed again. With their heads down and their
cloaks wrapped tight about them, Rupert and Louise had gone out
into the wind to push their way against it through mean little
streets with absurd names, the Street of the Green Lamb, of the
Raining House, towards their mother's house at the four-way
crossing of the Voorhout.

Rupert growled, "If he thinks I've got nothing better to do
than write down what happened at Edgehill and Naseby——"

"You had better, or in revenge he'll write badly of you or not
at all."

"So it's the first duty of a general to write himself up?"

"Oh yes. Lord Newcastle is even now busy priming his wife
as to what to write about him after he's dead. They all do."

"Well, you're wrong, for there's one who's had a book written
about him by the chaplain of a Scots regiment, and I can tell you
he's written it *con amore.*"

"Who is that?"

"Wishart, and his *Deeds of Montrose*. He saw something of his campaigns as Montrose's chaplain in Scotland."

"Oh, but I know about that—the 'Annus Mirabilis'—it ran through four editions in the Latin in one year, and now there's the translation, but every time I ask for it it is just sold out. Rupert, there is Jan Bardaens' little shop at the corner! If he has one, you shall give it me as your parting present."

"I've no time and no money, and I never intended to give you a parting present."

But Louey had run on full tilt, snatched the bookseller out of his little dark shop, and was already waving a small brown leather volume as Rupert caught her up.

"Here it is! He has it all ready for me this time. Where are your florins? How many, Mynheer? Now you need not send me anything from Ireland, Rupert."

"There's nothing there to send but whisky."

They hurried round the corner; he scarcely paused in his stride to toss the required florins to Mynheer Bardaens, whose round eyes opened indignantly at such abruptness, even from a prince, to a free burgher and, what was more, a scholar. But it was no good looking his thoughts at the Prince's back, just as it had been no good speaking to the Princess. The pair of them had already whisked round the corner and were now going out at the end of the street by the old Spanish prison.

Their Dutch cousins' palace of the Binnenhof rose to the right before them, carved out of a thunder-cloud in the bleak light of the easterly wind; they had seen it ever since they could remember, and generally double, all the walls and towers standing on their heads in the oblong lake on its south side. But now all that reflected image was broken up into turbulent dark ripples; the tiny bush-grown island in the middle of it had suddenly come alive in such a fury of blown bare branches that it was impossible to believe the storks that nested there each spring would ever find a calm enough resting-place in it again; the fine avenues of bare trees all along the walled bank opposite the Palace were transformed to angry skeletons, tossing and cracking their dry bones together.

"Listen to them!" cried Louey, "they are shouting to you of the sea."

They had turned to their left, in at the gates of their mother's house at the end of the Voorhout. Its main gables were pricked aloft like cats' ears into the stormy sky; the wind was racing round the courtyard like a trapped thing trying to get out, it tossed up whirlpools of dust and twigs and last year's leaves; it came from the east, from Poland and those icy mountain barriers of their father's kingdom of Bohemia that Louey had never seen and Rupert could not remember. The wind would take Rupert west to Ireland. She wished that it would take her too.

They were going up the steps into the house and as he went he was calling to his men to saddle the horses. They were going into the house together; in a few minutes he would come out alone and ride to Helvoetsluys to sail for Ireland, while she stayed here. But she held the little brown book in her hands, a talisman of adventure.

As Rupert halted, giving directions about Grey Day's harness—something about the saddle, and "Tighten that girth, the stirrup wants more length"—short words shooting through the keen, boisterous air, she opened the book, peered close at the first page and gave a little cry.

"There's no frontispiece. The picture of him has been torn out."

"Then old Bardaens cheated you."

"No. He was trying to tell me, I think, but we couldn't wait. It's always happening. People look at his books and steal the pictures—particularly *that* one. I've never seen Montrose's portrait yet."

"Draw it yourself then, one of your imaginary portraits, and see how near it is to the truth when he comes to The Hague."

"Is he coming?"

"If Lauderdale's faction don't prevent it.   That fellow's like a mad bull at the mention of him."

"Then he's an illogical fool.   How can they blame Montrose for having fought for his King, when they now propose to fight for him themselves?"

"Beaten men aren't logical.   And Montrose beat 'em."   He swore softly, going up the steps into the house.   Louey dared not ask more, but suddenly, striding along the passage, he told her, "I'd have gone to see him, I told Hyde so just now—but now that's all changed."

And it was she who had changed it, with this news of mutiny on his ships, news that she herself had hurried to take to him.   She could not have helped it, no one could have helped it.   Was it Montrose's fate that it should have happened at just this very moment to prevent the meeting with Rupert that Montrose had been urging for months past?   His fate?—or Rupert's?—perhaps even hers?

Here they were going along the passage to their mother's room in the house that she had lived in all her life; and a thing had just happened, fallen into all their lives like a stone falling into the canal that joined the river that joined the sea, breaking up the calm reflections of peaceful homes mirrored in the water, the ripples from it spreading out and out, reaching beyond where anyone could see.

III

THE plan of Rupert's mother, Elizabeth, the exiled Queen of Bohemia, was that she should pawn the jewels that had belonged to her grandmother, Mary Queen of Scots. She had not seen her brother, King Charles of England, since she was sixteen and he twelve, but he had helped her all he could through her stormy disastrous life, had sent money he could ill spare to try to win back the lost territories of her German husband, on whose death he had begged her to come and live with him in England, had had her sons to stay at his Court, the finest then in Europe, and wanted to give them whole colonies to govern when most royal uncles would have thought a stud of horses sufficient.

Now that he in his turn had had to fight for his throne and was a prisoner in the hands of his enemies, it was a matter of course to her that she should in her turn do what she could to help that well-loved, ill-remembered brother. So she had already sounded a pawnbroker as to the sum she could raise on the jewels, and even managed to get a considerable part of it paid in advance so that Rupert should have the cash ready to take with him to Helvoetsluys and the fleet he had raised for King Charles. She was now in high glee at her success, for nothing could daunt her spirits, not even the sordid transaction of her most treasured possessions; you would have thought it was for sheer delight in their beauty that she now sat counting them over with the help of her niece and especial favourite, Mary.

Mary was a slight girl of seventeen with a proud, rather plaintive mouth and the eyes of a gazelle—or, alternatively, of her father, King Charles. She was his eldest daughter and never forgot it, nor did anyone else, even the Dutch, for she was still called the Princess Royal though she had left England as a child to come to Holland to be the bride of the young Prince William of Orange. That had been seven years ago, but she had never got over her homesickness for England and that noisy crowd of brothers and sisters

30

and her vivid little mother and above all her adorably tender father.

As they now sat talking of him with those jewels in their hands, Elizabeth thought of the shy delicate little boy who had stood beside her, speaking very little because of his stammer, while they watched the fireworks over the Thames at her merry wedding festivities nearly thirty-seven years ago; while Mary remembered the quiet man with the pointed reddish-brown beard she had loved to stroke, it was so soft and silky, who had ridden up and down on the Dover cliffs for hours after her ship had put out to sea for Holland, that he might take his last view of her.

His *last* view? No, she should not have said that, even to herself. It was ill-omened, it was untrue,—she knew she must see her father again, for she had never loved anyone since then as much as she loved him.

But next to him she now loved her aunt, this glorious woman whose beauty was still as exuberant as her spirits, who had been the 'Winter Queen' of Bohemia for only one brief year but had been 'Queen of Hearts' ever since to the tens of thousands that had come from all countries to fight for her. The Palace of the Binnenhof was less than ten minutes' walk from her pleasant house among the lime trees at the end of the Voorhout, and Mary spent so much time in the latter that her mother-in-law, the Dowager Princess Amelia of Orange, was apt to be painfully sarcastic about it.

It was a sad fact of nature that, much as Mary loved her aunt and her father, she thought far more about her mother-in-law whom she detested. Her pensive and tearful mood at present as she sat on a cushion on the floor and leaned against her aunt's knee (wishing she were like her and then everyone would adore her, or, alternatively, that she were dead and then everyone would be sorry for her) was not, as she was trying to make out, solely on account of these glistening jewels that Queen Mary had worn and now must be sold.

Her aunt shrewdly suspected this, but was not going to show it. She was busy counting up her treasures in terms of their present value.

"This diamond my grandmother wore in France will pay for split peas and ships' biscuit for some months, and what better use could it have?" she said cheerfully. "Here are rubies, that is, rope and tar and sailcloth; and the emeralds the Dauphin gave her— glorious, aren't they? Would you think their value is only 9½d.—a day, I mean, since that's the daily wage of each of the crew, Rupert told me!"

Mary gasped, a little scandalized. It was all very well for her aunt to make an heroic sacrifice, but to do it in this farcical fashion was almost brutal.

"What would she have thought of your having to do this?" she exclaimed, trying to introduce a more reverent spirit. But her aunt would have none of it.

"My grandmother was a sensible woman, for all the nonsense people talked of her, and I am sure she would rather her jewels helped the present moment and the future than that we should gaze at them, thinking of the past, sighing, 'These diamonds she wore at her wedding with Darnley,' or even 'These black pearls were taken from her neck at her execution.'"

This last was a little too bracing; Mary shuddered and reached out her hand for the necklace. "Those very pearls! Oh, Aunt, can you bear to think your own grandmother was executed, and she a queen? Surely the world has grown better since then?"

"I have not observed it," said Elizabeth drily.

"No. Nor have I, really. I am sure my mother-in-law would execute me if she could."

And this, the true reason for Mary's melancholy, having slipped out in the most natural and inevitable way in the world, she subsided into sobs and even reproaches. "I can't think how you can be so friendly with her. She is wicked, jealous, she schemes against me all the time. *She* ought to be executed."

"My child, don't be so foolish. Please remember that Amelia von Solms was my maid-in-waiting and managed to marry my husband's uncle. Do you really think I could help you by quarrelling with my former maid and present aunt-in-law? Our village of The Hague is a small place; two royal ladies at each other's throats are as much as it can hold as it is."

This made Mary weep the more in self-defence. Her aunt was the most adorable woman on earth, but she had never quite understood, nobody could, all that Mary had had to endure ever since her marriage. She had been married in May, was it true that that was unlucky? It must be—and all her ill luck was bound up in the fat resplendent person of her mother-in-law, in her beady eyes, filled with malignity, as she was convinced, whenever they glanced at Mary, and even more alarming when they rested on any of her four daughters, or, still worse, on her only son, in a basilisk stare of maternal solicitude.

Impossible that William with his fastidious manners and fine straight hair, so gentle and grave (too grave, that was the trouble— he was always wanting other people to be lively for him, and Mary feared she was not lively enough), should have anything of his mother in him, or even, so she longed to believe, have any real affection for his mother.

"She tries to make William hate me, she encourages his flirtations with other girls, even with——" here she snatched at just enough sense through her sudden hysteria to remember that the name she had been going to say was the name that of all others she must not say, for it was that of Elizabeth's youngest daughter, Sophia. She tried to fill up her gap by hurrying on, but Elizabeth was too quick for her and demanded the missing name.

So Mary swerved violently from the point and said that she was not the only one to think the Dowager Amelia a dangerous woman, many others had said so.

"Pouf! All women are dangerous when they have four daughters to marry." (Elizabeth quite ignored her own position as the mother of four daughters as she spoke—as often happened, she had forgotten them for the moment.) "But it is a mistake to

c

let others talk of her. The peculiar feminine vice of discussing one's relatives is even more dangerous than maternity."

Mary could not bear it. She had to justify herself, to show that it was not all mere silly tittle-tattle; she sobbed out, "But William admires Sophie, and that is why his mother has arranged a ballet for them both to dance in, so that he can meet her for rehearsals here every evening."

"Have you taken leave of your senses? Why should Amelia do any such thing?"

"Because she wants my brother Charles to marry one of her daughters, and she is afraid of his liking Sophie better and so she is trying to damage her reputation through William. I thought I ought to tell you this for Sophie's sake, but I knew you'd be angry, and you see, you are."

There was a pause, a terrible silence. Mary, her head bent against that firm shapely knee, the knee of a rider, a handsome young cavalier, rather than of a woman over fifty, dared not look up, but she felt it tremble. She had to look up, she did so, and the shock she received sent the blood throbbing into her face; her neck, her whole body felt as though it were burning with blushes. She saw her aunt shaking, the tears running down her cheeks, but not from anger or sorrow as she had in the first wild instant imagined, but from laughter. Elizabeth tried to stop herself but could not; she shook and rocked to and fro, and at last gasped out, "Oh, my best niece! Who in the world can have told you such a farrago of nonsense?"

"Sophie herself," murmured Mary, driven to her last defence. "She was warned of the plot and she thought it right to warn me."

"So you two put your heads together and ought to have had them knocked together. I thought Sophie had more sense. But all young girls like to see themselves as heroines in the midst of plots and wicked designs." (To Mary's relief she did not trouble to ask who had 'warned' Sophie.) "I dare say with my usual vanity that William comes here for my sake even more than Sophie's. Are you going to consider me too as a rival? But the biggest nonsense is the notion that Charles should be deterred by another man's attentions. Your rascally young brother is much more likely to be spurred on by them. What was that rumour you mentioned of that trollop Lucy Walters being with child by him—a boy of his age!"

"He was eighteen last summer," corrected Mary, who had been too much ashamed even to cry, but found her self-respect somewhat restored by this new turn, her aunt talking to her again as an equal; "and I am only a year younger. It is high time I had a baby rather than he."

If she had a baby, William would love her and her only; Amelia, his mother, would not dare to interfere, she would be nowhere, and Mary would be free to do just as she liked, and she and William and their son, who would also be William, and her favourite brother, the delightful, irrepressible, highly reprehensible Charles, would all go back to England together, for by then the troubles would be sure to be over and her father on the throne again.

Her cousins swung into the room in a tremendous hurry, Rupert and Loucy. How tall they were, how careless and arrogant, unconscious of themselves and of all else, moving and speaking with the ease of gods, so they seemed to the homesick girl, quivering from her last encounter with her mother-in-law. You could not think of Louey or Rupert suffering from a mother-in-law: the one would laugh, the other shrug, and go their splendid indifferent way. Pictures or ships' tackle and mutiny, portraiture or piracy, these were their high impersonal element, filling Mary's soul with envious longing for the wings not of a dove but of a seagull.

They had heard Rupert calling orders as he came through the courtyard and up the stairs, for his and his servants' horses to be saddled on the instant. He was only here for that instant, and to sweep up into his pockets the cash his mother had already managed to raise. He did not even thank her so very much; he seemed to know that she would do it.

"This will get us to Ireland in any case," he said. "Once there, I believe we'll make a shift to live in spite of all factions. We'll conquer the Scillys from Kinsale and make a second Venice of 'em."

There was some very 'Scilly' joking over this boast, and Louey was telling her mother of some repulsive Scots lord she had just met, whose portrait she wished to paint, "but no picture could do him justice. I will carve his tombstone after his death of a debauch of pickled pork and onions swilled down with port and topped up with brandy, for all those airs attended his rich breath——"

"Nauseating girl! And how could you represent them in cold marble?"

"As bloated cherubs blowing their fat sighs about his effigy."

"You're talking in blank verse, very blank."

"And very rightly, to a mother who is always quoting Shakespeare."

How happy they were, the three of them together. It was not always like this. Mary usually found it a matter for wonder that her cousins, especially her female cousins, did not get on better with their charming mother. But this was one of those golden moments when they were sharing adventure together as three equals. Perhaps they would be still happier if she were not here—'a stranger shall not meddle with his joy'—she remembered her father quoting that.

Louey noticed that her cousin was so sensitive that she changed colour whenever one spoke to her; perhaps that was why she found it impossible to paint her, and even Honthorst had made a very poor job of it. Mary flushed, she smiled, the tears came up under her long dark eyelashes, and it was all because she was trying to think of some urgent reason why she should be gone that moment; but it was needless, for Rupert was going himself—his horse must be ready now, he said, and he would wait for none of his servants that were not also ready.

"You cannot reach Helvoetsluys before nightfall," exclaimed his mother. "Your horse might miss his footing in the dark and land you in a canal, and this wind makes it the more dangerous."

"The wind will be behind me, under Grey Day's tail; it will help, not hinder. I've ridden the distance in three hours before now. To-day it might take less."

And he took his leave of them as casually as if he would be back to-morrow. Mary need not mind being present, but was disappointed that she need not; it would have been pleasant to have seen a touch of the tender and intimate for once in her cousin who was so much the eldest and biggest of all of them, and with a strange dark splendour about him that made you long to see what he would be like when he was just a little different.

But he never was—not even now, when he might never see any of them again. That possibility was too frequent ever to occur to him.

He grumbled at having to leave without a word with his cousin Charles about Montrose, but when his mother begged him to find Charles as he rode out through the town, he said, "No, I can't wait to rout him out of whatever tavern or brothel he's in."

"Rupert!" (His mother had given a quick look at Charles' sister.) "You are not on the quarter-deck here!"

"Well, I soon must be—or there'll be no quarter-deck for me. Good-bye, Mother. Good-bye, Coz. Tell Charles to be a good boy and look out for Lauderdale. Good-bye, Louey, much the same advice would do for you if you could take it."

They heard him whistling as he leaped down the stairs two at a time.

"It is an odd thing," said Loucy, "that one never sees Rupert in really high spirits unless he has to sell half his ships, quell a mutiny, and get the fleet to sea, all in one day."

From below in high insolent triumph came his mare's shrill whinny, calling to the horses in the stables as her master swung into the saddle.

IV

*L*OUEY was right. This icy wind whistling and shrieking in his ears, twisting the few thin trees unavailingly planted for shelter on either side of the rough road, and already beginning to freeze the drops of rain on them into slanting splinters of ice, was shrill music to Rupert. In a few hours now this frost would harden the ground into slippery iron so that no horse could travel on it. But Grey Day, his big Flemish mare, was travelling magnificently at this moment, her hoofs pounding the hard earth, her long white mane streeling forward over her nose, her bulk responsive to the grip of his knees, the touch of his heel. This was the wind he had been wanting for weeks, the wind that was to set him and his ships free of their long-enforced idleness and take them west to Ireland. He would hold his own in the race against frost, against night, and against mutiny.

The road went straight as a ruled line before him through a country flat as the sea, rough hardening mud springing into dust under his horse's hoofs, the canal beside him a darker, rougher streak of broken water. Here and there he passed a peasant struggling to tow his barge of hay or cattle-fodder against the wind, driving the end of his spar into his chest in his frantic efforts to keep the blindly obstinate boat away from the shore. The men here wore boats even on their feet; he saw the heavy sabots clumping in and out of the puddles to fight their endless battle with the water, and pulled Grey Day's head straight again as she glanced and swerved from that plodding, pushing figure.

A shaft of sunlight cold as steel struck on a windmill's whirling arms, on a church tower, almost black before, now suddenly white, on a thatched farmhouse huddled among trees. It vanished, leaving the land interminably the same, endlessly flat, with not a hillock nor valley, scarce a landmark of any kind to show how far he had gone. In England, now, what clusters of cottages and village greens he would have passed already, manor houses set in tall trees, streams brawling down through wooded dales, and his mare now straining up-hill, now galloping down. Here there was nothing but the changeless grey scene under the changing sky, a vast sky filled with darkening, racing clouds.

'If I cross the Maas at Brielle in another hour I shall be in time,' thought Rupert.

He never really thought that he would not be in time, but all the way he was wondering what change each moment might not be bringing on his fleet, that fleet so subject to the winds of chance it might have been made of air and water like the cloud-ships sailing overhead. Only four fighting-ships left to him by now—no, three, since the *Roebuck* must go—four frigates, and the prize he had captured—and no money for them and their crews, perilously short in numbers as they were, but what he and now his mother had raised out of the pawnbrokers' pockets.

He had had his brother Maurice to help him, of course, and Maurice must be helping him now. He had left him in charge in his own ship the *Admiral*, and Captain Marshall and Captain Allen were with him, both men of experience and decision—and Maurice was Maurice, and what that was, Rupert had never thought to consider. Maurice, the faithful 'Twin' of their boyhood's nick-name, had at once become Rupert's Vice-Admiral, just as he had been his second-in-command all through the war in England when Rupert had been cavalry leader and then Commander-in-Chief of the armies of his uncle, King Charles.

All that was over now, that fury of shared endeavour up and down the English countryside, the forced marches, the sudden attacks, the comradeship with men seen once round a camp-fire and never again, the jokes, the lewd marching-songs, the nicknames and mad stories that had linked him with thousands of Englishmen. That was over; he had had to leave England, to fill up time in a foreign campaign that counted for nothing.

But now once again he was with his mother's countrymen, and

now once again and at long last he had got his chance to be Admiral
of the British fleet, as he had been promised at sixteen, when his
uncle, backed by the City of London, had proposed to give him the
island of Madagascar and a fleet of twelve ships of war and thirty-
six merchantmen to take out there.

What wouldn't he give for such a fleet as that now! Short work
he could then have made this autumn of his enemies the English
Parliament's fleet, which he had been able to beat only in the wild
race for neutral harbour in this country. He had won it by a short
neck, but with the result that his few ships had been penned up in
that Dutch harbour as close as if they were in prison, for they were
blockaded at its mouth by the English Parliament's navy, more
than twice their strength.

For more than two months the two enemy fleets had lain at
anchor within speaking distance of each other, and the amount of
bad language shouted from deck to deck had been enough, complained the peaceable Dutchmen, to stink out the harbour. The
shore was made hideous by the drunken brawls that rocked to and
fro between the King's men and the Parliament men in the taverns
and on the quayside, so that the Hollanders had only to hear a noise
in a back street to say, 'There are those English at it again!'

The Parliament's crews were well paid and their ships well
stocked from Rotterdam with food and stores; their agents worked
on Rupert's sailors until one after the other of the Royalist ships
went over to the enemy. Rupert took the law into his own hands,
defying both enemy and neutral powers, and fortified the harbour
with cannon on the treeheads and on his biggest ship, which lay
athwart on guard over the rest with her starboard side to the enemy's
to frighten off deserters. But his guns could not prevent the men
slipping out by night overland to the Parliament's fleet, and this they
still did by the score.

'So shaken a design' had the Royalist fleet become, and so confident were the Parliament officers that even Rupert must recognize
there was no more possible chance for it, that they actually proposed

that their Admiral Moulton should come and give a friendly talk to what remained of the Royalist crews. Rupert replied ominously that he would give leave for this—but that he would stand by all the time, and that if anything were said that he did not like, he would throw the orator overboard.

After that no more was said of friendly talks, and at last the Parliament's fleet had to sail back to England and leave the coast clear to Rupert to despatch his frigates and capture a couple of rich prizes that were carrying coal and cash to the Parliament merchants (and therefore, said the Royalists, were legitimate prizes of war. What the Parliament men said was, 'The Robber Prince is now the Pirate Prince'). That helped the good work—in more ways than one, for the London citizens made more outcry than since the beginning of the war. They had tolerated the Puritan army's outrages in condemning certain small shopkeepers to be whipped and imprisoned for life for speaking against the Parliament, but now that trade itself was endangered, that was too much. They declared that peace must instantly be declared and the King released from prison.

"Squeeze their pockets and they'll discover their loyalty fast enough," Rupert said in grim triumph. But most of the Council, including Hyde, were too anxious to conciliate the London merchants to pursue this policy—while, on the other hand, the little Court of beggared exiles at The Hague plainly said that the whole duty of the Prince and his fleet was to carry on piratical expeditions in order to provide them with food and clothes. Their need was indeed so desperate, and that of Prince Charles, that much of the prize money had to go to relieve it, but even so, charges of dishonesty and misappropriation of the money were brought against Rupert's officers.

Both 'friend' and foe alike seemed equally determined to wreck the remainder of his ships, and now the seamen themselves were yet again conspiring to do so—perhaps had already done so.

What would he find when he reached Helvoetsluys? Would he

ever reach it? This ride was a nightmare, through an unchanging land that had no end. The short winter daylight was fading, the sky darkening over him, the clouds no longer ships but torn like the wild hair of witches across the stormy evening light. The canals gleamed paler in the dusk, running in streaks of light through the dim land. That land had shortened before him, he could see less and less distance ahead, less and less into the future.

There was no future, no fleet awaiting him at Helvoetsluys, no Maurice even. His head was spinning as it sometimes did this last year; he was deadly tired, dead sick and weary of dealing month after month, year after year, with men who would not do as he willed—sick even of dealing with his mare, now flagging under the strain, her left fore-hoof going a little tender, her breath coming heavy and loud in the wind, shutting out the sound of it in his ears, for his mare must not flag, must not fail, must understand what he was telling her with the grip of his knees and the caress of his hand, that she must get him to Helvoetsluys in time.

He had crossed the Maas, and here at last was the Botlek and the second ferry. The great flat ferry-boat took the bulk of his horse like a sail. She neighed and stamped, her hoofs clattering on the wood as it spun round in mid-stream. ' Whoa, my girl, steady!' he said, passing his hand over the velvet ears, flattened back in terror against her head. The enormous glossy eyes, white-rimmed in their glancing fear, stared unseeing into his, unable to focus at that short range. He pulled down the beast's head against his chest so that she should not see the whipped grey water in the gathering dusk.

Looking down at that disturbed water, his aching body suddenly at rest from the saddle, he forgot for a moment to stare urgently, imperatively into the immediate future; he was looking down into the glossy canals of his boyhood at school here in Leyden, when he had punted his boat in and out of the dark reflections of the old college walls, under the gabled houses and their bright gardens, under the substantial stone lady and her surrounding merchants carved on the Weighing House where the boats weighed out their merchandise to be sold on the quays, wealth brought by water, won on water, gliding safely now up smooth waterways after tossing in a little ship across the mighty ocean from either Indies to its destined harbour.

Even then he had day-dreamed that he would grow up to be a British Admiral. And he had done so—here he was to prove it, and prove it he would, if he found but one ship left with which to do it. That dizzy spasm of exhaustion had swept over him like a wave, drowning him for the moment, but now he had struck through it and risen to the surface. He was strong and fresh again, and Grey Day knew the difference at once as he swung into the saddle, cheering on her heavy sagging flesh with his new life and purpose. She answered him nobly, straining each muscle to the top of its power as she pounded on, knowing thankfully that she was now near the end of her journey.

He could just see the lines of masts piercing the dusk above the dark fields as if the ships stood on dry land. It was quite dark by the time he reached the little wooden jetty that thrust out into the harbour at Helvoetsluys. Leaving his horse on the upper pier, he leaped down on to the jetty. He could see the ships, dim and shapeless as shadows, rocking in the windy harbour like huge sea-monsters. Men were moving on the quayside, talking in harsh voices that strained against the wind.

The doorway of a sailors' tavern flung a patch of smoky red light on to the quayside; dark figures came in and out against it, a man in a fur cap sat just inside the door playing the bagpipes, and every now and then jerked out his foot in joke to trip those who passed and cursed him. Voices were shouting inside, one voice louder, more insistent than the rest, arguing, complaining, going on and on through the interruptions of other men's shouts, drunken laughter, the squeal and snarl of the pipes and snatches of hoarse song bawled out in derision.

A boat was waiting for him under the jetty, and two of his own ship's officers hurried up out of the darkness as he approached it. He demanded first where was Prince Maurice, and was rowed out to him, the off-shore wind blowing back the little waves that hissed against the side of the boat, their spray streeling back in the light of the boat's lantern. He went straight to the stateroom in his ship, the *Admiral*, where Maurice was holding a council of war with four or five officers who sprang up at sight of him.

He still seemed to be swaying in the saddle; the faces before him looked long and unfamiliar as though reflected in a distorting mirror. Even Maurice's was different. But it was there—that was the chief thing.

"Well, what is it?" he asked.

"On the *Antelope*," Maurice told him, "that is, openly. There have been the usual complaints of food and lack of pay all through the fleet. This morning, early, when I sent for twenty of the *Antelope's* crew to come and help rig the *Admiral*, they sent back word they would not come."

"Where are her officers?"

"The men have barricaded them in their own quarters."

It was more serious even than Rupert had thought. But he showed nothing of his thoughts to the little group of officers who were watching his face so anxiously. He answered almost indifferently:

"Then we'll go fetch 'em out. Who'll come with me? You, Maurice, and you, Marshall, and you, Fielding—all of you, then."

He was unbuckling his sword and laying it on the cabin table. They exclaimed, protesting, but he said:

"It's more danger to me than to them. You, gentlemen, I trust, as I cannot myself, to obey my command not to draw any sword."

Then he led the way on to the deck, where he called for a boat and a hurricane-lamp. Three more officers joined him, doubtful, murmuring that it was madness for a handful like this to go now at night and practically unarmed on to a ship that had declared open mutiny. But all of them followed him down into the boat.

The dark bulk of the *Antelope* hung over them as they hailed her, and a row of heads appeared over the bulwarks, black against the faint glow of a ship's lanthorn. The men let down a ladder, were suspiciously ready to do so, thought some of those in the boat, and Rupert went up first on to the deck where the whole crew was quickly gathering, more and more men running up in the waving darkness.

He called out to them, "Let twenty of your best foremast men step forward. I want them to come aboard the *Admiral* at dawn and help rig her for action. We weigh anchor to-morrow, to catch this wind for Ireland."

His voice rang out in triumph as he said it. It had been the order he had longed to give for so many weeks that he was confident it would be enough in itself to dispel all disaffection.

But the men were gathering about him and his officers in a close-knit, dangerous crowd, muttering together; their faces grinned and snarled in the flickering light of the lanthorn; those that showed were silent, but those behind, emboldened by the darkness, were calling out jeers and defiance. Was it better to starve in Irish seas than in Dutch? Let them see their pay first before they saw Ireland! And one voice called out, "The Pauper Princes!" and another, shrill and cockney, "The bloody foreigners!"

A hot rage burned up in Rupert's head as all those faces grinned and mouthed silent in the light, and shouted in the dark. They were coming nearer and nearer to him, only waiting, it seemed, for some signal or command to spring all together.

It came, in that same cockney yelp from the back of the crowd, the mutineers' cry, "One and all!"

Rupert could not see who called it, but strode at once towards the sound, and on either side the men fell back, each afraid to be the first to attack. A short sturdy man fell back before him against the bulwarks, calling out again in that nasal snarl, "Now then you cowards—one and all!"; but in that instant, before any of them could move forward again, the Prince had seized him with both hands, pinning his arms to his sides, and lifted him, struggling and kicking as he was, clear over the side of the ship as if to drop him into the dark tossing waters below.

He yelled for mercy, and Rupert answered, "Order your officers' release, or I'll let go."

"Let 'em out!" shouted the man, but his fellows were staggered by Rupert's sudden action and the mighty strength that could swing a burly fellow over the bulwarks as though he were a puppy. They gaped at their bold ringleader dangling over that dark sea, and were too aghast at his howl for mercy to notice what he cried to them.

"Be quick and let out your officers before I drop this carrion!" Rupert called to them, and gave point to his warning by shaking his victim, who screamed, "Let 'em out for Christ's sake!"

They rushed then to let out their officers, they thronged round the Prince protesting their loyalty. Not till then did Rupert haul up the ringleader from his ignominious position over the bulwarks, give him a shake that rattled his teeth together like castanets, and throw him down on his feet, from which he promptly collapsed to his knees.

And Tom Smith proved his eternal devotion that night, sitting with his fellows in the fo'c'sle, by drinking the health again and again of a captain that was a captain, a captain who could pick you up in his hands and hold you over the side of the ship as easy as drowning kittens. And who cared if he was half a foreigner?—for if Oliver Cromwell was English, then he was only an English louse that their Prince could have killed with one hand, if that old snuffling high-hatted lout had ever had the guts to meet the young Devil face to face.

Next day, with that easterly wind behind them, bellying out what sails they dared set, the fleet sailed out to a grey choppy sea. Just as they were warping the *Admiral* out into midstream, a man came riding furiously down to the side of the low wooden jetty, and

Rupert said to his captain, "I know that fellow—the way he rides," but could not at once think who it was.

The man pulled in his horse close to the water's edge, waving and shouting into the wind that he must speak with Prince Rupert. They could not wait, the sails were already being set, but the man sprang into a rowing-boat below the jetty, and two fellows who were in it started to row furiously out to the ship. He stood up as they came near, and Rupert, leaning over the ship's side, recognized him just before he called out, "I am Sir John Hurry. I have a letter from my lord of Montrose."

"'Tie it to a weight and throw it," Rupert called back, for they had weighed anchor and the *Admiral* was fast slipping out of the harbour.

Hurry instantly drew his dirk and stabbed it through the folded paper, then cried, "'Ware the blade!" and flung it up above his head. It fell point downwards and stuck in a plank of the deck. Rupert pulled it up; the boat lagged behind, and the big ship sailed on.

"That's odd," said the captain, "for I remember Hurry left our side after Marston Moor and fought for the Scots Covenanters against Montrose."

"He went over to him at the end, though, when Montrose had made himself master of Scotland," said Rupert, and the two of them chuckled unkindly as he unfolded Montrose's letter with the gash through the centre folds.

There were few words in it, for he had evidently intended Hurry should speak of his design to Rupert, having had no idea that the fleet was sailing at this moment. A reference to the Lauderdale-Lanark group made Rupert smile grimly in agreement; 'there is nothing of honour amongst the stuff there.' He ended:

'I hope to let Your Highness see all is not yet gone, but that we may have a handsome pull for it—and rather win it or be sure to lose it fairly.'

The words raised a curious echo in Rupert's mind; he read them again; where had he heard them before, in Montrose's own voice ? but not spoken, for a wild tune was threading them together, a tune like those that his mother sang of the sad savage songs her nurse had taught her in her native country of Scotland. With that tune he remembered a small hot room up a rickety stair in a Yorkshire inn, a room filled with dusty sunshine and the smell of straw and sweat from outside, and the sounds of harness clanking and of hoofs against cobblestones, the neighing and champing of tired horses, the tired disillusioned voices of his men calling to each other. It was the first time he had heard their voices sound like that, with all the gay confidence he had inspired gone out of them, the first time he had heard their voices after defeat, his defeat at Marston Moor.

But now he saw, looking back into that mean despairing room, the keen outline of a man's head flung back against the dusty sunlight as he told Rupert of a desperate, an unbelievable plan to ride with two others in disguise through the armies of his enemies into his own country of Scotland and raise it for the King.

And he had done it, for that man was Montrose, and he had made and sung the gay ringing song that Rupert now remembered:

'He either fears his fate too much,
　Or his deserts are small,
That dares not put it to the touch,
　To win or lose it all.'

What plan had he now for 'a handsome pull for it,' that he would 'win or be sure to lose it fairly'? Whatever it might be, Rupert burned to share it with him. This was the only man that he had ever envied—a man of so 'clear a spirit,' as Hyde had put it, and so single of heart and purpose, that he could ride single-handed into a country armed against him. Within a year he won it for his King, and lost it, through the King. But the winning or losing was not what had moved Rupert—(What was it the man himself had said? —'That's not our concern, once it's done')—it was the flinging of himself into that desperate and lonely adventure. This was what made him remember Montrose with envy.

Give himself and that man but one campaign together away from the interference of the King's Court, and what might they not yet achieve?

He raised his head from the bold straggling writing on the paper and saw the long humped line of the dunes slipping away from him, the sands pale grey as a corpse in this cold light, scarred with dark patches of scrub. A church spire in the distance pierced the clouds, the arms of windmills whirled round and round behind the dunes, but so flat was the country that that low barrier of sand, only a few feet high, hid all the rest of it. He thought of the people he was leaving behind in that hidden land, the people he had just seen—fat Ned Hyde pegging away interminably at his papers, Lauderdale that Learned Pig, his mother gay among her bankrupt jewels, Louey.

In a short time now Montrose too would be there to adventure his plan.

A ray of watery sunshine straggled through the clouds, the church spire gleamed white in it, the sandhills silver-gold; then it passed, and only a low grey line remained of Holland.

D

V

The *Admiral* lay safely at anchor in Kinsale harbour off the south coast of Ireland, and Maurice's ship, the *Constant Reformation*, had just sailed in, two days later. The rest, owing to their inexpert pilots, had been driven to leeward, and Rupert had now to wait for them at this their rendezvous. He was not sorry for a few days' quiet, for the wind had reached gale strength soon after they had left the shores of Holland and he had been exhaustingly sick and with little chance to stay below, for his ship, which was used to a crew of three hundred men, now carried only forty seamen and eighty soldiers, so that the Lord High Admiral took his full share of the practical seamanship.

Few and weakly manned as they were, they had had to sail through the Channel, and there came in full view of the enemy's fleet, which rode at anchor in the Downs. The grumbling of the men at thus running into danger reached something like panic when Rupert, leaping down from the poop where he had been looking out through his telescope, shouted an order to charge straight at the enemy.

But—"There he is in the saddle again, sticking his spurs into the old ship's side!" Tom Smith jeered admiringly, and his determined backing of 'our trooper' helped more than the officers to prevent the crew's terrified disobedience.

"What's good enough in the army is good enough in the navy," Rupert told them, and proved it, for the very impudence of his little fleet 'charging' so boldly down on the far greater Parliament fleet bluffed them so badly that they did not stay to count the enemy but slipped their anchors and sheltered under the castles, while the Royalist ships sailed gaily on to Ireland.

There Rupert sat in his stateroom in the stern of the ship, with its two round windows (a new experiment that, to see if a circle of glass would weather better than a square), working out his 'Rule of Proportion' allotting what share in the booty should be taken, in capturing a prize, by every man in the ship down to the swabber and the swabber's mate and even the boy (half a share), when Maurice came on board and down into the stateroom and the two met again for the first time since Helvoetsluys. Maurice had been driven out of his course as far as Cork, had put in there for a few hours, and heard an astonishing report that had just been brought by a Dutch merchantman that had come straight from London.

"But there's no need to believe it just because it's bad," said Maurice. "They say Cromwell's brought the King to London."

"We'd heard that before: that the King had made a treaty with Parliament, and London was preparing an array for him."

"No. They say they've brought the King to London to make him stand his trial there."

"His *trial*? On what charge, in the name of God?"

"High treason," answered Maurice, as sullenly as if he were on trial himself, "for bearing arms against his subjects!"

Rupert turned on his brother, his face so dark with fury that even Maurice shrank from it. It was said that Rupert when angry looked like a devil in hell. He himself felt blasted by his rage, it tasted dry and bitter in his mouth since he could not assuage it in fight; his clenched fist tingled with the longing to smash it against all the injustice, cruelty, and slavish imbecility in the world.

He had to force himself to think reasonably, striding up and down that confined space.

"This cannot be true," he said. "Cromwell would never run himself into such a preposterous impasse. To find the King guilty would be to condemn him to death. And they could never carry out the sentence. Kings have been murdered, but not executed with a solemn show of law."

There was his own great-grandmother, Mary Queen of Scots, but even so, she had been beheaded by a rival queen, her lifelong foe, not by her own subjects. No, England might do many things, ridden as she was by that hard rider, General Cromwell, but not that.

Then, turning this way and that, he remembered how he had met General Cromwell at Bristol at the end of the war, and saw again the thick nose, the hot eyes, the bitterly repressed mouth. Sir Theodore Mayerne, King Charles' own doctor, had told him how he had once had to treat Cromwell for melancholia and had thought him a bad case unless he could contrive always to drug his tormented soul with action. He had certainly contrived it these late years, but that gave one no confidence as to whether the required action might not take some monstrous form.

"'A man who has a genius for practical organization plus a morbid hysteria,'" Rupert muttered, thinking of Sir Theodore's words, then added, "given such a man, whose genius is hampered by a certain obstacle, will he not then take steps to remove the obstacle? What is to prevent Cromwell from killing the King?"

"He would never dare," said Maurice.

"You have forgotten the hysteria. He would make himself think it was the will of God."

"He could never make others think it."

"You did not see him. I did."

A heavy silence fell on him, and when Maurice spoke later he did not hear him; he stood still and began shoving the papers here and there on the table, unable to push away the unbearable fear now in his mind. There was no escape among those papers. Charles' own writing struck up at him from the litter, the pointed handwriting piercing his heart as his eye fell carelessly upon it and saw what it was saying to him:

'Next my children (I say next), I shall have most care of you.'

The stammering precision of that repetition ('I say next—') was the very echo of his uncle's stammering speech; more poignant was that tender assurance of the loving care that the helpless prisoner intended to take of his nephew.

He took up the letter to tear it across—why was it still lying here? It was an old one and of no importance—but as the paper began to tear, he laid it down again. Why should he destroy this letter which spoke concern and gratitude towards him, when he had kept others in evidence against his uncle?

He had kept the letter in which King Charles in their bitterest quarrel had dismissed him from his service, banished him from England, and told him to seek employment elsewhere, 'somewhere beyond seas.'

And for years he had kept another of his letters, for no other purpose than the bitter, secret justification it gave to his pride to keep for himself the actual words in which his uncle had doomed him to his failure at Marston Moor.

Even now he could not say those words 'Marston Moor' to himself without checking the vigorous rush of life in his veins, just as that disastrous battle had checked and turned the mighty onrush of his success that had made his enemies as well as his friends declare him invincible. Marston Moor had turned the flow of that fierce tide; at Marston Moor he had gone down, and Oliver Cromwell, the cavalry leader for the English Parliament, had gone up, and had been going up and up ever since, until now he ruled all England.

It was this that mattered—nothing else. His uncle, King Charles, for whom he had fought in vain, was Cromwell's prisoner; and Cromwell was bringing him to trial—so they now said.

He swung round with a furious gesture, pushing the table back from him.

"We are fools to listen to every lying rumour!" he exclaimed. "If Cromwell runs mad, there's Fairfax ro restrain him, and he's a gentleman; there's all England, and for that matter all Europe. Cromwell has always had method in his madness, he'd not bring every country into line against him. Come up on deck. I must cool my head."

It felt dazed and empty after that blinding rage, a way it had had now and then ever since that bullet-wound in the head during that negligible Franco-Spanish campaign in which he had engaged last year to fill up time after the Civil War had ceased in England. It had destroyed his reputation as the Wizard Prince, Rupert the

Devil, whom no mortal-made weapon could touch. That bullet last year, fired from a stupid little ambush, had touched him quite severely, and though it had healed remarkably well, his head now sometimes ached abominably, and sometimes gave him a queer dizzy feeling as though he were walking in space, unable to bring his feet down to earth.

Now he felt at ease again, he no longer had any belief in that report—King Charles had been killed by rumour too often before now. He walked on deck with the sea-air on his bare head, and Maurice beside him, leaving that small dark room below for this vast pearl-coloured space. There was no sun and no wind for the moment; a spatter of rain fell like a sigh, whispered a little in the still air, then died on it as softly as it had begun. North of the ship lay the dim white lines of Kinsale harbour cutting into the towering rocks of the headland, a huddle of low white huts behind it, and the purple mist which showed where the bogs and wintry woods stretched away beyond the rocks.

This damp air destroyed distances both in memory and space, like the mist that blurred all outlines of the further scene, then suddenly rolled up over some brilliant patch of blue hill and crimson bog, showing it as dazzling clear as if it lay within a few yards. After the rich land of Holland, every inch of it tended and worked over, nursed into wealth that would repay the labour a million-fold, it was amazing, at first infuriating, to see, when he went ashore here, the starved, stony, uneven ground, where nothing seemed to grow but thorns and weeds.

Yet he had already ceased to wonder at the people's lack of effort; he, who had had all his nerves and energies strained to breaking-point these last months, now felt as though he had slipped from the immediate burning necessities of every day into the ramifications of a dream.

"Sir John Davies ought to have mentioned it among his 'True Causes why Ireland was Never Entirely Subdued,'" he remarked—"that you can't subdue men who are asleep—and dreaming."

And he told Maurice how every man he talked with when he went ashore told him that the first thing he must do if he hoped to consolidate Ireland for the King's cause was to get rid of the Protestant upstarts or alternately the Roman Catholic rebels, or else the English settlers or contrariwise the Irish rapparees; and how one could seldom make out if the invasion or the battle or the massacre or the famine of which one was hearing had happened a few years or a few centuries ago.

"Look at that spider on the water," he exclaimed, pointing at a long black boat rowed by two men, bobbing among the ships in the harbour. "They call that thing a curragh, it's made of wicker work and tarred canvas, and it's so light that a man has only to slip out one of the seats to carry it on his head down to the shore. Yet they'll go out in those boats in the roughest weather, wriggling up the big Atlantic waves and down again feet foremost into the trough of the wave. They say they're the boats the first settlers ever came in to Ireland, thousands of years ago, yet they still use them and always will, for no one ever wants to change anything here."

The wind had freshened again, it rose higher and higher as they walked the deck, talking of Ormonde's plan for Ireland which their fleet must now follow, but he wished he and Montrose could have got into conjunction over it.

"Montrose, Ormonde, you and I," he said, "we worked well together that night at Oxford in the King's rooms at Christ Church, do you remember?"

"I remember going to sleep," said Maurice frivolously; "and some drunken undergraduates going home from a supper-party singing that song from the play—

"'But did he take the fair Lucrece by the toe, sir?'
'Oh no, no, sir!'"

"'And did he somewhat nearer go, sir?'"

Rupert chimed in, and they finished in uproarious chorus,

"'Oh no no, no no, no no, sir!'"

"There's a pinnace to starboard, Your Highness," said the captain, coming down from the upper deck. "She's making for us with all sail set."

Rupert, still humming,

> "'But did he take the fair Lucrece by the thigh, sir?'
> 'Oh fie, fie, sir!'"

walked across to the upper deck and stared into the skirts of a cloud that was dropping rain as it passed only a little way off, though here where he stood it was not raining at all.

Through the grey slanting lines of rain the pinnace came flying to where the broken stump of rainbow that the sailors call a winddog splashed the cloud with iridescent light. A monstrous black bird was flapping its wings above the mast, following it so closely that it must have perched upon it. No raven would be that size, it could not be a bird at all, but before he could, or would, think what it might be, Rupert saw it for an instant as a black sail furled about the mast—and then the tail of the shower blotted out the boat and it disappeared.

The fancy came to him that this was no ship of the present world, but the black-sailed boat that came to Tristram as he lay dying, looking out to sea; the black sails told him that Iseult had not come, he turned his face to the wall, three times he called upon her name, at the third time he died.

He was making sound practical comments to the captain about the ship's course and probable nationality while beneath his spoken speech his mind was darting this way and that, trying to lose the meaning of that black thing above the mast in this fragment from a romance heard long ago at the English Court. It was the air of this western island, the sad rains and unnatural flying brilliance of the sky, the old memories of vanished glory, it was all these things, he told himself, and no real cause that wrapped his mind in foreboding and intangible sorrow as with its wreaths of white mist.

And then the pinnace came out again from behind that curtain of rain, and the black flag on its mast spread itself clear against the rainbow light in the sky.

'The captain has died on board.'

'By the cut of her jib she's a French pinnace. The young King of France must be dead.'

Rupert said these things to himself as precisely as if he were saying them aloud, while behind his reasoned conjectures, behind this vague cloud-curtained sky and sea, he saw, sharp and clear as at the wrong end of a telescope, a tiny picture of dense crowds mustered in the London streets to see King Charles go by, all standing still as death and in a deathly silence.

He had seen that picture before, in Hyde's room, in front of Lauderdale's gross face. Now he knew that it was true. He went down to his cabin and sat there staring at the round window, waiting for the news that they would bring.

But when they brought it, tramping down the ladder one after the other, Maurice and his captain and the captain of the pinnace, when they came and stood round him there as he sat at the table and said, "King Charles is dead. He has been beheaded by Cromwell's soldiers at Whitehall," the words he had known they would say fell like stones wide of their mark, he could neither understand nor believe them.

In that dark and narrow place where he sat, there was still the clear circle at which he had been staring all this time, a circle of greenish-whitish sea and white sky and the white wings of seagulls swooping and swirling. Now he could see nothing but that; the waiting men round him, the dark narrow walls had melted away, and he saw nothing but that circle of infinity, of cold space, of utter timelessness.

'Somewhere beyond seas'—Charles now was there, where he had once banished Rupert; he was beyond seas, beyond the world, and life, and time. There was nothing he could do now for Charles any more.

"This is the end of it all!" he cried in a great voice. He heard it as the voice of another man, of a wave crashing over his head. The white circle widened, rushed in on him, engulfed him.

This, then, is the end of it all, this white immensity, featureless, endless, not to be seen nor heard; this is what lies round life, waiting to release us, this is death. He had broken through the thin and brittle margin of time, he was in eternity.

But something was whispering, no, shouting at him; sound was coming back, and sense,—hands round him, fumbling at his neck, cold liquid splashing at his lips, the strong smell of brandy, an arm pushing round his shoulders, Maurice's face, long and yellow with fright, staring down into his own, dragging him back with his imploring eyes, refusing to let him go out through that white circle.

"Let me get back," he whispered.

It was no good; it was life that was coming back, familiar objects, faces, sounds, Maurice's voice claiming him, urging him—

"It is not the end. It is the beginning. We will avenge him. We will get his son back on to the throne. Charles shall not die forgotten."

A moment since he had been forgotten, with all else, and yet he had been there. There had been no memories beyond that white circle, only a vast discovery.

Some day Rupert would get back. He could not now. He dragged up his head from the table where he had fallen sideways, and looked round him in astonishment.

"I died just now," he said.

"You fainted," said Maurice. "You have never done that before, that is why it seemed like death."

"No," said his brother, "it seemed like life."

BOOK II

THE LOW LANDS

I

THAT easterly gale that had driven Rupert's ships to Ireland and there melted among the soft west air from the Atlantic had crystallized into an iron frost for the rest of Europe. It lasted several weeks. The later days of February found the little northern town of The Hague still ice-bound, as it had been when the news of King Charles I's execution had fallen on it like a thunderbolt. Horror of it had shaken not only the English Royalists but all the impartial countries of Europe. It was not merely 'this horrid murder,' but the pretence of legality in giving the King the form of a trial, that infuriated the nations. English hypocrisy had reached its apotheosis.

In France no Englishman was safe, since he belonged to the nation that had first tried and then killed their King. In Holland the populace howled round the house of the English Parliament's envoy and would have torn him in pieces if he had dared appear in the streets. Many of the sober Protestant democratic Dutch citizens clamoured that their country should go to war to avenge 'this barbarous and most inhuman action.'

But though kings died dreadfully, life had to go on all the same, and it would be wicked to waste this frost; righteous anger made the grand universal subject for conversation, but it cut no ice, and winter sports flourished gaily. There were carnivals on the ice at night, with ladies and their cavaliers skating hand-in-hand carrying torches; even the staid stout Dutch matrons were miraculously transformed into swiftly darting fireflies. There were games on the ice by day, curling and ball games and racing in sledges and little ice-boats on runners with sails.

The bereaved family of the dead King Charles' sister, the ex-Queen of Bohemia, could not take part in these pleasures; they wore deep mourning and had kept to the house for days, hearing the gay voices and the clang of bells on the sledges that raced down the

61

Voorhout below their windows, growing paler and crosser as the storm of bewildered and horrified grief was gradually frittered away by the effect of the sheer boredom of inactivity on healthy and vigorous young bodies.

For Queen Elizabeth's body at fifty-two and after bearing thirteen children was still that of a young woman though her face had grown lined and harsh when in repose, but it never was in repose. It was she who, after gazing into the fire for near an hour with brooding eyes, a crouched sibyl grim and passive as Fate herself, had cried out on a sudden yelp of boredom that it would do no good to have another death in the family, and dead she would be if she sat here another minute with nothing but sallow faces and black clothes all round her; and out she had gone to drive a sledge borrowed from Lord Craven, harnessed to her two fastest horses, at a break-neck pace over the ice.

She had taken her youngest daughter, Sophie, with her. Sophie was the one who amused her mother most at the moment. She was just grown up, and kind Englishmen had promised her she would be the prettiest of the family, a promise that had made her suddenly prettier than she had ever been before. This was something entirely new, for she was well accustomed to being clever, so sharp she'd cut herself if she didn't take care, her eldest sister Eliza always told her, quoting the homely wisdom of her dead father's old German mother, the Electress Juliana.

But Sophie always took care. She was not the twelfth child for nothing, and had always been sure that no one would look after her if she didn't look after herself. She even took care over this unexpected treat, for she wasn't going to risk her skin to please her mother, who as likely as not would rush out with the horses shod anyhow and never see to it that their shoes were properly cocked for the ice.

So Sophie saw to it and ordered the groom about, while her mother fed the champing and shivering beasts with sugar and told them they'd soon get warm at the rate she'd drive them, and that she'd been pining all this time for the sight and touch of their satin noses.

Eliza came down to the open door and called Sophie to her in a low voice.

"Can you find out if Lord Craven is really going to Amsterdam to-morrow?" she asked.

"If he is not, I can send someone for my new saddle. You have written another letter, I suppose?"

"Another? I have not written since his last."

Sophie thought how absurdly touchy Eliza was about her correspondence with that dry old philosopher Descartes. And with all her precautions lest her mother should know when she wrote to him, you might have thought he was a gay young gallant and their letters full of love-messages instead of learned discussions!

She did not see that in that case Eliza might be less self-conscious about them since disapproval is easier to bear than mockery. The Queen, whose own platonic friendships with men were innumerable, could laugh mercilessly at those of her daughters. It specially exasperated her that the most regularly beautiful of them all should waste hours in writing to 'that desiccated Descartes.' A helpless compunction mingled with the mother's annoyance. If Eliza had only married, it would not matter how many philosophers she wrote to,—and now the perception of this fell on Sophie like a revelation as her eldest sister turned a diffident and indignant back upon her.

'She had much better have married the King of Poland years ago, however unhappy it made her,' the girl decided; 'then at least she would not feel guilty for not having married at all.' Religion had prevented her, Eliza had refused to become a Catholic. 'Ideas matter more to her than facts,' Sophie added to her mental notes; the keen air and foretaste of new pleasure had put a sharp edge on her thoughts.

In one of those tremendous discoveries that one makes when one is just eighteen, so bright in their importance that it seems no one has ever discovered anything about life before, she had made up her mind at this moment, while discussing ways and means of sending a letter for Eliza to Amsterdam, that she would marry anyone, a Jew, a Turk, an infidel, rather than remain an old maid.

She sprang into the sledge beside her mother, waving her small fur muff, a present from 'kind little Craven.' Off they drove, their two faces raised laughing, a little shocked with themselves, absurdly alike at this moment, to the windows where Elizabeth and Louise and Henrietta (or Great Eliza and Louey and Etta, or a dozen other nicknames) were now three Cinderellas left behind, though their mother's action had left them free to go out too.

But Etta had got a cold and a new kind of sweet she was baking in the oven, and Eliza wanted to write her letter while her mother's satiric eyes were out of the house, and Louey was deep on a new book (which she had lost as soon as she had got it, and only recently discovered). Outside the windows the sky, shut down over the black trees and the huddled roofs, scarred with dirty snow, was heavy and relentless as a coffin-lid pressed down over the dead chill earth. 'Who wants to go out into *that*?' said they to each other, turning back to the bright fire and the sense of comfortable security that they all felt now that those two were out of the house.

Etta went off to the kitchen singing—most reprehensibly at such a time, but she just could not help it:

> " 'Si le roi m'avait donné
> Paris sa grande ville,
> J'aime mieux ma mie, oh gai!
> J'aime mieux ma mie.' "

Eliza heard her fresh childish voice with wonder. Etta still hoped, still believed that next year everything would be different, still did not understand that while their brothers left home to go out into the world on one fresh adventure after another, they themselves would always stay here and nothing would ever happen to them. Eliza had quarrelled with her mother and left home to stay with an aunt for a year, but she had come back, and everything had gone on as before, would always go on, and it was only because the others were so much younger, Eliza thought, that they did not know this.

She sat at a writing-table of Dutch marquetry inlaid with the scene of a little man with a big gun going out to shoot ducks as big as himself. Her pale carved face was so still, it might have been that of a statue but for the dark melancholy of her eyes.

She wrote: 'Is it possible that you can really wish to go to Sweden merely because Queen Christina has asked you? You are a philosopher. You have lived in Amsterdam for twenty years and have said again and again you would never leave it. Yet you would throw away the comfortable habits of a lifetime, your pleasant house in the Herrengracht, your garden small and exquisite as a jewel shining in the light from the canal below' (it was Louey who had said that, she remembered, and her scrupulous honesty paused for an instant over using another's metaphor—but why should not Louey help her all unconsciously?)—'you would throw away all this for the flimsy caprice of a silly eccentric young woman who wants to win a vicarious reputation for learning by getting the cleverest men in Europe round her in her barbarous freezing kingdom——'

Here she shivered, for she felt a ghost look over her shoulder, the ghost of her German grandmother, the sad strict religious old Dowager Electress Juliana who had brought up Eliza and had so disapproved of Eliza's mother, and was now whispering to her, asking was it indeed herself writing to grave courteous elderly ugly little Monsieur Descartes, to whose intellect she had always shown as much respect as he had to her rank?

Her mother might abuse elderly gentlemen in her letters, calling them 'little ape' or 'ugly filthy camel face,' but that was in joke, and that was her mother.

Well, why should she not for once be as free and untrammelled as her mother? She wrote on: 'Are your old friends nothing to you that you can wish to do this? But you do not wish it, you have said you do not, you have written of the deprivation it will be to

E

you, above even that of your flowers and your housekeeper and that
excellent oyster sauce she makes' (No, no, you cannot send this—
well then I cannot, but at least I have written it)—'as though you
acknowledge that it will mean, as it must, the loss of our friendship.
And I am to believe that because Christina of Sweden has asked
you to found an academy for her, this is a sacred call which must
be placed higher than your personal wishes. Oh my friend, remember your own words, that I have thought as noble as those of
Our Lord: "I think, therefore I am." You are not thinking now,
and therefore you are not being yourself.'

Here Eliza's long grey goose-quill stopped scratching. She
looked down at her words, 'You are a philosopher.' There was
venom in them, for Descartes had sought to console her for the
shock to her nerves and spirits given by her English uncle's appalling
death, by his opinion that that death 'would greatly enhance the
King's reputation.' What could one write in answer to such cold-
blooded philosophy? 'Nothing, nothing, nothing,' she muttered,
knowing that all this time she had been writing only to herself.
She took up the paper, tore it across and across, and continued to
stare in the same direction, though now only at the inlaid golden
wood that depicted the little man, his gun and his ducks.

Louey, lounging by the chimney-piece with her book in one
hand while she absent-mindedly ran the fingers of the other through
her hair, warming first one foot and then the other against the blazing logs, heard the savage rasping of the torn paper and hunched an
unwilling shoulder against it, wondering why women must always
do things noisily, even in letters, even in thoughts of absent friends—
absent enemies more likely.

It was no use reading on to herself. The air was too full of
angry bitter unhappy silence. There they were, two sisters in the
same room, and Eliza shut up in a fog of despair while she herself
had been marching in a blaze of glory; but now the fog had spread
outwards and caught the edges of her mood, damping and dimming
them; the whole room would be grey if they did not shake it off.

But she could not intrude on her sister's fierce solitude; Eliza must speak first.

Obediently, Eliza spoke, in a strained harsh voice, the first words that came to her as escape from her thoughts: "It's strange to see *you* reading anything so intently."

Eliza was the great reader in the family; little Sophie, frivolous as she appeared, was a good runner-up in this, but of the two intervening sisters Etta never read at all and Louey only when at a loose end. Louey never sat down to a book in the businesslike fashion of Eliza and Sophie, and it was really very odd how in pulling some book at random from the shelves and desultorily flicking over the pages as she stood, she yet managed as if by pure chance to tear the heart out of it. It was scarcely fair thus to gain the maximum of pleasure with the minimum of effort. There was therefore a faintly grudging note in the scholarly Eliza's comment—'strange —*you* reading——'

Louey swung round from the fire.

"Ah, but it's a brand-new book," she said, "and has been selling like the hot cakes on the ice out there."

Eliza was apt to despise modern literature, particularly when it was as popular as that. "The newest French romance, I suppose," she said.

"Not a novel, Ma Grecque" (it pleased Eliza to be called by their nickname of La Grecque, a tribute to her grave sculptured beauty). "Romance—yes it is, the wildest romance I've ever read, and yet, as the author tells you in his preface, he has done nothing but 'set down the simple and naked truth.'"

Eliza was tantalized into a smile. "Why can't you tell me what it is?"

"Wishart's *Deeds of Montrose* on his campaigns in Scotland four years ago."

"Why write a book about them?"

"Must books only be about ideas?"

"If you prefer to read of men, there is history."

"But this *will* be history," cried Louey, slamming the book in her impatience.

"It isn't *now*," continued the inexorable voice from the writing-table, vigorous and even cheerful in the joy of argument, "it is still part of 'the vulgar present.'"

"Is the present day always vulgar?"

"Always. One is blinded by it, personal, passionate. One cannot see what is happening at the moment."

"Some can, de Retz the great Coadjutor of Paris for instance; *he* has said that Montrose is 'le seul homme du monde qui m'ait rappelé l'idée de certains héros que l'on ne voit plus que dans les vies de Plutarque—une grandeur d'âme qui n'en avait point de pareille en ce siècle.'"

So Louey had troubled to learn the compliment by heart, but Eliza did not tease her for it, having suffered too much from teasing herself. If a brilliant and worldly French statesman had to go back to ancient history to find a parallel to a modern general's greatness of soul, well then it only helped to prove her case, and so she hastened to say, continuing to talk French without noticing it, since Louey had begun to do so, and then relapsing into English in their polyglot fashion: "It shows that we know more about Julius Caesar or Brutus to-day than about Oliver Cromwell."

"So you advise me to read Caesar's *Commentaries* rather than the *Deeds of Montrose*?"

"Certainly. The 'history of one's own day' is an anomaly. It cannot be history until it has undergone the balanced verdict of time."

"Balanced verdict be damned!" cried Louey. "The balance will go to the side of the winner and remain there, and that's all there is in your verdict of time. Cromwell will win it because he won the war."

"He's not won the peace yet," said Eliza, and the sudden note of reflective common-sense fell like a splash of cool water on their heated abstractions. But in the same instant her classic nose wrinkled sharply. "Your shoe is burning," she said, "I can smell it from here. Your new black shoes. There's no money for more. How can you be so careless!"

"Ough! You're right. It's burning my foot now."

Louey kicked off her shoe so high into the air that it executed a neat parabola and descended in some distant corner behind the furniture, unheeded by her as she nursed her toe, hopping on the other foot. There was a hole too in the stocking, she should have given it to the maid to mend, but it hadn't shown in the shoe.

There was a clatter of horses below. Were the others back already? Then something must have happened while they were out. Louey flew to the window. Eliza's interest in 'the vulgar present' was too slight to move her from her seat and that long, unseeing contemplation of the little man, his gun and ducks. But Louey's stillness at the window became strange, even alarming.

"What is it?" she asked, and her sister did not answer. "*Who* is it?" and she began to rise, though slowly, unwilling to confront any new emergency. Horses brought messengers, bad news; they had brought, not so very many days ago, the unbelievable news of the execution of their uncle, the King of England, by his subjects.

"I—don't—know—I—*think*——" said Louey, and stopped, unaware that she had not said what she thought.

She saw some horsemen dismounting in the smudgy trodden snow of the courtyard. She saw a man all in black on a great horse, who was obviously their leader. The porter had come out to greet him, bowing very low. Now he too had dismounted, was coming up the steps.

Eliza, peering out behind her sister, said, "It isn't anyone we know. New visitors." She sighed, hating the distraction of new visitors, endless talk between visitors and her mother while the rest of them had to play a sort of Greek chorus, speaking their part when required and never quite sure when it was required, sure rather that it never really was required, since nobody wanted to talk to anyone else when their mother was there. Yet their talk disturbed her solitude. Here she was just past thirty. Would she never be free to live her own life? Even her worries were not her own, for now her annoyance was extending beyond the casual interruption of a visit to its inopportune moment.

What would people think of a visit of condolence if they found that its object was out merry-making in a sledge on the ice? Years ago, when the English Puritans had come on a formal visit of condolence to her mother for the death of her German husband, they had been horribly scandalized to find her entire family of sons and daughters engaged in getting up a play and an absurd noisy masque for her amusement, and the palace (so called) a pandemonium of excited, prancing, hallooing boys and girls in every conceivable form of fancy dress. This mummery had taken place several months after her father's death, but that didn't shorten the long faces of the Puritan visitors, who were appalled that it should ever take place at all.

And now it was barely three weeks since they had heard of the dreadful death of their mother's brother. There was some fatality about visits of condolence to their mother; clearly she was unfitted by fate as well as nature ever to receive them.

Eliza, with the nervous desperation of an unready plotter, had just begun to say something of her fears to Louey, just begun to say, "We must say—what *can* we say?—A sick friend perhaps——" And Louey, with that blank angelic stare that showed she had not taken in a word, was softly answering, "Why a sick friend? Why not a sound one? And why say either of them to whom?" when a page came into the room and announced the Marquis of Montrose.

Louey saw him standing at the end of the long room in the cold grey light reflected through the windows from the snow outside, so still in that instant's pause that he might always have stood there between the door and the windows and only in this moment become visible, a spirit conjured up by her vehement thought of him.

'He is there—here in this room,' it was saying; 'now he is coming towards us, and I shall see his face clearly.'

But she had no need to see it, for already she had seen his eyes.

He had come forward; that pale light from the snow no longer hung over him, he was beside them in the warm firelight that danced over the inlaid marble floor and light painted walls, he was in this familiar room that glimmered with polished surfaces like a china bowl. She heard his voice, measured and grave, with the slight Scottish burr that gave each syllable so much more value than did the voices of their London visitors. She saw the irregular lines of his features, the faint jagged line of a scar at the side of his face, and that his lithe wiry figure made him look tall, but he would not seem so beside their giant brothers, Rupert and Maurice.

None of these things, nor the bows and greetings and Eliza's apologies for their mother's absence, broke the spell of that first sight of him.

Those eyes, keen and resolute, were inscrutable; they had looked on something that other men had not seen, something beyond sorrow or hope or despair, though it had once included all these things. She had just been reading how for two winters, bitter even for Scotland, wandering with his followers on the freezing mountains 'without quarters, without even tents, he had endured all war's hardships, with nothing to appease his thirst and hunger but icy water or melted snow, without bread and salt, and with only a scanty supply of lean and starveling cattle.'

Now he stood in their drawing-room and answered the correct things her sister was saying, and she might never get a chance again to hear him speak. She had heard him come riding into their courtyard, as all the great men in the world came riding to see her mother —and went away again. She saw them once, or perhaps twice, and often never spoke to them herself at all. This time she would speak to this man herself.

SIR EDWARD HYDE, Chancellor of the Exchequer, had gone to the Palace of the Binnenhof for an interview with his young master, the new King Charles II, who had been staying all this winter at the Binnenhof as guest of his brother-in-law, the young Prince William of Orange. But King Charles had forgotten the appointment and gone out skating.

In no hurry to get back to his draughty lodging, Hyde was strolling along the gallery that connected the outer buildings with the massive old central fort, talking extremely brilliantly to one of the Dutch officers of the household in the hope that he would appreciate his wit sufficiently to ask him out to dinner, when his companion must needs interrupt one of his best sallies to look out of the window and exclaim at something that was happening outside the Palace. A troop of horse, he said; some great personage must be arriving to see Prince William—or perhaps the English King.

Hyde had perforce to look out too, at which his whole train of lucid and sparkling thought was interrupted, his jaw dropped, and his round face turned as pale as it was possible for that choleric complexion to do.

"Yes, I know the leader," he replied abstractedly to his companion's question. It was five years since he had seen him among the King's Court at Oxford, but he was not likely to forget him, even at this distance and on horseback. "It is the Marquis of Montrose, come in his own person."

His companion's large face shone like the sun with satisfaction. "The Great Marquis! I have long wished to set eyes on him. Introduce me, I beg of you; it is something to say one has met the most famous soldier of one's day."

Hyde tried to acquiesce affably as they hurried down the stairs together, but he felt he would give a deal to avoid meeting the famous soldier at this moment, and yet see him he must as quickly as possible—warn him he must—but good God, when had he ever done anything else but warn him? And even in his last letters he had flatly forbidden him by command of his new Sovereign to approach The Hague.

Hyde had tried to meet him at Sevenbergen, but before he could do so the news of Charles I's death had fallen like a thunderbolt on them all, and it had been a messenger, not Hyde himself, that brought the news to Montrose. He had uttered no word in answer to that news, no message had come back, Montrose had remained shut in his room for two days, seeing nobody but his servants. His friend and chaplain, Wishart, had afterwards found a verse he had scribbled on a torn scrap of paper, in which his rage and pity and over-generous admiration burst from his heart like a gush of blood, and held up his own image of the King he had served with so great passion:

'Great, good and just, could I but rate
My grief, and thy too rigid fate'—

It was an odd way for a great soldier to take the blow, but it affected many people oddly, stunning some, driving others to despair and even suicide, while more than one had died simply of a broken heart. Personal loyalty was not the only cause for such violent grief; this death done in the open with a show of law, but in direct defiance of the laws of England, was more than the murder of a king; it was the death of a world, of all confidence in old beliefs. Nothing would ever be the same again.

To Hyde it was the death of law, of decency, of sanity, of all that he thought of when he thought of England. When he had been homesick for England it had been for a land which now had ceased to exist as utterly as if it had vanished under the sea. The sea might recede and something of England appear again, but never as it had been before.

His step was heavier now than it had been a month ago, and not by reason of the gout, as he plodded down the stairs and out over the drawbridge to meet the Marquis.

'He has changed,' he thought as he looked up at that spare active form in black, mounted on the big horse; but then which of them had not changed in these half-dozen years? Only, of most you could say, 'He is more worn,' or 'He is stouter,' or 'He is graver,' and you would not at first say any of these things of Montrose.

It was as though another man looked out of those steady and brilliant eyes down into Hyde's. Did Montrose even recognize him?—but surely he himself had not changed as much as that?—or was he seeing Hyde's thoughts so plainly that he had scarcely leisure to observe the man?

And here was this ridiculous Dutchman pulling at his sleeve for an introduction to a famous general, when they themselves could hardly wait to greet each other as persons.

"Is the King here?" said Montrose, and Hyde told him, no.

"If Your Lordship will come to my poor lodging——" He looked nervously at the Marquis' large retinue: Lauderdale and his faction would make trouble over that. He might as well have said it out aloud, for he saw Montrose's smile following his glance. Confused, unwontedly at a loss, he did not know how it happened that the Marquis had dismounted and dispersed most of his followers, while the Dutchman had disappeared.

They were now walking together beside the frozen lake of the Binnenhof on which people were skating and playing games. He was trying to give his reasons for attempting to keep Montrose from The Hague and realizing uncomfortably that he had already written them several times over,—and now all his balanced arguments were being brushed away.

Montrose was driving at him, demanding of him, "You write and ask my help with one hand while with the other you support Lauderdale and now Argyll. You pander to them and keep me at a distance. I have obeyed the King as long as I could—now I cannot. I have no apology to make for defying His Majesty's commands. The explanation is for you to give—why the King's recent enemies are to be trusted rather than his loyal servants."

Yet this was said, though sternly, without temper, or at any rate such temper as Rupert would have shown. There was an icy logic in it that worsted Lawyer Hyde, as he felt, at his own game. The result was to ruffle his own temper. He began desperately:

"If Your Lordship chooses to ignore His Majesty's commands——"

"His Majesty is not yet nineteen. His commands are prompted by his advisers. I am speaking to the chief of them."

"But not the only one. This Court is a whirlpool of contrary opinions. And we have only got him away this winter from his mother in Paris. All last year she was urging him, as she urged the late King, to ally himself with the Covenanters. Queen Henrietta Maria can see little difference between one Protestant and another; she has pinned her faith, as did the late King, to the split between Cromwell's army and their former allies in Scotland—a split that has certainly widened enormously in the last weeks. All Scotland is in uproar at King Charles' murder, the whole nation has gone into mourning. What's more, they have openly defied the English Parliament's decree to abolish Monarchy. Argyll himself——" he hesitated, then stopped altogether.

It was impossible to go on with those eyes upon him. In the silence that hung on the frost-still air, scarcely broken for them by the cries and laughter of the people playing on the ice, so near them yet as remote as the starved birds that also swooped and cried to each other, he heard Montrose's deep voice finish his sentence for him—not as Hyde had intended.

"Argyll himself," Montrose said, "is sending commissioners to the King. That is why I can no longer obey the King, and have come here at last myself. Argyll is my greatest enemy, I freely admit it. But Argyll is no more my enemy than he is the King's."

"My lord, you may well be right. I at any rate believe you to be—in part," he added judicially. "But at least it is something that Argyll is the present ruler of Scotland, if only by force and fear——"

"Add also by wealth and usury. There is scarce a family in

Scotland that is not bound in his toils.   Add also by the powers of death and hell.   Argyll as Chief Elder of the Kirk rules more by terror of excommunication and eternal damnation than by the armed forces of the Covenant.   The country is in the grip of a nightmare."

The passion with which the younger man spoke gave Hyde a momentary sense of advantage as the practical man of the world.

"My lord, let us keep to the main issue.   Whatever the reasons, the Marquis of Argyll is the ruling power of your country, and we cannot afford to ignore the fact that he has broken his alliance with Cromwell and is holding out his hand to King Charles II."

"Because that hand has been forced by the public opinion of his country.   Even Argyll has had to listen to the groan of horror that went up from every corner of Scotland at news of the King's murder.   Yet it is known that he sold the King to his murderers, it is believed that he and Cromwell discussed—planned rather—that murder together when he entertained him at his house in Edinburgh last autumn.   And now you'll take his hand and hope for his help, while you refuse mine!"

His anger, restrained till now, had broken into open fury.   Hyde made an attempt to calm him, but he himself was indignant, flustered, and in spite of himself unbearably anxious.   He reminded the Marquis that King Charles II, so far from refusing his help, had written through himself to beg for it, to which Montrose with a short laugh added, "With my hands bound!"

It was too much.   Hyde exploded with an oath, muttered an excuse that his gouty foot was troubling him (and so indeed it was, swathed inside a too large shoe, having to pad up and down keeping pace with this long springy stride), and asked whether Montrose would not take this opportunity, since King Charles was not at the Binnenhof, to present himself to the Dowager Princess of Orange, a greater power at present in Holland than her young son William.

"She hopes for a match between her daughter and the young King, and favours the Covenanters," replied Montrose coolly.   "I find myself well able to wait for another opportunity to be presented to the Princess Amelia. But will you direct me to the Queen of Bohemia's house?"

"You wish to go there this moment?"

"On the instant."

A round bright eye rolled indignantly up at the Marquis. This man was in a mighty hurry and, like Prince Rupert, determined to take his own way, and no one else's advice. But he seemed so unaware of his error that Hyde swallowed it with something of a gulp, and answered:

"It is behind you—the Wassanaar Hof, that big corner house, two houses rather, round to the right at the end of the Voorhout; it is just out of sight from here."

Montrose spun round so sharply on his heel that his spur clanked on the icy ground. In doing so he looked for the first time at the figures skimming over the ice in their thick bunched clothes, and stared at a little group standing at some distance round a man who was swinging a long clubbed stick backwards and forwards at a ball, which at last he struck and sent spinning to the end of the lake.

"If you must needs go and visit the King's aunt now——" Hyde began huffily, stuffily, and stopped, suddenly hearing how his voice sounded.

But Montrose did not seem to have heard it, nor his words. "I did not know they played golf on the ice here," he said. "It is a game I have played very often in my own country, but I have not seen it elsewhere."

"King James tried to introduce it into England," said Hyde, "but it has never proved popular. Its simplicity makes it more suitable for peasants than for a nation of tennis-players."

He cursed himself for his rudeness as Montrose, without seeming to notice it, took his leave of him with a cold and distant courtesy and strode back to the end of the lake where his personal attendants were waiting with his horse.

Hyde watched him go, and thought of Rupert whom Montrose

had wished to meet here. What a pair they would have made! They might well have been able together to sweep everything before them—sweep it indeed further than he himself approved.

These younger men, strong, active, indifferent to their elders, swinging through life on light, easy-moving feet, careless whether the next step were to their own death,—how insolent was their certainty, their contempt of brains better than their own, merely because those brains were cooped up in bodies less free and vigorous than their own. Confronted with them, even Hyde's self-satisfaction was forced to contrast that agile mind of his with his clumsy, aching body, grown too quickly old. He envied, and condemned.

Rupert blowing into his lodgings like the nor'-easterly gale that had driven his ships from these shores, disregarding, even despising Hyde's requests; Montrose marching openly with all his men into this sufficiently perturbed city in flat disobedience to the King's commands and Hyde's most urgent warnings—this was insolence, vanity, a harsh blot upon the nobility of the Marquis' character.

Hyde could recognize that nobility as well as anyone, but he could recognize faults too, and it gave him considerably more pleasure to do so. Did these soldiers, with all their showier opportunities for displaying their nobility, ever recognize Hyde's?

He knew how much he had it, and so, in unfortunate corollary, he felt he had earned full right to criticize even 'the clearest spirit and of the greatest honour' among the King's servants. He had acknowledged the Marquis to be that, and in firm hard handwriting, and laid down his considered opinion as solidly as a foundation-stone, that he believed 'his clear spirit to be most like to advance the King's service.' Yes, and he held to it, but there was another side to all things, and Montrose made it exceedingly difficult for others to get on with him.

'Damnable proud' had been the verdict on him ever since his first appearance as a youth at the English Court, when he had at once contrived to make an enemy of the very man who could best advance his interests, the Duke of Hamilton. He had been 'altogether too remarkable a young man' for Hamilton's taste. Hyde had now no opinion himself of the Duke of Hamilton, but that did not prevent his remembering Hamilton's opinion of Montrose with relish, and looking forward to his return to his cold lodging and the private notes for his *magnum opus* to which he could confide his own opinions. (These were sometimes inconsistent, since they were apt to vary according to whether the person described had lately agreed with him or not.)

And there was another obscure grievance, as yet undiscovered, that he had against the Marquis. Suddenly he discovered it.

"Damnation!" he swore. "And I never managed to introduce that Dutchman after all—there goes any hope of a dinner from him!"

III

AS Montrose turned and walked back towards his men they at once rode up with his horse for him to remount, and it took him only a minute or two to reach the Queen of Bohemia's house after turning at right angles at the end of the lake.

The game of golf he had just noticed had crowded out everything else in his mind in an absurd way. Here he was in yet another strange foreign city after travelling in the last two and a half years through Norway, Denmark, Germany, Flanders, France, Italy, Vienna, Prague, Poland, and Brussels; but he was not here, he was back in Scotland, up on the links of Old Montrose playing a match with his brother-in-law Sir John Colquhoun on the eve of his own wedding the next day to Magdalen Carnegie, daughter of the Earl of Southesk.

That familiar scene in the windy autumn twilight of nearly twenty years ago was more alive in his mind's eye than this frost-bound foreign city with people calling to each other in yet another strange language. He had ridden up to Kinnaird late that evening after the game on a sudden impulse to see Magdalen once more before she became his bride on the morrow. She had stood there so still, a girl of sixteen, looking at him with those deep eyes of hers. Had she in that instant seen all the agony that he would bring her?

What that agony had been to her, left in her father's house with their children while he went off to lead one campaign after another of wild Highlanders against the ruling powers of their country, and took their eldest son, a boy of fourteen, to his death in that winter mountain fighting,—what that long unrest had done to her, he never fully knew until he saw her as she lay dying, beyond the power of speech, yet still able to greet him with that secret smile of hers.

He had read its secret then: she, who had feared all their married

80

life to hear of his sudden death—or worse, not sudden, but by hanging, drawing and quartering—had, after all, cheated her fears; she had died first, and left him free to pursue his own end.

Nothing now could hurt her any more. He had said that since so often to himself, comforting himself, when it seemed that all that he had done had been in vain. They might have lived long years together at home and in peace, and brought up Johnnie, their eldest son, to be heir of his father's estates, that were now forfeited to the Estates of Scotland.

But he had fought for his King, and Johnnie had died in that fighting, and Magdalen his wife had died of it, nearly four years ago; and in the following spring King Charles I had given himself up to Argyll and asked Montrose, as he had asked his nephew Rupert, to lay down his arms and leave the country, since only so could he now serve his King.

There was no choice but to obey. Montrose, the King's Viceroy of Scotland, left his country, as he had come to it on the dawn of his 'Annus Mirabilis,' in the disguise of a servant; with two or three of his followers he sailed from the harbour of Old Montrose in a small Norwegian sloop and was nearly wrecked when his enemies cut her cable while the ship rode at anchor, so as to drive her upon the rocks.

That would have been an odd, ignominious end to his Year of Marvels, but it would not have mattered, since Magdalen was no longer alive to know of it. He was free by then to meet whatever end should come to him.

> ' I'll set my foot in yonder boat,
> Mither, Mither,
> I'll set my foot in yonder boat,
> And I'll fare o'er the sea, oh ! '

Years it had been since the tune of that old country song had swung into his head, and now it came back to him as he rode into the courtyard of an exiled queen's house in an unknown Dutch town.

F

He had 'set his foot in yonder boat,' and tossed through storms on the North Sea for a week's voyage before he reached Bergen in Norway, an exile, a condemned criminal, his estates forfeited—to be welcomed, as was Rupert, with offers of power and wealth from foreign princes who were eager to secure his services in the highest command of their armies.

But he refused them, as Rupert had done, and sought only to enlist help from the foreign powers for his helpless King, captive first to Argyll, then to Cromwell.

To gain that help he had wandered all through Europe and now was here, and his King was dead, and all that he had done had made no difference. His King was dead, as his wife and his eldest son were dead; tyranny had triumphed, and his country lay as in a dungeon under Argyll's rule, bound in a Covenant to the powers of death and hell.

'The griefs that astonish speak more by their silence,' he had written of the King's death. He still felt 'astonished,' stunned by that blow to all his hopes for his cause and country; he was indifferent to anything that might now happen to him, knowing only that he still had a task to perform, and that whatever was left to him of life was dedicated only to its performance.

So here he was at The Hague, and he had ridden through the gateway of the Wassanaar Hof, a big rambling red-brick house, all gables and ornamentally twisted chimneys and tiled roofs sloping in all directions like a miniature town.

The dead King's sister, Queen Elizabeth, was not at home, but some of her daughters were, and he had been so lost in that dream caused by the sight of a golf-club striking a ball over the ice that he had no thought of what he should do next, and so agreed to the servant's request that he should come in and wait for Her Majesty's return; he dismounted before he realized what he was doing, for it was important to meet the Queen as early as possible, but he was in no mood to meet extraneous princesses before it was necessary.

But it was done now, he was following the servant into a

lofty hall, floored with marble in black and white squares, and up a staircase and into a long L-shaped room with a ruddy glow flickering out from a great marble fireplace round the corner; and there he saw two tall young women in deep black, one of them standing by that fireplace, her face and form in shadow against the glow, and the other advancing towards him, making all the polite explanations and enquiries in a low, sad, mechanical voice, as though all the things that should be said by a princess and the daughter of an absent mother and the niece of a murdered king came into her mind by clockwork and out again in this even procession of suitable words.

This must be the Princess Elizabeth, eldest daughter of the Queen, and far the more regularly beautiful of the two in this room.

The other must be a good many years younger; she looked a young girl, or for that matter like a boy, and not at all like a young lady who had been cooped up in this neat Dutch house for three weeks, as she had doubtless been through the first period of mourning; she might have just been riding or running in the wind, her hair blown out all round her head in a glowing halo, a quick flush on her cheeks, and her eyes scanning the new visitor, bright and observant. The hand she had given him to kiss was not the soft white hand of a princess, but strong and hard, with long thin fingers and a black smudge right across them. She had only one shoe on and had evidently forgotten it until she saw her foot showing beneath her skirt with a hole in the toe of the stocking, when it hastily retreated behind the other foot.

Yet these absurd details did not seem to matter; she held her head high and her slight form straight, and the eyes that met his were fearless and eager, unconscious of herself, and of his talk, for it was plain she did not listen to a word while he courteously avoided her sister's guarded references to their uncle's death, and told her how strange and pleasant it was to him now to meet hospitality in his own tongue, since this was the eleventh country he had been in since he had left Scotland.

At the word 'Scotland' that slight silent figure by the chimney-piece plunged straight into what had evidently been the current of her thoughts.

"I was reading of you, my lord; this book was in my hand as I looked down and saw you in the courtyard. Do you read it yourself and wonder, 'Can this be I?'"

"Louey!" murmured her sister's low, pained voice.

"Am I talking nonsense? It sounds like it."

This then was the Princess Louise, the sixth or seventh member of the family; he had taken her for one still younger, both from her looks and the eager childlike candour of her gaze at him, and now her speech.

'Am I talking nonsense?' she had said, and cared nothing if it were so. "To read of one's own deeds," she was saying, "when the heat of action has passed and you are cold sober, sitting by the fire, it must be like remembering something you had dreamed when you were drunk."

"*Louey!*" came the bell-like note again from her sister, lower still, but even Louey heard it this time, swerved in mid-course to fling out an arm towards her sister, just touching her elegant hand but driven on in the wind of her own enthusiasm.

"Yes, I said that because I was reading of that action that they call—all the foreign generals who come here—a greater marvel than any of your victories."

He was struck by her likeness to Rupert as he had first seen him several years ago before his face had hardened. 'She dressed up once in an old out-grown suit I'd had as a boy, and they all said they might have mistaken her for me,' so Rupert had then told him with an odd shy pride, as though it were very considerate of any of his family to resemble him. Her talk showed her too to be as sudden and unconventional as he, but her freedom had more of gaiety and less of defiance in it; the laughter and love of life could not be shut out of her eyes, bright now with his own triumphs.

"What was the 'greater marvel'?" he asked.

It seemed the first time she had heard that deep voice—was it because he had now spoken to her? She answered him, "That time when you stormed Dundee and your 'breathless scouts' came dashing in with news of the enemy less than a mile off and six times your strength, and your men all grabbing their spoil, dead drunk——"

"No, only a bit overladen with drink," he corrected, "or I could never have got them going."

"How *did* you get them going, and on top of a twenty-mile march too before storming Dundee? The Prince de Condé says he'd give his soul for the secret of your power over your men."

"We have heard our brother Rupert too speak of that," Eliza chimed in, partly to add her praise, partly to extenuate by sharing her impulsive younger sister's emotion.

"Have you heard from him?" Montrose asked quickly.

"Not a word," said Louey.

"One never hears from Rupert," Eliza sighed in exasperation.

"Even when you'd beaten them off their loot," persisted Louey, "how could you get them into a line of march?"

This girl might have been his own son demanding details of his battles. Not a trace here of subtle feminine compliment such as he had met so often in foreign Courts and found wearisome enough to answer.

Women praising soldiers—it was an age-old activity and one that embarrassed him the more since his wife's death, for since then the ironic smile of her who never could nor would pay a compliment had become the more alive to him. But this intent interest was more a challenge than a compliment, and he met it as man to man.

"They'd had a few hours' rest after their all-night march," he said, "they'd been full fed after starving, and got stout clothes on their backs instead of rags against the rain, and that had put them in good fettle. Once they were pushed and kicked out of the town we shook them somehow into their line of march as they went, the worst of 'em in the van with the few horse hurrying them on from the rear, and the musketeers in support."

"And then led them nearly thirty miles! But how could you shake off the pursuers?"

"I know the country—and I knew that Hurry and Baillie knew it. I had, as always, to get back to the hills, while their move was to cut me off from them. So I took the line they expected until midnight, then turned on my tracks and slipped round behind them."

"And their scouts never saw it?"

"It was a wet night, pitch dark. And they'd hardly expect troops to march first east and north, then south-west, then north again."

"In that dripping darkness," breathed Louey, "what blind confidence they must have had in you, tacking, swerving like an unsteady ship in a gale, yet knowing that mad contrary course to be right because they knew their leader!"

It was extraordinary to find himself living those wild hours over again—and through the mind of this girl, unknown before to him, who showed her admiration with such passionate innocence.

"Your Highness speaks as though you had been there yourself," he said with a slow, amused smile.

"Why not, my lord? Other people's experiences are often much more real than one's own."

Eliza seized the chance to explain and excuse her sister. "Because you cultivate imagination at the expense of intellect. That is why she talks so wildly, my lord. She is an artist like Rupert."

The word 'artist' seemed to annoy Louey.

"Then all those staggering drunkards on the retreat were artists —or something bigger. The only moments worth living are those when you lose yourself."

"In drink?" asked Eliza, annoyed in her turn.

"Drink can be one way, I suppose; art, love, religion are others —or some overmastering faith and purpose. When Rupert leads a charge or works up a fleet out of nothing as he did here this autumn; when young Jan Steen paints those pictures of old women warming their feet on their charcoal boxes and adding their cracked voices to the singing-party while the children steal tit-bits out of their dish, the men swilling beer and kissing anyone within reach, the dogs gnawing bones—life runs roaring through them and they are so caught up in it that they never hear that strange force that sings so loud in them."

"Nor does she hear it," thought Eliza, looking in amazement at her sister. What had happened to her? Eager, impulsive, Louey had often been that with visitors, though more often casual and distraite, but never had Eliza seen her like this, 'caught up,' as she had said herself, like a flame blown in the wind.

Did *he* see it now he was silent, but with a silence so watchful, aware, amused, that it stimulated Louey more than any polite questions? Eliza felt that he saw a great deal, but what did he make of it? Did he think Louey was shamelessly setting her cap at him? Many men with far less reason had thought it, and Louey had not cared, had laughed richly and whole-heartedly over them, never minding a jot whether she had given them occasion to laugh at her.

This was different. Eliza could not bear it, nor, she knew, could Louey, if this man should think lightly of her.

But as she looked at those eyes that watched her sister, she felt that she need not fear, that explanations or excuses would make no difference to him; he would form his own opinion independent of them, and it would not be ignoble. That slower Scottish voice was now answering even Louey's talk of pictures with easier intimacy; Eliza warmed to the sense of surprised understanding that was growing between these two strangers so utterly unlike each other.

"When I first visited the English Court," he said, "the Duke of Hamilton advised me to make a good impression by admiring the King's new Mantegnas at Hampton Court, or else the Breughel. 'Admire the snow effects' was a sentence that stuck in my mind— and my throat."

"And turned you against pictures ever since? Wait till you have seen Rembrandt van Rijn's at Amsterdam. But is it true that Cromwell is going to sell that glorious collection of my uncle's at Hampton Court?"

She wished she had not said it, for his face had shut again into the mask it had worn when Eliza had spoken of King Charles' death. She hurried on about pictures instead, but faltered, caught Eliza's eye and was listening, but not to what he would say; and now Eliza too was taut, both attentive to a distant sound as light as castanets in the frosty air.

What was happening to them? He spoke, but they were not even listening. Puzzled, amused, he wondered what it was that had scared this glancing creature whose moods sped faster than he could follow—yes, and the elder one too; something was breaking up their thoughts, scattering them uneasily here and there.

They were listening to the sound of horses again in the courtyard; the sledge had returned with their mother, she would be coming upstairs and into this room, and their moment was going from them.

Desperately they tried to hold it, to go on talking as they had done, but it was no use, they were conscious now of what they were saying and how it would sound. Eliza frowned, Louey laughed, and their mother came into the room.

Was that really all that had happened? Poets knew better.

'And then my mother came into the room,' said Louey to herself with the queer little half-smile that had settled on her face instead of that former radiance, like a bird sailing down the wind and folding its wings.

Poets in England years ago had known what happened when her mother came into the room.

> 'You meaner beauties of the night
> That poorly satisfy our eyes
> More by your number than your light,
> You common people of the skies,
> What are you when the moon shall rise?'

So now she 'rose,' 'Th' eclipse and glory of her kind,' upon the famous stranger; and her attendant satellites who had shone like stars now paled before her splendour and shrank back, while their mother's glorious welcome warmed the dim room.

IV

ONCE again she had been Diana that 'Goddess excellently bright,' enjoying her native element, immortal and immune from human cares, losing all sense of time and purpose, and purpose disappointed, in the impersonal rapture of driving her horses at top speed over the frozen world. And now when this 'Winter Queen' entered on the rush of that rare air, the joyous life that filled her body and shone in her eyes and cheeks flowed even into her sense of the tragedy that had befallen her family, since with that tragedy was involved the heroic endeavour of this man who had fought and lost all for her brother.

She swept towards him with her cloak billowing out behind her, both hands outstretched, and the tears rushing unheeded into her splendid eyes.

"You were his friend," she said, "you did all that man could do, and yet he died the death of a criminal."

He could not answer her, but she did not notice that.

"Assassination," she said, "*that* we had long feared possible— but that it should be done in the light of the sun!"

She had taken his hands when he kissed hers, and stood holding them while he looked into the face for which so many thousand men had gone to fight, in a quarrel not their own. Her beauty was radiant, time could not touch it, not care nor sorrow, and she was giving no thought to it.

"I had not seen him since he was a child," she said, "and I can remember him in his cradle at Dunfermline Castle where his nurse once saw a black pall soaked in blood lying across the sleeping baby. Poor 'Baby Charles,' as our father called him to the end of his life! Even in his infancy he was fey."

She broke off, she could say no more of him, nor did Montrose. It was as though he had taken a vow of silence on the subject of his murdered master.

And the Queen in the same instant had flown to the duties of hospitality—had these careless girls offered him nothing on arrival after his long journey? There was Great Eliza with her head in the clouds as absent-minded as her own professor, and Louey so flighty and scatter-brained, would she never learn to grow up?

Her airy scolding reduced them to awkward shamefacedness in spite of his protests that he had dined quite lately and would not take wine, but for all that she was sending for some when Eliza whispered to her and she exclaimed, "What, only that sour stuff of Carl's left!—He sent us a handsome present of wine from Heidelberg some time ago and it's clean undrinkable," she explained to her guest with a wry face at the meanness of her eldest son, "and you who have had your fill of the finest Rhenish in Germany!"

"I never drank it when I could get their light ale," he replied.

She was enchanted. She always had ale brewed at her country house at Rhenen according to the English recipe, and he must taste it instantly. A page brought some in immensely long slender glasses, and the Queen drank too.

She sat in a great carved and gilded chair by the fire, holding that long fluted glass of liquid amber in its light, her black dress and cloak framed in a golden throne, and the firelight flickering on her face. He sat opposite her and could scarcely believe in her beauty; it put that of her daughters utterly in the shade, and shadows now they both seemed to have become, sitting a little further from the fire in the colder light of the departing day.

Eliza had taken up some knitting which she did for the Lutheran nuns to dispose of in charity; it was her compensation for the waste of time imposed by her mother's endless succession of visitors.

Louey, crouched on a stool, twisting her long fingers together, gazed at those two figures by the fire. Never had she seen her mother lovelier, and growing more so every minute; she drew fresh life from each new admirer in proportion to her interest in them. At worst it was 'I never lack a fool to laugh at; when one goes, another comes.' And at best—yes, Louey had never seen her mother at her best, not even in her mad infatuation two or three years ago for de l'Epinay, for that had been a restless frenzy burning rather than illumining her,—never until now, when she talked with this man who sat so still, leaning forward in his chair, his elbow on his knee, his deep-set eyes scanning her face.

What was he thinking of her? Was he falling headlong in love with her like everyone else who came here, and on less than a hundredth part of the attention that she was giving him? If he were not doing so he'd be an insensate dolt, she decided in an unwilling glow of admiration at the new and lovely life in her mother's face.

Yet they were speaking on a far from lively subject, the news that was now reaching the Continent of more and more executions in England. The Duke of Hamilton had just testified to his belated loyalty by the loss of his head, though, as the Queen heartlessly said, it was little loss to the cause he had once betrayed. But the oddest thing was that as he had escaped from the Tower for a few days the judges argued his recapture as a sign that God desired his death—"a sign rather," Montrose was saying, "that reason is dead in England, and only superstition rules. They have substituted the Code of Moses for the laws of England."

"And yet we had thought Fairfax was at the head of affairs there," the Queen answered, "and Rupert has spoken well of him."

(It was always Rupert's opinion that was quoted now; it used to be Carl's.)

"Fairfax must be the figure-head only," Montrose answered; "it is Cromwell who reigns."

"A reign of terror," she cried. "That man must be the Beast in the Book of Revelation."

"I have always heard that Beast was the Roman Catholic Church," observed Eliza dryly over her knitting. "Two such enemies should not share the same symbol!"

Louey nearly cried out to stop her. How frivolous pedantry could be in the wrong place! Eliza was making a strident effort to catch on to some shred, however tattered, of the conversation that was slipping away so fast from her and her sister, but their mother naturally did not find it worthy of notice and turned impulsively to her visitor with fresh subjects: the crimson baton that the Emperor of Germany had just presented to him, creating him a Field-Marshal of the Empire with power to raise troops anywhere in his dominions; Rupert's great disappointment at having to leave Holland without meeting him, "the worst luck in the world."

"That was not luck," he answered sternly, "it was arranged."

By whom, she knew as well as he. Queen Henrietta Maria, though far away in Paris, still directed her son Charles' policy, and there had been some bad passages-at-arms between her and the Marquis of Montrose. So that Elizabeth's next remark was more to the point than it appeared when it flicked out like a whiplash at her absent sister-in-law.

"My poor brother *lived* a martyr to his Church as well as died it, for his wife burdened his whole life with her efforts to change his religion. Has she written to you since his death?"

"She has, Madam, asking me to unite with all my countrymen and forget all former differences."

There was a gasp, an instant's silence, and then an irrepressible burst of laughter from the Queen.

"And how," she exclaimed, "you are to unite with the men who begin all their discussions by demanding that the King must banish you for ever from his Court is beyond the wit of man—but not, it seems, of woman!"

"How does the King take their demands?"

"He is only eighteen, remember, and his mother's grip still on him. Lord, how I hate these maternal women, it is not easy to distinguish 'em from tigresses. Their savage simplicity! That grim Solemn League and Covenant of the Scottish Kirk—and the Church of England for which my brother died,—the Queen Henrietta Maria can see no difference between them, so you are to 'forget all differences,' and her son Charles to ignore them!"

"And he?" he asked again with quiet insistence, for in the pleasure of criticizing her sister-in-law the Queen seemed to forget that it was her nephew who was now King of England.

"He has no love for Lauderdale," she assured him. "He is anything but squeamish, but he tells me he wants to rinse his mouth out from Lauderdale's foul after-dinner talk when he shows himself off as an affable man of the world. But I doubt if Lauderdale ever guesses that."

"It would need a hatchet to make him do so."

It was Louey now who had made a brief snatch at the conversation, but it at once rolled past her again.

"Charles hates to express disapproval or dislike," said her mother. "Ned Hyde says it will break his heart if he does not outgrow that infirmity. But is it always an infirmity? Some of us—Charles for one—might wish that fat old Ned himself had a touch of it."

She never cared what she said, she could never be afraid either of persons, opinions, or consequences, and that was one reason why men adored her.

She had never seen Montrose before, and seemed to have known him all her life; she even knew that he had been born in that wild stormy winter when she had married at sixteen and her brother Henry Prince of Wales had died, that strong, splendid youth, and left Baby Charles, whom no one had expected to live, as heir to the English throne.

"How that one winter has linked all our fates!" she exclaimed, her lustrous eyes filled with wonder at the pitiful tangle of human life, thinking of her two brothers' deaths, and this man's birth, and her own marriage, when every poet in England had written in praise of her—John Donne and Ben Jonson and Will Shakespeare.

"'Stands Scotland where it did?'" she asked with a glancing smile at her visitor which alarmed Louey, who knew how men's reputations rose or fell in her mother's estimation according to their ability to recognize a quotation from her favourite playwright. But to her relief he capped it.

"'Alas, poor country!'" he said slowly. "Wasn't that the answer?"

"Yes, yes—'where nothing is once seen to smile.' Shakespeare must have forgotten Macbeth when he wrote that, and prophesied this present day of the Solemn League and Covenant. Is it true that it is now a criminal offence to laugh on the Sabbath—or pluck berries—or dance even in the week? What has happened to the land I remember as a child?"

"Darkness has fallen on it. But what does Your Majesty remember?"

"My nurse singing—my elder brother and I dancing with other children to the shrill skirling music of the pipes,—such memories as you must have of your childhood, my lord. Were you not one of the scarlet-gowned scholars at St. Andrews and won the archery medal for your college there?"

How had she heard that? There were moments when Louey credited her mother with witchcraft. And of course it was no magic but sheer inborn knowledge of men that made her say the very thing that would please him better than any praise of his famous deeds of war. He looked years younger now in talking to her; Louey could even see what he had been like as a boy, shy and proud, with the corners of his mouth upturned like a faun's, and freakish eyebrows peaked slightly in the middle.

"Yes," he said, "I was up at St. Salvator's, but little enough of the scholar. There was too much golf to be had on the links by the sea—I still think St. Andrews the best links in Scotland—and the Cupar races, and the archery contests down at Butts Wynd——"

"Which you won——"

"Which I won, and well I mind the supper-party we had after it with fiddlers and pipers from the town!"

There was more of the Scot in his voice than there had been since he entered—than there had been for years, Louey guessed. Oh, how had her mother done it, built up the picture of him complete so that he could live his boyhood over again for her benefit?

And what picture was she building now for his? The picture of herself homesick all her life for the Scotland she had known only in early childhood. "It is true what the Jesuits say," she said; "given the first seven years of a life, it does not matter who has the rest. I was seven when I came south to England and I have never seen Scotland since, but I have seen it always—in those placid fields by the Thames (and I have not seen those since I was sixteen), and when I went as a bride to Heidelberg and one April morning got up so early that no one saw me steal out of the Castle in a man's coat and riding-breeches, and galloped over that covered wooden bridge to the woods on the other side where the sun would strike earliest—I could not wait for it to reach the Castle ground, by then it might all be gone—and came to a hillside where the sharp grey rocks and young springing birches made me think I was home in Scotland; and now I have not seen Heidelberg for thirty years and our Castle there is a haunted ruin—'The bread is eaten and the company broke up.' Those days are gone," she cried, "they are gone and they cannot come back."

Louey, watching her, forgot even that Montrose was doing so. 'This is my mother,' she thought, 'who is old (though he'll never know it) and was young, a girl riding through the woods on an April morning. And these things are still there,' she thought, seeing them reflected in her mother's great eyes as they were when Louey herself was not born nor thought of—that incredible condition of human affairs!

Montrose was thinking there could never have been a woman like this but one, and that her own grandmother. He had sat in the house of Mary Queen of Scots in St. Andrews and looked out on the bright garden that she had made within its grey stone walls, and a thousand times he had passed the thorn tree she had planted in the courtyard of St. Mary's College, a tiny sapling now grown to a tall tree showering its white blossom above his head in the stormy winds of May, and often he had wondered what that queen had been like.

Now he thought he knew.

"They still speak of Queen Mary at St. Andrews," he told her. "Has it ever been said that Your Majesty resembles her?"

"I don't think so," she answered carelessly. "The portraits of her are bad—old-fashioned and wooden—and my father, I believe, never saw his mother, certainly he never spoke of her. For the rest, who cares to compare one old woman with another, dead more than half a century ago? Except myself—for I think I must have inherited something of her spirit that so wished to be a man, 'to know what life it was to lie all night in the fields or to walk upon the causeway with a knapsack, a Glasgow buckler and a broadsword.' But what a fool I am to talk so, sitting tamely here, with all these great girls round me!"

Since their poverty and rank had prevented their marrying, she preferred not to think of them as of marriageable age, and the 'great girls,' submitted to the schoolroom by that phrase, exchanged glances, Eliza of anger, Louey of rather desperate amusement.

Louey made another haphazard dash into the conversation, not realizing that by her efforts to intrude her talk she lost the charm of its fresh sincerity. "All the great girls aren't round you. What have you done with Sophie, Maman? Thrown her out of the sledge to the wolves?"

There, she had done it, and it pleased her that she had made her mother pause in bewilderment, even some slight confusion. Her chance shot had evidently gone home to something the Queen did not wish to confess; there was a faint hesitation, an air of conscious guilt behind her airy reply.

"To the wolves? Is that how you interpret the English lion? Sophie is skating with her cousin Charles whom we met on the ice, and I thought the exercise would do her good," she added in rather superfluous explanation.

Louey at once felt unchivalrous, pulling her mother from her high status as goddess and great adventurer to that of an impoverished widow and mother of an enormous family with matchmaking designs. And she had done herself no good; Montrose had not even turned his head towards her, only flicked a narrow glance in her direction which she feared despairingly was one of impatience at her interruption into the delightful flow of her mother's talk.

The interruption was brief, her mother had at once shaken off the tiresome reminder of maternity, led a fresh charge into the conversation and was galloping off the field. Certainly Montrose did not want to talk with Louey any more, did not want to talk himself, but only to sit and listen and watch.

Elizabeth's beauty, amazing as it was at her age, was the least of her charms. It was her frankness, courage and gaiety that enchanted him, and a certain simple directness of thought that would make it possible to talk with her as straightforwardly as with a man, a very welcome change from the princesses he had met in other Courts.

Already he had been pleased with that quality in her younger daughter, but in her it had been cruder, more abrupt, as she had just now shown in the untimely remark that annoyed her mother. But the Queen, with a spirit as unquenchably young as her daughter's, had a lifelong knowledge of the world and experience of men, and the complete easy certainty of her power over them that these had taught her.

All this her daughter saw as plainly as himself, and ruefully resigned herself to push her stool a little further back behind her mother to where she could watch the firelight carve deep shadows on his still face.

'It is no use,' she thought, and gave up all hope that he would look at herself again, 'she has "risen" on him, and like everyone else he can see no one else.'

V

SOPHIE had had the forethought to tell Carey to put their skates in the sleigh. Carey was Sophie's maid-in-waiting, a pleasant rosy girl, daughter of an impoverished English lord. At the last minute the Queen had invited Carey too to jump into the sleigh, for it was a relief to see a girl about who was not a daughter. So that Sophie was well equipped with skates and chaperon when they met the new young English King skating with Lord Craven, the Queen's oldest and most devoted friend.

It was Lord Craven who had lent the sleigh, and earlier had given the horses, and now happened to be skating with the King on the broad canal that went all round the town, just where they were most likely to drive. Even a prosy little old gentleman, Sophie reflected (and Will Craven must be at least fifty) could sometimes be very useful. Now he was talking to Carey, chaffing her in his humorous inconsequent fashion and encouraging her to prattle to him while King Charles' long legs led Sophie further and further ahead of them.

She did not much wish this at first, for it was the first time she had talked alone with him since the news of his father's death, and she did not know whether she ought to talk in a different voice from that which she generally used (he himself did not sound different, but he looked it, he looked much older, or was that just his black clothes?). It was spoiling all the pleasure of skating with him.

He said in a grave yet amused voice, "Don't try, Cousin; even if you think of the right thing to say, I shan't think of the right answer. There *are* no right things to be said about this," he added on a sudden savage note, and shot so far ahead on a few rapid strides that Sophie thought he must be intending to leave her, and pulled up short on her skates to wait for the others, her cheeks flaming at the rebuff.

But he wheeled sharp round, sped back to her and close round

98

her in a series of circles, said, "There! That is how it is done," as though he had been teaching her the manœuvre, took her hand, telling her she would keep up better with him like that, and led her on over the ice at a pace that left her no breath to speak condolences nor time to think of them. A pair of skimming swallows in the eager air, that was all they were for the moment. His hand felt hard and strong through his glove and warm with exercise, his rather gawky young form was taller than anyone they passed, and moved with the muscular ease of a healthy young animal; she felt she would have been proud to be skating with him even if he were not the King of England.

A weak gleam of sunshine had split the leaden sky, it painted the surface of the ice a dull copper and turned all the faces deep pink that came towards them, round Dutch faces smiling good-humouredly. "Look at all the Dutch cheeses stuck on top of bolsters," said Charles, and Sophie giggled at the comparison, could not stop giggling. The sharp air had caught her breath, so she said in excuse, they were going so fast, and where were the others? They were nowhere in sight. He told her they would let the others catch them up presently, but she must get warmed first; he could feel her hand was frozen even through their two gloves.

So they sped on past a cluster of men who were playing at curling, and a line of little boys who had made a slide that glowed in the opaque sunlight; they were shooting down it one after the other with arms outstretched, a frieze of goblin figures on a streak of fire. Stout matrons were being pushed along on runner-chairs by sweating and panting men; the bunched-up figures of women were sitting on the banks of the canal while their cavaliers put on their skates; men with skates to hire were bawling their wares and prices, so were the sellers of hot cakes and hot drinks in front of their burning braziers.

Sophie was warm now, but would be warmer still with some of these inside her, Charles told her, and this would give her Watchdog Will (one of her mother's names for Craven) a chance to catch up with them—if he wished to, "but it's my opinion he's counting your pretty Mother Carey's chickens before they're hatched," he added shamelessly.

Sophie wondered if there were not something rather indecent in this remark; she had been told that her cousin was a wild lad and that she must not laugh at all he said. But it was difficult not to laugh for sheer pleasure in escaping from what seemed weeks and weeks of being cooped up indoors with cross elder sisters and a gloomy mother, in finding herself free to move like a bird through the sharp air, free to sit on the crisp frosted grass and eat hot buttery cake and drink warm wine that made her glow and tingle all down her throat and chest and stomach and right into the ends of her toes and fingers, free to talk all alone with a young man who, in spite of the tragedy that had lately made him so much more important, was looking at her with pleasure and amusement.

Too much amusement perhaps. Why was he smiling? She had a sudden panic lest the mulled wine had made the cold tip of her nose burn red, and tried to see if this were so by squinting down at it. There was no question about Charles' amusement now. He burst into a roar of laughter and demanded to know why she was making those frightful faces. Whatever the colour of her nose, her cheeks had come up into line with it—that was some consolation for going crimson all over. Not for worlds would she have told him the true reason for her anxious squint.

"Oh," she said airily, "I was just going to tell you that that was what old 'Gargoyle' was like,—I mean Galen, my waiting-maid before Carey. She was so frightful that I used to hide from her for hours behind the bed-curtains."

"Was it so necessary to set dragons to guard you?"

"I don't know, but they did. I inherited my father's governess, Madame de Pless, so you can guess how old she was. And she had two daughters still older than herself."

"Is it possible?" observed Charles.

"It is not possible, but it is true. They made faces at me in turn while I said the Catechism."

"To test your reverence for it?"

"No, to save time. I had to get up at seven o'clock and recite the Precepts of Pibrac to one or other of them every morning while she cleaned her teeth, which she did with a bit of rag—like this."

Sophie demonstrated with a corner of her delicate lace handkerchief. She made gargling noises at the back of her throat, now suave and eagerly conversational, now indignant as a clucking hen, now sanctimonious as though she were intoning a psalm in the Calvinistic manner.

Charles was enchanted. Most pretty girls he knew, particularly those of high birth, thought all the time of being pretty, and would never dream of making themselves ugly for amusement.

"You are as good a mimic as a monkey," he said; and she told him proudly, "I am the Elected Queen of all Her Majesty's Monkeys. The French Ambassador appointed me that years ago. He gave me the sealed charter for it in front of a large company, pretending it was some grand new honour. He hoped to tease me into a rage, but he didn't succeed at all. I laughed as much as any of them."

Yes, it would not be easy to get the better of Sophie, and it was surprising how much prettier she had grown lately, softer and plumper; she could use those bright mocking eyes of hers now, and her lips looked as though they would like to be kissed as well as to laugh.

"You are far too clever for a princess," he told her, "you should be an actress. They have actresses in France and I shall bring them into England when I go back. Will you come and act for me in England?"

He said it on a note of cousinly chaff, but his dark liquid eyes (the only good feature in that ugly face, Sophie had decided) were looking at her in a way that excited her deliciously.

"I dare say I shall be glad of the offer," she said. "The youngest

of twelve ought to work for a living.   It's true I have £40 a year
of my own——"

"No, Cousin!   I never knew you were an heiress!"

"Oh yes, I'm on an equality with your other first cousin, that
tall girl your mother wants you to marry."

"La Grande Mademoiselle!" he exclaimed.   "You are on no
equality with her, Sophie."

"She has more than £40 a year?" asked Sophie demurely, who
knew well that Mademoiselle was the richest heiress in France.

"Yes, she has rather more than that.   And in matters more
essential you also fall short of her—by nearly a head in height, and
by nearly an inch in the length of your nose."

"Is hers—so very big?" she asked yearningly.

"It is enormous."

She drew a deep breath.   There was nothing more of life she
wished to ask.   But yes there was, there was the Dowager Princess
Amelia's daughter Agnes, and though Agnes was negligible, her
mother was a redoubtable old campaigner; she had climbed to her
position over Great-Uncle Maurice's dying body, for on his death-
bed he had told his brother Henry to marry her.   'What was
Mother about to allow it?'   Sophie indignantly demanded of herself, for Amelia von Solms had been her mother's maid-in-waiting.
It could not be that the King of England would ever marry the
daughter of a maid-in-waiting?

"You like Prince William very much, don't you?" she asked
suddenly.

"I do, surprisingly so, seeing that I owe him even for this suit
of mourning I'm wearing—a severe test for any friend, let alone a
brother-in-law."

"And do you like his sisters—do you like Agnes?" she continued
more tentatively.

"A good solid obedient girl," he said solemnly, "she would
make an admirable wife to any man."

She shot an agonized glance at him, caught his eye, and they

both rocked to and fro in uproarious laughter. Sophie was ecstatic-
ally happy. So he did not like Mademoiselle; he could not like
the pudding-faced Agnes; and there was no one else at all suitable
for him to marry but herself.

Charles, seeing her glowing satisfaction, wondered if this were
not going a bit faster than he had intended. Sophie's rank and
position as child of the Protestant champions of Europe made her
a very desirable match for him in the eyes of most of his followers,
for prestige would count as high now in the game as fortune. And
if he had got to tie himself up with a wife already, he would rather
have her than any. But he had not yet decided to commit himself.
Finance was a safer subject than comparisons between cousins.

"Who gave you your fortune, my pretty maid?" he asked in a
bantering tone that made it safe, he hoped, to pick up her hand,
and a very pretty hand it was.

"My godfathers and godmothers in my baptism," she replied;
"that is, the States of Holland. They are Louey's godfathers too,
that is why she has that hideous second name, Hollandina, but they
were kind enough to give me an income and not a name—in fact,
nobody gave me a name. My eleven elder brothers and sisters had
used up all in the family. I only got mine by chance—out of a hat."

"Were you drawn lots for, out of a hat? That ought to make
you adventurous, Sophie."

"No," she answered, suddenly serious, "it ought to make me
cautious. If nobody else looks after me, I must look after myself."
She had noticed his change of subject and tone just now. Had she
given herself away? She must show him she was not really such
a fool.

But her resolution was not becoming. Sophie could look as ugly
as she chose in the sacred cause of buffoonery and was only the more
attractive, but she was not nearly so charming when she showed
sound hard sense. Charles could see the pert angular fledgling again
in her when she looked like that; he could also see in an odd
glimpse of foresight how she would look when she was old, with

nutcracker nose and grim, corroded mouth. The disconcerting vision passed in a flash; Sophie was merely looking rather sulky because she was afraid she would not have all the good things of life that a pretty girl expected as her right; she would be jolly again on another glass of this mulled wine.

He felt in his pockets to see how much money he had left on him and found he had none at all. Turning to his cousin with a pensive smile, he asked if she had any of that £40 on her now. But, as he had expected from his precocious experience of her sex, she had left her purse behind. They would have to ask for credit, and Heaven alone knew whose was the worst.

"My mother has owed bills to all the tradesmen here for years," said Sophie.

"Mine are newer, but I'd back their weight against yours any day," said Charles. "The difficulty is to find anyone to back either of them."

"Heaven has heard you, Cousin. There is someone riding towards us. Is he one of your suite?"

"No. Wears a plaid. He's a Scot."

"*Do* Scots have money?" enquired Sophie innocently.

"Not often. I'm a Scot myself, remember."

"Just as much as I am, and no more. If my father was German, your mother is French."

There was a determined note in her voice; she did not know why she wished to insist that she was as much of a Stuart as Charles. Perhaps because, as the youngest of twelve, it was necessary to insist on any point that showed her importance.

The horseman she had observed was riding along the bank towards them from the direction of the town; they could still get a glimpse of it in the distance, a neat little etching of towers and walls surrounded by bare wintry woods, looking too remote and small in the flat grey light for real people to be moving about in it and doing things that might even now be affecting herself and Charles.

This man who had ridden out from that delicate background, a

tall figure in a rough frieze cloak, came up to the bank, leaped from
his horse, gave the bridle to one of the little boys who were hovering
like flies round the brazier of hot cakes, strode up to King Charles
with a stately swagger, and went down on one knee before him.
He had broad shoulders, the long lean bowed legs of a cavalry man,
a ruddy weatherbeaten face, light-coloured reckless eyes set rather
near together and hard as pebbles under their white lashes, and the
long scar of some old sword-cut, purple in this cold air, down the
side of one shiny red cheek.   He looked what he was, a soldier of
fortune; and he sounded what he was, a Lowland Scot, in the two
words he uttered before Charles recognized him.

"Your Majesty——" he began.

"Hurry, by God!" cried Charles.   "Then is your General
here?"

"He arrived this afternoon, sir, and sought you at the Binnenhof.
On finding you absent, he went to pay his respects to the Queen of
Bohemia while I rode out to look for Your Majesty."

"He's losing no time then!" exclaimed Charles.   Sophie noticed
with interest the look of fear behind his excitement, though it was
shot through with a certain schoolboy glee.   "*Now* the fat will be
in the fire, especially Lauderdale's fat!" he said.

There was fire in his own eyes, usually so sleepy.   Alarm, anger,
in spite of these he could not check the look of pride and awakened
courage which is a young man's admiration.

Montrose must be a remarkable man if his mere name could
transform her rather lethargic cousin like this.   If she had gone back
with her mother she would have seen him—but then she would not
have been skating with Charles; it was a pity there were so many
excitements in the world that you could not have one without missing another.   She sighed greedily and looked at this rugged tawny
Scot and wondered if that were what his master was like, a splendid
figure of a man as he stood up now with that rough cloak swung
across his shoulders, and his bold eyes scanning herself with curiosity
and, she hoped, appreciation.

"This is Major-General Sir John Hurry," King Charles told her.

"Urré," murmured the General in involuntary correction and then tried to check himself, so that his audience, instead of grasping the true quality of his fine old Norman name, only imagined that he was suppressing a hiccup. He made a good recovery in kissing Sophie's hand on being told that she was the youngest daughter of the Queen of Bohemia.

Charles asked one eager question after another. Why had Montrose come here in spite of his commands? What hope had he in Germany? And from that odd little fish, Queen Christina of Sweden?

"The situation in Scotland, Your Majesty, holds bigger hopes than that," Hurry told him portentously.

"The situation here," said Charles with equal solemnity, "is on the contrary without any hope, unless you can save it."

The hard eyes of the Scot swivelled round on his King in astonished enquiry.

"The Princess Sophia and myself," explained Charles, "have consumed four hot cakes and two cups of mulled wine and have not a farthing between us to pay for them. Will you then save the situation—and my face—by following our example first?"

And Hurry, while the warm drink and his pride glowed together in his stomach, thought, 'Here am I paying for the King's drinks!' as yet innocently unaware how common that honour could be.

The two men had plunged into discussion that made Sophie feel a frivolous alien. Why was it that men talked so differently together from when they talked with a girl? She had as good a brain as any of her brothers, but neither of the men gave her any chance to show it.

Hurry was speaking of the chances in Scotland. Scots had insulted their kings in times past, called them 'God's silly vassals' to their faces, rebelled and fought against them, occasionally murdered them; but never had they solemnly tried one for resisting rebellion and condemned him to death, then abolished the Monarchy for ever as an ' unnecessary, burdensome and dangerous' institution, as the English had just done.

Scotland's answer to that had been the public Proclamation in Edinburgh of Charles II as King of Great Britain.

Hurry spoke of this with the elation of a gambler who has just witnessed some unexpected throw of the dice; his eyes sparkled with excitement and optimism, he evidently had some difficulty in restraining himself from telling Charles that the murder of his father had been the best stroke of luck that could have happened to him.

Argyll was actually sending emissaries to The Hague with offers of the Scottish crown—"Your Majesty has only to deal the cards and you will have the whole game in Scotland in your hands."

Sophie was shocked. Scots and Englishmen always liked to talk of high affairs of state as a game, it was part of their schoolboy bravado, but surely in this case it showed a great lack of delicacy of feeling.

"What does Montrose say to all this?" Charles was asking.

"He'll hate Argyll to the death whatever happens," Hurry told him. "He owes Argyll a long score."

"All the more reason why Argyll should pay some of it cash down," replied Charles.

Hurry laughed loudly. "Lauderdale might even use Argyll's wealth and influence to raise new armies for Montrose. Your Majesty's well-known skill and finesse will discover how to humour all parties."

('So he's known for that already, is he?' asked Sophie of herself. 'Has he been humouring *me*?')

"Not easy to humour a man into fighting side by side with his former enemy," said Charles.

Hurry grinned in a way that made him look almost boyish. "It can be done, sir. Look at me. I fought with the Covenanters against Montrose, and many a knock he gave us. God, shall I ever forget how my cavalry and fat old Baillie's 3000 foot all but caught him and his handful of men when they were storming Dundee? The wild dance he led us through that foul night!"

Sophie could bear her silence no longer.

"Why did you change over, Sir John?" she asked in a chill little voice.

He was startled, for he had quite obviously forgotten the slight black figure sitting on the bank on the other side of King Charles. But he was pleased at the opportunity thus given him to state his case before his King.

"Why, Your Highness," he told her in his bluff fashion, "I'm just a plain soldier of fortune, no more nor less, and it's all I was brought up to be. The Urrés are gentle, but poor, and there was no money else to keep up our little place of Pitfichie in Aberdeenshire, so as soon as I was old enough my family sent me out to earn my keep in the German wars."

Where this hearty ruffian had earned it in some far from reputable ways, Charles could swear, remembering the stories of loot and rape he had listened to so eagerly as a boy whenever he could play truant among the soldiers. But only a decorous comment would be suitable now.

"They say Gustavus Adolphus only won his victories because half his Swedes were Scots," he said with his accustomed politeness, which Hurry accepted as no more than a statement of fact.

"That is so, Your Majesty, and more thanks to those of the lower than the higher command. My superior officer was that scrubby twisted little bastard, Sandy Leslie" ('So he's already forgotten again I'm here!' thought Sophie) "and to hear him say every minute, 'As Gustavus said to me,' you'd think he was bloodbrother to the Swedish King. *That* was how he got his reputation as a great general at home when he brought us all back to Scotland a dozen years ago to fight for the independence of the Scottish Kirk."

'A dozen years ago' Charles had seen his father start off with an army for Scotland when Charles himself was a little boy, wild to go too, cheering that jolly poet fellow Suckling as he rode past at the head of the troop he'd raised and put into white doublets and scarlet coats and huge feathers at his own expense—and then found there was no money to feed them!

"Yes," said Charles pensively, "that was when it all began, first Scotland and then down into England."

"And mighty well did Sandy do out of it." Hurry's attention was still on the really important matter. "Got himself made Earl of Leven in no time—and all *I* ever got out of it was a barren knighthood, won when I could stand those smug English gentle-men-amateurs no longer, for I'd had the bad luck to be quartered with the Parliament armies in England. They were always sneer-ing at their Scottish allies, particularly those from Aberdeen."

"I'm supposed to have some faint appreciation of wit myself," said Charles gravely, "but I have never understood the intense amusement given by the name of Aberdeen."

"May God of His goodness keep Your Majesty in that blessed state of mind! Those sanctimonious hypocritical English gentry's one idea of good fellowship was to tell a funny story about a man from Aberdeen, and always to show his meanness about money. That came well from Mr. John Hampden, rich enough to buy all Aberdeen, and too mean to pay a trifling tax towards the King's navy! Objected 'for conscience sake'—pah! As if the rest of us hadn't worse objections than conscience to paying money! But here was this damned conscientious objector, who'd never seen active service in his life, as my commanding officer. With a fellow like that, what chance could I get for promotion?"

"Or for a woman and a bottle or two either, hey, Sir John? You've finished your wine?"

"Too fast to notice it, sir. May I double the reckoning before I pay it, for the honour of Aberdeen?"

Charles graciously accepted, and he and Hurry took two cups more each to compensate for Sophie's refusal to have any more.

She was disgusted by Charles' manners towards ladies. She might freeze sitting here on the bank for all he'd care. Yet she dared not complain nor even call attention to herself; the training of her many elder brothers had been too severe, and she dreaded lest Charles should think her 'that nuisance of a girl.' And only a moment since he had been talking to her, looking at her, as though she were the most delightful woman in the world! This turncoat soldier had spoilt it all.

She silently endured her chilling toes and fingers and tip of her nose as the warmth of the wine died down and her pride would not let her renew it, and the air got colder and colder and that glorious moment just now when she had been sure that Charles wanted her for his queen, the Queen of Great Britain, got colder too, so cold it must be quite dead by now, and the two men talked and talked, Hurry telling how from the first he had longed to serve under the leaders on the other side, "nobles who'd fought in the German wars, George Goring and Wilmot, above all that Prince of cavalry leaders, Rupert of the Rhine! It was more than flesh and blood could stand, and so one night in June I rode for it instead, to the King's camp at Oxford, to the Prince himself.

"God, what a ride we had with Rupert! I was beside him as we rode over Magdalen Bridge, he on that black horse of his, and all the townsfolk running out to gape at him. Fifty miles all through the enemy's own country, and soundly beating them three times over in less than two days, and leaving Mr. Conscientious Hampden with his death-wound at Chalgrove Field—while we trotted back to Oxford with a loss of only twelve men in all, and I got my spurs and promotion and saw myself, poor fool, as the coming man on the King's side!"

He gave a short laugh like a bark, and a tug at his scrubby moustache as he glanced sideways to see how the young man beside him was taking it.

Charles was taking it well, for he much preferred impudence to professions of disinterested loyalty, a sentiment he had begun to distrust, having found how far from disinterested were many of his immediate followers. This hard-bitten rough rider was being frank on purpose, no doubt, to produce a right impression, but it was something to have such impressions tried out on him with laughter rather than with tears of devotion.

"I had good reason to be grateful to you," he said, "for I remember getting a half-holiday from my tutor at Merton on the strength of Chalgrove Field."

A hot June day it had been, and he had spent it fishing in the Cherwell with the new rod his father had just given him for his thirteenth birthday—but it hadn't made up (nothing could do that) for not being allowed to ride out with Rupert, his tall arrogant superbly adventurous cousin, ten years his senior and Commander of all the King's cavalry, on that lightning foray into the surrounding hills.

In that strange Oxford, transformed into court and camp, young Charles had lodged with his mother at Merton and done lessons in the little rooms over the gateway, watched the gun-park at Magdalen and the undergraduates drilling in Christ Church meadow, and wished passionately he were a few years older. How this tall fellow was bringing it all back to him!

"So that's how you came over to us," he said. "But what prevented your coming further with us? Was Rupert the Devil himself too slow to keep pace with Colonel Hurry?"

Hurry's debonair ease had darkened on him and he did not at once answer.

"I fell out with the Prince at Marston Moor," he blurted out at last. "I had interspersed the cavalry with musketeers in the Swedish manner; it was what Gustavus would have done, but——"

"But Gustavus had been dead more than a dozen years, and Rupert was alive," Charles insinuated ironically.

"Alive and kicking, Your Majesty, and I got kicked for it. There was no hope of advancement for me after that. Besides, the whole of the North was lost by Marston Moor, and all Scotland

held by the Covenanters against the King ; and what was to happen to my little place of Pitfichie in Aberdeenshire and my wife,
honest decent body that she is, installed there with a fresh brat every
year or so, though all girls, worse luck, five of them now and not
a single boy yet to carry on the name I mean to make so proud for
him,—was *she* to pay fines on my account to the Covenanters when
she'd barely enough to get porridge for her brats ?"

"So you heard the bells ringing, 'Turn again, Sir John Hurry' ?"

There was a saturnine note in Charles' voice which Hurry recklessly ignored, now well away on hot wine and the headier fumes
of egoism.

"Yes, sir, and turn I did, a Covenanter all over again, and swore
allegiance to Archibald Campbell, Marquis of Argyll, as head of the
Scots Government, and was given a new cavalry command with a
brand-new hope of getting reward at last. How the Devil who
tempted me must have laughed! For *this* was my reward—that at
that very moment, when all was lost for the King in Scotland, Montrose pushed north alone into the land, collected a handful of Highlanders together, swung them here, there and everywhere, now
east, now west, smashed the Covenanters at Tippermuir, at
Aberdeen, at Fyvie, at Alford and Auldearn, swooped down over
the winter mountains where no army had ever passed before, and
routed Argyll himself, the old Campbell fox, out of his lair at
Inveraray, drove the best part of the Campbell clan into the sea at
Inverlochy, and—Christ! what wouldn't I have given to be with
the man who outwitted and out-marched myself when I'd all but
got him at Dundee!"

There was no 'playing up' now in Hurry's tones; here if ever
was the real man, the born adventurer who could forgive himself
for the most unscrupulous desertion in search of luck, but not for
the ill luck that had landed him against instead of with Montrose.

"There was he doing all the things I had longed to do myself
ever since I was a schoolboy!"

And that Charles too had longed to do as a schoolboy, sitting disconsolate over his books in that sleepy western air of Oxford while news came crashing into the little university town of one furious battle after another fought up in those mountains of the north and won against incredible odds by Montrose and his small band of Highlanders.

"All this must be God's work, for it is above the power of man," Lord Digby, his father's handsome secretary, had exclaimed, his blue eyes blazing with excitement so that he looked like the warrior Archangel Michael himself.

But Digby had not behaved like him; it had been mainly his doing, Rupert said, that Montrose had never got the backing from the English Royalists that would have helped him to defeat the Parliament armies as well as the Covenanters. What a fool Digby had been—and this turncoat swashbuckler too, belatedly bemoaning his 'luck'!

"There was I," he was saying, staring like a sick dog into his empty cup, "with Argyll, a Commander-in-Chief like an old woman in his skull-cap and black robes, a limping lawyer-brained coward, a Campbell! Baillie at least was a soldier, though a stout stodgy old slow-coach, and Argyll carted about on all the campaigns a flock of hen-witted civilians as a pocket committee of the Government—I could vomit at the thought of them, and of his bilious face squinting in through the flap of Baillie's tent at dawn on the morning of Kilsyth, insisting on calling his precious Committee together and botching the whole battle with his choplogical civilian notions before ever it began.

"I swear it was the *beginning* of that battle that made me change sides again—not its ending, with Argyll flying headlong into England and Baillie across the sea, and Montrose the acknowledged conqueror of Scotland, the King's Lieutenant-Governor, with his camp a royal Court, and all the statesmen and poets acclaiming him as the man who had worked a year of miracles, and brought the Golden Age."

"Alas, Sir John Jonah! Was it your second advent to our side

H

that tipped down the ship of state when it was so fairly launched? Wasn't it within one month of the victory of Kilsyth that Montrose's small remnant of an army was surprised and massacred at Philiphaugh?"

Charles' urbanity was not able to resist making this thrust. He had played the affable young prince long enough, and was sick of the rôle; was he never to show anybody what he felt?

He showed it now; his smile was as sardonic as his cousin Rupert's could be.

For one instant the two men looked at each other with their eyes bared. Hurry could have killed Charles for calling him Jonah.

"Your Majesty is right to condemn me," he said slowly, "for to be unlucky is the greatest of all crimes. Call a man a scoundrel and he can shake it off with a smile or a blow, but call him unlucky and you poison the sap in his veins, you destroy all hope and belief in his life, for he knows then it would be better for him if he had never been born. Failure is shabby, shameful, dreary beyond words. Who does not shun the man who has failed? My crime was not in joining the winning side, but that never did I join it in time to share any of its gay triumphs. Just as I missed Rupert's great charge at Edgehill, to be with him at the breaking of his power and prestige at Marston Moor, so I missed every one of Montrose's six astounding victories, missed all the night rides, the forced marches over the mountains, the jolly forays upon fat purse-proud psalm-singing towns snugly locking up their stores in the security of the Covenant troops (and finding what that security was worth!)—missed all of it, all,—to share only his last fight, his only defeat."

He was mad to be saying this, to be rubbing in the very impression of ill luck which he longed to avoid. His hasty temper had run away with him again, and now he found it impossible to say what he had been leading up to all this time—that he had disliked Hampden, quarrelled with Rupert, despised Baillie, and loathed Argyll, but that now at last he had found his leader in Montrose. 'I've fought against him and I've fought with him, and I ask nothing better than to go on doing the latter for the rest of my life.' Those were the words he had wanted to say, but now they stuck in his throat. They were true, but he was angry, and they would not sound true.

He was not the only one to be angry. Charles was already smiling good-humouredly at him again, thinking this was an honest rascal as rascals go, and telling him that the luck would surely turn for them all now. But Sophie was speechless from rage as well as from necessity. They had never once noticed her—and she had never heard anything so shamelessly abandoned as the sentiments of this low adventurer, which Charles so obviously approved.

Thank heaven she had had her eyes opened to her cousin's true character in time. In time for what? Well, that was not quite clear, but no doubt God would punish such scheming selfishness, 'and *then* they will find themselves on the wrong side,' she told herself, *then* they would know that God was on the side of the right and would not permit it to fail.

But was He? Was there not some inkling of truth in those dreadful opinions—that to be unlucky, to be a failure, was worse than the worst crime; that men might hate you for being wicked, but would only despise you for being defeated? They would do worse than despise you, they would forget all about you, as these two men were forgetting her now, a princess and pretty, but nobody who mattered, the youngest brat of twelve, whose fortune was £40 a year.

She had often told herself these unpalatable truths, wondering how the chance would come to her to change them, for it must be that she would change them. She could not be herself, she, Sophie, the youngest but also the cleverest of the family,—well, no, not quite that, for there was always Eliza (though what use were her 'heavy guns of learning' as Rupert called them?)—but at any rate the most aware and the most determined, and, what was better, growing prettier every day,—she could not be all this and not, at last, become Somebody.

But now all that she had thought and hoped had suffered this harsh travesty from a crude Scots adventurer.

She had been longing to meet Montrose, and now she did not want to, for she might feel him superior not only to Hurry but to herself. And it would not be very satisfactory to see him for the first time at the meeting between him and his new King; she had a notion that at such a moment he might not have much attention to spare for herself.

VI

CHARLES had met Montrose briefly last year in Paris, where Charles had been staying with his mother. She had not approved of the Marquis' plans, since they were a stumbling-block in the way of reconcilement with the 'Moderate Covenanters' who were then beginning to come round to the Royalist side. So she had discouraged Charles' friendship with him, though she tried to conciliate the great soldier by offering his niece Lilias Napier a place at the little Court of exiles, but this the proud Scot had forbidden Lilias to accept, for in his blunt opinion 'so lewd and worthless a place' was no fit training for a girl still in her teens.

In this he showed himself a wise uncle but, as Henrietta Maria had already complained, no diplomat, for her ardent angry busy little brain became fixed in the notion that he was her enemy and working against her influence over her son.

That influence was strong; Charles had not seen his father since he was fifteen, his brothers and sisters were scattered, three of them in an English prison as his father had been, and his mother was the only firm relic of the intensely happy and tender home he had known in childhood. She was very apt to scold him as though he were a naughty little boy, and, what he minded much worse, to burst into tears, but she was passionately devoted to him. With their family life wrecked round them, he felt tenderly responsible for her. He greatly admired her amusing brilliance, had generally found it saved trouble to follow her advice, and his father's last commands had been that he should be 'totally directed by his mother.'

But it was something of a relief to have been at The Hague all this winter staying with his brother-in-law, Prince William, only four years or so older than himself, while she remained in Paris. It was also a relief to Hyde and others of his counsellors.

In his mother's absence, but with Lauderdale at head of the new Moderate Covenanters dogging his every step, Charles had ordered

Hyde to write to Montrose at Brussels to ask his help and arrange a secret meeting with him.

This was the letter that Rupert had found Hyde writing when he called on him at The Hague on the afternoon of his ride to Helvoetsluys for his departure to Ireland. With it, Charles had written also in person to Montrose as 'your affectionate friend,' urging that 'there must be great secrecy in this business.'

In answer Montrose warned Prince Charles plainly to 'vouch-safe a little faith unto your loyal servants and stand at guard with others'; he also declared his wish to serve him as he had done his father: 'I never had passion upon earth so strong as to do the King, your father, service.'

That simple expression of loyalty together with his advice, indeed rebuke, fell on Charles at a moment when he was not likely to forget it. For the letter was dated January 28th, 1649, and two days later the King his father was executed.

Now Montrose was here himself; Charles must deal with him direct, and felt uneasily that, when it came to direct dealing, Montrose would quickly prove the master.

But he was King, wasn't he? King Charles II—how strange it sounded! He remembered his mother's little quick brown hands thumping on his father's chest as she urged him to remember he was King and to 'pull out these rogues by the ears.' It was all very well when it was a question of rogues, but his father had never had to stand up to Montrose.

In escorting Sophie back to her home together with Hurry he was precipitating his interview, but he had best get it over quickly he thought as he tried to disguise his anxiety from himself, squaring his shoulders as he went up the stairs in that pleasant, shabby, familiar house of his aunt's; silently cursing this swaggering Scots knight who was so complacently dogging his heels (Sophie had had the sense to vanish on entering the house); saying to himself, 'Now for it, now I've got to show Montrose he can't come marching in on me with all his men like this against my orders—I'm not going to

let him wreck all my other plans as though his were the only one—
and I've got to do it without offending him; I'll flatter him, show
him I know damned well he's the biggest man we've got.'

That last should be easy, for Charles was particularly good at
showing this even when he did not, as now, believe it.

And with his face set he braced himself to the interview.

The ground for it was quickly prepared for him; he had a glimpse
of two of his pretty cousins leaving at the other end of the room as
he entered it, and the Queen with heroic self-denial forbore to stay
and direct the talk into the channels she hoped for. His aunt's
influence over Charles was not as strong as his mother's, but it was
much more pleasant, and she would use it unscrupulously on behalf
of this man who she had long felt certain was the only one to save
the royal cause in Scotland. But she was wiser than her wishes and
at once realized that here was the perfect opportunity for a private
unofficial meeting as if by chance between Montrose and his King.

So with the bare minimum of greeting and excuse she swept off
General Hurry with her to the stables to give his opinion as an
expert on horseflesh on the poor remnant of her stud. There was
a roan mare that might be worth breeding from, came of a good
stock, she said, swinging the cloak round her that had slipped from
her shoulders in the warm room and catching and tearing it on
Hurry's spur, but she laughed it off with the glee of a schoolboy
who has torn his breeches, and prevented Hurry's apologies by
instant questions of his service under Gustavus Adolphus (thereby
showing her swift tact, since talk of his part in the Scottish wars
would so clearly be fraught with embarrassment). She would have
given her eyes to have seen King Gustavus go off to a carnival disguised as a waiter, with her husband as a Jesuit friar! And had Sir
John come across her greatest friend Will Craven in the earlier
campaigns?

Dazzled by her royal air that could so quickly become one of gay
camaraderie, Hurry had been carefully silent, but now prayed to
Heaven for the right answer and told her, "I saw Lord Craven

fighting like a wild cat, Your Majesty, when the Swedish King asked the name of the little man who was in such a mighty hurry to die."

It was certainly the right answer, for she laughed delightedly as she went down the stair beside that lean figure with the massive shoulders. The tough imperturbability of his bearing belied his thoughts, which were leaping and singing in his head, 'Here have I been drinking with the King of England and been in the same room with him and my general and left it with the most famous and beautiful queen in the world, and eh but if Maggie could see me the now!'

Charles found himself alone, face to face with Montrose. The candles had been lit in the great bronze chandelier, the faded stamped velvet curtains drawn across the shuttered windows. Their pattern, now spread out, showed itself heavily encrusted with darns, and Charles stared at the long centipede shape of one of them in the instant's pause that followed the Queen's departure with Hurry. Those clear grey eyes before him seemed to be scanning every one of his carefully prepared thoughts, driving them shamefacedly to hide behind each other and anxiously wonder how best to express themselves.

Montrose saved him the trouble by striking at the root of them.

"I have disobeyed Your Majesty's commands in coming here."

Charles' quick flush made him look very young, uncomfortable, and rather indignant.

"Those commands were not my wishes. There is no one I would rather have had by me at this juncture than you, my lord, the truest and bravest friend my father ever had. But when I wrote to you and asked your help I *dared* not have you here, and that's the plain truth of it. Your old enemies from Scotland have been pestering me for weeks not to let you come near me—but you know that."

"I know it, sir, too well. They are still my enemies—and yours, sir, if you do not do all they ask."

"I'll never do that. But *I'll* get them to do what *I* ask." He had settled himself in the big chair where his beautiful aunt had sat, and his dark face, ugly as it was, had a great look of hers there in the softening firelight. He waited for Montrose's answer, but as none came he went on with increasing confidence, "The whole of the Covenanters are coming round to me now. These Lords of the Covenant, why shouldn't their money and influence with the Kirk help your enterprise in Scotland?"

"Sir, how should they help it? To them I am a dead man. In all their Government's papers I am referred to only as 'the late Marquis,' since I stand condemned by them to be hanged, drawn, and quartered."

Charles looked up at the 'dead man' who was telling him this so quietly as he stood in front of him, erect, alert, but very still.

"Of all monstrous insanities! But this foul murder of my father is bound to bring them to their senses."

"I doubt it," said Montrose.

"But Argyll himself is sending Commissioners to me here to offer me the Crown of Scotland. He wants nothing better than to crown me at Scone with his own hands."

"Two years ago, sir, Argyll sold your father to Cromwell's army. On the day he handed over the King to his butchers, the carts of English gold trundled into Argyll's camp. There is no refuting that. If Your Majesty puts your head too under his hands, he will keep it his prisoner and his pawn, whether he puts a crown on it or not."

"Not if I shackle them first," said Charles. "This game will have to be played with finesse as well as strength."

The word struck an unpleasant chord in Montrose's memory. It was the belief in his own finesse, in his ability to outwit his enemies even when he was their prisoner, that had helped to knot the noose round the neck of Charles I.

He thought of Argyll, that 'bottled spider,' whose delight it had always been to keep himself in the background and weave the intricate net of the Covenant's power that now bound the whole or Scotland—and he looked at this boy of eighteen with the sad eyes and the charming smile, who hoped to outwit him.

When he spoke, his voice was more grave.

"In this tangle," he said, "the direct method has the best chance to win through."

"The best chance," said Charles eagerly, "is in your military genius and power to win men to your side. Turenne, Condé, the greatest foreign captains, say how you beat them all there—that you bind men to you with a chain to follow wherever you wish."

Montrose did not seem to hear the flattery.

"Where do you wish them to follow me?"

"Why, to raise Scotland yet again."

"And how am I to do this in secret, without Your Majesty's sanction?"

This was awkward.

"It is only the preparations that should be secret. I would of course acknowledge the expedition once it was launched."

He wished Montrose would move; he himself seemed to have crossed and uncrossed his legs half a dozen times as he sprawled in that chair.

"And in the meantime," asked that deliberate voice, "does Your Majesty mean to receive the Commissioners from Argyll?"

"I shall hear what they have to say, certainly. I should be mad if I refused to consider any possible way out of this desperate situation."

Here he was actually excusing himself, when he had meant to tax Montrose for his insubordination in marching to The Hague against his orders.

And Montrose's next words took him completely by surprise.

"The Earl of Huntly, chief of the Gordon clan," he said, "has been executed within this week by Argyll's Government for his attempt last year to rise on behalf of the late King."

Now why should he have told him that? He could have no reason to regret Huntly, who in his jealousy of Montrose had refused ever to join with him in his campaigns in Scotland. Charles answered contemptuously in his annoyance at having had to undergo those last difficult moments:

"Why do you speak of Huntly? If the old Cock o' the North has crowed his last, that's about all his loyalty ever amounted to— some mighty loyal speeches."

"He never made a better than on the scaffold," said Montrose, "when he 'wished his life had been more use to his royal master, for whom he was at least content to die.' But I am asking Your Majesty to consider this—*why* was he made to die, now, at the very moment when Scotland has proclaimed you as Charles II, King of Great Britain? For this reason: to show that that proclamation need not be taken seriously."

"Show whom?"

"Cromwell himself. Words are only so much breath wasted, but the chop of an axe is a definite and substantial proof to Cromwell that Argyll is still Cromwell's ally."

"But your country," cried Charles, "is dead against Cromwell."

"They know little of Cromwell, sir. To rise for the King means in Scotland to rise against the tyranny of Argyll. The country is groaning under it, as in a nightmare. But if Your Majesty enters into treaties with him, of what use is it for me to try and raise the country against him?"

Charles pushed a worried hand up over his forehead, rumpling his black hair. "If only Scotland could sometimes forget!" he exclaimed with the petulance of a boy. "Why can't they forget their differences and unite together?"

They were almost the very words that his mother had used in writing to Montrose. But this unthinking echo of them encouraged their hearer; it showed that Charles' reason had practically given up the contest and admitted Montrose's argument. What he needed now was conviction.

"I tell you," Charles was saying, "I am sick and tired of it all. Lauderdale gives me no rest, nor anyone else. He prods at everyone to do as he wants, and he's got the force of a mad bull. There's never a moment's peace to be had among them all."

"You had it once, sir, of late."

"What do you mean?"

"Did you have any doubts, sir, of what you were doing when you gave your enemies 'carte blanche,' as people are now calling it, to do what they would with yourself if they would spare your father?"

A dark painful flush came slowly up over the young man's face. Had Montrose read even that inner secret thought of his that had hovered at the back of his mind ever since he had faced those eyes— the wish that this man could know that he too had done what he could to save his father?

He had done it by sending a blank sheet of paper signed with his name for the Parliament to fill in their own terms, for he was willing to resign his right to the throne or give himself up as their prisoner if they would spare his father's life. He had felt that moment of nobility wasted—more humiliating still, utterly ignored, for the Parliament never even troubled to answer him.

But Montrose knew of it, and the grave admiration in his voice as he spoke of it made Charles feel as though he had been knighted on the field of battle.

His head went up, his hands gripped the arms of his chair. "You are right," he said. "There were no doubts then."

How he envied this man before him who stood free as on an open heath, seeing only the thing that he knew he must do.

But himself, Charles, was standing at the cross-roads. He could see this way and that: the political advantages of an alliance with Argyll, of being crowned King of Scots by him, of making friends with at least the half of his enemies—and against that, the help, to the death, of this man who was almost single-handed.

If only he could have them both!

He flung himself out of his chair to stride through the room on long restless uneven steps.

"I had no choice then," he said.

"Nor have you now, sir."

A new confidence came to Charles at the sound of that deep voice behind him. The man who stood there so still, while he himself drifted up and down, was saying nothing that could comfort him —rather, it made his situation the more desperate. Yet it gave him hope as nothing else had done through this bleak winter.

He turned sharply on his heel and came back to him.

"What shall I do?" he said, and his voice had a new ring in it.

"Give me a free hand in Scotland. Do not send me there with one hand bound behind my back. Commit yourself to nothing with these men, or you destroy my venture before I start."

"I'll never do that. How would you start?"

"Land in the Highlands and raise the country in Your Majesty's name."

"With no help from its rulers?"

"They did not help me before," said Montrose grimly.

Charles stood still, gazing at this man, remembering the strange things he had heard of him.

"Yes," he said thoughtfully, "you did it once before."

He swung himself back into the chair, a long black leg dangling over one of its carved arms, but too intent to notice his uncomfortable position.

"Didn't you," he asked "walk over the moor with only one companion to find Alasdair Macdonald and his handful of Highlanders?"

"Alasdair is dead," said Montrose, "killed last year in Ireland. I'll never find a better ally. But I'll find others. From all over the country I hear from men begging me to return."

'Oh for one hour of Montrose!' From all over the country that cry had gone up last summer after the blundering campaign of

Lauderdale and the 'Moderate Covenanters.' Charles had heard of that. But Montrose did not mention it, he was counting up his most likely allies.

"'There's Seaforth and his Mackenzies in the far north. There are the Gordons, though scattered now for lack of a leader—they'd help from the east. There are the Macdonalds whom the Campbells drove over to Ireland."

"Rupert's ships would come in handy there! He's grown an absolute old sea-dog now, though they say he still gives the order to 'charge'! God, how I wanted to sail with him to Ireland! And now I long to go to Scotland with you."

Montrose did not speak at once. He was looking at that eager face leaning towards him in the firelight; he was considering it, and his answer. For once it came unwillingly.

"Wait," he said at last, "till you can come—I will not even say 'as a king,' but at least as a free man. Wait till I have got Scotland for you. I have done it once, when the country had not half the reason to rise against Argyll that it has now."

"Let me come with you! What does it matter what happens? It would be better to lose my life in action with you than waste it here among these squabblers."

Once again that day Charles was afire with the longing to prove himself a man beside this man.

It was the desire that Montrose had seen burn in the eyes of many men, but now in the eyes of the man he hoped to make king.

"Take me with you," Charles urged. "Am I to go on kicking my heels here, eating my brother-in-law's meals, even wearing the clothes he gives me, while you and Rupert go off on your adventures? I've seen fighting as a boy, it's time I saw it once more."

He was moving restlessly about the room again, picking things up and laying them down, Eliza's dreary knitting, a thick stocking nearly finished, his aunt's embroidery-frame with scarcely a stitch on it, and even, behind a chair, one of the girls' shoes,—all women's things in a house full of women, and here he was left behind as though he were one of them.

He burst out in a sudden fury, "God, how I hate women! For two years now my mother's been worrying me to marry that French heiress with the Bourbon nose, pestered me to pay her compliments —that's the best way, she thinks, for me to win my throne. And the Dowager Princess Amelia here, *she* is scheming for me to marry one of her stupid daughters; she dangles an alliance with Holland and all other Calvinist countries before me as reward, and she'll intrigue for that with Argyll's Commissioners. I'm sick to death of their schemes—and I'm in a mess here, I don't suppose it will amount to much, but it might—I wish to God I were out of this place and away from all women."

Yes, he was right enough there. It would do him no harm to get him away from the women and toughen him a bit in camp or at sea. There were already lines of dissipation engraved round the eyes and the mouth that fell so easily into the lazy cynical smile of a much older man—and he had endured enough without that to make him older than his age. Yet now, with all his defences broken down, quite off that careful guard he had laid on himself at the beginning, and longing only to do what Montrose advised, he seemed no more than a boy.

"What shall I do?" he said, thinking evidently of his last words, this scrape he had got into with some woman, but Montrose did not trouble himself with that.

It was his turn now to have to choose, and never did so strong a temptation look so like the right choice. Here was his chance to take this youth with him and influence him as he wished and as he knew he could. To have the King in person would of course strengthen his hand enormously against both his rivals and his enemies. But the chief temptation lay in the King himself, still impressionable and enthusiastic in spite of being dragged about for the last half-dozen years through England and Europe with a 'Court' that for the most part had become a mere pack of needy adventurers.

It lay now in Montrose's power to retrieve him from that pack, to train him to his own ideal of kingship, an ideal not merely of soldiering, but of government in all its aspects as he had worked it out in his masterly treatise on 'Sovereign Power.'

But he had no right to hurl the King's life, and through it his country, into such danger. Waste his life here as Charles might, it was not for Montrose to risk throwing it away or handing it over to his enemies.

"Your life is not your own now, sir," he said at last.

Charles' face that had been watching him so anxiously fell in disappointment. He was growing too well accustomed to disappointment. No doubt he would make it up to himself somehow, he thought with a faint disillusioned grin.

Montrose saw it, saw all that he feared growing more clear before his eyes, but did not swerve from his decision. The King's life was not his, any more than it was his own.

"I wish for your sake it were," he said gravely, "for I shall leave you here to a harder and more distasteful task than mine—one that will require a greater courage if you give me your whole-hearted support."

"You shall have that, I swear." The heavy eyes had opened full again, almost begging the older man to trust him. "I will back you against them all," he said, "though not openly as yet. I *must* see the Commissioners first, now they are on their way here."

Montrose had to concede that. And there could be no doubt of Charles' purpose now. Charles himself could not believe that he had ever doubted it. His father's last letter before his death came into his mind: 'Whatever you promise, keep. Do not think anything in this world worth obtaining by foul or unjust means.'

Whatever foul or unjust means he might have to use hereafter against his enemies, he would keep his promise to Montrose.

"But what shall *I* do?" the young man repeated, and his tone was that of a lieutenant asking his superior officer his marching orders.

"Join your cousin in Ireland, sir." That would be the best way to keep him out of mischief both political and personal, but Montrose naturally did not advance that among his reasons. "Your presence there will bind together all the contrary parties. And when you have raised your troops you and Prince Rupert can sail with them in his ships to Scotland when I have made my country securely yours—a country ready heart and soul to follow you and the Prince and myself down into England against the King's murderers."

It was done with some art. 'You and the Prince and myself'— Charles to be one of that trilogy, to join Rupert in Ireland and then Montrose in Scotland and fight by their side! If he had heard those words four years ago he could not have believed them, so delirious would he have been with joy and pride. And it was the same now —but no, it was not quite the same.

There were more things in his life to enjoy than there had been four years ago. The longing for danger and hard campaigning, and the chance to prove himself a man beside the two men he most admired, had now to compete with the freedom of rollicking company and drink and pretty, laughing, easy-going women. He could give up these latter pleasures on the instant if need be, but they had already blunted the edges of that earlier sense of rapture. He knew it; and Montrose, looking at him, knew it too.

I

VII

SOPHIE found Etta in her own little kitchen, her fair head bent lovingly over a tray of pink bonbons shaped like hearts and flat Tudor roses, yellow ones like crowns, and green ones like clover leaves.

"All for me!" exclaimed Sophie. "Don't shake your head. You always make your sweets for me."

"You always eat most of them. But you say you have just been guzzling hot cakes."

"After that miserable dinner and that run on the ice I could eat the whole trayful."

She seemed in a fair way to do so, and with some reason, since the household funds were depressingly low at the moment; for all the horrified sympathy of the Dutch citizens, the death of the English King had not increased their tradesmen's hopes that his sister would ever be able to pay her butchers' and grocers' bills. "Our meals might be the famous feasts of Cleopatra—plenty of pearls and diamonds but nothing else to eat," Sophie grumbled, "and now even they are gone, the best of them, to feed Rupert's sailors instead of us!"

She rattled out her adventures, feeling twice as gay and successful as she had done even at the outset, and almost forgetting that annoying return journey *à trois*.

Etta was always ready to be impressed, particularly by Sophie, the baby of the family, who had delighted them all with her childish high spirits and precocious wits when at nine years old she left the care of her severe old governesses and came to live with the family for good. 'Even the Queen took pleasure in me,' Sophie herself had noticed, and recorded later with pride. That 'even' was a slap at her un-maternal mother, but it was also a record of her achievement. However deeply Sophie disapproved of her mother, to please her was the highest criterion, a difficult and often a dangerous game, for you never knew whether the Queen might order you out of the room for a pert brat, or break into delicious laughter and call you her rival Majesty, the Queen of monkeys.

But it was easy to amuse Louey, to sharpen her wits on Eliza, to be petted and admired by Etta, who was more simple than her sisters and far more maternal than her mother, had always loved to dress dolls for Sophie in her childhood (in fact, Sophie had outgrown the dolls considerably quicker than her elder sister's secret passion for them), and now was as eager to listen to her adventures as if nobody had ever admired her own gentle loveliness. She was thrilled to hear of the impromptu skating-party, delightfully certain that it was entirely due to Sophie's attractions.

"He took you quite away from Carey and Craven to talk to you all alone! Sophie, is he in love with you?"

Sophie answered airily, "Oh, as to that, I believe he is in love with any pretty girl he happens to be with—and I *am* pretty now, aren't I, Etta?" she added with a sudden drop into earnest anxiety that quite destroyed her effect as the woman of the world.

Etta's reassurance left no possible doubt on this point.

"You are, my darling, and what is more, you love life so much you make one glad to be alive."

"Oh, Etta!" Sophie breathed in ecstasy, "you have always been pretty, you cannot guess what it is like to learn suddenly that one is. I'll never forget my eighth birthday, how miserable I was because some English visitors were admiring poor little Gustavus, 'such a beautiful child,' and then said, 'It is a pity the girl is not more like him, she is so scraggy and ugly—by the way, I hope she doesn't speak English!' 'Doesn't speak English'—could anyone be so stupid as to think that because I had been talking French and German I shouldn't know my own mother-tongue? How I envied Gustavus, poor angel! But then you see he died the next year, and I was alive, and came among you all here and saw such crowds of people and all sorts of different life going on—so I have the best of it after all."

Etta's heart was torn with pity and longing when she thought of Gustavus, the unlucky thirteenth child, christened in honour of Gustavus Adolphus and his ill-fated campaign in company with their father which had cost them both their lives—had cost little Gustavus his life too in all probability, since their mother's anxiety had made her very ill for the first time in her life at the birth of this her last child. He had always been wretchedly delicate, but Etta felt that if she had only been older and had had the charge of him he might not perhaps have died in great suffering before he was nine years old.

Sophie felt her sister's silence uncomfortable; she knew she had sounded heartless, and it exasperated her, for she had not felt heartless at all; she could never bear to think of Gustavus' illness and death—it would wake her even now sometimes in the middle of the night in a cold sweat of terror lest she, who had never known what it was to have an ache or pain, might suddenly find herself ill and dying. She had only spoken with common sense and logic such as Monsieur Descartes himself would have commended. The plain fact was that it was better to be alive than dead, and so she had the better of it.

She twirled away from Etta, hopping and clapping her hands to warm her toes and fingers, singing defiantly,

> "'So I will dance and I will sing,
> For sure it is the very best thing
> To drive the plague away—away—
> To drive the plague away,'"

then seized Etta's recipe book, pulled out a blank page, wrote with a flourish, 'Sophia, Queen of Great Britain,' but would not show it to Etta, then remembered that it was as unlucky to do that as to wear your wedding-dress before you were married, and crumpled it up and tossed it into the fire as Eliza and Louey came into the kitchen.

She at once asked them about Montrose. Louey did not answer, and Eliza said, "He did not speak much."

"He did not have much chance to," said Louey.

Sophie was scanning them both with the critical eye of the younger sister. How unpractical they both were! Why did they never contrive to look their best when anybody important or interesting came to the house? Eliza for all her beauty had no animation, was distraite as usual; Louey, on the other hand, looked so vivid that even her silence shone, but her hair was more untidy than Sophie's after all her driving and skating.

Etta in innocent admiration told of Sophie's triumphs on the ice with the young King, but Eliza was very disapproving; what had Craven and Carey been about to allow it?

"They could not keep up with us, that is all, and if our old True Towser didn't think it mattered, who should? You know everything is different on the ice—it is a law to itself."

"I am not thinking only of appearances, though that is bad enough. But it is better for you not to talk too freely with King Charles."

"But supposing he should want to marry me?" faltered Sophie. "His Court think it probable, that's plain, for they have all been trying to curry favour with me. I am the right age for him, and there is no Protestant princess of superior or indeed equal birth."

"Is that how he's been wooing you?" asked Louey casually as she ate a sweet.

"Of course not," Sophie flushed indignantly. "But at least I need not fear a rival in his Catholic cousin, La Grande Mademoiselle. He went out of his way to assure me that her nose is enormous."

"It's not as big as her fortune," murmured Louey.

Sophie rushed on in her anxiety to prove her claim to that prospective title she had scrawled and now, thank Heaven, safely burnt. "He said I amused him better than any actress and he wished I would come with him to England."

Eliza gasped in indignation. "*That* is not the way the marriages of great princes are arranged."

How detestable elder sisters were, particularly when they echoed one's own misgivings! Eliza now reminded Sophie that she herself had complained of the Dowager Princess Amelia's 'plots' against her reputation, encouraging her own son Prince William to flirt with her so that Charles should think lightly of her—and at this Louey swept in with a burst of laughter that threatened to blow the whole heated discussion up the chimney.

But Sophie was as much annoyed by the laxity of one of her elders as by the strictness of the other. "You of all people shouldn't laugh. Just look at the things Amelia says of you!"

"I can't very well, as I'm naturally the last person to hear them. What does it matter?"

"Mud sticks," said Sophie sombrely, her pretty face suddenly gone heavy.

"Only to those who stick in the mud. Climb out of it and leave that fat envious old woman to wallow in it."

But Sophie, determined on being taken seriously, assured her that 'good old faithful Fritz' had himself warned her of Amelia's plot.

"Faithful Fritz? Is that the busy officious German footman Carl bequeathed to us when he went to Heidelberg?—a worse legacy even than his sour wine!"

Sophie flared up. Her eldest brother was her favourite, for her rather tart wit suited his own vein of cynicism ('Timon the Cynic' had always been Carl's nickname). "You are never fair to him just because you adore Rupert, but they can't *all* be knights-errant— and Rupert has never given Mother a moment's peace."

"Nor has Carl ever given her a moment's pride."

Louey was not as unkind as she seemed, for by heading the argument away from Charles she was trying to prevent Eliza from saying something that she had been brooding over for the last few minutes, but she was not successful, for Eliza after two broken starts ('I think you ought to know'—'I am afraid I must tell you—') now informed Sophie that Charles was not only a dissolute but an imprudent young man whose mistress, Lucy Walters, would shortly bear him a child and, if it were a boy, was determined to lay claim to his legitimacy.

Lucy was of good family, her father a Welsh gentleman of Castle Rock in Pembrokeshire; she was very beautiful in her brown, rather bucolic way, and not a day older than Charles himself—there was nothing so very improbable in the idea that he might have married her secretly. He had flatly denied it, but that might only mean that he had tired of her.

"And that he has no more honesty than I ever dreamed of his possessing!" cried Sophie in a strained angry voice.

"Open your mouth," said Louey, swinging round on her, and crammed a sweet into it, then another and another. "Don't talk about Charles," she said, "you don't know him yet, we none of us do. You had much better eat." She wanted to cry, to hit Eliza, to hug Sophie. It was a shame to spoil things like this for the pretty, eager child. Even her prettiness was spoiled now she was looking such a little shrew.

If only she could marry Charles at once before that look became a habit with her. But might he not spoil things for her himself? He might, but at least that would be their own affair, and they were both so young and gay and charming that they should stand a better chance together than most royal couples. So don't look like that, Sophie, smooth your face out and smile, for that is your best, your only weapon.

'Love to be loved whilst thou art lovely,
Lest thou love too late.'

Could she tell her that now? No she couldn't; she could only say to Etta, "If I cooked like you, I'd never paint."

"Humbug!" sighed Etta on a long gasp of relief. "Your pictures will last for centuries."

"And what's the point of that—three minutes or three centuries at the end of time, when they're all gone together? Our cook is the only true artist, *she* isn't always looking at the future like a looking-

---

glass, not even till next morning. Take one of these, Eliza, and tell me I'm right."

"You are not. Art must be directed to a purpose."

"A whole school of purposes if you wish. You had better take one before I take them all."

She collected a saucerful, whistling a dance tune as she did so; her nerves felt as taut and sensitive as a violin string. What would happen to Sophie, to Charles, to the man who was even now talking with him in that room above them? However bold and successful a soldier he was, everything for him must depend ultimately on his King's character and strength to stand by him.

And here they all stood about and ate sweets and talked of scandals and flirtations and a bastard baby as though they were the most important things in the world.

She went to her room and shut the door and knew that she need not see any of her family again that evening.

'Now I have entered my kingdom,' said Louey; 'freedom and power are in my hands, there is no one to dispute them.'

A single deep-mouthed stroke answered her out of the dark stillness beyond her room. 'Yes, there is time,' she added, 'but even time can speak only from outside the kingdom.'

One o'clock, and for hours now she had been enjoying the fierce deep pleasure of reading alone in her room, knowing the rest of the household to be asleep. As long as the night lasted, then only the length of the candles, and they were long, and the amount of logs for the fire, and there were still several, could set a term to that pleasure. She had got rid of her maid-in-waiting, Moll Butler, an Irish girl, a relative of Lord Ormonde's, as soon as Moll had helped her out of her stiff whale-boned bodice and into an old loose gown lined with soft white fur, and her feet into fur-lined scarlet velvet boots.

What an orgy of comfort it was to get into such clothes after enduring those extraneous bones! Their points always seemed to find out the tender spots in her own, they were far worse for thin people than for fat, she was sure of it, and was guilty of removing first one and then another until her mother's roving eye would rest on her in abstract speculation while she asked heaven how it was that Louey's clothes always looked as though they were just falling off her?

And if Louey complained of instruments of torture, then girls nowadays had no control, they did not know how well off they were, they should have lived as *she* had done at the Court of King James I of England and seen her mother Anne of Denmark so pinched in and barricaded behind bone and buckram between the monstrous hoops of her farthingale and the bristling fortress of her ruff that she had looked like a thing carved out of painted wood—and Elizabeth rocked with laughter at the memory, quite careless how she destroyed her example by mocking it.

Eliza, devoted to the pious memory of their German grandmother, the Dowager Electress Juliana, whose long yellow face they had all known, framed in her widow's weeds, could not bear to acknowledge that they had had also this unknown bedizened grandmother glittering with enormous jewels, who had danced and acted in public and blacked her face and arms to take the part of a negress and caused scandals with handsome young men and got drunk like her husband and everybody else at his gorgeous, disgraceful Court. They had never seen her, thank heaven, and it was better never to speak of her, said Eliza; but Louey said, 'It was she brought the best looks into the family, you can thank her for that, for if our long noses came from the Stuarts, then all the great mournful eyes that go rolling round the family come out of *her* portrait above her cast-iron ruff.'

It was no doubt her training as a portrait-painter that made her like to think of the unknown people, their eyes and noses, their passions and tricks of speech and twists of mind, now all dead and gone, that yet lived on in themselves.

Now that she had finished reading she roamed up and down the room and watched her shadow leap up from the red pool of firelight and shoot across the wall, a black shape now tall as a goddess, now shrinking to a crouched witch; went over to the corner cupboard for another of Etta's sweets, tasting in it the delicious flavour of a stolen feast snatched when everyone else is asleep; pulled back a curtain, then a shutter, then a window opening on to an ice-still, ice-bright sky, spangled with stars that winked and popped like fireworks.

To breathe this air made one gasp, to watch those stars crackling with inhuman energy made one proud to be alive. They had no power over our fate, so her mother always said, for so her tutor, Lord Harington, long ago in England had taught her; the art of astrology was all nonsense, and one's fate was one's own affair.

From this upper window she could see the black mass of the roofs of the Binnenhof rising here and there into towers above the trees of the Voorhout. No light came up from it; the Palace, like this house, was dark and silent, the people in it all asleep—her cousin Charles, who should now be in his own palace of Whitehall far away in London, and his sensitive little sister Mary, who had come from there to marry young William of Orange. Were their fates indeed all their own affair—or had her mother's tutor been wrong, and their future written long ago in the strange movements of the unseeing stars? And her own? And that new visitor's, the Marquis of Montrose?

She shivered, pulled the window to, turned back into the room and sat at the dressing-table. She hated to have her hair arranged, that tiresome niggling business, having it tied here and pinned there, but it was delightful to brush it like this with long rhythmic strokes when it was loose and free, stretching to the length of her arm on the brush and then springing away from it, fizzing and crackling with sparks in the frosty night like a cat's fur rubbed the wrong way.

All the small inanimate objects on the dressing-table, encircled in the pool of candle-light, had a strange bright awareness, as though now, and now only, when all else slept in the darkness, they knew their own significance. The cameo brooch with the head of Apollo carved in coral looked up at her from the pin-cushion. The old silver mirror lay like clear water on the table. She picked it up and sat staring at the dim reflection of her face; it showed only a pale oval set in the misty cloud of her hair. The faces of other women had gazed into this glass as she was gazing now, the face of her mother, of her mother's mother, gaudy Queen Anne, and of her husband King James' mother, Mary Queen of Scots.

This mirror had been Louey's since she was a child, when her mother had given it for a birthday present as no other was handy. It had always been the 'birthday mirror,' but now she was thinking how her mother had spoken this afternoon of Queen Mary.

It was into this mirror Queen Mary had looked for the last time before she walked to her execution, and now her great-grand-daughter held it in her hand. What had that face looked like as it took leave of itself? What had the woman felt behind the dim reflection of living flesh? Had she believed 'now hast thou but one bare hour to live,' laid down this mirror and walked out, knowing that life was over?

Louey could not think it. For Mary, dying long ago, as for herself so sharply tingling with life in this freezing night of earliest spring, life was always beginning anew—even in the hour of her death it had done so. She had left proof of it in her death in the song of praise and thanksgiving written in those last hours, the Latin rhymes pealing out like a carillon of bells in their abundance of spirit. She had left proof of it in her life, in the tireless rides at the head of her troops, dressed as a man, sharing their hardships in the wild Scots weather.

What a companion she would have been to a man of her spirit! But there were no men of that spirit in Scotland—then. If there had been, she might not have had to lay her gallant head upon the block. If Montrose had lived then——

And with that Louey came back to the deep under-current of her thoughts that had run steady and unbroken by any interruption these two hours, carried on through one vivid picture after another, conjured up by those magic lines of print that she had been reading. Not the dead Queen Mary who 'so wished to be a man,' nor her mother in whom burned the same spirit, but herself had marched and galloped with Montrose all through those fantastic campaigns of his in Scotland four years ago.

And now that the last page was turned, the book shut, and she, as if to escape from the rapt intensity of her pleasure, had wandered here and there in her room, turning her attention this way and that, only now did it come back into her mind that there was still the consummation to be reached, the fruit of that book and her imagination, to be tested now by experience.

She took the candle in her hand and went through the door at the end of the room that led to her studio, opened a drawer and pulled out a red-chalk drawing that she had sketched days ago, before Montrose had ridden into the courtyard and come into their house, before she had ever seen him.

Underneath it was written, 'Imaginary Portrait of the Marquis of Montrose.'

What could have possessed her to draw it thus ? 'Possessed' was the literal word, for some force outside herself must surely have taken charge of her eyes and hand when she did this. When *did* she do it ? She could not remember, nor what impulse had suddenly led her to imagine thus the face of the man that Rupert had so wished to meet again.

Her imaginary portraits were famous in a small way; she was apt to catch an extraordinarily close likeness to people she had never known by sight, merely through what she had heard of their sayings and doings; for whatever she heard made a picture in her mind, and that picture was generally right in expression if not in feature. Often they turned out wickedly clever caricatures, sometimes they showed a strange and sensitive fancy. Her portrait of her eldest brother Henry, who had been drowned in a public packet-boat off Amsterdam when she was still too much of a baby to remember him, was a curiously appealing study; those who had known the dead boy said that his very soul looked out through the tender and wistful eyes of her portrait.

No, it was not the actual likeness of her sketch of Montrose that now took her breath away, though that was indeed far nearer than in any she had ever done which she could compare with the original. The keen eyes under rough peaked eyebrows, the long, rather irregular and bumpy nose with its high bridge, the unusually broad forehead and wide mouth that went up a little at the corners, these were the very same in their proportions as in the living face she had seen for the first time this afternoon.

Yet the most striking thing in the comparison between the two was the one great difference between them. The face she had watched that afternoon had been waiting, hopeful, knowing he had not yet reached what he waited for and hoped. The face she had drawn showed the joy of absolute fulfilment in one who has achieved the utmost that his present life could hold.

Someone had come into the room just as she had finished drawing it, so she now remembered; it was Etta, and she had looked over her shoulder at it and asked who it was, and Loucy had told her to guess, hoping Etta would say a great soldier or something that would show she had succeeded in what she had attempted.

But Etta's answer had been utterly unexpected; she had said, 'It is the face of a bridegroom.'

Louey had laughed it off at the moment, half annoyed. Etta's mind ran so on wedding bells and tender happy-ending romances that she would discover them even in the cannon's mouth. This man was the boldest adventurer of any of this age, excepting their knight-errant brother, Rupert, and Rupert himself looked to him as to a greater spirit than his own,—'and yet all you say of him is that he looks like a bridegroom. Would you say the same if I did Rupert's portrait?'

'No,' Etta had replied, quite unshaken, 'I would not. I have never seen Rupert look so, and I don't think he ever could.'

Louey had forgotten all about it, forgotten also this sketch and what it looked like, as was her way with anything that she had done. But now, seeing it afresh, she saw that Etta had been right. Why had she all unconsciously drawn Montrose like this? Was it because of her own secret wish?

Nearly three years ago Rupert had come home from the Civil War in England, and had sat beside her at a family dinner given to all the brothers and sisters and their young Stuart cousins who were then at The Hague, and had talked to her of Montrose in such a way that she had said, 'I believe he is the only man with whom I could ever really fall in love.' She did not know then that his wife was dead, and when Rupert had told her this, she had said lightly that now indeed had he destroyed her hopes, for there was no rivalry so strong as that of the dead.

Had their careless talk lain unthought of at the back of her mind all this time, and come out now in this swift sketch, drawn while she was brooding on the deeds of which she had since heard so much? She felt the blood mount to her head, she put up her hand to her cheek and found it burning. She could listen and join unabashed in the coarse and jovial talk of the Dutch painters with a freedom that had gained her so warm a reputation for bonhomie that it had endangered her reputation as a princess; but she was now blushing as hotly as a schoolgirl alone in the darkness at her own secret thoughts, so secret that her hand had discovered them here on the paper before her heart had known them.

In sudden panic she took the drawing to hold it over the flame of the candle, but the face that looked back so serenely at her arrested her. 'He could never look so for me,' she told herself, and then, as she looked longer, 'nor for any woman'; and then her very thoughts fell silent as she gazed on what she had drawn, and wondered what she saw.

VIII

AMONG the Royalist exiles at The Hague was that charming young woman, Kate d'Aubigny, who had been a dancingly happy bride for a few weeks, and then a war widow since almost the beginning of the war. Her handsome gallant young husband, George Lord d'Aubigny, younger brother to the Duke of Richmond, had been killed nearly seven years ago while following Rupert in his terrific charge at Edgehill.

Since then, public affairs and platonic friendships had been her two chief distractions; she had corresponded copiously in political plots with Prince Rupert, who had no eyes to spare for her charms since he was deep in love with her sister-in-law, the lovely Duchess of Richmond; when all England was at war, she had smuggled important documents into London, hidden in her curls.

Lately she had been remarried, to young Lord Newburgh, but nobody seemed to remember it, not even herself; everybody still called her Kate d'Aubigny when they did not call her 'Clever Kate,' 'Pretty Kate.' With her new husband, a boy who had not been old enough for the war but had come straight from school in France to wait on the late King in prison, she had attempted and all but effected the King's escape from Hampton Court; it was said indeed that she had married young Newburgh largely for the sake of this opportunity.

Now that she had come to The Hague she was an intimate friend of such contrary types as the aggressively legal Sir Edward Hyde and the elegant and debonair Lord Lanark, who had just inherited the ducal coronet of Hamilton since his elder brother's execution by Cromwell. That execution had been an ironic fulfilment of the prophecy that had always clouded the first Duke's loyalty, for he had been told he would succeed to King Charles' crown—and within a month of King Charles' death he did so, but it proved to be a martyr's crown and not a royal one.

Now his younger brother Lanark was the second Duke of Hamilton, and showed signs of the same tendency as his brother to run with the hare and hunt with the hounds, for he had joined Lauderdale last summer in breaking away from Argyll's extreme Covenanters, yet still declared that they continued to uphold the Covenant.

"But if the new Duke of Hamilton is, as you say he is, a reasonable man," Hyde argued with Kate d'Aubigny, frowning at the pretty bird-like creature with his bushy brows and thinking it almost a pity that such attractive looks should be balanced with so much good sense (the times were bringing women to the fore in a way that was good for their brains but not for their characters, or anyway not for men's characters)—"*if*, as you say, a *reasonable* man," he repeated portentously, thinking that the new Hamilton or any other man would doubtless show himself just as reasonable with Kate as she wanted him to be, "then he is bound to see how impossible this position is of the 'Moderate Covenanters' as they call themselves."

"So he would," she cried, "if only it weren't for his precious cousin and ally, Lauderdale. And it is that gross pig who is making all the mischief against Montrose, I am convinced of it," she continued in her eager glancing fashion, picking up things on her table and laying them down again, for nothing, no, nothing that she saw and handled could cease to remind her of George d'Aubigny, not this enamelled box of his for wax and letter wafers, nor the tiny jewelled figure of Saint George and the Dragon he had worn, nor least of all the carved walnut-shell for a thimble-case that he had got her at a country fair.

This last she opened and shut and turned all round in her thin fingers and then closed them tightly over it, never looking at it, but at Hyde, brightly and intently as if she saw him for the first time, while she said, "Yes, I see what we must do. You shall meet Lanark—I beg his pardon, Hamilton—at my house as if by chance, with other people here, and then you can talk naturally, not in a

set interview, and make friends. If only everybody would always
do that, it would save a deal of trouble."

She sighed, opened her hand and looked at the nut-shell for the
first time, laid it on the table, brushed her fingers together, laughed
and got up, saying, "Lauderdale hates Montrose because he is so
unlike him that he knows it is hopeless his ever wishing to be like
him. But Hamilton *does* wish it; he has told me how he admires
Montrose and wishes his poor brother had not fallen out with him."

"As far as I remember," said Hyde a little stiffly, "it was the
first Duke of Hamilton who made mischief between Montrose and
the late King from the very beginning, and did as much as any man
to put Scotland under the tyranny of Argyll and the Kirk."

"He's paid for it now with his life," said Kate sadly.

Hyde, knitting his brows, reflected with exasperation that even
the most intelligent women were illogical. The first Duke of
Hamilton had played into Argyll's and Cromwell's hands, but had
paid, not for that, but for the fact that he had turned against them
last summer and headed a Royalist rising which had been squashed
by Cromwell.

But Kate showed sense over this meeting and he was glad to fall
in with it and see the new Duke apart from his jovially bullying
mentor and jailer, Lauderdale.

Her pretty feminine room, so modernly furnished with the com-
forts that one could get more easily in Holland than anywhere else
—rugs from Persia, curtains and cushion-covers of Chinese silk,
two charming still-life paintings of flowers by a Dutch artist, and
even flowers themselves, grown from bulbs in a shining porcelain
bowl, so that though it was still winter outside, yet here in the warm
scented firelight it was already spring,—this her temporary lodging
was instantly her home, the perfect setting for her, herself bright
and brittle as some piece of glass.

It was also the favourite rendezvous of Cavaliers and Covenanters, Dutch and English royalties, foreign ambassadors and the
senators of the States of Holland.   And there in the most natural

K

way in the world Hyde happened to come in when the new Duke of Hamilton was there among half a dozen others, and Kate d'Aubigny led them both up to the window to pay their devoirs to her growing flowers—"and the bowl, holding all that heavy earth, came all the way from China—is it conceivable that anything so fragile should be so strong? And look, there is a picture on it of one of their heathen temples; and why is it only the Dutch can trade with China and we of Britain are so backward?"

She had darted away to a new arrival before they could answer, and Hyde and Hamilton were left with their backs to the company, their eyes on a painted bowl, and their tongues wagging on the enormous advance of Holland as a seafaring and commercial Power. From there it was a short step to England, to Scotland, and their hopes of restoring the young King to both these countries.

They talked amicably and moderately, as people do who talk politics in a drawing-room; each was surprised to find how reasonable was the other; each wished to continue the conversation and was annoyed when it had to break up under pressure of the amenities and they had to take part in the general talk again. 'But it's led nowhere,' thought Hyde, as they decided that they must join the others, 'these friendly chats never do. He'll say I'm a good sort of fellow and I'll say as much by him, and we'll continue to oppose each other's plans as before.'

But as they walked slowly back into the centre of the room he was astonished to hear Hamilton murmur in an elaborately casual but very low tone, "Do you rise early? You might come and see me to-morrow morning, if you come before——"

"Before what?"

"Before a lazy fellow is out of bed," Hamilton finished in his accustomed voice, smiling, for they had now reached the others. But Hyde was sure it had not been what he was going to say.

He went to Hamilton's rooms before eight o'clock next morning, stumping in his soft shoes down the wet street (for the thaw had come at last), and was at once taken straight to the Duke's bedroom. Hamilton was sitting up in his curtained bed with a furred robe thrown over his shoulders, his long dark curls framing a face as melancholy and anxious as a spaniel's. He told the servant who showed Hyde in to tell anyone who wanted to see him that he was asleep.

That was encouraging, Hyde thought, but as soon as the door had closed behind the servant he shied away from his visitor, increasing his resemblance to a nervous dog, and when Hyde spoke of Montrose, the great things he had done for the King's cause and hoped to do again, Hamilton started impatiently, drew his cloak more closely round him and said, "It's no good, it's no good; one swallow doesn't make a summer, nor one great man a nation. I tell you Scotland *is* the Covenant now, and the Covenant Scotland, and whoever speaks against the one speaks against the other. I tell you," he repeated, leaning forward on his elbow on the pillows and agitatedly beating them up in support with his other hand, "there is *nothing* that can lessen the power of the Covenant now in Scotland, only time and patience. Montrose has shown himself its enemy; he is therefore regarded, will always be regarded, as Scotland's enemy."

"Have *all* your countrymen then so deep a sense of religion?" asked Hyde dryly.

The younger man fell back on his pillows as if to give up the struggle. Nothing could make this crass Englishman understand what was happening in Scotland now. His eyes were half-shut, seeing, not the rational, highly intellectual face of his stout visitor, nor the comfortable healthily warmed and airy room round him, but stone castles that were never warm, narrow windows that never opened, grey streets that were never washed nor swept.

And in those streets men walked with averted eyes on Christmas Day and the days that used to be called holy, lest they should be seen to greet a neighbour and so be charged with the crime of Popery in giving him the compliments of the season; in those freezing and stuffy rooms families huddled round the fire, afraid to dance to make them warm, or sing to make them merry, lest it should be reported to the spies that the Elders of the Kirk appointed in every parish, in closer because more intimate family inquisition than had ever been known in the days of the Old Church.

Men had lately been fined heavily for a careless oath in the company of their neighbours; they had been punished more severely for picking their own gooseberries on a Sunday than if they had stolen them on a week-day; in fact, it was safer not to go out at all on a Sunday lest they should be reported for taking any pleasure on that day.

And under this black oppression, since natural pleasures had no chance to live, unnatural ones were growing hideously frequent. The Devil, for all the warfare against him, seemed to be taking fresh life and power; the number of witches, male and female, was increasing everywhere in spite of all the tortures and burnings urged by the Kirk against them.

"Religion!" Hamilton flung out bitterly at last. "The Covenant is more than a religion, it is a superstition!"

Hyde was impressed by the distinction and prepared to question it, but was forestalled by Hamilton, who cried, "Can you not see? It is not fear of God but fear of the Devil that holds Scotland cowering together like children in the dark? The Covenant says that what they have sworn on earth God will bind in heaven, that they have power in excommunicating a man to condemn not only his body on the scaffold but his soul to hell. They have excommunicated Montrose. To you that is nothing more than banishment from the Presbyterian Kirk, and as you are not a Presbyterian yourself it is nothing to you. You think more of the fact that his estates and titles have been forfeited by the government of the Kirk and himself condemned to be hanged, drawn, and quartered as a traitor to that Kirk—should his enemies ever get the chance to lay their hands on him. But in Scotland we do not talk of Presbyterians and the Church of England. There, there is one Church of God and one only, the Kirk as established by Calvin, and he who has belonged to it and been cast out of it, is damned to hell fire for ever.

To his countrymen Montrose is a thing accursed, and whoever would join with him will be dragged down to hell with him."

"I see," said Hyde slowly, "that that foul-mouthed pamphleteer of Cromwell's (I should, more correctly, say foul-penned) wrote the truth for once in his life in that line,

'New Presbyter is but old Priest writ large.'"

"Who wrote that?" exclaimed Hamilton.

"A writer who was a charming poet till he took to politics, a Mr. Milton."

"I never heard of him. But he never wrote a truer word than that. Good God, what am I saying? If you ever repeat a word of this to any soul alive——"

"I shall not think of it," said Hyde, shutting his full lips firmly together as if not to let even his breath escape him from now on, his eyes bright, not to say beady, with satisfaction at the remarkable confidence he must have inspired in this well-meaning though excitable and unbalanced young man. People were astonishingly interesting, they were so weak, so foolish, so incapable of managing their lives to advantage. How was it that anyone so personable and intelligent as this young Scots noble should have got himself enslaved to an institution he loathed as much as the Kirk, and to a man so much his inferior as Lauderdale?

"Yet Your Grace has taken the Covenant yourself?" he suggested, "and I believe agrees publicly with most of the Earl of Lauderdale's opinions on it?"

Hamilton's answer was a curse which should have called down on him a specially heavy fine.

"I wish to God I had never taken it," he added presently. "I detest it utterly. But I am caught and held in its bonds. And Lauderdale, I am in his hold too. I am tied and bound, there's no way I can turn."

He was turning though, this way and that, in a fury of restlessness.

'He owes Lauderdale money—Lauderdale knows something against him—now I shall hear it,' Hyde was saying to himself with complacent expectancy. But it was not fulfilled. When the wretched man in the bed began to speak again, he only said:

"He is my cousin, you know."

"Ah yes, you set great store by that in Scotland," said Hyde, still hopeful.

"And older, and wiser in some ways. You Englishmen may think him uncouth, for he has not lived in Courts like some of us, and the late King Charles' Court is acknowledged, now it has ceased, to have been the best education for a gentleman in all Europe. But all the same, my cousin's understanding is equal to any," he continued in the same oddly defensive manner, "and I have a great affection for him. Besides, he counts for more in Scotland than you can guess."

"I thought Argyll had managed to oust him from any share in the Government for some years to come," said Hyde with an almost surly note in his voice. This was a slippery fish after all; here he was sliding away as fast as Hyde had thought he was holding him.

"Oh, but he'll bob up again, you'll see," said Hamilton almost cheerfully now. "Men like Lauderdale aren't to be either ousted or squashed, and whatever happens to Argyll in the long run, you'll find Lauderdale sitting on top, I'll swear."

Hyde gave it up. "Then you hold by him and would never be reconciled to serving by the side of Montrose?" he said. "I suppose indeed it is impossible. You took up arms against him. You would hardly take a subordinate position under the man who had been your enemy."

But there was no telling what Hamilton would do. Now, at the very moment that Hyde thought he had 'placed' him so that he knew exactly what he could and could not expect from him, Hamilton swerved again, started forward and declared with passionate intensity, "What do I care about a subordinate position?

Would I be such a fool as to expect to command the greatest commander alive? I'd be glad and proud to serve as a sergeant under Montrose—would to God I could ever do so!" he added on so wretched a note that it was like the sigh of a prisoner for free air.

The solid Englishman, trying to make consistent sense of all these contradictions, stared at him, determined to discover some evidence of the suave duplicity he had been accustomed to find in his brother, the first Duke of Hamilton. But his bright stare could detect no hint of it, the young man was obviously and even painfully sincere, so Hyde decided almost regretfully, for it would make everything much easier to understand if he were just a liar, and simpler for him to write about in his history. 'But no,' he said to himself, 'I must do him justice, and I shall write him down as still the same man that he seems to be.'

Hamilton, unaware of the momentous phrase that was hanging over him like an inscription on his tombstone, could not think why the little man was staring and blinking so owlishly at him; in sudden exasperation he very nearly endangered his obituary notice by telling Hyde what a fool he looked.

Didn't he understand what one soldier could feel about another, on whatever side he was, and even to whatever clan he belonged?

"His house has always been the enemy of ours," he said, "and in Scotland we have an old saying,

'From the pride of the Grahams,
Good Lord, deliver us!'

"But it makes no odds, I would be proud to serve that pride."

"Umph," said Hyde. He began to think the young man was going too far to be quite sensible. There was no need to extenuate Montrose's pride—Hyde had been a good deal annoyed by it himself; in fact, he had had more than one stiffish passage-at-arms with Montrose, though he was not going to admit that to Hamilton. But this high-flown Scot here was really making himself ridiculous by talking so exaggeratedly.

"If you feel such admiration for him, why not flout your cousin and serve with him?" he said bluntly. "You talk so eloquently you might even persuade Lauderdale to join you too."

"He would rather kill me than join with me," said Hamilton earnestly. "If he ever knew I had even discussed it——" He broke off, his eyes dilated, he said low and hurriedly, "I should lose every friend I have, every bit of property, and most probably my head. They are too much for me, as they will be for everyone who is against them, mark that."

He made a grimace that startled Hyde until he saw its purpose. The door just behind the bed was opening, there was the smell of tobacco, and the shapeless bulk of a stout man in a loose dark velvet nightgown was coming round the door, the purple face of Lauderdale puffing at a long clay pipe, his large clouded eyes blinking suspiciously at Hamilton's visitor.

Hamilton hastily introduced them, forgetting they already knew each other, and began to talk about the Council meeting they were to have that day with the King, as though that had been the subject of their conversation.

But Hyde saw no reason to maintain the fiction; he began at once, "Since the Marquis of Montrose will be there, I have come on behalf of the King to express his earnest desire that you will meet the Marquis in a friendly spirit, since only so is there any chance of furthering His Majesty's cause."

For answer Lauderdale removed his pipe from his mouth and spat into the fire. Hyde got up in disgust and looked round for his hat. Hamilton gave him a despairing glance. Lauderdale's bulky figure blocked the way to the door. He did not seem to notice that Hyde was wishing to pass him.

"Ask me to make friends with Satan," he said, "and out of friendship to yourself I might try and do it. But with a man whose hands are stained with the blood of his countrymen, whose hideous barbarities have made his name the terror of Scotland——"

He was deliberately working himself up into a frenzy, his bloodshot eyes rolling in his head as though he had lost control of his reason, and yet they flickered out a sharp enough glance at Hamilton to see if he were taking this as he should, without any sign of weakening.

Hyde determined to have this out and sat down to a judicial enquiry.

"It being the unfortunate nature of civil war," he said, "that whoever fights in it must kill his countrymen, it seems highly ridiculous to all sober men that you should blame Montrose for what every general in the war was doing."

"Three thousand of the Clan Campbell in one field of battle!" Lauderdale exclaimed, and flopped down on the edge of Hamilton's bed to take breath.

Hyde patiently asked what atrocities had Montrose been guilty of apart from the field of battle.

"*Apart* from the field—oh, well, I don't know of any *apart* from that, but for what was done there Scotland will *never pardon him*," he finished, glaring at Hyde with such a glazed and bulbous stare from those protuberant eyes that the Chancellor was alarmed lest he should be called upon to witness the unpleasant spectacle of a fit.

Seeing that he had made an impression, Lauderdale hastened to follow it up by declaring that he wished for King Charles' restoration above all things, "but for all that," said he, staring harder than ever, "I would much rather he were never restored than that James Graham should be permitted to come into his Court."

This sounded so mad that Hyde nearly gave it up, but a dogged obstinacy, combined with a growing fear of a force so volcanically irrational, made him make one last effort on behalf of reason.

"You know, then, of nothing but what was done by his soldiers in the heat of action?"

Lauderdale, unable to work up another explosion, took a pull at his pipe, spat again, but this time in an impartial manner, and at last had to say "No."

"Then," said Hyde, "may I beg you will observe how very absurd you have shown your objections to be?"

Not unnaturally, Lauderdale failed to make the required answer. He ignored his judge and shot another side-glance at the silent figure in the bed.

"Argyll's Commissioners," he said, "have just arrived at The Hague."

The words were as much a threat as an announcement.

IX

KING CHARLES held his formal reception of Argyll's Commissioners in the house of his brother-in-law, Prince William of Orange, the only place, as he said to him, where he could still hold anything.

To this Dutch Prince of twenty-two, only four years his senior, he owed a comfortable roof over his head all this winter, good and regular meals, and even the clothes he was wearing. On the other hand, William with his pretty but proud and rather plaintive young English wife the Princess Mary, and his overpowering German mother the Princess Amelia and her brood of harassed daughters, owed to this dispossessed English lad, the son of a murdered king, more gaiety and amusement through these few months than he had had in the whole of his life.

William had a passion for amusement but no ability to provide it for himself; he needed someone like young Charles who could communicate to him his overflowing power of enjoyment. His delicate and melancholy beauty had a maternal effect on women which exasperated him. He had an excellent brain, which was often of good service to Charles, but he was not nearly as proud of this as of being almost as good a sportsman as his young brother-in-law; and sadly conscious that for all his determined pursuit of pleasure he would never be as natural and easy a rake.

How did this lad Charles, so much his junior, manage to be so casual, insolent, assured in all matters of the world? (William might have revised his judgment had he seen him with Montrose.)

Here he was just returned from a stroll to the lodgings of pretty Lucy Walters and discussing with some annoyance the fact that she was now as big as a barrel, "and she says, by me, but how do I know? It might as easily be Bob Sidney or even one or two others, possibly yourself, Will? Or what do you say to my young prig of a brother, James? He told me as solemnly as a judge just before he went off to Paris that she might be very good-looking but that he preferred women to be intelligent. Good for a fifteen-year-old, hey? Suspicious too, throwing me off the scent!"

And he would not take seriously any of William's warnings as to the mischief Lucy might do with her reports as to the legitimacy of her baby.

"It's absurd," he said. "All the world knows she came here as Colonel Sidney's mistress and left him—or didn't leave him—for me. What point would there have been in my marrying her?"

And he nonchalantly passed on to his forthcoming reception of the Commissioners from Argyll as to a companion annoyance with that of Lucy's bastard.

"The glimpse I've had of those five old crows in steeples turned my stomach at the start. Think of it—no less than three lots of Scots here now, and all at each other's throats!"

Prince William had thought of it and had already talked with the minister Mr. Robert Baillie (who represented the Kirk, but showed far more comfortable common sense than the lay representative Lord Cassillis), to sound him as to their point of view. He had been very tactful in impressing on Mr. Baillie the enormous weight of the ministers' advice in the State, and in trying to modify it to some faint shadow of tolerance.

"'Malignant!'" he now exclaimed to Charles. "I am sick of the very sound of that word, and, as I told him to his face, it has lost all meaning, for they call any man malignant that they please. As for your Marquis of Montrose, the Brethren can't speak of him without abusing his 'apostacy and unheard-of cruelty.'"

"'Unheard-of' is the correct term, I fancy. They'd had a 'day of humiliation' at Delft, you know, before coming here—nothing like a day of humiliation to cocker up their pride. They're own Brethren to Christ after it, and wouldn't have a word to fling to the Holy Ghost."

"For God's sake don't be blasphemous in their hearing, Charles. You've made a good first impression—stick to it."

"What is it?"

"'Very sweet and courteous'—'the most gentle and innocent and virtuously inclined of princes.' Your only fault is your inclination to Montrose, and Mr. Baillie thinks it would be the greatest pity in the world you should not be in good company."

"Very sound of him—it's the greatest pity in the world I've had to leave Lucy's company for his. I'd better take off this cravat she's given me, it might give me away."

"You have a real chance in the way you charmed them, God knows how. They'd curse you to hell if they knew anything of you really."

Charles gave his gay triumphant laugh as he stood at the mirror, untying Lucy's cravat. It pleased him to think how well he could manage men, even these furiously pious fanatics. In spite of Montrose's warnings, the chances were that he would find he could manage them even in Scotland. He asked Will his opinion as to this. Will, looking affectionately at the young rascal, thought it more than likely.

"Montrose doesn't," said Charles.

"He knows them. But he doesn't know you."

"Isn't 'charmed' by me, you mean. I wish I knew which of you is right."

He did know. He didn't wish to know. It was easier and pleasanter to believe the amused admiration of this quiet young man who assured him that—"set a foot in Scotland and you'll have the whole country following you to a man—*and*, which counts as much, to a woman."

Charles grinned back at him. "To the hips and haws of Scotland!" he cried as he pulled off Lucy's cravat and waved it round his head like a flag. "And now for the high hats! I can't run to a steeple crown myself, but you'll observe, dear Will, that there's no trace left of frivolity in my dress."

Will answered soberly in an attempt to draw Charles down to the real matter in hand: "These Moderate Covenanters of Lauderdale's and Hamilton's party, they, I suppose, support the earlier, the National League and Covenant, that Montrose himself upheld at its beginning?"

But Charles was irrepressible. Mounting on a stool, in a high snuffling whine he intoned: "There is not one Covenant but three Covenants, all of them incomprehensible. First the Scots made a Covenant against the Pope and the Roman Mass, and nobody minded it. So then they made another, the National League and Covenant against the English Prayer Book, and nobody minded that. So Argyll made yet another and called it the Solemn League and Covenant because it had ceased to be national and grown a damned sight too solemn—and nobody minded that, but he said they'd go to hell if they didn't, so they had to. Have I expounded this doctrine well and truly unto you, my feeble-minded brother?"

"Get down, you fool!" exclaimed Will. "They're coming!"

There were two ministers among the Commissioners and two advocates with the Earl of Cassillis at their head, but all looked overpoweringly clerical in their high hats and severely plain clothes, representing as they did the extreme clerical party in Scotland. Their bearing towards Charles, once they had performed a fairly low bow, was not that of subjects towards their King but of ambassadors from an equal Power, and it was noted that they gave their formal condolences on the lamented 'violent death' of King Charles I, not his 'murder,' as even the most severely Calvinistic of their sympathizers in Holland had not hesitated to call it.

They went straight from the King's presence to his aunt the ex-Queen of Bohemia, where at least they should find sympathy, in the martyred saint of the Protestant cause, whose husband had died fighting the great powers of Rome.

But Elizabeth, with ruthless feminine logic, could see no connection between this and the hostility she was expected to bear to Montrose.

"What in God's name has Rome to do with the matter?" she exclaimed in her downright fashion that always managed to wear the appearance of a compliment, as if to say, 'To sensible people like yourself I can afford to speak frankly.' "Here on the Continent we see Rome where she is, and big and dangerous enough in all conscience. But in those cloudy islands of my home, and yours, you see her in impossible places, like an old maid looking under her bed every night for the man she's never found there yet. You would suspect a poppy of wearing a Cardinal's hat! What has Rome to do with the Marquis of Montrose, who is and has been a Presbyterian all his life?"

In a sharp swerve to a new point of attack Mr. Robert Baillie answered by condemning the Popish practices in the Church of England Prayer Book and begging her to reclaim her own child the Princess Sophia and the young King her nephew from this insidious influence and to lead them back into the one true Presbyterian Church of Calvin.

"And you can see what *that* means!" she burst out to her faithful Craven as soon as she had rid herself of them, a little sooner than was quite decent. "Amelia has already got at them with tales against Sophie—met them at the Palace gates, no doubt, to tell them to marry Charles to her own pure Protestant girl. The presumption of these steeple crowns! What is Cassillis doing in a high hat? But the Kennedys have had to show themselves off as unco guid Reformers ever since they part-roasted an Abbot to get his lands. And so here's this wizened elder of an earl complaining to me of my daughter going to the Church of England service with her own first cousin!"

"Ah well," said little Lord Craven in his sleepy fashion, "it's as good a place for meeting as any, now that the ice has melted."

Elizabeth laughed wickedly. 'True Towser' could get in a shrewd nip on occasion.

But for all her mockery, her concern for Sophie's hopes was more eager and personal than she had ever felt for any of her daughters. She could not imagine a more pleasant son-in-law than Charles— what jokes they would have together!—and then to think of her youngest daughter becoming the Queen of England, as she herself was intended to be by nature and had so nearly been by fate.

That plot of Guy Fawkes to blow up her father and brothers in Parliament and put herself, then a child of ten, on the throne,—horrible as it had been, she could not but admit now, looking back, that she would have made a far better business of it as Queen Elizabeth II than her brother had done as King Charles I. But now if poor Charles' son and her daughter could reclaim the family fortunes and England together, what splendid justification it would give to all past failures!

"And you and I, old friend, should then see dear England once again," she said to Craven, her eyes bright and tender with the vision of the England she had left at sixteen, the Merry England of her father King James' heyday.

Martial law now ruled England, forbidding football and horse-racing and dancing round the maypole. The soldiers were rebelling against the preparations for the invasion of Ireland. They had set fire to the cannon foundries that were making munitions for it, and had arrested their officers and elected new ones under the principles of democracy.

But Oliver Cromwell had put all that down with an iron hand, and men were thrown into prison who dared to say that England was now under no law but that of the sword. The sword and the Code of Moses now reigned together over what had been so lately the most modern and enlightened nation in Europe.

The Scots Commissioners at The Hague were a sore reminder to Elizabeth of that alien rule, yet she was charming to them, both from policy and habit. She told the acid, prematurely withered Earl of Cassillis, nicknamed the Solemn, how well she remembered visiting his father in his lovely and ancient castle on the banks of the little river in the wooded valley on the way to Glasgow. (She had visited it, as it happened, at the age of one, but she did not mention that—what difference did it make if she remembered it or only remembered hearing about it afterwards?)

And she told the sturdy and loquacious Mr. Robert Baillie (the only human being among the lot, she declared) how much interested she was to hear he kept a diary and hoped she might some day be allowed a glimpse of it. She would like to see his first impressions of London eight years ago at the beginning of the troubles, when he had gone there as Commissioner at Lord Strafford's trial.

He gave her his impressions then and there very tersely; the London lodging-house keepers had grossly overcharged him and his fellows, he told her, and it was the first and he hoped the last time he would ever be charged 40 shillings Scots for a dish of partridges as small as sparrows.

She laughed herself into fits telling this afterwards to Montrose. Then suddenly her splendid eyes flashed in scorn and she reminded him how Mr. Baillie's cousin, General Baillie, had boasted publicly that he and Argyll had caught Montrose and his handful of Highlanders in a trap, and 'if we get not the life of these worms chirted out of them, the reproach will stick on us for ever.'

"And the reproach has stuck, and it was the life of some 3000 of Argyll's clan that was chirted out of them by 'these worms'!" So she now cried gleefully, declaring that it was no wonder these Brethren fled whenever they heard the very name of Jamie Graham.

"I must have a portrait of you to be my rescuer when you are gone. I will get that fat lazy Gerard to do a large one that I can hang in my room to frighten away those carrion crows when they flap their black wings at me and caw their dismal prophecies and would peck if they dare."

"So Your Majesty dubs me your scarecrow," he said, smiling with pleasure at her laughter. He had never seen a woman who could laugh like this. It made no odds what happened to her, that 'unhappy,' 'unfortunate' were what all men called her and her family; there was a rich world of happiness within her, wider than any circumstance without.

Her daughter Louise watched in amusement, annoyance and agony the rapid growth of the friendship between them. She too

L

could recognize in her mother a true grandeur of spirit preserved through all the dragging poverty of her conditions. But a lifetime with her could make her see in it also that touch of exaggeration, of consciousness, that makes for travesty. There is no insurmountable gulf between the heroine and the charlatan, and the heroine who is everlastingly deprived of the natural exercise of her immense vitality, thwarted and suppressed, an empress in a lodging-house, is apt to be forced to play up to herself.

Elizabeth I made the England of the Elizabethan age; but she who might have been Elizabeth II, with a spirit equally imperial, had to bother about the butchers' and the bakers' bills. The inequality of her fate could not lower her pride, but it inclined her to caricature it. 'I am still of my mad humour to be merry,' she declared when things were at the worst with her, and her high spirits seemed at times uncomfortably excessive to her daughters. Why should she sit up so much later than they wished to do at any Court function, as though determined to show that five-in-the-morning had no terrors for a fifty-year-old? Why must she swear so often, make even that sour stick Cassillis and that podgy wind-bag Baillie her slaves, call her men friends such nicknames as 'little ape' or 'ugly filthy camel's face'?

"And what does she call the Marquis of Montrose?" asked Eliza dryly when Louey had burst out in these indignant questions.

"No worse than 'Jamie Graham' so far, or it may be—God forgive her!—'Gentle Jamie.' But he likes it—likes being praised and laughed at as though he were a little boy! And this is the 'Great Marquis,' so grave and aloof, of whom everybody stands in awe, or rather fear!"

"That is probably the reason of his liking it," said Eliza as though quoting from a Jesuit's manual of psychology.

"Oh, you are right! That is the secret of Mother's success with men. She is never afraid of anybody or anything, least of all of the effect she might have upon them. And so they would give their lives for her. While I——"

"While you——?"

'Wish only that I could give my life for him,' thought Louey.

But she did not say it. She smiled at her sister as they rode over the flat pasture lands beyond the town towards the sunset that lay in bars of cloud and fire above the flat horizon, and said, "Was one so able as a child to enjoy a sunset such as this, a little flat mud, and above us an immeasurable immensity of heaven, because one had then no thought of *what to do with it*? Artists are mere merchants after all; they muddy all their precious merchandise by bringing it to market. And the artist and the lover 'Are of imagination all compact.'"

"What do you want then, Louey?"

Louey did not answer.

But Eliza, even while putting her question, still heard only her sister's low voice that had wandered so far away from this present moment. She thought that of all their family Louey was the most fascinating although the most unsure of herself, the gayest though the most troubled in spirit, because the waters of that spirit ran deeper and broader than the others', more open to every wind of heaven to stir with its breath—and what word is that but inspiration?

X

*L*ESS than two miles from The Hague was the House in the Wood which Prince William's father, Prince Frederick Henry of Orange, had begun to build before his death two years ago. It was the perfect summer palace, surrounded by woods and water, with long windows opening on to a lake of swans set among the curtains of great trees; it enshrined the most perfect treasures that had yet been acquired by Holland's adventurous sea trade on the other side of the world.

There was to be an Indian room, a Japanese room, a Chinese room; huge jars of cloisonné filled with sweet-smelling spices stood about in corners; a rhinoceros horn set on a stand of carved ivory bore witness to the fable of the unicorn; a baby's rattle showed six carved balls enclosed each inside the other so that only a miracle of the Eastern magicians could have placed them there. The floor was a spider-web pattern of inlaid woods, the walls were covered with enormous canvases representing Prince Henry's victories, all by different artists, or indifferent, as Louey complained.

There was her Great-Uncle Henry fighting Hate, Envy and Calumny all at once while the skeleton figure of Death aimed his javelin at him; there he was again, making a triumphal entry into Bois-le-Duc, his red cheeks sagging rather than burly, and his figure rather small and insignificant, looking embarrassingly over-dressed in full Court armour among so many large naked females, allegorical of course, but painted so realistically in all their bulging curves that they looked like a party of good burghers' wives taking a bathe, which God forbid they should ever do, especially in front of Great-Uncle Henry in full dress. And there too was the skeleton Death dodging through a welter of naked women, angels, magnificent horses and dogs, and the artist himself who leaned forward from a corner of his own picture in a blue cap and grey whiskers to gaze shrewdly at the scene he had conjured up.

Death, after pursuing Great-Uncle Henry through so many
pictures, got him in the end after a banquet at which he would eat
(and drink) all the things that were the worst possible for his gout,
while his wife Amelia sat in helpless tears, obliged at last to give up
even saying 'Do remember!'

From the moment of his death the House in the Wood under-
went a curious transformation; it was no longer Henry's but
Amelia's. The same pictures remained on the walls, but others were
added—of his son Prince William when a boy with his English
child-bride, the Princess Mary; of Mary's father, King Charles I
of England, as a Roman knight riding into a thundercloud—bad
portraits all of these and hung in a very bad light.

But the pictures that now began to dominate the House in the
Wood were the pictures of Amelia—Amelia as a blooming matron
surrounded by her four daughters, blazoning her opulent maternity
in ermine and yellow satin studded with jewels like the harness on
a Flanders mare; Amelia as a solitary widow in black on a dark
ground surrounded by white immortelles of an unpleasant greyish
hue like rather dusty feathers moulting from angels' wings; Amelia
above all and in the middle of all, at the top of the dome that sur-
mounted the whole vast structure, her hard eye staring down past
the musicians' gallery into the body of the Great Hall, supervising
everybody and everything that went on there.

You could only see her by cricking your head back till it hurt
your neck, but all the time she was seeing you. The very workmen
felt the effect of the Dowager's eye and worked more continuously
in that central banqueting-hall than anywhere else, forbearing to
slink off with their accustomed frequency for another pot of beer.

For the Summer Palace was by no means finished yet; it would
not be finished for years, and for that very reason made the easiest
and most informal rendezvous, since there was always the excuse to
come out and see how such a room or picture or bulb garden was
getting on.

And to the House in the Wood went Argyll's Commissioners for an informal conference with King Charles and his counsellors and were most graciously received by the Dowager Princess, who told them it had always been her husband's policy, and was now her son's and her own, to uphold the united Church of Calvin as the one hope of peace in Europe.

"They talk about the Thirty Years' War that has now at last ended in Germany," she said, "but for us here in Holland it was the end of eighty years' fighting for our faith, and not one jot or tittle of it must now be yielded to Rome, or to Rome's jackal the Church of England. Calvin and his disciple John Knox—the man who swerves from them by as much as one syllable is a traitor to his God. My daughter Agnes here has never been inside any church but the Calvinist or, as you would say, Presbyterian."

They were enchanted with her orthodoxy, the staunchest they had yet found in even this most Protestant country. King Charles had, of course, the appalling disadvantage of a Papist mother, though his youth, and sweet and virtuous disposition, coupled with severe training from now on, might reclaim him in time from even this error. But they admitted their disappointment in not finding more of Amelia's spirit in that martyr to the Protestant cause, the Queen of Bohemia.

The Dowager smiled so witheringly at such expectations that even the early spring flowers she clenched in her hand hung their heads. Had not the Commissioners seen for themselves, even as she had warned them, that the Princess Sophia attended the Church of England services and, what was worse, led her cousin King Charles into accompanying her there? They even listened to Wishart's preaching, Montrose's chaplain who had written that book in praise of his master's victories over the Covenanters in Scotland. Were the Commissioners going to suffer this insult in silence?

They were not. Mr. Robert Baillie busily pulled out a little book and made a note that they should lodge a protest against Wishart and the Church of England services together.

But Amelia was not yet going to leave the subject of Elizabeth and her daughters' unorthodoxy. It was not only a question of the Anglican services, but (and she dropped her voice to a hollow whisper) the Princess Louise had been seen coming out of the Queen Henrietta Maria's Papist chapel after they had been saying Mass, her eyes red with crying.

"But the Queen Henrietta Maria has not been at The Hague for seven years," said Mr. Baillie innocently.

"Seven years ago then," snapped Amelia; "what odds does it make? What's begun early is continued ill. The Princess Louise worships her Papist aunt, and so does her sister Sophia."

"Oh, but, Mamma," her daughter Agnes expostulated, "Sophia said she was an ugly little woman with thin arms, and teeth sticking out of her mouth like guns out of a fort."

Mr. Baillie chuckled richly; even Lord Cassillis made a wry grin, for laughter at the enemies of the Lord might be permissible; but Amelia rapped her daughter over the knuckles, not for her pertness, as she said, but for taking Sophia's part.

Agnes had not realized she was taking it, she had spoken only with her usual honesty and stupidity. She stood beside her mother in a blue-and-white striped dress, rather too tight across her full bosom, looked dully at these ugly old men in black and wondered if they could really help her to marry the young English King. Here they were talking for hours with her mother, who promised them the support of all the Continental Calvinist countries as though that painted eye of hers in the dome commanded the whole of Europe as well as the House in the Wood.

But it could not command the young King, and he, Agnes knew, was walking at this very moment with her cousin Sophia in the new tulip walk at the other side of the Palace.

For the last few weeks Sophie had been in process of having her head turned. She had always been popular as a butt for teasing, one who gave as good as she got, gave a good deal better in the case of slow-witted young men who were frankly terrified of her; the Prince de Tarente would fly at the sight of her, and the young Englishman Vane never forgave the verses she wrote on his 'shoe-horn chin.' But those were not the victories she was wishing for, or getting now.

The Hague was the perfect place for flirtations. 'I never lack a fool to laugh at,' said Sophie's mother; 'as soon as one goes, another comes.' Now Sophie was taking her share of these multitudinous admirers and finding it more intoxicating than amusing.

Among all the visitors who had begun to show her how attractive she had grown was a young German prince, Ernest Augustus, who had seemed quite lost and homesick on his visit to this foreign city, since he was travelling for once without his elder brother, George William of Hanover, for the two of them went everywhere together, he assured Sophie, especially to Venice—ah the gay life in Venice! He could not mention Venice without giggling, it seemed it was not quite proper to mention it.

Ernest Augustus, who possessed the boneless buoyancy of those beginning to be fat, danced with her as lightly as a bubble bouncing, and all the time his solemn sentimental eyes above his blandly smiling mouth looked admiringly at the brown curls that bobbed up and down on her bare shoulders as she danced opposite him in the set, and at the feathers that streeled out from the back of her head like those of some fluttering bird of paradise. He played the guitar with her too, showing off a pair of beautifully kept, plump white hands. He taught her tender German ditties and new airs from the Italian operas—but he did not propose. 'They never do,' thought Sophie bitterly.

He was not an eligible *parti* himself, a third son; moreover, he and his brother George were so fond of each other's company and the gay life in Venice that they had promised each other to remain bachelors always, unless George's Hanoverian subjects insisted on an heir, in which case George had said he would hand over Hanover and the tiresome obligation of matrimony together to Ernest—and that was the only, and unflattering chance in that quarter of an 'establishment' for Sophie.

Elizabeth teased her daughter about it just as her own mother had teased herself. Was Sophie going to settle down as a German *Hausfrau*, as Sophia, Electress of Hanover, when she might be Sophia, Queen of Great Britain?

Sophie took fright and abruptly broke off the lengthy correspondence that Ernest had started as soon as he had left The Hague, on the pretext of sending her some of Corbetti's guitar music. She was not going to do anything to endanger her chances of the English throne, especially now that there was no doubt that King Charles' followers had come to look on her, the least important of her family, as the most likely person to be their future Queen. They gave her unwanted presents to which she had to make an adequate return, out of Lord Craven's purse. They paid her so many compliments that she began to keep a diary in which to catalogue them, for each was as carefully treasured as a pearl added to a necklace.

Some day she would rewrite that diary as the story of her life, and she was determined it should be a story with a happy ending. What a heroine for romance she would prove, the Cinderella princess, youngest of a family of paupers, who became the Queen of England!

That she was indeed the sole heroine of the story she had not a shadow of doubt; her young egoism centred the whole complicated structure of Charles' hopes, Montrose's plans for him, and the Covenanters' counter-plans and hatred of Montrose, into factions that were fighting either in her interests or in those of Amelia's daughter, Agnes.

She was in a nervous and excitable state. Then came a real shock; she heard that Lucy Walters had just given birth to a fine boy, that he had big dark eyes and was the squalling image of Charles in miniature, that Charles had acknowledged him as his son, promised Lucy a pension, and would have the boy christened James after his grandfather King James I of England and his young brother and heir the Duke of York. How *could* Charles thus endanger his legitimate heirs, whoever they might come to be, for the sake of his careless pleasures?

And he was not nearly so friendly with her when those odious Commissioners were by; he had been careful to get her out of the Palace before they arrived, and she was sure he pretended to them that he liked Agnes better than her.

This was what Sophie was thinking while poor Agnes envied her enjoyment as Sophie walked beside the young King on the light brittle shell-gravel brought from the seashore three miles away. Scrunch, scrunch went the shells underfoot while the birds shouted overhead in the morning sunlight, and they two were both silent, wondering how the other would begin.

Charles guessed she had heard something and regarded her with a wary amusement, as though he would enjoy seeing how far he could tease her without getting scratched.

"Will you walk with me to the lake?" he asked, looking down at her with roguish eyes, and his tone suggested to her that he was having a bet with himself (or perhaps, horrid thought, with some-one else!) as to whether she would or not.

She would show him she could meet him on his own ground.

"I am sorry, Cousin," she said brightly, "but I should find it too painful in my condition."

"I had no knowledge of your condition. Is it interesting?"

"To myself, very. I have a corn on my little toe." She swung round in a pirouette and dropped him a curtsey.

"Ah, I can see how it has crippled you. You should swathe it in flannel as Ned Hyde does his gout. What a pair you'd make!" He added, a touch more seriously, "Why avoid me? You can't be pining for that German fellow, you weren't really interested in him."

"One cannot be really interested in a third son, can one?—unless one lives in a fairy-tale, and life these days, God knows, is no fairy-tale."

He laughed delightedly, "So that's why you've given up answering his letters."

"How do you know that?"

"I make it my business to know what concerns me."

She began to pick the early tulip buds, regardless of their value and of the sticky juice from the stems that ran over her fingers; she said, fast and low, "Do I concern you? I thought Lucy Walters concerned you. She is very handsome and she has borne you a son and——" she stopped, shocked at her own daring.

"And you have been remiss in that last particular. We might see what could be done to remedy it. Would you like to?"

Before his bold gaze her own fell; she blushed hotly, with rage she thought, but there was excitement in it and a strange new fear of him.

Here was a girl worth loving, with the quick blood now warming and wakening to life at last. Strange to think she was but six months his junior and still a virgin (he would not be a girl for much!). Her jealousy, her curiosity, showed how ripe she was for him.

"Would you not like to?" he repeated, his head bent so that now his eyes were level with her own.

'I hate him, I hate him!' she told herself and struggled for words. Out they came, squeaky, gawky, ridiculous, how she hated him for that! "You've no need of me in that respect, Cousin. You had best return to your handsome Lucy."

He took her hand and said, "You do not know how pretty you are looking. You are far handsomer than Lucy Walters."

There was no one in sight; the cherry trees, already spangled with rosily-white blossom, shut them off from the Palace windows. His face came down towards her, shutting out the sun. If she let him have his way she would be no more than the slack-lipped women who let him have his way and then saw him go his way.

She jerked back her head, tore away her hand and cried in a harsh strained voice, "That indeed is a compliment, to compare me with your mistress! Your Majesty does me too much honour!"

"It was rather a lame proposal," he admitted. "But what do

you expect when the lady too is lame, of a corn on her toe? How should I propose to you?"

"I don't know," she said miserably. She must show how she should be treated—it was that that mattered, her whole future life, not any mere momentary question of feelings; she clutched at her memory of Eliza's words: "'It is not thus,'" she said, "'that the marriages of great princes are arranged.'"

"In fact, you don't trust me. 'Infirm of purpose,' is that it?"

She replied with dignity, "I wish I could be as sure of your firmness of purpose as of your friends who are seeking their own fortune in my service."

"Whom do you mean?"

It was a slip to have said 'my' service, to Charles of all people; her ears went pink, but she was determined to brazen it out.

"Of the Marquis of Montrose."

"*He*—seek his own fortune—in *your* service?"

"Certainly," said Sophie, now more composedly. "I look on him as the best of my servants. You do not imagine that *he* supports the faction to make Agnes your Queen, as do his enemies the Covenanters?"

"And do *you* imagine he is seeking his own fortune?"

"What else should he seek? We are past the days when knights went about the world merely to rescue distressed damsels and forlorn kings without a thought of their own profit."

An odd little silence fell into the air. It hung there in the sunshine among the clear colours of the spring flowers, like an invisible and alien presence.

The silence grew, it spread between them, a whole world stretched between them. Even Sophie felt that hush fall on her brisk and confident mind and wondered if she had shocked him by referring, even so indirectly, to the possibility of their marriage.

"Is it shocking to face the facts?" she said aloud.

"By no means," he answered dryly, "if you are sure it is the facts you are facing. But you can't see other people if you look only in the glass at your own face. You can never have seen Montrose."

"I cannot abide parables," said Sophie furiously, grinding her foot into the little shells sprinkled on the path, scattering the fragments here and there. That this young libertine should presume to read her a moral lecture was not to be borne.

But it did not have to be borne, for Charles was leaving her. He bowed very low, with mockingly exaggerated respect, and said something—nothing—what was it? 'I am sorry to have offended you, Cousin,' that was all it could have been.

She saw him straighten that tall back of his and stalk away, a boy's long figure, thin and stiff and black in his mourning-clothes among the fruit blossom frothing like foam in the bright sunshine; and as she saw him go away, not to the gates to ride back to The Hague to speak to her mother as she had half hoped, but up the terrace into the Palace, she had an absurd, miserable feeling that it was indeed her whole future life that she saw marching away from her up through the cherry trees into the Palace, that she had lost it as irretrievably as those momentary feelings that she had just now sacrificed for its sake.

XI

'WOMEN,' said Charles to himself as he went up the steps between the silly placid statues all curling themselves into affected positions—'it doesn't matter whether it's the virgin cat Sophie or the strumpet Lucy, they are all playing their own game, seeing what they can get out of you, and they've not even the wit to see that anybody else can be different.'

It hit him the harder because he himself had begun to think that nobody else could really be different, that if men showed loyalty it was because they thought his side had the best chance to win in the long run. But he had not thought so when he had seen and talked with Montrose.

At least he was that much superior to Sophie; he might be a rake and get drunk too often, and make his mother cry over his faults, and know that they would have disgusted his father; but at any rate he had been able to see what Montrose was like, and Sophie had not.

The very fact that this did not affect him directly, opened the gates to his anger by lifting it away from just another petty quarrel. He had had personal reasons enough for irritation and disillusion— his mother nagging at him, women making demands on him, Lucy losing her shape and her looks, growing peevish and exacting, teasing him into binding his bonds to her all the closer, when he had hoped to avoid forging them altogether.

He was suffering a physical revulsion from her big olive-smooth breasts and stupid reproachful brown eyes (though God knows she had little enough to reproach him with!) when Sophie's contrasting freshness and bright wits had begun to attract him—but it made no odds, you could turn to a dozen women one after the other and find them all alike in their hearts, however stupid or clever their minds, and their bodies were the only thing about them worth considering.

'So that's ended it,' he said to himself as he went into the Palace, 'I've done with women.' But he knew that he hadn't—that he

174

never would have done. He saw himself leading troops from Ireland with Rupert, fighting by the side of Montrose, freed of all feminine entanglements, feminine tyranny. And he knew that vision to be not even a hope, but only a wish, and one that he would never win.

Even now, going out of the sunlight into the cold draughty noisy halls where workmen hammered and called to each other and passed in and out in ceaseless hoarse pursuit of some other workman or their tools, even now he was going at the arrangement of a woman, and the woman he disliked most in the world, the Dowager Princess Amelia, to attend an informal conference of the Commissioners together with the Moderate Covenanters and some of his own Council.

It is true that her son, his friend William, favoured the notion and would be present, but that made him none the better pleased that he had agreed to it. William was the best of good fellows, but he was damned if he'd have his affairs managed by the female Oranges. Only this moment he had planned an overt act of rebellion, a walk to the lake with Sophie in full view of the Palace windows, which would have shown these religious meddlers *and* their hostess Amelia *and* her dumpling of a daughter exactly how much attention he meant to pay to their combined matrimonial schemes for him. It would have kept the Commissioners waiting too, and only by such unkingly bad manners could he show them what he thought of theirs.

But Sophie would not walk with him, and here he was walking through these empty echoing rooms instead with his hostess, being just as polite as ever to that hard-faced officious thruster ('if she could only know how I long to wring her neck!'), and as polite now to the Brethren who were already waiting for him in the Chinese room, although, owing to his tiff with Sophie, he had come there sooner than had been expected.

No doubt they had hoped for an earlier and private consultation with the Moderates, for there was Lauderdale goggling in a corner at Baillie, whose friend and patron he was, and the minister pursing up his precious lips like a cat that's been lapping cream but too well-bred to show appreciation.   The Duke of Hamilton, too, was being very affable to Lord Cassillis (there was no doubt these Moderates would soon manage to make their peace with Argyll), and Charles observed that he seemed ill at ease with Hyde after the somewhat short-winded entry of the Chancellor, who had found a two-mile ride a by no means pleasant preliminary to this informal conference.

The Dowager left them, the conference began, but the Commissioners declared that before they could submit Argyll's proposals to the King he must instantly banish all persons from his Court who had been excommunicated by the Covenant, especially James Graham, sometime Earl of Montrose.

Charles had been prepared for this by Hyde and had his answer ready.

"I will hear the whole of your conditions before I consider any part of them," he said.

They consulted together in whispers, then tried again to press their demand for Montrose's banishment from the Court, and this time for that of his chaplain, Wishart, also—a still more directly personal attack, since the King had been to hear him preach last Sunday.

Charles only repeated his former words; he would hear the whole before he would answer any part.

There was a little more whispering, and then Mr. Robert Baillie, the principal of the two ministers and reader of the address, announced in his majestic preacher's voice that Charles should be acknowledged their true and lawful King 'upon condition of his good behaviour and strict observation of the Covenant and his entertaining no other persons about him but such as were godly men and faithful to that obligation.'

There was a rustle of indignation, and the Chancellor of the Exchequer pointed out that this was scarcely the way in which to address their King.

But the Earl of Cassillis, speaking on behalf of the Kingdom and Parliament of Scotland, in a voice as harsh as Baillie's had been unctuous, declared that, despite the Proclamation, Charles was not to be King there at all until he had first signed the Covenant and promised to enforce it on all his subjects in England and Ireland as well as Scotland, 'to submit himself to the Kirk's censure and renounce the sins of his father's house and the iniquity of his mother.'

At this staggering conclusion there started an outcry from the King's Council which the King checked himself, though his face had gone a dark and painful red.

"It comes to this," he said at last slowly, "I have and shall have no intention of altering the laws of Scotland—yet the Scots wish me to alter the laws of both the other kingdoms that I should rule."

He looked at Hyde, who took up the cudgels, rising to his infirm feet with an air as sturdy and tenacious as a bull-dog's.

"Is His Majesty right even to say 'the Scots'?" he demanded. "He is not, for you gentlemen have a Government that is neither legal nor representative, one that is entirely under the domination of the Chief Elder of the Kirk, the Marquis of Argyll—a Government from which he has excluded more than four-fifths of your nobility and gentry and allowed them no jot nor tittle of a share in it—no, not even to these two noblemen present, the Duke of Hamilton and the Earl of Lauderdale. While as for the Marquis of Montrose, to give him his proper title, which you deny him, who served the late King better than any other in your country, he has been sentenced to death for that service by your Government."

He pulled himself up sharply, aware that his anger had made him say more than he had intended. But before he could retreat from or even qualify his rashness in his usual judicial manner, he was answered by such a storm of protest from all the Scots present as made the scene more like one of those Parliamentary riots of his youth, which he had such good reason to remember, than the council-chamber of a king.

M

There were cries all round him against Montrose—"the cursh of our country," as Lauderdale was spluttering from his already reeking lips ("Brandy for Breakfast, that's his motto," muttered Charles in a swift aside to his brother-in-law), Cassillis was grinding out accusations of Montrose's barbarities, while Baillie, with the steadier persistence in oratory gained by long practice in the pulpit, wore down the rest as he declared in an encroaching roar that Montrose's most heinous offence was that "he still to this day continues in the highest contempt against God, under the fearful sentence of excommunication without the least sign of repentance."

Baillie won to the end of his sentence in a hush that gave him no small satisfaction; everyone was looking at him in positively frozen attention, even horror; never had he gained so triumphant an effect. But the triumph was short-lived, the company were not looking at him but just over his head to where, close behind him in the doorway, as he saw when he wheeled heavily round, there stood the Marquis of Montrose.

In a silence that after the recent uproar struck like the chill of sudden death, the Marquis came forward, knelt and kissed the King's hand.

"Your Majesty," he said, "since I knew that accusations were to be made against me to you and your counsellors, I have come to answer them myself. Have I your leave to do so?"

The King did not speak at once. These men had just insulted him to his face, and not only him but his father's memory, and his mother. His policy of conciliation, of seeing what could be got out of all parties, howsoever opposed to each other, had already had a bad jar that day.

He had wanted to prove himself a man beside Montrose. Here was his chance; breathing rather quickly, he determined to take it.

"My lord," he said, staring into the older man's eyes as though his courage were holding on by them, "I had hoped to confer with you as with the rest of your countrymen to see what can be done for my return to my kingdom of Scotland. These gentlemen refuse to confer with you. But since they have given so frank an opinion of you, I may ask you in your turn to tell me with equal frankness your opinion of their proposals. The Chancellor will repeat them to you."

He motioned him to take his seat with the rest while Hyde in a somewhat grumpy voice repeated the proposals, striving to modify them slightly in his rendering. But Cassillis would have none of such hedging; he rose to enforce the conditions of the King's 'good behaviour' and 'submission to the Kirk's censure' as rigorously as before.

Montrose stood up as quickly as if a sword had been drawn: "Your Majesty, there can be but one motive for these proposals—that they shall be of such a nature as to prevent your ever accepting them. That will leave Argyll safe in his secret pact with Cromwell."

"It is a lie of the Devil's," broke out Cassillis; "that pact has been broken by the late King's trial and death."

"That pact," answered Montrose, "led to the late King's trial and death. Argyll promised the King safety—and sold him to Cromwell. That treachery led to the King's trial. It raised such outcry in Scotland that even Argyll was forced to bow to it and send protests to Cromwell's Army."

Baillie was on his feet again, his face redder than ever, his voice now too breathlessly eager to keep any of its organ notes. "I took those protests. I did all that could be done. My loyalty is beyond question. I even went as far as to say that it would indeed be shocking if my master Argyll were to desert the King in those straits! I offered to attend the King myself on the scaffold when my protests had failed."

Montrose turned to Hyde. "Has the Chancellor kept the words of the protests from Argyll's Government?"

"They amount to this," Hyde answered: "that Argyll's Government 'declared their dissent from the taking away of His Majesty's life' and their hope that they at any rate would be 'free from all the evil consequences that might follow thereupon.'"

"That amounts," said Montrose, "to no more than that King Charles I should have been kept always in prison, while Cromwell and Argyll should continue to rule England and Scotland. And that, in exact repetition, is what these proposals now amount to—with this difference—that King Charles II shall be kept in exile instead of prison."

"Man, are you daft?" burst out Lauderdale. "The Chancellor of Scotland, old Loudoun himself, has proclaimed him King Charles II at the Mercat Cross in Edinburgh."

"In a proclamation so clogged with conditions he might as well have been proclaimed slave as king. You have to-day heard some of those conditions. What can they mean but that Argyll is to continue to govern, with the help of his brother dictator? It is Cromwell who is Argyll's ally, it was Cromwell whose army invaded Scotland last summer——"

"As *your* army invaded it like a raging fire—barbarian!—monster!"

There were two or three Scots voices calling out against him now. Montrose turned towards them.

"Will you tell me what I did," he asked, "in comparison with your ally Cromwell, whose soldiers stripped some of their prisoners naked and put out their eyes, and were under orders to sell most of them for slaves to the Turks at two shillings apiece? That was a fitting judgment on a nation whose usurper had sold its king for £200,000."

There was terror now in the outcry against him. Would this man make the King believe they were Cromwell's agents?

"Cromwell has foresworn our Covenant," cried Baillie, "he has told all the world how he loathes the Presbyterian religion—how can we have anything to do with Cromwell?"

"Only this—that you have made him your ruler by upholding his deputy Argyll. You have given him the ultimate say in all your councils. You have betrayed your country into the hands of her enemy. It is for Cromwell that Argyll has beheaded Huntly, has banished you, my Lord Hamilton, and you, my Lord Lauderdale, though I do not think your banishment will be for long. You will soon go back in safety to Scotland, for you have your secret pact with Argyll, as he has his with Cromwell."

Lauderdale raised his fists in the air as though he would hurl himself upon his enemy, but Cassillis held him back, telling him to have patience. As for Hamilton, who 'would have been glad and proud to serve as a sergeant under Montrose,' he had avoided looking at him ever since the Marquis entered, and now sat as though stunned. All hopes that Hyde had had of reconciling these two men were crushed by Montrose's attack. Mr. Baillie, who had recovered his ringing pulpit voice, was calling down God's judgment on 'this ravening lion.'

Montrose answered:

"You say 'God, God,' and follow the Devil's counsel. Is it God's work to sell the King to death, to whom you had promised safety? To behead men for loyalty to their King? You have destroyed law in the name of the law of God, and you interpret God as you wish—a God who delights in blood sacrifices, in the smell of burning flesh. You bribe children to spy on their parents, and wives on their husbands; you have brought a darkness unutterable upon the land, where evil things crawl in the slime of men's fearful hearts. You have broken away from Rome; but you have set up a tyranny as cruel and more private than the Inquisition. You have put your country in prison."

There was no more hope for the conference after that. The King rose and left with Prince William; Montrose immediately went out of the Palace to where Sir John Hurry was waiting for him with his orderly and the horses; the Council and the Commissioners split up into separate groups, each talking with low and furious volubility, and soon, to Hyde's deep dissatisfaction, Lauderdale found an occasion to thrust himself into talk with Cassillis and was not too ill received; Hamilton too was presently drawn in. It was just as Hyde had feared; their common hatred of

Montrose would draw together the extreme and the Moderate Covenanters.

Mr. Baillie had not waited to hear these aftermaths of indignation. Mr. Baillie was apt to be impatient and hasty of movement; for all his solid consistency of flesh, he could change his mind as quickly and frequently as men of more flimsy metal: he had declared 'Bishops I love' not so very long before he had refused a bishopric as a snare of the devil; he had declared his nation to be 'possessed of a bloody devil' at the beginning of their rebellion against the King, and then become one of the clerical leaders of that rebellion; he had called Montrose 'a generous and noble youth' years ago, and now denounced him as 'a ravening lion.'

It had not been his own choice that Robert Baillie had been led, thrust rather, right into the forefront of this troubled, angry, topsy-turvy time. All he had wanted had been to stay comfortably installed first as Parish Minister at Kilwinning in the county of Ayr and then Professor of Divinity at Glasgow, with all his busy duties and his collection of rare Dutch theological books and his wife, good soul, whom he instructed to read morning and evening prayers with the servants whenever he was away, and pray in private too (though that came second) and to buy him bobbin waistcoats and beware of lawyers' 'subdolous contracts' and look after their boys Rob and Harry at school and teach them 'some little beginnings of God's fear,' and especially to 'have a care of my little Lillie.' All this had made his life diligent enough to fill a century, but it was not enough for God, who had called him to take such an active part in public affairs.

God had marked him out from the very beginning of the troubles, had sent him down to London to share the great work of bringing King Charles I's Lord Lieutenant in Ireland, the Earl of Strafford, to his doom; so that it was only fit that he, Robert Baillie, who had seen Strafford, the King's greatest servant, walking with his proud 'glooming' expression through the staring crowd at his trial, no man capping him, 'before whom that morning the greatest in England would have stood uncovered,'—it was very fit that he should be God's instrument to warn this equally proud nobleman.

And as he saw that free erect figure of the Marquis of Montrose turning away from them all, he remembered his former opinion of him in a flash of indignant regret that he should now be against them instead of with them. Could nothing be done to recall him to the fold? On a sudden impulse he left his colleagues who were fuming together over their wrath, padded after Montrose and even broke into the undignified motion of a trot in order to catch up with that swinging stride.

By the time Montrose had reached the terrace, that stout determined black figure was fairly scampering in such haste that he did not even observe the two young princes in deep consultation at the end of the terrace; but if he had, it would scarcely have deterred him from the mighty sense of his mission from God, which led to the somewhat unmannerly action of laying his hand on the Marquis' cloak.

The Marquis swung sharply round to see Mr. Baillie's light blue eyes peering up at him, shrewd, canny, and almost glassy with excitement. At that quick movement of Montrose, and still more at sight of his face dark with anger so near his own, the minister flinched and his eyes fell; for an instant he wished heartily he had not been so impetuous. But was he not a minister of the Lord? Had he not the power to bind on earth what God would infallibly ratify in heaven? Not merely death but damnation was in his hands, and not only the Marquis' splendid head, but his very soul to all eternity must hang upon the word of Robert Baillie.

"Will Your Lordship show such hardness of heart, such contempt of God's word and salvation?" he demanded. "It is not too late to repent, remember."

Montrose looked down on the short stout figure, whose black robes were flapping in the keen April air. He was of the same build exactly as the man's cousin, General Baillie, whose rounded back Montrose had seen flying from one battlefield after another in that Year of Miracles four years ago.

Mr. Robert Baillie grew uneasy under that cold, inflexible stare. Could nothing shake this man, stir him even?

He had been moved by a genuine impulse to heal (if that were possible) as well as rebuke the Marquis' conscience, but now it was plain that sharper weapons must be used.

A sure instinct prompted him to probe now with forgiveness rather than threats. "Harden not your heart for ever, my lord. God is of infinite mercy and has forgiven crimes near as great as your own."

That opaque blue eye rolled up again in a shrewd glance as he dealt his final thrust: "Your Lordship's own brother-in-law, Sir John Colquhoun, has even now met forgiveness from the Kirk for his rape upon your youngest sister, his seduction of her, rather, with the help of witchcraft."

He had succeeded just too well. If he had not stumbled as he leaped back in terror from the face before him, Montrose's clenched fist would have crashed him down on to the stone flags. As it was, he suffered nothing worse than an ignominious roll on them, and it was the young King himself who came rushing forward to pick him up.

Montrose had already flung off in the opposite direction with Sir John Hurry.

"Is this true?" he demanded of the knight, who was doing his best not to look too well pleased at the minister's tumble.

"True for months past, my lord, but I would not trouble you with it. Sir John Colquhoun has taken the Covenant, had all his estates restored to him, and is about to marry again."

A sideways glance at his Commander's grim face made him wish he had not said so much even now. It was natural enough that Montrose should wish to stick a knife into his brother-in-law for being respectably reinstated in the country that had condemned himself, but Hurry knew that the hurt to his master had gone deeper than that. What the devil was the matter with the man that he should mind about a family scandal almost twenty years old? It was the present moment that he should mind, the King's opinion, and the danger of it being influenced by these fellows.

There was a touch of exasperated affection in his concern as he laid a hand on his master's arm. "Won't you say something to the King, my lord, to get him away from the minister's complaints?"

Montrose gave him the flash of a smile. "It's no good, Hurry. I'm too angry for it to be any use."

It was an apology, for he saw well enough what Hurry was thinking. The difference between them was admitted, and never had it mattered so little. Hurry knew he could not alter him— more, that he would never really wish to do so, howsoever it might affect both their fates.

He saw his master swing into the saddle and ride back towards the town.

'There he goes, God damn him and save him!' he said to himself, an odd emotion tugging at him that he, Jack Hurry, had never till now had any occasion to recognize. For, apart from any questions of self-interest, or even recognition, he felt an almost painful desire to be of service to this man. He thought for a moment, then returned to the Palace to spread a scandal he had been hopefully inventing of Mr. Baillie's secret visits to a certain brothel in Slop Street behind the east canal.

XII

'OUR Court is full of distraction—our Court is full of Scots.'
So Hyde wrote despairingly that same morning to Rupert,
telling him, though, that in spite of it all the King 'keeps himself
upon his guard—and really he carries himself very well.'

This tutorial touch was followed with a more encouraging piece
of news than even Hyde's approval of his King. 'Here is likewise
the Marquis of Montrose, who in truth is a very gallant person,'
('And did it take him till now to discover that?' muttered Rupert
when he came to read it), 'and though the Presbyterians are as busy
as ever, yet I believe the next news I shall send you will be that His
Majesty entirely trusts Montrose and puts the business of Scotland
wholly into his conduct—so that I doubt not the Covenanters'
design of having the King into Scotland will be disappointed.'

But that Hyde could not feel quite as confident as he wrote was
shown in his last urgent request: 'I beseech Your Highness, vouch-
safe two or three lines to Charles II, who will be much encouraged
by it.'

But *would* Rupert 'vouchsafe two or three lines'? It was as hard
to get blood out of a stone as a letter out of Rupert; even little Kate
d'Aubigny had not been able to coax answers out of him when she
had written him most urgently about the political intrigues in which
she had then been engaged.

And Kate d'Aubigny herself could not help Hyde any more, for
Kate had just died, quite suddenly and for no reason that anyone
found it worth while to mention, and that gay, sad, active brain
found at last a deeper rest than politics and plots could give it. The
drawing-room meeting she had staged so prettily between Hyde and
Hamilton had been her last dragonfly dart into history before she
disappeared for ever from her crowded scene; people said, 'Poor
Kate,' 'Pretty Kate,' for a little time and then no more of her.

But Ned Hyde sat thinking of her for several minutes in the

bright morning sunshine that showed up all the dust in his dingy lodging, when he should have been telling Rupert how he had contracted with a merchant of Rotterdam to send corn into Ireland; sat thinking of her quick laughing ways, that yet hinted at something lost and appealing, like the flutterings of a bird whose wing is broken —as indeed the mainspring of her life had been broken in the young glorious body of George d'Aubigny, trampled underfoot in that cavalry charge at Edgehill.

'And now she's dead too, and I, twice her age, go fumbling on,' muttered Hyde, scratching a pattern with his pen on the table, for how odd it was that not only a young thing should die, but that he too would one day be here no longer to make plans for his master, and send news and business to Prince Rupert, and hope for a jaunt to Spain, and think of that unsatisfied, unspoken longing he had had for Kate d'Aubigny's delicate, eager body.

"Compare you favourably with his mistress? Why, you silly child, that is a compliment most wives would give their ears for!"

Elizabeth, full of jovial tolerance for the weaknesses of gay young men, had none for the nervous qualms of young girls.

Sophie had hurried straight from the House in the Wood to Lord Craven's house, which was always ready for any member of their family—it was like part of their own furniture, but more useful. It was more exciting to tell her adventure to a man, even old Craven, who must be nearly fifty, than to her sisters.

Unfortunately she found her mother there. Elizabeth thought Charles had shown himself rather charmingly ingenuous, and that Sophie was a little prude. Poor Sophie longed to tell more of her encounter with Charles, to justify herself. (Those remarks of his about her bearing him a child as Lucy had done—what would her mother have to say to *that*?) But caution won, and it was her caution that her mother now condemned.

"These girls to-day!" she exclaimed, "*they* take no chances."

It was a pity really, for one can only be young once, "but these modern girls aren't young, they know too much, they look at people with bleak critical eyes, they are hard, calculating, deliberate——"

She forgot how angry she often was with Louey for exactly the opposite qualities—slapdash, reckless, casual—which she also labelled modern. Now she declared that girls to-day were not more good than those of her generation, only more careful: "'Our Sophie is a careful girl!' What a motto for a great-granddaughter of Queen Mary of Scotland!"

And she swept out of the room, brandishing a trowel, to dig up some precious bulbs Craven had promised her and which she would trust to no other hand but her own.

Sophie turned for refuge to the sideboard, where there were always nice things standing ready to eat and drink, sweet wines, pastries, and piled-up dishes of marchpane and sugar-plums. Further consolation came when Lord Craven silently fished out a trinket from his pocket and tossed it over to her; he had an inexhaustible store of such ornaments from the curio-dealers at Amsterdam, who commissioned sailors to bring them from China and India.

Sophie pinned the spray of blue enamelled flowers in her dress, nodding her thanks to him; these gifts were merely a wise and necessary provision, for he needed such extra attractions since he was elderly, small and plain and not of good family, his enormous fortune, the chief support of them all for the past quarter of a century, having been made by his father, a Lord Mayor of London, in trade. But he was a good friend to her, and she could at once pour out her doubts and fears of Charles and all those courtiers of his who were trying to curry favour with her and even, she had heard, hoping to secure Craven's money for Charles' schemes through his kindness for herself.

"Did you know that, my True Towser? You see they have designs on you too. What do you think of it all? Wake up and tell me."

He had shut his eyes in that annoying way he sometimes had when she was chattering to him, but now opened them, blinking like an owl, and said, "I am not thinking just now."

"But you must be thinking of something? What is it?"

"Nothing. It is a great art, to think of nothing, I can do it whenever I like."

"But why should you like?" she asked indignantly.

"I hope it may help me to shine in such conversation as yours," he told her.

Sophie gave him an uncertain eye; she wondered if he were not practically senile. She was certain of it when he began to trot out a pedantic theory of his about spelling French like Latin.

"But the two languages are utterly unlike," she declared, and thought he was quizzing her when he told her the one was derived from the other. And who cared if it were or not?

"Tell me what you think of Charles," she demanded.

"I think his best hope for his crown is in your hope of it," he replied, taking up his clarionet and picking out a tune on it.

"Then you do think I was right to break with Ernest Augustus? I'd never get the English crown for myself or my heirs if I married a prince of Brunswick or Hanover."

"Your will is so strong, my dear, there's no knowing what you might compass even then."

That cheered her with a sense of power; *she* would never spoil her chances by the vagueness and unworldliness, in such different ways, of her two eldest sisters.

Gay, but poised and sure of herself, she would tread the path of her life exactly as she intended, like the new dance steps she now began to practise to his music on the chequered marble floor, tapping her toes so precisely now on the black square, now on the white.

But she could not keep it up; a queer mood was falling on her, making her feel lonely and frightened as she had done sometimes when a child, remembering in the dark all the terrible stories she had heard of hell-fire and the eternal wrath of God against those who cared only for this world.

She remembered them now, though she was not in the dark but dancing to this tiny tripping tune in the morning, dancing in and out of this long sunbeam that sent its whirling golden specks spinning round her in the bright room. Yet it seemed as though a shadow had fallen on the earth that none could see, not even herself, who felt only the inexplicable chill strike at her heart.

Greedy of life as she was, life itself was not enough; she might grasp all she desired within her hands and find it withered, turned tasteless and foul. Was there nothing beyond it to give it sense and form? But what then could ever satisfy her, if life was not enough?

"How is it I can feel so melancholy when all nature means us to be gay?" she broke out passionately.

But her eccentric old friend only removed the clarionet from his lips for an instant, and replied that statistics had proved suicides to be most frequent in the spring.

Sophie preferred to diagnose her case as one of religion. A violent fit of devotion, that was what it was. She at once made use of it to propitiate herself with God by the offering of a devotional poem.

Sitting at Craven's writing-table, wielding a big white quill, she wrote, in the space of half an hour, the same half-hour in which Hyde was writing to Rupert a few streets away:

> 'Lord, how can I, a child of Thine,
> For ever play the castanet,
> For ever aim to be coquette
> And dance away my time?
>
> That this alone would please Thee, Lord,
> How happy would I be to know!
> I'd take my pleasure here below,
> And in the next world, my reward.'

To make the best of both worlds, was that after all the sum of her 'devotion'? She did not feel quite satisfied about it. In tiresome comparison she remembered a couplet from some verses her mother had once written in a like 'fit of devotion,' at the much earlier age of twelve, and had shown her daughters in a burst of laughter at her youthful heroics:

'Oh my soul of heavenly birth,
  Do thou scorn this basest earth!'

That echo from Elizabeth's proud childhood was now vaguely disturbing. Never, even at twelve years old, could Sophie have managed to 'scorn this basest earth.'

While Hyde wrote his letter and Sophie her verse, and Montrose rode by Scheveningen to cool his head in the sea-breeze, Louey sat watching Gerard Honthorst paint in the big studio he used while in her mother's house. He was at work on the portrait of the Marquis of Montrose that had been commissioned by her mother; he had to work at it mostly in the Marquis' absence, and complained loudly of the fact.

"Says two sittings are enough for any portrait, since it's all that Jamesone needed when he painted him as a youth. What's Jamesone? A beggarly Scots painter that never learned his trade in Italy as far as I can make out. And a boy of seventeen or so is easy work compared with the job I have to do now. Look at it. Do you like it?"

"No," said Louey.

"I know," echoed her master despondently. "That air of greatness, yet unconscious of it—is it there?"

She did not think so. She answered, "The eyes are good; you have got them, though not entirely. That left eyelid lower than the other, and the steady way they watch people."

"Yes, yes, I've got something there."

He stepped backwards to where she was sitting and flumped down beside her, a heavy man whose jovial round face had turned suddenly elderly as it sagged with disappointment. But now those lines of age and weariness tautened in the effort of concentration; he stared frowning at his painting, determined to wrest from it the secret of his failure. Louey, sitting doubled up beside him, leaning forward with her elbow on her knee and her chin propped on her fist, knew, without even glancing round at him, how his face was hardening, remodelling itself. Gerard was working at this portrait as he had not worked for years.

He was doing more, he was admitting it had gone wrong, and to a pupil. Once or twice lately he had done this to her, and she had been more impressed by so singular a trust than by the most passionate avowal of devotion.

"He is very difficult," she said.

"Damnably. If you had ever tried to paint him yourself you would know. And why don't you?"

"Too difficult. I wouldn't dare——now I have seen him," she added under her breath. Not for worlds would she have told of that imaginary sketch she had drawn before she had ever seen Montrose. Its unconscious guess had caught something nearer the truth than this large deliberate oil-painting, three-quarter length, by the practised Court-painter——though this too was aiming, she could see, at the same effect. Honthorst had painted Montrose in armour such as was now worn for State occasions and portraits rather than on the battlefield——black armour for the death of his master King Charles, as befitted the portrait of a great soldier vowed to vengeance of his murdered King.

But in this face, as in the rough sketch of Louey's, shone a strange serenity, not to be expected of such a man in such a mood of grim determination as all now recognized in him.

"Yet I haven't got it," Honthorst was muttering, "that look, alert and keen, though the face keeps so still. He's got the eyes of a hawk and the nose of one; but look what I have done instead: smoothed everything down, taken all that look of rugged power out of the face, made it just another conventional portrait of a soldier, if that. *Does* he look a soldier?"

"He looks more 'a veray parfait gentil knight,'" said Louey, and translated her quotation into the corresponding old Flemish words before he could swear at her for talking English.

"That is the language of chivalry, *hein*? Like that armour, obsolete, picturesque, for formal occasions only, fit for a lady's chamber, like this portrait that's been ordered for your lady mother's chamber."

He turned his great black curled head and looked full at her, his eyes those of a mischievous schoolboy. She met them with a smile of acknowledgment. It was not worth the trouble to hide her thoughts from Gerard. But he must have seen more even than she intended, for he laid his broad hand on her shoulder and shook it gently and told her in bluff kindly clumsy fashion that she had nothing to fear. "A man can't really love a woman over fifty," he said with coarse simplicity.

"I've seen them do it often enough," remarked Louey.

"Ah, your mother's a wonderful woman, I'm not saying anything else, but nature counts most in the long run."

"I doubt it. I'd back reputation against nature any day, especially with our countrymen. When they've heard a woman is fascinating for nearly forty years they begin to believe it."

He roared with laughter, wagging a strong stubby forefinger at her, and his head in rhythm with it. "You and your clever sisters, the eldest and the youngest, you've tongues like needles all three of you, and it's that that stands in your way more than any mother. Are you sure you haven't frightened the Great Marquis now? That's what it is, I'll be bound, you've scared the mighty General as stiff as any schoolboy."

"I wish I had. He's never heard me speak that I'm aware of." ('But yes, he did at first. Before my mother came into the room.' But she did not say that.) "Even if he ever looks at me, he is listening to my mother."

"He'll hear you. Wait. You have all her courage and honesty —no, you've more, for you're an honest worker, you never shirk what you see when you're painting."

N

"And to what man, dear Gerard, would that ever make a penny's odds?"

"It makes many pounds odds to the price of your pictures," he chuckled, and then with one of his sudden changes of expression he said ruefully, "And to me."

He was looking at her with great tenderness. She was no goddess like her mother, who was indeed a bit too titanic for him, but she was as pretty as a nymph, and an amusing little devil, and the only girl who had ever understood him—it was astonishing the things he didn't mind saying to her. It was just his luck that she should be a princess. "And I'm only an old hack of a job painter, and what I think don't make any odds."

Louey knew her drawing-master. Some sentiment he certainly had for her, but more for himself; it was that that must have been jarred lately. She uncoiled herself from her cramped, curled-up position, getting taller and taller as she rose, and stretched her arms above her head.

"Let us have a pipe together," she said. "That is, if you have got a new one for me."

"I have, but it's an expensive business if you insist on a fresh pipe every time you try one."

"Not very. This is only the third, and I'm still not sure I like it."

He opened a cupboard, pulled out two long clay pipes, two tall tapering glasses, and a bottle of wine. He filled the pipes, handed her one, and lit it from a burning coal which he took from the fire in a pair of tongs. They settled themselves comfortably on either side of the table that held his paints and palette, looking rather like a couple of convivial Carthusian monks, for both wore their white painting-coats, shapeless linen sacks held in by belts at the waist. She waited till he had drunk a glass and drawn two or three times at his pipe, watching the smoke-wreaths that rose from it through the sun-laden air in thin spirals, blue on the one side, faint brown on the other, before she tried to probe his discontent.

"You have seen the art-dealers at Amsterdam?" she said. "They haven't lowered your prices, have they?"

"No, they've raised them. I am getting more for my portraits than any painter in Holland at the moment. The Dutch are all very well for their gross little plebeian scenes, but when it comes to a portrait of a lady or gentleman that can show any grace or distinction they've still got to go to a Fleming."

"That's why that gross Dutch painter at Amsterdam, Rembrandt van Rijn, has to go on painting his own portrait, I suppose," said Louey, not looking at her master, who was twirling his fine upturned moustaches in renewed self-satisfaction. But at her apparently careless remark that satisfaction exploded like a bubble in a long sigh. He tugged instead of twirled at the silky, still brown hairs, then burst out:

"That fellow's a fool. He'll never be a success again. He's had it all and chucked it away. He's deep in debt, his house is a hugger-mugger of dirty splendour. He drinks—well, we all do that, but he drinks with the wrong people. He does everything with the wrong people. He quarrels with the dealers, he paints Jews, he sleeps with his housekeeper, he never went to Italy, he worships ugliness, all he cares to paint are vulgar cunning peasants or lousy beggars or greasy Jews bound up in bundles of cloths; he even paints the characters in the Bible as Jews———"

"But the characters in the Bible *were* Jews."

"So they were, I never thought of that. But it's downright blasphemy to paint Our Lord as a Jew."

"Since it was only on His mother's side?" suggested Louey.

"Historical accuracy can be carried too far," replied the painter, shocked, not for the first time, by his pupil's flippancy. "And anyway it's done Rembrandt no good; after all his grand start and success he's getting nowhere. They've refused his designs for a picture of the Peace Treaty of Westphalia and given the job to Gerard Ter Borch. Rembrandt is sick as a dog about it, but lord! I saw his sketches for it at Amsterdam and you never saw such stuff. Classic allegorical figures, he can't do that sort of thing; he's never been to Italy, never studied the masters of classic form, he's no sense of beauty, can't paint a beautiful woman, especially a nude—barrels ot wrinkled fat, that's all he ever sees in 'em. Mind you, the colour's lovely, those rose-pink flesh tints, the warm cream of the skin, the lighting above all——" He broke off, musing; he had lost the thread of his diatribe, he had forgotten Louey, he was staring at nothing, at the pictures he had seen at Amsterdam.

When he spoke again it was softly, truly, in the voice in which a man speaks to himself. "I saw his 'Christ before Pilate,'" he said.

How odd and sad it was! Here was Rembrandt 'sick as a dog' at missing the well-paid jobs, and Gerard at only getting them. One man's meat was another man's poison.

"But you painted Christ before Pilate yourself, Gerard, your best picture——"

"Painted thirty years ago."

"What does it matter *when*? You did it."

They were both sharing for an instant their vision of that night interior he had painted with the single candle-flame illumining those two faces, lords of two different worlds—the eager, argumentative, logical face of Pilate seated at the table, looking up into that ineffable other-worldly calm of his prisoner. Gherardo della Notte he had been nicknamed after that picture, acknowledged master of chiaro-scuro even by the Italians, the supreme arbiters of taste.

"You lit a candle in the night," she said slowly, "and focussed two worlds, divine and human wisdom, in the single flare of that painted flame."

He burst out, "But if I did it then, did it once, look at what Rembrandt has done since, look at *his* 'Christ before Pilate'—that crowded whirra-whirra of all humanity jostling the divine, and a light falling on it such as never fell on earth."

He picked up a brush from the table, looked at it in disgust, and flung it at his portrait of Montrose. "That's what I think of *that*," he said. "Rembrandt could do him. I can't." He heaved a great sigh out of himself as he got up from his stool.

"What's the odds?" he said, picking up his hat and cloak. "People may go on gaping at Rembrandt's pictures when they've forgotten mine, but is that going to make any difference to me then when I'm food for the worms? Rembrandt is making a mess of his life and I'm going to dine with some good fellows and the best art-dealers of the day in the best tavern in the town, and it's that that makes the difference now."

He whipped off his painting-coat, swung his cloak round his great shoulders and made a swaggering bow to Louey, flourishing the wide cavalier hat in his hand. He was still floridly handsome, his big upturned moustaches only partly grey. Once, when she had been just grown-up, she had let him kiss her (what a scene there had been with her mother over that!) in much the same experimental spirit as she had now tried smoking, though she had not, as in this latter case, repeated the experiment,—and now, suddenly remembering it, she looked at poor Gerard's coarsely complacent good looks, grown too quickly elderly in the few years since then, with an exasperation, almost disgust, that did not in the least impair her friendliness.

"You look just like Hals' 'Laughing Cavalier,'" she said, knowing how it would please him.

"Poor old Frans. Eighty this year if he's a day. He may be joining us at dinner if the gout and his mistress—his nurse rather—lets him. And you, Princess? There's no hope of your Marquis, you know. He wouldn't promise me another sitting. Do you stay and work?"

"Yes," she said with a sigh, "since I can't come and dine with you." And how she wished she could! She could not bear banquets or Court entertainments, but she longed to see something for herself of the jovial tavern life which was so warming the heart of this newly free and vital country that it was giving its art the most vigorous fresh inspiration it had had for centuries. And all she could see of it was on painted canvas—or at best some sudden glimpse through a low lighted doorway into a little bright scene of soldiers singing and shouting, a group of card-players, of firelight playing on flushed faces.

"I'd give a deal not to be a princess," she said.

"And I'd double it," he muttered, but she paid no heed to that.

"I could be a Roaring Boy with the best or the worst of you," she said, "but you'd all know me, so I can't dress up as a young man and come with you."

"It's a pity you can't. Young Adrian is bringing his lute and there'll be some pretty playing and some jolly drinking-songs where we can all join in. And he's got a mighty fine eating-song too, all in honour of grease and gravy and the crisp little crackle of the pig, with a refrain—

"'More fat! More fat!
What's better than that?'"

He shouted with laughter as he sang it, and she joined in, though laughing so much she could hardly sing. But his laugh stiffened on his lips, he stared before him at the open doorway with an expression of dismay. Louey turned and saw that he was looking into the next room at someone who was coming through the open doors towards them.

"Who is it?"

"The Lord Montrose!" he just breathed.

'Just my cursed luck!' thought Louey. He must have heard their singing and bursts of laughter. Here she was, caught drinking and smoking with her drawing-master like any roystering trollop, and by this austere soldier of all people.

But he did not seem disgusted (if he were he would never let her see it), only amused. He explained that he had come to see her mother, who was out, and as he was here he had remembered Honthorst's appeals for another sitting. "But you too are just going, Mynheer."

"It was nothing, my lord, nothing," stammered Honthorst unhappily.

But Burgomaster Six wasn't nothing. He couldn't offend such a patron, nor the art-dealers; but he couldn't offend his patroness the Queen either, nor yet the great foreign lord. But wouldn't it please him to be left alone with a charming girl? And Gerard was certain it would please his little princess.

"My lord," he said, "it is most unfortunately true that I have to go to—ah—a meeting of considerable importance. But may I confess a professional secret? You may have heard that we overworked artists sometimes employ our pupils to do parts of our pictures. The Princess Louise is the best of my pupils. I have sometimes sold her pictures under my name as my own work——"

"And did you allow that?" Montrose asked Louise.

"Yes, for they fetch a better price with his name," she replied casually. "It helps pay the household bills, though not many of them."

He was looking at her with surprise and interest. "I knew Your Highness to be accomplished," he said. "I did not know you to be so true an artist."

"What do you mean, my lord?"

"That you paint so well, yet care nothing for your reward."

"But my reward is good hard cash."

"To pay household bills. Few women would care for that where they can have fame."

Honthorst felt that this was going just as he had hoped—at least it should have been as he had hoped. If he were such an old fool as to feel a futile prick of jealousy he would soon forget that among the company to which he was going.

"Your Lordship will know her work better when you see her at work," he said. "And if you will agree, Princess, I should be grateful if you would work in this background while His Lordship is here, and see if that would pull the face better into tone. The light has changed since I began, the sunshine is stronger. Would Your Highness have that great goodness?"

He bowed profusely to them both and left as fast as he respectfully could. Louey heard his heavy hurried steps go padding through the next room and the next and down the stairs.

"Oh well——" she murmured. She could not help it. She took up his palette.

XIII

HE stood facing the western-looking window, and she, in silhouette against it, turned towards the easel. The sunlight, reflected from the water below the window, rippled up over the white ceiling above her head in a faint, endlessly glimmering pattern; it shimmered round the edges of the shapeless white coat that hung very straight on her slight body; it made a halo of the loose shining hair that floated so lightly round her head. She looked like an untidy angel—he thought he had once heard her so described but could not remember by whom.

Her head had been bent as she dabbled the paints on the palette, but now she lifted it, looked intently at him and then only at the canvas, which he could not see, one loose-sleeved arm outstretched with the long brush between her fingers. The action, the attention to the work in hand, restored her confidence enough for her to speak, if only to express something of her confusion. There was Gerard pounding away through the garden below, damn him!

"It's not much use his being so respectful," she observed, "with these glasses and pipes on the table. Do you smoke, my lord?"

"No," he replied, "I never liked it, though my father smoked so much he had almost as many pipe-racks as bookshelves at Kincardine."

Clipped, abrupt, businesslike, their words fell between them. What nonsense it was! They couldn't cover over the fact that he had found her smoking and drinking with her drawing-master.

"Have you ever seen a woman smoke, my lord?"

"Often," he replied gravely. "Old Lady Ann Cunningham used to ride over to smoke with my father-in-law, Lord Southesk, and spit too, as much as any sailor."

She was not sure that she liked this. If he were laughing at her, he could do it openly. "Over here," she said, "it's only vulgar old washerwomen who smoke at their oyster feasts and village carousals. It is not even dashing, as it is for a young man."

"Do you want to be a young man?"

"Very much.   I could work then for myself and not only under a master's shadow.   I could lead a jolly and disreputable life and not have to think about it.   I could go and fight with you in Scotland."

She was working in the background, talking the while in so absent and preoccupied a tone that he wondered if she knew what she was saying.   It was as though she were talking in her sleep.   It gave him an extraordinary sense of release, weary as he was after the furious and heated use to which words had been put this morning in the House in the Wood—words as fiercely directed at their aim as weapons.

Watching her work, watching her think of it, while the words she spoke dropped quietly from some unguarded part of her mind, made his mind also lower its guard, relax from its angry tension into a surprising peace.   He had never heard a woman talk as she did, except perhaps one, and she had not been a woman then.   For the first time since he had lost her, he found himself speaking of the girl who had broken his youth.

"My younger sister," he said slowly, "talked as you do.   She too wished to be a man, to have adventure."

"Is she dead?"

"I don't know.   She was seduced by the husband of our eldest sister, and he fled to Italy with her and his foreign servant, Carlippis, who was accused of helping his schemes with magic.   He left his wife, his children, his lands at Luss on the shores of Loch Lomond where we used to stay on our holidays, I and—Kat."

It was seventeen years since he had used that name, or indeed since he had voluntarily thought of those long summer days at Ross-dhu Castle, trolling for salmon with Kat on Loch Lomond or wandering with her over the mountain-slopes, he with a gun or cross-bow in case he might get a roe-buck,—getting drenched through together in the rain, and then, when the sun came out, lying on the heather to dry, staring up the loch towards the purple head of old Ben Lomond, the guardian of the Highlands, and talking of what he would do when he was full-grown.

It had always been of what he would do, so it struck him now, never what she would do. It was not surprising Kat too had wished to be a young man, or even perhaps to 'lead a jolly and disreputable life and not have to think about it,' as this girl here so casually avowed. Looking at her, he began to see again, and see more clearly, that wild little creature who had always wanted to do the dangerous, the forbidden thing, even to play with magic, a crime equal to treason or murder.

Louey had never heard so extraordinary a tale. For a man to commit adultery, or, as it was held by law, incest, with his sister-in-law, was surprising enough in one of the greatest families in Scotland, but it would have been less startling to have murdered his wife than to have run away from her, his home, and his country.

"Who was he?"

"He is Sir John Colquhoun. I have just heard within this hour that he has returned to Scotland. He had been under sentence of death for his crime, his estates forfeited, but he has made his peace with the Kirk, taken the Covenant, had all his lands restored to him, and has just remarried. His wife, my sister Lilias, has been dead some years, thank God."

"And you are an exile, condemned to death by your country, while he goes back to it to enjoy his estates and be accepted by its Church! The Covenant has strange bedfellows. But your sister, Kat——?"

"I could never find her. I followed them to Italy, but she had already left him."

But he did not want to think of that bitter search, that bitterer discovery. It had struck him how odd it was he should be speaking of Kat, and so naturally, as though to stretch out a hand to her across all these years.

It must be something in this strange girl that had made him wish to do it. Since their first meeting, her mother had so delighted and dazzled him that all her daughters had sunk back as it were and become merged together as a crowd of girls, good-looking and intelligent, who pleased him by smiling sympathetically rather than gazing in adoration like so many women. There had even been a hint of irony, or so he now fancied, in the smiles of the Princess Louise.

He began to notice again, as he had done at first, the swift light and shadow, the baffling changes of expression on her curious face. He had never seen so many contradictions in a face. Her mouth was tender and yet sarcastic, her eyes observant and yet absent-minded; when she smiled she looked as subtle as the Sibyl, and when she frowned as she was doing now, intent on her work, her hair ruffled with one wandering hand while the other plied her paint-brush, she looked like an eager child.

She was working in the cloudy broken light round the head in the portrait, now concentrating on her painting, now on his own face in almost fierce absorption.

She saw how thoughtfully he was considering her—or was it something quite different?—and how sternly his mouth shut when he was silent; she wished he would speak again. He must still be thinking of that strange and terrible thing he had told her.

"You have never told this before?"

"No."

"Nor spoken of her since—even to your wife?"

"Least of all to my wife. She was very different from her. She feared Kat, I think, that she would come between us, as indeed she did when I left my wife and our eldest son and went in search of her."

"And was there no one else to whom you could talk of her?"

"I did not wish to. Her memory had dried and hardened in me —till this moment."

Louey flung herself back on to her painting. It was no use. His last words were hammering in her brain. Why 'this moment'? What had happened in 'this moment'?

"You came in this moment and found me carousing with my drawing-master," she said. "Why should that make you forgive

your sister? But the things that happen inside one have no sense.
You are right" (what had he said that was right?). "It is not
sound to love adventure if one is a woman. Your wife was much
happier without it—she must have been very happy," added Louey
on so low a note that his quick ears only just caught it, and he could
have left it, pretending not to hear, for why should he trouble himself with this girl, sensitive and bright as water, when women could
no longer be anything to him?

"She had small happiness with me," he said. "Her life was a
torment of anxiety. It killed her, I think."

"Ah, doesn't that show how happy she was? Happy—unhappy
—what does one mean by words like that? But one would rather
die of what one loves than live without it."

What was happening in this moment, where was it leading them?
He had come in and Gerard had gone out; he had spoken of his
sister, which he had not done for many years, and she had spoken of
his wife, and he was looking at her, looking through her, she felt,
into the desperate thoughts that now hammered in her brain. 'I love
you,' they said, 'I would rather die of that love than live without it.'

Did he see them, would he speak of them? She longed for him
to do so, she prayed he would not. He was speaking again now,
what was he saying? She scarcely heard how he began; then with
a stab of disappointment she realized that he was speaking of the
wars, and of the dead King.

"It is the death of a world," he said, "of both worlds, of both
sides in this struggle, for it is the death of all that was best in our
enemies, of all their hopes of liberty and a brave new order in the
land. Those hopes were true enough once, as I well know, for I
believed in them so passionately in my youth that I took up arms
for them—to prevent England imposing her religious government
on Scotland. But that revolt to defend liberty became a worse
tyranny itself; it denied liberty to all others. Scotland rose to prevent the English Church being forced on her, and has tried ever
since to force her Kirk on England. And Cromwell's army fought

for the liberties of Parliament, but Parliament is now the mere rump of that former body, kicked into slavish obedience by the very army that was to secure its freedom. The rebellion to defend the liberty of the subject has crushed all liberty of the subject. Members of Parliament are imprisoned for refusing to break the laws. The 'brave new world' that men hoped for is a tyranny of hypocrisy and lies, it is a republic that dares not appeal to the people."

He was talking as if to himself, he had forgotten that he was standing for his portrait, he was walking up and down the long light room, past the easel and herself, seeing neither. She had never seen him like this; usually he kept so still and said so little. Her disappointment when he began just now to speak had quickly died, for she knew that he was talking with her (though scarcely to her) as he had not talked even with her mother.

"And I helped start it," he said, "as did each of us who thought he could pull a single brick out of the interwoven structure of the State, each pursuing his own separate end, even though it be an ideal. But you cannot do that, or in time the whole vast edifice comes crashing down—as it has done now—and crimes are committed in the name of religion and righteousness. This is the worst crime of all, to sicken and turn men away from the right, because of what has been done in its name. It would have been honester and cleanlier to have assassinated the King in the dark of his prison than to execute him in the name of God. Error is infinite. There is no end to it. All one can do is to pay one's own debt."

She cried out at that. "You fought for the King against worse odds than any man on his side! And you never got one scrap of the help from his armies that had been promised you. How can you speak of debt? Whatever you owed has been cleared a thousand times."

"Are such debts ever cleared? King Charles himself was glad to die on the scaffold to clear his."

"What do you mean?"

She felt cold at heart. She wished he had not said that.

"You know now," he answered, "of King Charles' last words on the scaffold.   He said he had done wrong in having consented to the death of his faithful servant Strafford, and for that was content to die."

Louey sat down, laid down her palette, rubbed at the paint on her fingers, found they were chill and numb.   Staring at them, she said in a voice that sounded very weak, "I think you were going to say something else.   What was it?"

"I don't remember.   Yes I do now, but it wasn't to say anything —if I'd said it, I'd have sung it, for I was remembering a scrap of an old song which our country people still sing near the Border———" And standing beside her he sang in a low voice to a wild, simple tune,

> " 'But I ha'e dreamed a dreary dream
> Ayont the Isle o' Skye.
> I dreamed a dead man won a fight,
> And I think that man was I.'

I was thinking," he said, "that King Charles won his fight when he went to die, and that I hope when I go I may do the same."

So that was where this moment had been leading them.   He had come in and Gerard had gone out, and they had spoken of his sister, of his wife, of his king.   Those lives and his life had gone on for years before this moment, tying up their several fates into these knots.   They had come before she could meet him, and so had all the tangles of this present perturbed age.

How could one find happiness if it depended on so many chances, public and private, if such an intricate spider-web pattern had to be woven in its perfection to catch it?   One could not: that was the answer.   So deep was her despair that it could not matter now what she said.

"I love you," she said, "and you could have loved me.   You know it too, I think," and then fell silent, gazing not at him but at his portrait, at the eyes that watched her there, as his own eyes were now watching her, she knew, and did not dare to look.

He had not guessed she loved him, had never thought of it, but now he felt he could not have talked to her as he had just done if he had not known it deep within himself.   He stood looking down on that small ruffled uptilted head like a wind-blown flower on the long stem of her neck.   Had he ever before noticed the wild grace of that head?   Yes he had, and would not let himself do so.   Why then was he doing it now?

For a moment he saw his life as it might yet begin again for him —then he shut it out.

"Listen to me," he said brutally.   "I dare not hope for your love. I do not want to hope for it.   My life is no longer my own.   I have other things to do with it than think of happiness, my own or another's."

Now she would cry, and that would be well, for it would relieve her feelings and spare him his; it would remind him that the work he had to do must never again be mixed up with a woman's grief.

But she did not cry.   She said almost indifferently, "Hope?   If I'd had any hope of you I should not have dared speak of it.   You cannot give me your love, I know that.   But I shall have to give mine, whether you can take it or not.   Wherever you go, whatever you do when you go from here to fight for the King, I shall know it, I think, long, long before the news of it can reach us."

"That might well be martyrdom," he said.   "My wife suffered it, as I now know better than when she lived."

"She would not have had it otherwise."

"She had other things.   She had our home together and our children, some years before that torturing anxiety.   But you would have nothing but the anxiety, nothing but the suffering, if it should come to that.   It would be cruel, unjust to you."

Then how was it, he asked himself, he had come so near to her? And how was it that whatever he said or thought about women did not seem to apply to her?

In all the different Courts of Europe who had lately welcomed him as an honoured guest, many women had made love to him openly, flagrantly, attracted by his world-wide reputation as a great soldier, by his grave and polished manners, and his indifference to themselves. But they and their methods had been so totally different from this girl that the comparison did not even occur to him.

This casual, curious, untidy, lovely creature did not, like most women, demand happiness as the reward of love.

But he could not ignore it for her.

"You are much younger than I," he said. "You have beauty and great gifts, you will marry some prince and make him happier than he has ever dreamed, if you wish,—and if you do not wish, then God help him!"

She turned her head and looked at him at last, and saw his eyes, grave and tender, smiling at her. She smiled too.

They should not have done that. They forgot what they had been saying, they saw only each other's eyes. She stood up, she was tall, her face nearly on a level with his own; he put his hand over her bright hair, behind that small, back-tossed head, he held her in his arms and they kissed.

It was done now, what he had meant never to do. Her moment of triumphant happiness was shot through with the guilty knowledge that he would regret it.

She broke from him, retreated from him. "We couldn't help it," she said. "It shan't make any difference."

Her voice was troubled, pleading against herself; she slipped through the doorway and was gone. He checked his fierce impulse to follow and snatch her back into his arms. She had given him these few seconds' respite and he seized them, staying rigidly where he was, staring at the empty doorway through which that slight white figure had fled.

Certainly this was not like other women he had met. In another moment he could smile in amused gratitude at her chivalry. She might not be a young man as she wished, but she was a gentleman.

And would that moment's madness make no difference as she had promised?

He was not so sure.

o

XIV

FOR Louey, at any rate, everything was different after that; everything came alive and moved more quickly, too quickly; never had the year rushed on them at so quick a rate. The windmills spun madly in the spring gales, now this way, now that, as ir trying always to snatch at the torn strips of cloud scurrying past in the blue sky above. Birds shouted in the lime trees of the Voorhout among the purple twigs that were now all spangled with tiny points of green light; half-grown birds hopped about on the garden paths; grave portly shopkeepers pounding down the streets, counting up figures in their heads, had suddenly to hop too, to avoid tripping over a spinning-top, a hoop bowled furiously between their legs, or a ball bouncing down the street to splash among yells of disaster into the canal.

For little boys, like the birds, had suddenly appeared in noisy profusion; they hung over the canal edge, their round faces gaping and grinning back at them from the gleaming water, and pushed bits of wood, into which they had stuck a stick and a piece of rag, as far out as they could without toppling over; then, as the wind caught their craft and sent them proudly down-stream, they ran screaming after them, proclaiming that their ships were of the East or the West India Companies and racing against each other.

The sad sodden fields in the rains that followed the great frost suddenly burgeoned, and the precious bulb-growing patches showed flecks of scarlet, purple and orange among the enormous flat expanse of green; stout men in breeches, with thick red necks and arms sticking out of their flapping shirts, tended and guarded them all day long, while stouter men in cloaks and stockings and big important hats, sitting in fine stuffy halls, bid enormous sums against each other as the price of a single flower: 16,000 florins for one tulip bulb from Haarlem—that showed how mad even the stout Dutch business men could run in the spring.

All this had happened in other springs, but never so quickly, so flamboyantly, with such a sense of the year rushing on towards some tremendous goal. Everyone was hoping different things, hoping to go somewhere, do something different.

Lucy Walters was teasing Charles with her demands; Sophie was telling him she meant to go and stay with her brother Carl in Germany; and Charles himself, bothered between the two, talked of agreeing to his mother's ever more pressing demands that he should go back to her in Paris. Hyde objected urgently, for far stronger than the Covenanters' own influence was Queen Henrietta Maria's in their favour.

But Hyde himself was longing, though still secretly, for that ambassadorial trip he might make with his friend Cottington to Spain, which would remove him from these nagging disputes; and with every fresh gust of harsh wind that marred this northerly spring sunshine, he wished it more and more.

Eliza had heard that Descartes had caught a severe cold on the chest owing to Queen Christina's peculiar desire to discuss philosophy with him in an unheated library at five o'clock in the morning; she was in a fever to go to Sweden and nurse him, but could only write letters to him and to Christina, which latter she always tore up.

The Queen of Bohemia began to talk of her country house at Rhenen, to plan whom she would have to stay there to ride and hunt with her and boat on the river and take part in her archery contests. She was a fine shot; she had brought down sixteen buck with her own cross-bow in one morning, "but Jamie Graham is a better, to judge by his college record." It would be perfect to have Jamie Graham at Rhenen; they would have music-parties in the evenings, sitting on the terrace, and she would get him to sing the songs she had heard he had composed himself.

She had not yet been successful in her attempts at this, though she did induce him to sing to the lute one or two of the rough old country-songs of their native land that she could just remember having heard as a small child, but only from her nurse or the gardeners singing below the castle walls. Other cavaliers here had sung her the works of modern English poets, Lovelace's tender love-songs, Suckling's impudent, amusing verses; some of them even sang the old-fashioned charming lyrics of Queen Elizabeth's day that had sprung into fashion from the innumerable plays of that time.

To the Queen and her daughter Louise there was, however, an odd charm in hearing the simple words and tunes of his countryside, sung by this quiet and courtly Scots Marquis.

> " 'The deer runs wild on hill and dale,
> The birds fly wild from tree to tree,
> But there is neither bread nor kail
> To fend my men and me.' "

His deep voice echoed through the long room where the shadows were gathering in a stormy sunset. To Louey the song echoed down through the years, from the rough Scots peasants who had sung it for centuries, to Montrose as he sang it to her and her mother on this April evening; and others would sing it for centuries after the three of them were dead. It seemed strange to her that people do not last, that their voices are stilled in death, but that the things they make and do and think go on and on.

The Queen sat before him in her flowing black dress, her proud neck rising from a broad collar of fine lace and the short necklace of big pearls which she always wore. He did not look at her daughter, who sat at a little distance, but her bright image danced before his eyes—unduly bright as it happened, for Louey had suddenly revolted against all this endless black and put on a pale yellow dress she had got just before her uncle's death.

It could not matter while she was at home and alone, she had said in disingenuous answer to Eliza's expostulations, for, as it happened, she had known that Montrose was likely to come that evening. And she wore one of the absurd new little Turkish caps of green velvet, undeniably becoming, since for once she had arranged the hair beneath it with care. She had even considered cutting it in a straight fringe or else in short ringlets (both were fashionable) to cover up her broad high forehead, but had fortunately been prevented by the usual loss of her scissors.

The music was interrupted by a message for the Queen, who, it seemed, had forgotten that she had promised her 'best niece' Mary to go with her to the Dowager Princess Amelia's reception in the Mauritzhuis. Swearing volubly, the Queen departed, threatening that Jamie Graham should make up for this disappointment to her at Rhenen.

But 'Jamie Graham,' now alone with Louey for the first time since she had worked at his portrait, told her he was only waiting for King Charles' definite signed agreement before he too would be off once more to the Northern capitals of Europe, to collect money and munitions for his enterprise. It was not likely that he would return to The Hague before that enterprise, still less likely that he could spare time to stay with the Queen at Rhenen.

He stood up to take his leave as he told Louey this. He took her hand in his to kiss it, and told her to put him out of her head, and she looked up at him and laughed.

"What do you wish me to put in it instead?" she asked in her nonchalant manner. "Marriage to some prince, you said, but the only firm offer I ever got from one was too weak to withstand a grandmother."

"Whose grandmother?"

"His and mine. She was the Dowager Electress Juliana, and he my cousin Prince William of Brandenburg."

That quick flush of hers flew over her face as she spoke, and never had she been so furious at her inability to control it, as now under his keen scrutiny. "No, you are wrong," she said. "I did not care for him a scrap, I don't know why, for he was very good-looking."

"And mad for love of you."

"How do you know? Did Rupert tell you?"

He smiled at her idea of his conversations with Rupert and shook his head. But he had remembered how during the war King Charles I had been so concerned to get together a sufficient dowry to appease the relatives of the handsome young Prince of Brandenburg who waited four years in such desperate anxiety to marry his fascinating cousin.

"What became of your uncle's dowry for you?"

"Carl took it, I believe. That is usually what becomes of money raised for our family. You need not look so angry. I have told you I did not really care for him."

"Though you turn crimson at mention of him."

"No, it was only,—oh, damn your eyes and all they see!—only that—that was when I—why I——" But she could not tell him that that was when, for no reason she could think of (unless it were because her handsome young lover had gone away from that first visit without any chance to declare his passion to her), she had allowed Gerard Honthorst to give her her first kiss. If it had been anyone more attractive—but not poor coarse old full-blown Gerard!

So to avoid his eyes (as he could very well see) she pulled at the little shoulder-flaps that fluted out like petals round her voluminous sleeves, and went on hurriedly, "No, it was the Dowager Amelia walked off with Brandenburg for her eldest daughter, and my mother made me attend the wedding with my sisters, quite rightly. We couldn't wear mourning for the Pauper Palatines who had stayed unmarried—and probably always will."

But he would not take her at her word. "You have had scores of men in love with you," he said quietly.

"Who told you that?"

"My own eyes and senses."

But not only that, she was sure of it. There had been talk enough about her at one time and another, scandal too, some started, all nursed and multiplied by the Dowager Amelia.

"Love and marriage are clean different things," she said, still trying to keep that light careless tone that had always come instinctively to her till this moment, when she most needed it. "A man does not want to marry a princess without a penny, but with a line of kings for ancestors which would necessitate all her relatives going in to dinner before all his. And I'm just on twenty-six," she added inconsequently.

He had thought her some years younger. "But you are still more than ten years younger than myself. I have had the best of my life, but you have yours before you."

"Ah, but in what direction? In friendships with funny gross artists, in flirtations with scamps such as poor de l'Epinay? My young brother Philip killed him, you know, for making love to my mother and myself and boasting of it."

He knew, but he did not show it, and she wished she had not said it. She leaned back against the table, her hands outstretched on either side of her, playing uneasily with the dark crimson Persian rug that covered it, folding it and twisting it round her fingers. Her dress gleamed and shimmered against the rich background, her up-turned face under the peaked cap was tilted towards him like the thin mocking slip of the crescent moon.

It was the first time he had seen her in anything but dead-black or the loose white painter's coat, impersonal and sexless as a monastic robe, and the new effect of this brilliant and piquant dress was not what she would have wished. For she had charmed him by her un-likeness to all the other women he had met abroad, and now she annoyed him by looking as they did, sophisticated, provocative—and he could not take his eyes off her.

His silence made her reckless; something was going wrong and she could not stop it, would not, rather, for she was damned if she'd play for his good opinion!

"Or would you advise George Goring?" she asked; "that jolly ruffian Rupert hated so in England. I wrote, or rather drew him a letter there which he showed all round the camp, Rupert told me."

"Yes, I remember."

Goring was still doing it when he had met him at Oxford nearly a year later, and still pretending he had only just got it.

She saw that he had seen the letter, but did not seem to care what he thought of her, or expect him to think at all of her. She expected nothing, and he must expect nothing of her, he told himself, while unwillingly, unbelievingly, there came into his mind a sudden jealous memory of Goring's winking innuendoes, unheeded at the time.

But Goring could boast of a woman he had never met. It was impossible that Goring, the most brilliant but the most scurrilous wit in King Charles' Court, should have had his way with this elusive wisp of humanity rather than womanhood—or so she had seemed until to-day. But to-day somehow she was different.

And would she not have been different with Goring?

His eyes fastened on her with a look so searching that her heart seemed to turn over inside her.

"I remember that letter," he repeated, and his voice was now hard. "It was exquisitely decorated, riotously witty, those caricatures and illustrations to private jokes between you—a string of pearls to send to that debauched swine!"

She was trembling, but her fear of his anger had roused her own. "My mother thought him the most amusing visitor we ever had, she laughed for hours at *her* 'private jokes' with him, and why shouldn't I have mine? Don't tell me the case is quite different because I've not had a husband and thirteen children—I've heard it too often, and I don't believe in it as a necessary preliminary to amusement."

He burst out laughing, as so often happened with Louey; all might have been well even now, had she not been still hot on justifying Goring. "Why, even the Parliament were so charmed by him that they had to let him go free instead of executing him. Ned Hyde told me it was simply because they all found him irresistible."

As she had done?

He caught at the hand she was waving in expostulation, crushing it in his grasp. "Stop praising that sot!" he said. "Do you want to drive me mad?"

"Yes," she replied instantly on a flash of laughter, though once again she was shaking, it was ridiculous, her teeth were chattering. She saw his face swoop towards her and he kissed her—not as he had done that first time, but savagely, again and again, with all the un-recognized power of emotion that had been pent up in him these last lonely years released in sudden fury.

"Is that what you want of me?" he asked her. "And that? And that?" But as she began to struggle he let her go as quickly as he had attacked. She collapsed into a chair, her green cap fallen off, her carefully arranged hair tumbling over her shoulders, and he saw, not without satisfaction, how shaken she was. He could not trust himself to stay; he turned sharply on his heel and left her.

Goring, no, that made it impossible. Anybody else might not have mattered, even de l'Epinay (it did not occur to him that this might be because he had never seen de l'Epinay), but 'Roaring Goring,' with his bloated beauty, his insolent upturned moustaches, his swagger, his smile, his limp (a perfectly genuine limp from an old wound got in the German wars, but he managed to convert even that into an amusing mannerism and another attraction); Goring, who had won half his battles with the courage and dash of a born cavalry leader but lost the other half when drunk; Goring, who would betray a friend or a woman or his king and make a joke and brag of it,—so Goring was the man no one could resist !

She had said it openly—and doubtless she had not resisted him.

He had been amused and touched by the wild innocence of her enthusiasm when she had first talked with him; but now that he had begun to be in love, his jealousy would not let him recognize any such quality in her. 'Love and marriage are clean different things,' that light laughing voice echoed in his head. With that as her own expressed opinion, it was scarcely necessary to remember Goring's, that 'princesses are cheaper than prostitutes.'

Well, Goring had settled this matter for him; it was over now, and a very good thing it was, almost before it had begun, for he would be a fool to get himself tied up now with anything that might distract him from his one purpose.

But Goring had not settled the matter; it was not over, and it was not a good thing. Since his wife's death nearly four years ago, Montrose had shut out all thought of women; but now he paid the price for that restraint, and they would no longer be shut out. For years the image of Magdalen had haunted him, her anxious and watchful eyes, her silence, her smile that had once been ironic but had learned a greater courage, a happiness in spite of fear.

It was no good angel now that haunted his dreams, but a mocking sensual witch with loose flying hair and subtle eyes, the hair and eyes of the Princess Louise, who tormented him with desire, then turned and jeered at him from Goring's arms. He could drive her with contempt from his waking thoughts, but his sleep, and that uneasy passage between sleeping and waking, became hag-ridden with the longing to tear her from those arms and make her his own, brutally, as he had never yet taken a woman.

These dreams did not distract him from his one purpose, but they began to embitter it. 'Woman' became a synonym for disloyalty and treachery and all annoyance: Ned Hyde for all his massive brain was a fussy old woman; the ministers' raucous nagging derived straight from the beldams that they persecuted in thousands as witches; young Charles himself, smooth-spoken, watchful, for all his air of careless ease, striving perpetually to charm all men to his advantage, however untrustworthy he knew them to be, was employing all the methods of a practised whore, and was as little likely to keep faith with him.

Even the formula of Montrose's hopes and fears for his purpose began to follow that of an angry lover, for they kept jigging into rhymes so persistent that to get rid of them he dashed some of them down on paper. But as fast as he did so, more sprang up, jeering, abusive.

They followed the rhythm of the ballad to his 'dear and only love' which he had made and sung long ago to Magdalen, when she had repudiated it in indignation, demanding to know who had ever brought such a word as 'committees' into a love-song? For then, as now, his ballad had been as much to his loyalty to his King and hope for 'purest monarchy,' as to his love.

And the refrain was the threat of the loyal servant as of the faithful lover, that, if tried too far, he would 'never love thee more.'

So now when he rode over the marshes beyond The Hague, baffled by some tussle with his enemies, or, worse, by some fresh glimpse of Charles' friendly dealings with them, the thud of his horse's hoofs on the muddy road hammered out the old tune in his head to the throb of new, angry rhymes.

> 'And if by fraud or by consent
>   Thy heart to ruin come,
> I'll sound no trumpet as my wont,
>   Nor march by tuck of drum.'

Would he not? It was a lie, he knew, yet it gave him satisfaction to believe it of himself. All his warning and remonstrance with the King had been rigorously but fiercely controlled, both in his present speech and his former letters ('If Your Highness shall but vouchsafe a little faith unto your loyal servants, and stand at guard with others' had been a very mild translation of his thought); but now it broke out in the scorn of a defiance that he could express only to himself, and only in the guise of a lover's indignation.

Nor was that guise a disguise. For he himself could not tell at what point the dark suave face of the young King faded before the long swift-glancing eyes of the Princess Louise, as his anger against both their false and fickle souls burned up his heart to the tune of an old love-song.

> 'Then shall thy heart be set by mine
>   But in far different case.
> For mine was true, so was not thine,
>   But looked like Janus' face.
> For as the waves with every wind
>   So sail'st thou every shore,
> And leaves my constant heart behind.
>   —How *can* I love thee more?'

XV

LOUEY too told herself, 'It's over now—he'll not look at me nor speak to me again if he can avoid it, and I'll never dare to as I did before.' But she could not entirely believe it, not in such fine weather. The market-women spread out their booths in the open with oyster-barrels and fish and vegetables, and oranges brought in ships from China, and flowers the colour of sunshine and of blood; and news came from England of the enormous army Cromwell was gathering together with taxes fifteen times as much as King Charles had ever dared impose, and all to invade Ireland.

What would become of Montrose's scheme if Cromwell conquered Ireland first? And how could he fail to conquer the scattered forces in that distracted country when he had a huge army trained and organized through seven years of civil war, and behind it the wealth and greed of the London merchants with their vested interests in Ireland?

And still the Scots Commissioners hissed and screamed their threats against Montrose, and their dire prophecies as to what would happen to King Charles if he touched the hand of the accursed thing.

And Charles, after his rashness in the House in the Wood, no longer dared to meet Montrose openly, since he had been warned that the moment he did so the Commissioners would give the signal to the Head of their Government to break off all relations with the Court at The Hague; and this at the present stage of affairs would, Hyde declared, mean the loss not only of the official Scottish support, but that of the Dutch Calvinists also.

The year was slipping on, would soon slip past them, and what would next year bring?

Worst of all, thought Louey, Montrose despised her, believed the worst of her. Let him then, and he should have some reason to do so! As with Rupert, bad opinion made her defiant, in this case almost desperate. She tried to fling herself into work, but what good did that do anyone?

A good deal of good, said her mother, who was in despair at the shortage of candles since the chandler had refused to supply any more till his bill was paid; "and next week we shall all be sitting in the dark!" she declared. Never was there more reason to be thankful that the days were drawing out, and no doubt one could plead health and go to bed early. But Elizabeth detested going to bed. It was much better that Louey should work.

Louey's work, however, refused to be profitable. It had turned rebellious, like everything else in her at this moment, and she only wanted to do caricatures or malicious subjects that were impossible to put out for sale on the picture-booths along the canal, by the side of Vermeer's latest from Delft or a Peter de Hooch. She pulled out a canvas she had begun some months ago of herself and the two elder of her sisters dressing their mother's hair for a State ball at the Binnenhof, a cruel thing, for it was done at a moment when her mother, who had had to sell her horses and in consequence give up hunting, had grown rather stout and much older looking for lack of her accustomed exercise. That was quickly repaired by Lord Craven's gift of fresh horses, and Elizabeth soon 'rumbled away in riding' her advancing years, as she used to do any ill effects from her children's births.

But the sketch of the three slender girls with lovely serious faces, intent only on adorning that elderly lady in all her gorgeous Court finery, as she sat with her eyes complacently fixed upon the mirror, now gave Louey a bitter amusement as a prophecy rather than a recollection. So would they stand all their lives, attendant only on their mother's charms, long after she had ceased to possess them. She worked at it with feverish amusement, a joke that she shared with no one, not even Honthorst, though the temptation to do so grew hourly greater, for it was turning into a superb painting.

Then came a counter-attraction. Honthorst had a commission to paint Lauderdale, and Louey seized the chance to do so too. It had been no mere joke when she had declared her longing to paint him at her first meeting. That grossly sensual face had at once fired her ironic fancy and made her want to do a grandiose allegorical figure of him, as Mammon perhaps, or the World and the Flesh, with one of her imaginary portraits of Argyll, squinting and sallow as she had heard, whispering into his ear as the Devil.

So while Honthorst worked at his large canvas on the easel, she sat in a corner and made sketches so grotesquely hideous that they had always to be hidden before Lauderdale could see them, and substituted by some charming genial portrait-study worked up in his absence.

This amused her and Honthorst too; they shared a deal of low jokes about it together, but for all that, her master was not too easy in the matter. His Princess was in one of her most reckless moods, flirting with this obscene satyr in a way to turn the head of a far less complacent rake. *He* didn't know, as Honthorst did from experience, that she was adding him to her collection of oddities, studying his character just as she did his face for his portrait, absorbed in that extraordinary mixture of his tremendous will and utter unscrupulousness, his acute judgment of men (as long as they were not too much his superior) and skill in handling them, his enormous knowledge of foreign languages, abstruse classical learning, theology and divinity, as well as all forms of debauchery throughout Europe, of comic tales and characters, odd anecdotes, some merely gross but many undeniably witty.

"If old Ben Jonson had put you into a play all by yourself, my lord, he might still have called it 'Every Man in his Humour,'" Louey exclaimed in genuine appreciation.

"And the result would have been to put 'Every Man out of his Humour,'" muttered Honthorst, and repeated his quip aloud to Louey as soon as he was alone with her. "God save us from these Scots, they seem to have driven you crazy between them—but I wish you'd mind the advice to the cobbler to 'Stick to your last.' There's a gentleman and a great man, and you've turned from him to set your cap at this rotten sack of iniquity and his worst enemy."

"That last might have something to do with it," replied Louey.

"If you're hoping to get any of his plans or secrets out of Lauderdale, you're mistaken. He may talk as expansively as a drunken woman, but he's as cunning as a fox."

"Lay in a bottle of brandy for him next time, dear Gerard, and see if that helps. No, better and cheaper, hint to him that he can bring his own."

"Do you think t'other lord would be grateful for any information you could get that way? You're wrong. And do you never think of the danger you're running?"

Louey did not, since she had been extremely careful never to be alone in the studio with Lauderdale for one moment, in spite of his efforts to get Honthorst out of the way.

But Honthorst only snorted when she mentioned these precautions;—"A fellow like that would stick at nothing. He has his own bravoes, and half of those in the town are in his pocket as well. A job of kidnapping is nothing to them. There's that cut-throat, Bastard Aank, he's got more money than he knows what to do with these days, and boasted to his whore one night he got it from a Scots lord who's none so mean as his countrymen are made out to be."

"Did she tell you that? Who is she? You know her then?" asked Louey all in a breath.

"I did," he said significantly.

"Then, Gerard, you must get her to tell you more."

"She'd no more to tell."

"Make her get it out of Aank, then. I *know* there's something wrong."

"So do I," growled her master, still convinced of her danger, which she refused even to consider.

But she had her own fears. Only yesterday Lauderdale had come in for a sitting, after a Dutch banquet at which even his hard Scots head had to own itself inferior to those of his phlegmatic Dutch hosts. In his slightly maudlin and homesick mood she had encouraged him to talk of Scotland, of his own fine woods that surrounded his splendid castle with the great gates that opened near to the little town of Lauder,—"and not so little neither, it's one of the widest in Scotland, splitting in two to hold the old Town Hall in the middle of it like an old tappit hen with her brood of chicks tailing away behind on either side of her—and let you not be making the mistake of thinking a tappit hen is only a pint measure and nothing else, for it's as good a fowl as ever shed fleas. Ay, they call us 'Lousy Lauder,' and where's the harm in that? since closeness is company and 'as snug as a bug in a rug' is the saying for comfort all the world over."

Which seemed just the right moment to ogle the Princess, who smiled back in delicious encouragement, but only led him imperceptibly on to tell her other homely Scots soubriquets that linked places and their attendant great families together.

"Have Lord Cassillis and the Kennedy family or their place any nickname such as Lousy Lauder?" she demanded.

"Ay, the Kennedys have their tag right enough.

> "'Tween Wigtown and the town o' Ayr,
> Portpatrick and the Cruives o' Cree,
> Ye shall not get a lodging there
> Except ye court a Kennedy.'"

Louey clapped her hands in delight. "That's grim and inhospitable enough even for the present Cassillis, stalking The Hague in his scowl and steeple hat. More, I say, I must have more."

He told her that the Leslies got their name from the Less Lee, and that

> "'Between the Less Lee and the Mair
> Leslie slew a knight and left him there.'"

He told her the Gordons' Gramercie,

> "'To curse and swear and damn and lee,
> And that's the Gordons' Gramercie.'"

"And old Huntly, the head of the Gordons, kept up the family reputation until they cut off his head this spring and he'd none to do it with, the more's the pity, for I like a good swearer, I like a good liar too, I hate your damned insipid lies."

"Have Montrose and the Grahams their password too?"

He admitted rather reluctantly that they were called the Gallant Grahams, but chuckled slyly as he repeated the rhyme:

> "'Wad the Gallant Grahams but stand by me,
> The dogs might douk in English bluid
> Ere a foot's breadth I wad flinch or flee!'"

Louey kept her head down over her drawing so as not to show her pleasure that even some country minstrel long ago should know so well what like were the Grahams, and their leader now here to-day.

But she had not cared for the sound of that chuckle. "I suppose," she said in a tone of careless contempt, "that is why that soldier of fortune Sir John Hurry swaggers so insolently here, since he's got the leader of the Grahams to 'stand by him.'"

Lauderdale exploded with an oath that startled Honthorst, who understood it, more than herself. But it was she who heard Lauderdale exclaim in the same breath, "He'll not have him here long then!"

She tried to get more from him, but he shut up his full mouth like a puckered seam in the middle of his baggy face, and she dared not rouse his suspicion.

It was enough though to convince her that if Lauderdale were plotting mischief, it was against Montrose.

Now it was Honthorst's job, so she told him as soon as the Scots lord had unsteadily departed, to find out what he could from his end; and very comically rueful he was about it, being sent back to his old bad haunts just as he had grown respectable, back to a woman of the town that he had abjured, in order to bribe her present client's secrets out of her, and all for the sake of his lady's love for another man. "Did ever a true knight in romance do as much?"

P

With superhuman restraint he just refrained from adding, 'for nothing.' It would not have been true, for in answer she flung her arms round his neck and kissed him as she had once done years ago and never since,—but not as she had done it then, out of mischief and piqued curiosity, but with such deep warmth of affection as made him know that he had his own place in her heart, and for ever.

After that he set to work with the cunning of a Machiavelli and the persistence of Lauderdale himself, and discovered that there was indeed a design for Aank and his gang to set on Montrose and kill him when riding alone, except for a single attendant, when sent for by the King (as he would suppose) to a secret interview with King Charles at a country house outside The Hague.

This arrangement would have a very fair show of truth, since Charles was now so beset with spies that it was all but impossible for him to discuss anything of real private importance with Montrose; moreover, Charles was in actual fact going to Amsterdam soon on a short visit on an equally private matter, since it was to visit no less and no more a person than Lucy Walters, who had been bundled out of the way there with her baby. As soon as he should depart, the false summons would be sent to Montrose, and Aank and his gang would attack him either on the road or at his own house when he returned to it alone.

This was discovered on the afternoon of Easter Eve, and Honthorst at once went to Montrose's house to warn him beforehand, but found it empty, the servants all absent, presumably for the Carnival. He promised Louey to go back again the first thing next morning—Charles was sure to be at the Easter Eve reception at the Binnenhof that evening, and nothing could happen as long as he was at The Hague.

But it was that very evening, at that very reception, that Louey learned of Charles' departure. Most of the guests wore masks and fancy-dress; it was late in the evening, just on eleven o'clock, when the Princess Mary interrupted a long complaint to her cousin (she had not been able to wear her dress as an Amazon with a delicious little silver bow, because she was in mourning) to whisper indignantly, "Do you know why that wicked Charles is not here? He has this afternoon ridden off to that horrible woman, and wouldn't your mother be angry! Oh yes, she laughs and won't let anyone else say a word against him, but for all that she's scolded him soundly."

Louey could hardly wait to hear her as far as that. Since Charles had already gone, it meant that Lauderdale's spies knew of it and would be even now sending the message to Montrose that would take him out to a secret interview with his King—but really to the ambush for his death. She could not lose a moment in trying to find Honthorst or anyone else whom she might trust to go and warn him, if indeed he had returned.

All she did was to catch Etta aside, whisper to her to cover her departure and say that she had already left to go home, and then slip out by herself in a borrowed mask and her dark cloak, in the confusion of all those fantastic figures coming and going, while the music thrummed and spun its intricate spider-dance about them.

Like Cinderella, she fled out of the Palace, and that thin music and the roar of voices faded away behind her.

XVI

*L*UCKILY there was no moon, and the streets showed only here and there the lighted doorway of a tavern or a lantern hung at a cross-road. It was raining too—a good thing, as it would keep people indoors—and the mud squelched underfoot. She kept to the darkest side of the road and ran too fast and desperately for any of the decent though drunken Dutch citizens returning from a supper-party to try to molest her, though they hailed her jovially. Then, as that silent black figure flew past them, they crossed themselves surreptitiously, those determined anti-Romanists, in anxious reversion to that forbidden charm, thinking a ghost or witch might have flitted past them through the night.

But now some cavalier, short and stout and also drunk, was making for her with more determination, hailed her with one or two of the gross words in Dutch that every Englishman at The Hague knew by now, and barred her way, putting a hand on her arm and holding it tight as she tried to shake it off. She had a heavy ring on her right hand which Rupert had once remarked would make a useful knuckle-duster, and at once lunged out, crashing it into his face with so sudden and swift an action that he staggered back with a cry of pain, slipped in the mud and fell sprawling at her feet. In another instant he was clawing for her cloak, but she had already leaped past him and was tearing down the dark street quicker than any drunkard could follow.

She had reached the house now. There was a light in one of the upper windows. Then Montrose had returned, alone, as Lauderdale had planned, and she was most likely in time. The side door had been left unfastened. Was that the servants' carelessness or because *they* had already come? Her heart beat so quick and loud as she went up those silent stairs that it seemed to echo through the house. What would she see when she went through that door—Montrose dead, or alive?

But she *must* be in time; she would see him sitting at his table perhaps, or walking up and down, and she would tell him very quickly—'you must go; they are coming here to kill you'—and he would be kind and comforting and they would get away at once from this dreadful, silent, waiting house. Her fingers fumbled at the door; lifting the latch, she went in.

Yes, he was sitting at the table, writing. She tore off her mask, —it was not he, it was General Sir John Hurry who was rising slowly, getting taller and scrawnier and more astonished every instant. His enormously wide shoulders stooped forward as if they were holding up the ceiling, his long thin slightly bowed legs narrowed sharply to his feet; he was a long triangle standing on its point, and his scarred face lowered forward, leered forward, the lamplight striking on his shining red jaw—the hard-bitten, driven-in red of a fair, weather-beaten Scot.

She gasped out : "Where is Montrose ?"

"He is expecting Your Highness ?"

"No, you idiot!" she snapped, in answer to his tone rather than his question, and he started, actually believing for a flash that it was the mother and not the daughter who stood there, words and voice were so exactly what she would have used. But the next moment he forgot her and all women, for she told him of Lauderdale's plot.

"If he is still on the road," she said, "they will try to get him there."

He turned his back on her to pick up a couple of horse-pistols, which he loaded and rammed into his belt.

"Are you going to ride and meet him ?"

His answer was a surly grunt, inarticulate, but in the accent of Aberdeen. ('What did the woman need asking such fool questions ?')

"But he might come by the other road," she said.

"Not if I ride fast enough to reach him before the cross-roads. There's a risk, but I must take it."

"If they miss him on the road, they'll come after him here. Some of them may come here anyway. Is there no one you could leave here to warn him?"

"Not a soul in the house, and I'll not wait to fetch any."

"I'll wait here, then."

He gave her a nod and a narrow glance under his light red eyelashes. 'I've thrown finer lumps of flesh than yon on their backs, but none with more spirit,' he thought, and aloud said, "Ay."

She heard him clattering downstairs, then leading his horse out of the stable. It must have been all ready saddled and bridled, for there was no pause. She heard the hoofs splash in the mud and then thud away.

The house shut down round her, all dark outside this room, all silent, waiting. She drew her cloak tight round her to try to stop herself shivering. She felt very cold. At any moment Montrose might come in—or his murderers. The clock on the chimney-piece was ticking heavily, its pendulum swinging to and fro in time to that loud ticking, a ticking that sounded more and more like the steady clatter of hoofs on the cobblestones outside, of steps in the paved courtyard. Yet whenever she looked at it the time was the same as when she had looked last.

But this night too must pass as other nights had done; time must go on past this moment and tell her whether Montrose was alive or not. He *must* be alive, it was unthinkable his great design should end like this before it began, God could not allow it, Fate itself would have too much sense to allow such a thing to happen. The moments would move on, and someone would come to tell her all was well.

But supposing there was no God, no Fate even; only the blind working of chance?

She crammed her hand into her mouth to stop herself from screaming, for she heard someone—more than one—coming up the stair. She looked round frantically for a place to hide, but what was the use of that? They would ferret into all possible hiding-places. Now they would burst the door open. She must stand up stiffly and not show she was afraid.

But there was no sound now. Had they stopped at the door to listen, to peer through the keyhole? The thought that someone might be watching her, unseen, was more unbearable than any other fear. She went to the door and flung it open. There was no one that she could see outside. The stairs yawned in a deep well of darkness. No one had come up them; she had imagined it all.

'In another hour I shall be mad,' thought Louey. She went back into the room and walked round the table with her fingers in her ears to shut out the innumerable unnamable sounds one hears at night in an empty house. But that made it worse.

She began deliberately to look at different things in the room— there were not many. His lute lay on a stool. She took it up and plucked out the beginning of a jerky little tune on the strings; but the sounds went echoing away through the silence and terrified her.

There was a shelf of books. She pulled out the biggest, a thick brown folio. It was Sir Walter Raleigh's *History of the World*, published in 1614, when he had still been alive and in the Tower where he wrote it. Montrose's name was at the beginning, but as James Graham, and the date and a brief inscription from his father, showing the book to have been a gift from him for his son's twelfth birthday in October 1624. She dipped here and there; the pages fell open of themselves in several places as if from long usage.

One had a thin, crushed, withered stem of some herb to mark the place; all the leaves had fallen from it long ago and only the faintest dusty scent remained, nothing to show if it had once been lavender or lad's love or rosemary; nothing to show if it had been he or some woman, his wife, walking in his garden, their garden, who had plucked it and laid it there. It left a faint stained dent in the margin beside these words: 'Only those few black swans I must except, who behold death without dread, and the grave without fear, and embrace both, as necessary guides to endless glory.'

This had been written by Raleigh in the Tower, who had been let out of the Tower, a man nearing seventy, weakened by fourteen years of imprisonment and disappointment, to try his luck once more in his ship named *The Destiny*, to break the huge power of Spain and to found an empire for the king who behind his back was already conspiring with that enemy against him.

And she remembered how that voyage had taken four times as long as that distance had ever taken before, and a hurricane had sunk one of his pinnaces, and a raging epidemic destroyed half his men, and for weeks they lay becalmed and Raleigh's log was one long catalogue of death day by day, and Raleigh himself was sick of the fever and with the pleurisy he had already had in the Tower, and so weakened he could scarcely hold his pen.

And on that voyage his son was killed in the attack on the Spanish town on the Orinoco.

Then at the end he might have escaped as his friends urged him to do, but on his way to the French ship that was to rescue him he turned back to meet his destiny, and so became immortal.

She sat there with her chin between her hands, her elbows on the table, seeing these things so clear before her mind that for the first time the house was filled with silence—until she could no longer bear the silence, and the echoes of that past that could be heard in it throbbing away into the future. She picked up Hurry's pen and pulled towards her the paper on which he had been writing, and scrawled a caricature of Hurry rising, an immense raw-boned ruffian, against the ceiling.

There were more sheets of paper beneath Hurry's crabbed scrawl; she drew one out to make another sketch, and saw straggling short lines of verse scribbled on it. She knew them, from one or two notes he had sent her mother, to be in Montrose's handwriting. He might be fighting his death-battle even now, living his poem to its sharp end instead of writing it, and these disjointed verses might be his last words, whether said or written. She must not read them; she must read them; she read:

> 'My dear and only love, take heed
>   How thou thyself dispose.
> Let not all longing lovers feed
>   Upon such looks as those.
> I'll marble-wall thee round about
>   Myself shall be the door,
> And if thy heart dare to slide out
>   I'll never love thee more.'

Doggerel? With a certain wild swinging, or indeed swingeing vigour perhaps, but not much else? Louey tried to read it as critically as Eliza would do, but it was no good. There was only one question in her mind: To whom was this written? Could it be herself?

Her cheeks that had felt so cold with fear against her hands were now burning, and a vein pulsed madly in her forehead; she looked here and there over the scattered lines, scarcely daring to choose which to read next, for words caught her unawares:

> 'Thou traitorous and untrue!'

Was that for her? And—

> 'Thy spirit grown so poor.'

And this?

> 'Thy beauty shined at first so bright
>   And woe is me therefore
> That ever I found thy love so light
>   That I could love no more.'

That 'damnable iteration'! And there again, scrawled along the side, a cruelly mocking jest,—

> 'If thou turn a Commonwealth
>   I'll never love thee more.'

Since this was what he thought of her, why did he not choose the obvious rhyme to that insistent refrain? Perhaps that final stone was flung at her here down in the corner where something almost illegible had been scribbled about 'that tracing goddess Fame,' who

'Shall record it to thy shame
How thou hast lovéd me!
And how in odds our love was such
As few have been before.
Thou lovedst too many, I too much,
So I can love no more.'

Nor could she read more. She felt she had been stripped and beaten. She put her hands over her face, trying to see herself as Honthorst saw her, and all the other men who had loved her and told her they had to do so for ever, howsoever she had treated them.

But she could not shut out that brutal, jeering vision of her in Montrose's eyes, and her despairing certainty that that vision was the last he had seen of her, that he would never know how she indeed loved him, would never come back to know it, that he was lying out there on the marshes outside the town, his eyes shut fast in darkness for ever.

Death mattered most, after all.

What did it matter what he thought of her, since now he thought no more? (Still that refrain was knocking at her mind with the relentless throbbing of a witch's curse.)

But that was a lie. He had died hating and despising her, and that would matter to the end of her life. She would have no courage now to take up any of the threads of it again, but would let them take their own course and do with her what they would.

She did not even hear when first the sound of horses' hoofs came into the distance, came nearer, galloping fast, nearer and nearer the house. They stopped outside; someone was coming into the house, up the stair. She sprang up and saw the door flung open, saw Montrose enter with his drawn sword in his hand and bring it to the ready at the sight of someone in the room.

Then he saw who it was and lowered its point, but his eyes were still bright and dangerous, she knew now how he looked in battle. He came towards her, flinging his sword on the table; she saw blood on it and on his hand, in the same flash as she saw his fierce amazement at her presence.

She backed in terror before his eyes.

"Wait," she cried. "Didn't Hurry tell you I'm here?"

"I can see you are here!"

He was breathing fast from his gallop—and what else?

"Are you hurt? There's blood——"

"It's not mine."

"Did Hurry miss you? Did you fight them alone?"

He flung back his head and laughed.

"Don't!" she cried sharply, more frightened by his face than when she had been alone. "I don't know you. You are someone different."

"That is what you want, isn't it? That I should be different?"

He seized her arms and looked hard at her face with those bright, dangerous eyes. His grip was agony, but she did not wince under it. She cried out in fury and in desperate haste, for in another instant he would hear nothing that she said. "*Will* you listen? I found out about this to-night, and came here to warn you, and Hurry was here, so he went after you and I stayed in case they should come to get you here."

He dropped his hands. He was still staring at her, but differently now, incredulous, shocked—and, was it possible, disappointed?

But at least he had heard her.

"And you think," she gasped out, "just as your oaf of a general did——"

"I was not thinking at all." He turned from her and walked up and down the room before he spoke, and now he did not look at her. "I had been fighting and riding for life or death, I came in, saw someone waiting for me, another assassin, and then it was you. Why didn't you tell me this before?"

"I did—or didn't I? It's all been so desperate." She looked at the naked sword on the table and began to shake. "I thought you were wounded. Then you wouldn't hear—wouldn't see. They might still come here."

"Not now. My man has gone to rouse the Prince's guards. They'll know that—they daren't enter the city. And you've been waiting here—how long?"

She looked at the clock. "I don't know. I've looked at it too often. It's close on one o'clock now. I don't think I came later than eleven. That only makes two hours after all."

It was inconceivable it should have been only two hours; inconceivable that that clock should still be ticking so loud and calm, would still be ticking whatever had happened just now in this room. Her breath was coming as sharp and painful as if she had run a race. So she had, against him and time. Had she won it? She was still too shaken to be certain, still playing for time.

She pushed the Raleigh over the paper with the verses, it was somehow desperately important to hide them. "I've been reading this," she said, showing him the passage by the sprig. "Was that why you put a marker in it, for the black swans?"

He could not speak. He was glad not to look at her. He bent his head in obedience and read the familiar words to himself. It was many years since he had done so.

"I did not put the marker," he said.

"Do you remember that bit?"

"I knew it once by heart."

Once he had quoted it to Magdalen when he had been a boy home for the holidays from St. Andrews, and she a shy lovely child of fifteen. He remembered the evening he had done that, the songs and dances with his sisters and the friends he had brought from college—over twenty years ago. It must have been Magdalen who had put that sprig of herb between the pages.

Less than ever now could he look at this girl beside him who had waited in such danger to save his life, and whom he had outraged in thought.

He stood staring down at the open book, seeing no more of it, pulling himself together as best he could; but it was not easy, for all his recent thoughts of her had been darkened by the violence of his desire and hatred, and it was hard to realize how different was this witch with the wild hair and subtle eyes from his unjust imagination of her.

"You must have learned it by heart again now," said Louey.

But he still did not move. He said slowly, "What can I say to you, who have done this for me?"

"Nothing, for I've done nothing."

She fell into a chair, feeling utterly weary and disillusioned, the reaction against all her terrors telling her that nothing had been worth them. And she knew now who had put that marker, she had known all along.

"It's all worked out without me and I might just as well have never done anything—it's always the way when one thinks one is being heroic."

"It doesn't make it any the less heroic."

But he still would not look at her. He was still standing by the table, staring down at that book. And under that book were the verses he had written—about her?

All she had gone through had been a fuss about nothing. "They wouldn't have killed me anyway," she said.

"Not if you'd time to explain who you were. But they'd have wanted no witness of their crime and might have struck quickly. In any case, your name would have been blasted for ever."

"Oh well, you know now how little value it is to me."

"I know now how little value I need attach to that," he said, able at last to turn and smile at her. "I don't know why you want me to believe the worst of you, but you lose your pains. I know now what you are."

'And I know now what you believe,' she thought, but found she did not dare to say it, only—"What is that?"

He looked at the pale face framed in the hood, the long line of her throat within the black folds of her cloak, at the proud unconscious grace of her; he went down on one knee and took her hands in his, and kissed them very gently.

"Oh rare black swan," he said.

It was too much. She began to cry softly, helplessly, the tears rolling down her cheeks. "No, no, you are all wrong about me. I am not rare at all." ('A Commonwealth' he had written—he should judge how common.) "I will tell you——" but he interrupted her with a gesture, shaking his head.

"You don't want to hear, then? You think it will be so bad?" But what did it matter? "It doesn't matter to you what I am."

"It will matter to me all my life," he said, "and after, I think." He was standing there by the table as before, but now he was looking down at her and not at the book. "I can promise you nothing of my future," he said, "so why should you give me of your past? It was lived before you met or thought of me. It cannot be mine. Nor is my past free to give you."

"Ah, but whoever thinks of a man's past follies?"

"I was not thinking of them. I was thinking of all those years with my wife, a companionship reaching even further back than our marriage, right into our childhood's days together, and forward into our children. All that has been taken from you. We meet only here and now."

"I know that. Your life has been made up without me. You have no need of me. I can give you nothing."

"You have given affection and hostility, both dear to me."

She was startled into a smile. "Take care," she said. "I have not much to give of the latter."

"And now I have got to get you home. How did you come?"

She told him as she stood up, stumbling with fatigue, and about the man she had knocked down with her ring. "Rupert once showed me how to use it."

He cursed, a thing unusual with him. "Did he see your face?"

"No, I'd a mask, and it was pitch dark; all I could see was that he was short and stout, and his voice was English—or Scottish. We can look at them all in the next few days and see who's got a black eye. It would be too good to be true if it's Lauderdale. Or perhaps the Reverend Robert Baillie. Or even Ned Hyde!"

She was shaking with a sudden wild spurt of laughter, her cloak slipped from her shoulder, and he saw the deep bruised marks of his fingers where he had gripped her arm in that blind moment of passion. She hastily covered it again, blushing furiously and trying to go on talking fast, but it was no good. He was looking at her without hearing anything she said. He did not speak. He put the cloak round her and held her for a moment in his arms, and she put up her face and he kissed it.

Then he took up the sword from the table and held it under his cloak but did not sheath it, and they walked down the stairs and into the streets where now no light showed at all, and along to the door in the wall of the garden at the end of the Voorhout, and there she slipped through and he heard her bolt it after her.

All the way they had never spoken, for it was safer not; and now he walked back alone and up into his empty room where the clock ticked so loud and the lamp that had been lit so long was burning low at last, and looked down at the table, at the *History of the World* that he used to carry himself on his saddle-bow when he rode back to school. He took it up to put away, for he was always careful of that book, and saw beneath it the letter that Hurry had begun to write to him, and the caricature of Hurry that Louey had sketched. He picked that up too to look at it, smiling in delight at its cleverness, and at the courage that could do anything so acute and witty at such a moment.

Beside it was the sheet of paper with the rhymes that he had scribbled at odd moments. These then were what she had been reading and had covered with that quick nervous gesture when she showed him the Raleigh.　He stood looking down at them, and wished she had not read them.

Then he sat down and wrote:

> 'The golden laws of love shall be
> 　Beneath thine image hung.
> A single heart—a simple eye—
> 　A true and constant tongue.
> Let no man for more loves pretend
> 　Than he has hearts in store.
> True love begun will never end—
> 　Love one and love no more.'

XVII

NEXT morning Montrose went to see the Queen of Bohemia and told her that if he succeeded in his enterprise in Scotland he would have the presumption on his return to ask for the hand of her daughter Louise.

They were walking in her garden where the sun was shining again and the birds shouting for joy after last night's rain. Elizabeth paused to observe a blackbird that was pulling a particularly juicy fat worm out of the lawn; all her attention seemed to be focussed on this fascinating object.

At last she said in a low voice that seemed to come from a long way off, "I am so glad it is Louey. She is my favourite too, really, though I had begun to think Sophie might prove even more amusing." Then she moved on towards the bench in the summer-house, for she suddenly found that she was tired, a discovery so remarkable that she was convinced she must be ill; or perhaps she had grown old, all in a few minutes, and no doubt it was quite right she should do so. She was fifty-three, though she could never believe it, nor anyone else, and this man beside her, whom she had been thinking of as near her own age, was not quite thirty-seven and wanted to marry her daughter.

She struggled with a suffocating sense of indignation. She did not know why she should have given that complacent answer without thinking it over first. He had startled her into it and she had spoken to gain time, but why should she be discreet and unlike herself, why should she be afraid of him? And she struggled now to find reasons for that unreasoning indignation, but here her inveterate honesty gave her small chance.

He was too old for Louey, that was it; eleven years were too big a difference, there had only been a few months between herself and her husband. Well, but there were sixteen years between herself and Montrose, and she had never noticed it.

And rank (it was odd she had not thought of that first), he was not of royal birth. But he was chief of as proud a family in Scotland as hers, and her own Scots blood and traditions told her that that was of more worth than any of these petty European princelings.

But what was this she had heard (and here her indignation did indeed swell till she felt it would choke her) of his being so devoted to his wife that he had never even looked at another woman since her death?——except perhaps herself, came the inevitable afterthought, her humour now also taking sides against her, while her sense and knowledge of the world insisted on reminding her that his wife had been dead four years now, and that a man of his age who had been happily married so long was unlikely to live without any woman for the rest of his life.

No, it was all quite natural, and that was what made it so depressing, she supposed. People did not live in fairy-tales any longer, and it was no use wishing they did.

She smiled as they sat down on the seat, and told him she had been expecting this for some time.

"Liar! Liar! Liar!" shouted the blackbird, who had swallowed his worm. Why on earth should she say all these ridiculous things like any other mother with marrying daughters, even like that humbug Amelia? And she flatly contradicted herself.

"I didn't expect it one bit," she said, "though I'd thought perhaps you might be in love."

That was true, for he had been more distrait with her lately, and damnably polite, she had wondered if anything were wrong. She had noticed nothing in Louey—perhaps she did not notice her daughters enough.

"But why Louey?" she asked. Yes, why indeed? When Etta would have made him such a much better wife, so neat and sweet and pretty and good, with all the meekness and domestic virtues that she credited to the late Lady of Montrose. From all she had heard, his wife must have been very like Etta—it would have been more faithful of him to have loved Etta. And Louey would not make a good wife at all, he must see that, yet how perverse men were!

He was answering her question with a smile: "For all the reasons, no doubt, that make her your favourite, her laughter and her candour and her likeness to you."

"Oh, Jamie Graham, you're a wise man and I'm an old fool."

"To give consent? For you have given it, haven't you?"

"Would I dare refuse it to a Graham? Your house has got the better of the Stuarts too often for that. You'll have to ask King Charles' consent too—but he'll never refuse that to his Viceroy in Scotland, since your betrothal is not to be till then. But why wait for it till you return?"

"Because that will make it the worse for her if I do not return. I do not wish her to be tied to me in any way until I have a fairer chance of life to offer her."

"Then why speak to me of it now at all?"

"Because," he said simply, "I wish to be tied to her."

She laughed, and wondered if it had as cracked and harsh a sound in his ears as it had in hers. "Go and find her," she said, "and when you have told her, send her to me here. But perhaps you have already told her."

"No, I have not done that."

"Send her to me first," she said, "and then she can return to you. I can't wait for the lovers' scene to finish."

He went; and she watched him go through the sunlit garden and into the dark doorway of the house, straight and vigorous, walking with the long easy springy stride of a man who finds it nothing to walk twenty miles in a day over the heather. She had never known a man like this before; if she had, her life would have been very different. But men like this were not born in every generation. It was Louey, of the next generation, and not yet twenty-six, who had the luck.

Why Louey? Louey was like her, he had said, and not for flattery, for he did not flatter. Unintrospective, she had never thought that Louey was like her. Now she thought of it and wondered with a slight shock if that were why they were apt to be attracted by the same man. That handsome rascal Goring, how they had laughed together with him! Nothing was sacred to him, not even Sir Philip Sidney's dying words. 'My greed is greater than thine,' he had said as he snatched Louey's glass of wine.

And de l'Epinay, poor de l'Epinay—no laughing matter there. Her youngest son, that reckless, furious boy Philip, had killed de l'Epinay and she had never been able to give him her real forgiveness, though Rupert had forced her to make a show of it. She knew now, three years later, what de l'Epinay had been, a charming scamp, a professional lover, a boaster of his conquests. That made no difference to the fact that for the first time in her life, at fifty, she had been conquered by his appeal to her senses.

But Louey had never been really in love with de l'Epinay: that was what had made it so cruel. She had only amused herself with him and taken him away from herself as much as she could.

It flashed across her mind for the first time that this might have been in part to protect her mother from making too great a fool of herself. Unbearable fancy! It would be better to believe what Amelia had so industriously insinuated, that Louey had been de l'Epinay's mistress. No, it would not—good God, it would not! And all the less now that she was to go to Montrose.

She sat stiff and cold in the sunlight, and all she said when Louey stood before her was, "Were you ever de l'Epinay's mistress?"

"No, Mother."

Elizabeth raised her great melancholy eyes from under their arched lids and saw her daughter's eyes answer her as clearly as her words. So that was well. Odd that she should have wanted to ask it all this time and never been able to till now.

Then she saw her daughter's face on its own account and was shocked at its pallor and the heavy rings under the eyes.

"What has Jamie Graham been saying to you?"

"Nothing. He told me you wanted me here."

"Then is there any reason for your looking like a piece of white paper with two ink smudges? You might have been up all night."

"I might," said Louey recklessly, "but I wasn't. I went to bed late, though."

"Bah! I've no patience with girls who need eight hours' sleep always. I often sit up till five and it makes no odds. Run away and apply your paint-box to your cheeks, it's the best use you can make of it."

"But, Mother, why did you send for me? Did you only want to ask that of de l'Epinay?"

"Only? Is that 'only' to you? I've waited three years to ask it. Now go back to your lover and answer what he asks you."

"My—lover? What has he been saying?"

"Get him to tell you. He's still there?"

"In the studio, where he found me."

"Ah yes, painting is far more useful to a girl than music. I ought to have remembered that, when I made Honthorst do his portrait."

"Mother?"

"What the devil is the matter with the girl? Why do you look at me like that?"

"You sound so"—('old' was what Louey had nearly said)—"so sad."

Elizabeth boxed her ears.

The bewildered Louey ran to the studio. Montrose was sitting at the table, looking at a drawing which he laid down as she burst into the room.

"What have you been saying to Mother? I think she's mad. She sends for me, and then all she asks is, was I de l'Epinay's mistress?"

"Is that so small an 'all'? Of how many should she have asked it?"

"No—but don't laugh. What does it all mean?"

"That I have asked her consent for me to propose for your hand when or if I return from Scotland."

That paper-white face of hers went a deep pink, the 'ink smudges' blazed. "And why, in the name of God?"

"For some, at least, of the usual reasons," he said, still amused, but in the same instant realized that she was as unhappy as she was angry.

"The other reasons, I suppose, being that I was at your house half last night and that you owe me reparation in case it should be discovered—oh yes, and to clear me in Hurry's squinny eyes! As if it mattered what he thinks!"

"I have seen Hurry this morning," he said sternly. "You have no need to defy what he thinks. And you pay me small compliment in bringing him into the question."

She hung her head ruefully, her face already white again, all courage draining out of her at his tone.

He took her hands and looked down at her tired eyelids; had she slept at all after he had taken her back last night?

"Don't you think," he said, smiling at her, "that I'm more likely to consider my wishes than Hurry's opinions?"

"Ah, but it isn't your wish. You don't want to be mixed up with a woman at all—or when you do, it's against your true will and you are angry both with yourself and me. You hated me last night when you came into your room and found me there, and you'd been hating me for days before that. Oh, but now," she cried, tearing her hands from his, "you have made me more ashamed than if you—than if——" But with all her outspokenness she could not say it. She turned from him and fell into a chair, pressing her hands over her eyes, but still seeing his face as it had been last night when he had thrown his sword on the table and come towards her.

He looked at her bowed head and wished he had not hurt her.

"Every word you say is true," he said. "What you are remembering against me from last night is true also. Will you remember it against me always? I did not ask you to forgive me for it, but I suppose I hoped it. Are you telling me I may not hope it?"

She shook her head, but she still could not look at him. He was walking up and down the studio when he next spoke. "I have mis-judged you more badly than any man had any right to do. In spite of that, I insist on your not misjudging me. You have got to believe this, do you hear? I did not want ever to love again, I told you I never could, and in telling you that, I have come to do so."

He walked to the end of the room and back, then stopped before her chair.

"Well?" he said in a low voice, and then, "Are you never going to look at me again?"

She raised her head at last; her strange slanting eyes were smiling at him, though her mouth trembled. "I will try to believe that I persuaded rather than tricked you into loving me."

"Of all damnable sophistries!" He sat on the table opposite her and took that pointed chin between his finger and thumb, tilting it towards him. "You exasperate me into loving you, that's the truth of it. I can't dispense with the pleasure of quarrelling with you."

He turned her chin this way and that. "I've been wanting to do this ever since I first saw it," he said reflectively, and his deep voice made her shiver with delight. "There was a line in a play I once saw:

> 'View well her face, and in that little round
> You may discern a world's variety.'"

"I remember," she said quickly, "and the name of the play gives the best rhyme and the best reason to your refrain of 'never loving more'; and it is this, ''Tis Pity She's a Whore.'"

He seized her by the shoulders and shook her hard, then caught her to him and kissed her, both laughing until they kissed again. They seemed suddenly to have known each other for years.

"Well," he said, "have I your consent?"

"Consent? When you have given me your marching-orders?"

"If I only could!"

If only she were not a princess, first cousin to his King, he could have insisted on marriage now, and they would have had at least these few brief weeks together. But 'it is not thus that the marriages of princes are arranged,' and no one would believe that the scandal of such a hasty match had any other reason than to avoid the still worse scandal of an illegitimate birth. And she would be left to face it alone.

He did not speak his wish, and hoped she did not read it, for the deeper they went in love, the worse might be her fate.

But she was following her own thoughts. "One thing I will mutiny for," she said.—"No, I'll tell you later."

"Why not now?"

But she was silent except for a deep sigh of peace, leaning against him as he sat on the edge of the table, her head on his shoulder. The downward curves of her face were curiously beautiful now that he could see them thus at rest; Leonardo would have painted her like this. Her body was limp with fatigue, yet he could feel the strength and vitality of those slender limbs; she made him think of the bluebells on the moor at home, harebells she would call them, the drooping delicate head and thread-like stem that seemed too fragile to survive a breeze, yet could rise and live again after the most savage storm had beaten them to the earth. This girl had her mother's tireless spirit and physique, she was not like Magdalen.

'It's well she's strong,' he thought, and the fear of what she might suffer through him, the fear he had sworn he would never feel again on behalf of a woman, stood before him once again so sharp and clear that he pressed her face against his shoulder as if to prevent her seeing it also.

With her eyes shut against his coat she felt the tenderness of that protective hand as poignant as the stab of a knife. 'Oh, why can't we stay safe for ever?' she thought, and then—'but if we were safe, he would not be wanting to protect me.'

She could feel his heart beating in strong steady strokes under her cheek. "Don't think so hard," she said. "I can hear every word you don't say."

"What do you hear?"

"That you are afraid for me. You need not be. If I have

nothing else to look back on all my life but this moment, it will make me glad to have lived."

"I thank God for your courage."

"No, it's sheer sense. You cannot be bound, so let us not bind ourselves even by hope. We'll give no hostages to fortune."

"Not yet certainly, if you speak of our children," he answered, smiling down at that sweet serious face that flashed instantly into laughter.

"You are too quick," she complained. "I did not think you would have read Bacon."

"Are these, then, the grounds of your mutiny—that I am not to hope for you?"

"As I promise not to hope for you. We know we love—is that so small a thing? No one and nothing—*nothing*—can take it from us."

She was clinging to him now, burrowing her face into his coat like a frightened child, all her instinctive action belying the high courage of her words.

He soothed her head with his hand, stroking it again and again, without words, for there was nothing he could say.

Time took on another perspective. Years did not count; they had passed as unnoticeably as the forgotten days in childhood. But this moment, a thing as light and transitory as a butterfly's wing, blown towards them on the winds of chance among all the cross-currents of that violent and uncertain time, this moment between them now mercifully expanded as a bubble expands when it is blown—it became a world free of the outside world, where almost every country was tortured by civil wars, and this little town where they loved was a battlefield of opposing hates; a world free of time, of before and after, as long as life itself.

XVIII

*T*HEY had gone to Rhenen for the summer; there was no point in staying on at The Hague, for Charles had gone to Breda, and with him Montrose, who had not needed Elizabeth's passionate warnings 'for God's sake' not to leave the King's side or 'Your enemies will work all to the ruin of yourself and your friends.'

Queen Henrietta Maria was sending her Majordomo, the jolly Lord Jermyn, to Holland, and that boded no good; whatever the pretext of his visit, Elizabeth, speaking out of her knowledge and suspicion of her sister-in-law, was certain that its real purpose was to get in touch with Lauderdale and the Commissioners and work together against 'wicked Jamie Graham,' though she tried hard to assure herself as well as him that this could 'lead to nothing, as the King is constant to his principles.'

What Montrose thought of that he did not say, nor did Louey; but Sophie thought that Charles, like the rest of men, would be 'to one thing constant never.' She spoke of her sister's betrothal to Montrose as his reward for his service to the King in Scotland, 'and if it succeeds and he is made Viceroy of Scotland again it will not, I suppose, be too much for him to ask, since he will have done it through his courage and ability alone.'

This patronizing tone from her younger sister had small power now to annoy Louey; she was too anxious. And she knew how anxious poor Sophie was too for her own concerns, and that pride of rank was only one small extra piece of armour for her to buckle on in her struggle with fortune.

Louey, whose handsome young cousin William of Brandenburg had waited four years for her, since she was fifteen, until in sheer desperation he had married the Dowager Amelia's eldest daughter instead, knew well that in one's teens it is harder to wait than to do anything else. To give up is easier. Sophie was showing strong signs of giving up, or at least of securing another string to her bow.

Her eldest brother, Carl, now installed at last as the Elector Palatine as his father had been, had invited his youngest and favourite sister to come and stay with him. The country of Germany had been a shambles during the Thirty Years' War and was now a wreck; the beautiful old castle of rose-red brick at Heidelberg, that had been their father's and mother's happy and peaceful home for the first few years of their married life, was mostly in ruins. Carl was losing no time in getting it repaired, and hoped that part of it at any rate would be habitable by the time Sophie came to him.

Sophie hoped so too, for at present Carl was living down in a square in the town below the Castle, at a private citizen's house called Commissariat House, which had a low sound; there was certainly not much point in being royal these days.

But she firmly intended to visit him for all that her mother, who had never yet tried to manage any of her daughter's matrimonial affairs, begged her to consider seriously how she would be throwing away her chances with Charles. Sophie was in that mood of piqued pride that made her long to throw them away, if only they were sufficiently solid for the rejection to be noticed.

She would talk of nothing but Heidelberg and Carl, and hotly defended his demand for the gilded leather hangings that used to be in their father's palace and now covered the many cracks in the walls of the Wassenaar Hof. Of course Carl ought to have all the former belongings he could collect, to patch up his residence and give it some semblance of royalty again; she would not admit in the many arguments with her sisters that it was hard on their mother to find herself poorer instead of better off through her son's inheritance to the property for which she had struggled on his behalf for nearly thirty years.

Elizabeth was indeed so much the poorer that she had once again to set about selling her hunters, and this at Rhenen, where the hares and deer in the woods above the house, and the springy heathy soil, gave such good sport, was agonizing. A bay gelding was left for

Louey, since the girl was the only one of her daughters who loved riding as much as herself, and it was a shame to deprive her of it at her age.

Elizabeth was determined not to let herself sag under the lack of her wonted riding as she had done before. Hard walking, sawing wood, and shooting at a butt with the long-bow were now her chief exercises, and she urged 'Jamie Graham' to pay them a visit and see if his archery had stood the test of time since the days when he had been champion at St. Andrews. But she knew that he could not come, indeed she urged him not to leave the King, 'for without question there is nothing that will be omitted to ruin you and your friends, and so the King at last.'

And always she begged him to believe that she was 'ever your most constant affectionate friend, Elizabeth.'

There were many visitors at Rhenen. Lord Craven was there on and off through the summer, helping with the expenses as usual, but allowing himself an occasional private treat. He found a superb floridly carved chimney-piece in the little town when out walking there one day with Louey, and for once did not present it to her mother, but had it packed up at great expense and labour and sent to his old manor-house of Stokesay near the Shropshire village that bore his name, Craven Arms. An enchanting place it sounded to Louey, in its deep wooded valley with the Tudor rooms at one end perching like nests on top of the massive Norman structure. But he had not seen it since he had lived there as a boy with his mother.

"Are you not homesick for it?" she demanded, and he replied, "Sometimes. But what would 'home' be if you were none of you there with me?"

Would he then never marry and have children of his own to inherit his great wealth and the beautiful houses that he let to strangers? She did not ask him, for she knew he would not, and that as long as her mother was in exile, so would he be.

At least his love brought him more happiness than poor Eliza, who had lost all spirit since she had heard of Descartes' death from his pneumonia. It was all the fault of the young Queen Christina of Sweden, Eliza said. "He has been killed by the perverse vanity of that woman who can do nothing like anyone else and so must have him drive to her palace at five o'clock in the morning to read and talk philosophy with her. Well, he's passed out of her collection," she added cruelly.

For the bereavement of her friend was not the worst thing that had happened to Eliza; it was the bitterness of her disillusionment in him. He had left behind him a letter of fulsome thanks and gratification in answer to Christina's invitation to her Court, which Christina had made public in self-justification at his death. It proved a tragic testimony to the limitations of philosophy.

"And all that he got by it is death," said Eliza.

"'Death is a tremendous thing,'" Louey quoted. "He would appreciate it better than Christina's Court."

"Do you then truly believe in a future life?"

"Ask me later. I don't know yet."

There were visitors from the French Court too, talking twice as much and twice as fast as their Dutch guests. They told of the poor Queen Henrietta Maria in Paris, an inconsolable widow, only longing for the return of her son Charles, to whom she was devoted. It was cruelty to keep them apart, so they said in their bright practical voices; her only comfort had been in her little girl Minette, whose childish prattle had saved her mother's reason under the shock of her husband's dreadful death.

They sat and talked and talked. It rained, and the garden and the waving trees, and the rustling river seen here and there through them, were like a country at the bottom of the sea—so Louey thought, talking in her heart to Montrose, as she moved restlessly through the shining rooms, noticing the blue tiles running along in a little dotted line at the base of the white walls, the china bowls of flowers, the treasures from India and Japan. This idle busy house was full of people talking, playing games, making music, thinking thoughts all so different from her own. She leaned against the window-sill and looked out on the great green shapes of the trees in the rain, and the roses on the terrace drowned in rain, and heard the quacking of ducks in the moat below, that was now domesticated to a pond.

Behind her through the open doorway came the sound of the French voices talking neatly and precisely as if for the sheer sensual pleasure of the sound of the words—'a gross delicatesse,' thought Louey, 'of the earth earthy, and yet exquisite in appreciation.' For they were talking of music, saying charming and witty things about it, and as they talked, someone picked up his lute, and the tiny music of a minuet came stealing in on all those words, intruding on them, covering that rattle of words with a tinkling yet eternal sound, 'like the ticking of the old French clock here in this room, where the Cupids hammer out their arrows on an anvil to count the hours of advancing time '—until those gross and appreciative voices died into listening silence, and the tune played on alone a little time, then died too.

But the clock ticked on, the Cupids lifted and struck their hammers to tell four o'clock (and so long a time since they had struck three), the voices began talking about something else, the rain cleared and the sun shone, those visitors went away and others came, and still Montrose could not say in his letters when he would come.

Then he came, suddenly, with no warning, one afternoon while she was out riding in a man's coat and breeches such as she often wore while riding in the country, and she came up through the garden to see him walking on the terrace with her mother, talking low and earnestly, and her first wild throb of delight was shot through with pain that she had been away.

"How long have you been here?" she cried as she ran up the terrace steps. ('How much time have I missed of him?') But he had not been long, less than half an hour, Elizabeth assured her, laughing at her, yet in spite of that, Louey could see how grave she was. "What has happened?" she asked at once; and now the fact that he was there was a fear, a terror, for what had happened to bring him there so suddenly and to make her mother look so grave?

He kissed her hand, the hair falling forward over his face with suitable cavalier grace as he did so in the gesture he would make before all the world; but the grasp of those strong nervous fingers round hers was for her alone, and the hard pressure of his lips.

It was her mother who answered her, over that bent gracious head.

"They have killed Dorislaus," she said.

"Dorislaus?" For a moment Louey could not remember, it seemed so oddly unimportant. Dorislaus, the renegade Dutch lawyer, whom the Parliament had had to call in to try King Charles, since they could find no English lawyer to consent to such a travesty of English justice? What could it matter that he was killed?

"How can that affect you?"

"It affects all of us," he said. "The Dutch have no sympathy with him, they are saying that this is more rightly to be called an 'execution' than the King's murder, to which he gave a false legality. But they cannot let one of their citizens be killed out of hand without protest, and the men who killed him were my servants and have been warned to leave the city to escape trial. That shows how little the authorities wish to proceed against them. For all that, they are bound to act, for Holland is alarmed; they complain that they cannot have all these warring factions at such close quarters in their city without danger to themselves."

"Just what they said when Rupert's ships and the Parliament's were shut up in the same harbour together," exclaimed Elizabeth, "and very reasonably no doubt, but they stood it, and why not now?"

"They have stood it too long, Madam, that is why. There have been other plots, an attempt made by the Covenanters to murder me some time ago." (He did not look at Louey as he said it, but gave the information carelessly, to both her and her mother.) "They say that with all these attacks from one faction and another their own peaceable lives will not be safe. Prince William has had to tell King Charles that he can give him shelter no longer, and he and his followers must leave at once."

"Where for?" asked Louey. "For Ireland then?"

"It is not possible yet. Ormonde has not been able to co-ordinate Ireland as he had hoped, and Cromwell's army is shortly setting out for there. It would be too dangerous for the King. No, he is going to Paris, to the Queen-Mother."

"Oh, but———!" she cried, and stopped. There was no need to say it. All three of them knew the danger of that.

"And Ned Hyde?"

"Will go to Spain with Cottington."

"Is that necessary?"

"It is to him, it seems. He is well satisfied, and so should we all be, for King Charles has now finally rejected the Covenanters' terms. He has broken with them altogether. He has given me my commission, and sworn in writing that he will do nothing in any matter relating to Scotland without first consulting me. So there is nothing left for me to do now but start on my travels again."

"And when to Scotland?"

"As soon as I have revisited Sweden and Germany, where King Charles has nominated me as his ambassador, to raise money loans and war material. And the sooner, the more likely to succeed."

"So you will leave here———?"

"This evening," he said, "for Breda."

It was Elizabeth who exclaimed, "But you cannot ride all night!"

"There is a full moon, clear sky, and a road—better conditions than I've had on most night marches!"

Louey was silent, wondering what was troubling her most. That he must leave to-night? No, that did not matter. Whenever he left, it would be as though he had spent only a moment here. Already he was half away, thinking of what he must next do, and next and next, now that at last his work was to begin.

That Charles was going to Paris?—Hyde to Spain? Yes, that was it. These were worse news than that Montrose would now leave Holland. But were they? Wasn't she being nervous, foolish, losing her courage really only because Montrose was leaving—just as she had vowed she would not do?

Charles had rejected Argyll and openly declared for Montrose, appointed him his ambassador, had sworn in writing that he would do nothing in Scottish matters without him—and Hyde, who knew him best, was 'satisfied.'

"Satisfied because he is going to Spain, the selfish pig!" she broke out. "Hyde's been wanting that for weeks past, I know!"

Her mother laughed. "Poor faithful Ned! He's less selfish by a long way than most of them."

"There's no room for anyone to be selfish in this game."

"You can't alter human nature," said Elizabeth.

She left them abruptly. It would be tiresome to see him looking at Louey, but it was more tiresome to see him avoid looking at her.

They walked down the terraces towards the river. He seemed suddenly to have finished all there was to tell.

"I've never seen you wear the breeches before," he said; "is it a warning for our married life?"

"Or for your next campaign? Shall I join you in Scotland? Why should I not? Wasn't there a woman led a troop under your command in your earlier campaigns?"

"A Dalziel. That family are all wild as wolves."

"And am I too tame?"

"I'm not. I was not in love with her, that is the difference."

Princesses had fought in the Fronde wars in France, King Charles' own first cousin, La Grande Mademoiselle, was even now showing herself off as a warrior. Why should it be impossible for her?

But looking at his face, she knew it was, and would not waste more time on it. But there was no time, however much she saved it, to say one-millionth part of all she had wanted to say when next

R

they met again; nor would the words come into her head; they had fled, all of them, and all her thoughts.

She knew only that she was walking here beside him down to the river, and that he was no longer reaching out towards his enterprise, as he had been when with her and her mother, but was with her now utterly.

"What will you do when I am gone?" he asked.

"Paint, and pray. I think I shall pray best while I am painting."

He thought how love to Magdalen had meant possession and all the sweet earthly cares of home and children, the quiet continuity of life; but that it was Louey's art, and power of faith in things outside her own experience, that had set him free to love her. Whatever happened to him, her true life should be beyond the power of human wreckage.

"Pray for what will last," he said, "then your prayers will be answered. What we get out of life is nothing, what we give to it is all."

"Shall I not pray for your victory and your life?"

"Yes, if it be God's will. But we can neither read nor force that will. 'Oh Lord, *do* it, or it will be the worse for you!' I've heard Warriston pray so."

She looked up to see the laugh in his face while he said that, and saw it pass like a shadow as his gaze grew clear and grave again, holding her own.

But in rebellion she cried out, "How could I ever believe in God if He let you be defeated?"

"One cannot always tell defeat at the time. God sees further than we do. A cause has been won by its defeats."

"Oh, but is this cause worth it? Young Charles is not—and Scotland turned sour and hideous under Argyll. Why should you give all—all—perhaps your life?" She gasped, for she had been trying not to say it, but now it came and she could not help it, and she cried, "If you give your life, it will be for nothing."

He said, "Did the three Wise Men ever trouble as to what had become of their gifts, when the Babe to whom they gave them had died upon the Cross?"

She hid her face from him till it should be calmer, turned aside and looked down at the river that flowed on and on through the trees towards the sea. She knew that his words would echo on and on through her mind to the end of her life.

The reflected light from the river glimmered up over her face, giving it the clear and mobile look of water. He stood by her, watching it; then he put his hands on her shoulders and turned her towards him. "Do you wish you had never met me?" he asked.

"No, no, *no!*"

"Yet I'm leaving you to the worst of it. To go out and fight, perhaps to die for what we love, that would be easy; to live for it, on through the years, keeping it fresh and living, that is a harder thing. If I have to die for what we both love, then remember that I leave it to you to cherish and pray for."

She knew that he meant more than her uncle's and her cousin's cause.

He sat with them there that evening at dinner; they had two or three paid musicians playing from time to time in the little painted gallery, an unusual luxury, and doubtless paid for, like most other luxuries in their odd establishment, by the little man with the pleasant ugly face who sat at the further end of the table, 'True Towser,' the first Earl of Craven.

He had been here most evenings since they came; and everything else was the same as on other evenings, the shining glass and porcelain, the great bowl of glossy fruit, the wide-awake faces of the flowers; everything was the same, but everything was different, for Montrose was sitting there on their mother's right hand. Louey could see his face across the table, its strong lines softened by the light of the long heart-shaped flames of the tall candles in the centre,

and those clear steady eyes that looked towards her mother as she
talked, but rested in the pauses on herself.

Behind him the door windows stood open on to the terrace, and
she could see the bats spinning their mazy dance through the twilit
air, looping the shadows together, minute harbingers of the darkness
that had already swallowed up the great shapes of the further trees
by the river, and was now advancing slowly round the house.

White moths fluttered in from that dimming scene; they spun
above the white flowers on the table and round the candles; notes
of music fell soft and sparkling through the warm air, and through
it all came the sound of her mother's voice, varied, vivid, in brilliant
gay talk, the voice of all the charming women in the world, rippling
on and on through men's lives to make them forget the darkness of
pain and death by bloody wars and cruel fortune, forget that kings
have died horribly and their servants must fight for them, to make
them believe that life is a glorious thing that lasts for ever.

Behind that voice Louey listened to the murmur of the river
flowing out there through their garden down to the sea, into the
North Sea—and on the other side of it, sailing north, to the land
called Scotland, cold and mountainous, where hundreds and thousands of men lay in wait to kill the man who sat here at table with
them, and whose eyes were resting on herself.

Sometimes she tried to tug her thoughts into shape, to attend, not
to the light talk now glancing round her and into which she found
it quite easy every now and then to fling some laughing comment or
scrap of mocking description, but to what he had told them this
afternoon of Dorislaus' death and its effect on all their plans. Perhaps it was a good thing it had happened—you could never tell
results, and it had certainly hurried matters and brought them to a
climax.

They were all setting off now on their different paths, and as
Montrose himself had said, the sooner the better. Cromwell was
planning this enormous expeditionary force to Ireland, and that had
seemed disastrous, but it would give Montrose his best possible

chance in Scotland. With Scotland behind him as it had been before, he might sweep down into England before Cromwell could get back from Ireland—yes, it might all be the best thing that could have happened.

Why was it so important for her to discover what was the best thing that could have happened? She could not tell what that was now; no one could, not even the man who sat there beside her mother, the light of the candles shining on his eyes and that grave smile. How could he look so quiet, so secure?—yes, that was the word. Wasn't he tossing these questions over and over in his mind as she was?

But looking at him she knew that he was not, that he had made his decisions and did not feel their possible event was for him to decide. 'Do your duty, gentlemen; leave the management to me, the event to God.' That was what he had told his terrified officers when their small remnant of an army had been surprised at Dundee. Looking at him, she too could take those marching-orders to herself.

But that was because he was there—and he would not be there for ever, not even for half an hour more; another quarter of an hour and he would have gone out into that darkness outside, and to-morrow they would sit here without him, and the next day and the next,—for how long—'how long, oh Lord, how long?' These summer nights glittering with relentless starlight when she would wake to find herself so awake, so alive, how many would have to string themselves together before she could know—know for certain—that she would see him again?

'Know for certain'—that one might never know, however peaceful and secure life lay around them. This moment must pass, and all the other moments in their lives, and their lives too, however long they lived, they too would be things of the past, and that gallant head be laid low in the grave, however peacefully death might come to it. How then could he be secure?

And suddenly she knew that she could only find security by

attaching it to where it belonged. Her love was secure because it belonged to eternity, not time; all her agony of spirit came from confusing their issues, from trying to attach her happiness to the material results of chance, like the small spider that this morning attached the end of its web to her knee as she sat drawing in the garden, and never saw that its whole elaborate structure would be destroyed the moment she moved.

Happiness must be independent of luck or success or the conditions of this troubled world, of wars and revolutions, or it would wave like a torn cobweb in the wind. 'Lay up for yourselves treasures in heaven, where neither moth nor rust doth corrupt, and where thieves do not break through nor steal.'

Now for the first time she saw that 'heaven' was not hereafter, but round us and within us, a condition not of the body but the soul, not of time but eternity.

In that instant, as compellingly as if she had seen a vision of Him, she knew that God was there with them, all around them and in them: in little Craven's tender smile for her mother, in her mother's gay courage now flaunting for others with no consciousness of herself, in Eliza's sad thoughts of Descartes, yes, and in Etta's fantastic dishes of salads and sweets prettier than she had ever made them, to adorn this evening for her sister and the man to whom she must say good-bye,—'And in him,' she thought finally, her eyes, that had roved startled round the table in the shock of this discovery, coming to rest again upon his face.

And he, watching her as he had been doing all through this evening, saw the strange light come into her face, a sudden peace that moved him more than had all her attempts to conquer the fear in her eyes.

He asked her when they came to say good-bye what it had been, and she said in that light voice of hers, "I think that for an instant I saw God, and not even only in your face! Give me a charm that I may do so again."

They were out on the terrace in the thin blue darkness of the summer night, for all the company had left the dining-room and the lights there had been put out.

He said, "I will tell you a hymn so old that it has the ring in it of a heathen charm, as all my good Presbyterian Scots held it to be, for it was sung by my wild Irishry whom they called savages. It is Saint Patrick's own charm, the Irish say,—they called it his Breast-Plate."

"And you a good Presbyterian to be telling me that! What is it?"

He took her hands and put them together, those long supple fingers, in the attitude of prayer, and held them so between his own, against his heart, his face dark above them, his eyes dark hollows, yet she could feel them upon her as his deep voice came close to her out of the night, in the insurgent rhythm of those mighty words:

> "'I bind unto myself this day
> The strong Name of the Trinity.
> I bind unto myself this day
> The power of Heaven,
> The light of the Sun,
> The whiteness of Snow,
> The force of Fire.
>
> "'The power of the Resurrection with the Ascension,
> The power of the Coming to the sentence of Judgment,
> I have set around me all these powers
> Against the incantations of false prophets,
> Against all knowledge which blinds the soul of man.'"

As if to answer and accompany that incantation from more than a thousand years ago, the church tower that overhung the garden wall broke into a peal of bells; their triumphant notes sprang out and galloped away through the night like the clarions of an army with banners.

Louey laughed wildly, clinging to him in that turmoil of magnificent sound. "Saint Kunera is answering you," she said, "and she was a princess of Orkney as long ago as Saint Patrick in Ireland."

"It is to Orkney that I am going."

"You take her blessing with you, then, with Saint Patrick's charm——"

"Which is in the name of Christ," he answered.

> "'Christ with me, Christ before me,
>   Christ behind me, Christ within me,
>   Christ in the fort,
>   Christ in the chariot seat,
>   Christ in the poop,
>   Christ in the heart of every man who thinks of me,
>   Christ in the mouth of every man who speaks to me.'"

As he and his men rode away, she heard those words still thundering against her heart, long after the thud of his horses' hoofs had been swallowed up by the engulfing night.

BOOK III

THE HIGH LANDS

I

NOT till the following spring was Montrose back again in Scotland. He was no longer staying as the honoured and flattered guest of one reigning monarch after another, with the Kings of Denmark and Poland, the restlessly brilliant young Queen of Sweden, the princely Electors of Germany. Since he had left Holland a few months ago, all of these had been his hosts and vied with each other in promising help to his Sovereign, the Emperor even calling a meeting at Frankfort for the purpose. A recruiting sergeant on a superior, even imperial scale, that was what Montrose called himself, using his scarlet baton of Field-Marshal of the Empire for the purpose, and in the imperially sumptuous surroundings which he disliked; but, "once a recruiting sergeant always a recruiting sergeant, and it's what I've always had to waste more than half my time on," he now said on the jovially grumbling note that showed him to be at last at ease again in the old soldierly surroundings that he had missed so long.

"*Waste?*" interpolated Jack Hurry, cocking an ironic eyebrow like a jagged tuft of straw.

The two had met again in Caithness. Hurry had done his job well. Sent on with an advance guard to make the first landing, he had marched south and secured the Ord of Caithness, where Montrose joined him after landing near John o' Groats and making a preliminary dash on Thurso to summon the lairds of the country-side to take the oath of allegiance. The island of Orkney had been the base of the little expeditionary force, once they could make it from the ice-bound harbours of Denmark. Some of their ships could not make it, and had been dashed to pieces on the rocks of the islands, losing all the troops and ammunition on board.

And in that strange little town of Kirkwall in Orkney, where the clear spring daylight never seemed to fade, but painted all the outlines of the harbour and the grey stone houses, the breaking waves and the low hills, with a pale luminous edge until far into the night, there in that remote Northern air that was yet as strangely mild and soft as of one of the Islands of the Blest, two of the best leaders of the expedition died of pneumonia contracted on the frightful voyage to that temperate climate through the intemperate winter seas. These were the Earls of Kinnoull and of Morton.

Morton's wife was governess to the little Princess Henriette, youngest child of the late King. Now she would have to leave the little girl, 'Minette' (her brother Charles always called her that because she was small and dainty as a kitten), with her mother, the Queen Henrietta Maria, in Paris, and return to her own children and estates in Scotland.

Like the faintest echo of some plaintively courtly tune played all those hundreds of miles away, Montrose could imagine the minor storm against him that this would arouse in Henrietta Maria's breast, her certainty that whatever was done by him or happened to him was somehow contrived by his own perverse inclination to plague herself. He could smile at it here on the north-east coast of Scotland, yet could he afford to smile even at a crumpled rose-leaf in the bed of a far-off queen ? For the Queen's opinions and prejudices profoundly influenced her son Charles. Who would be left to influence her in Montrose's favour now Lady Morton, his passionate partisan, had gone ?

Worst of all, the Commissioners held a warrant under the Great Seal of Scotland to borrow £300,000 to give King Charles, if he would come to terms with them; if not, they were to give him no money at all. To all those who knew the really desperate straits of the young King, his family and followers, such a bribe seemed as though it must prove irresistible. 'I do not yet know of any actual death from lack of bread, which yet I wonder at,' Hyde had written lately in his carefully moderate fashion.

Hyde himself was no longer with Charles. He had at last accomplished that appointment on a mission as foreign ambassador, and was slowly journeying south in the early spring sunshine to-

wards the golden fruit and heavy-scented white blossom of the
orange groves of Spain that had dangled so temptingly in his dreams
as he lay racked with rheumatism in his damp Dutch lodging. To
be a traveller and ambassador without money was proving no such
idyll, as he was bitterly learning. But his experience was bought
at heavier cost than his own discomfort; his 'unnecessary and un-
skilful absence,' as Montrose's friends were calling it, had left the
King without the very adviser that he needed at this moment.

Rupert would have been even better. But Rupert and his ships,
and indeed all Ireland, might have been sunk beneath the stormy
waves of the Atlantic for all that could now be learned of them.
His mother, who still wrote almost as constantly as his sister Louise
to Montrose, had first told 'her most affectionate friend' that all
Irish affairs were 'so in a cloud as we hear nothing of certainty,
which I hope is a good sign'—a vain hope, as she recognized when
she wrote a little later that 'Rupert le Diable is out of Kinsale and
most believe him now at Jersey.' Charles also was then at Jersey
and 'without question the King will go with Rupert's ships. But
whither, God knows, since many letters say all goes ill in Ireland.'
And then came the last report: 'Since Rupert was at Cape St.
Vincent on the coast of Portugal I have not heard from him.'

Montrose must reckon without Rupert as without Hyde. Whatever had 'gone ill' in Ireland (and there were horrible rumours of
massacre and devastation and artificially induced famine wrought by
that enormous iron machine of Cromwell's invading army), that
country was clearly out of action now as far as the Scottish campaign
was concerned. But Rupert had had to go to Ireland when he did,
as it had been the most necessary thing at that moment. And now
the whole Parliamentary fleet with Admiral Blake at its head
must be preventing Rupert's handful of ships from sailing north
to Montrose.

But Cromwell's army was still out of England, and this should
give Montrose his best chance of mustering an army to meet him
on that return. On the Continent he was being cited by all the

military experts as the one commander in Europe whose genius for war was superior to Cromwell's.

Politically, too, the odds were in his favour. The Irish invasion was unpopular in England; the Parliament was clamouring for Cromwell's return to quell the risings at home. If Cromwell met with one disaster on top of this year of tyranny and discontent, the bulk of England would take heart to join in rebellion against his rule.

It was the golden moment for Montrose's enterprise, if all could be done on the moment and not a moment wasted.

'In regard of the shortness and pressingness of the time,' Montrose had written to Hurry when giving him his marching-orders from shipboard, and the phrase stuck in both their heads in the midst of all the maddening delays that beset them.

Time was their chief enemy. No commander should have less reason to fear it than Montrose, whose lightning speed in forced marches had been the wonder of Europe. But when all was ready to embark he had had to wait at the Swedish port for a despatch from Charles at Jersey until it was impossible to wait longer, and the King's messenger had to follow him to Orkney, bearing with him the Order of the Garter. Montrose would gladly have forgone it for a different pair of letters.

For there were two from Charles; the one, private to Montrose, again warned him 'not to take alarm at any reports' he might hear; the other, public, showed what grave reason there was for alarm. In it Charles told him that he would discuss terms with the Commissioners, assured him that if they arrived at an agreement he would so provide for Montrose's 'honour and interest as shall let the whole world see the high esteem we have for you'; and also besought him yet again to 'proceed vigorously and effectively in your undertaking.'

With Montrose victorious, it was obvious that Charles could make better terms for himself with the Commissioners; but the very fact that he was considering a treaty with Montrose's enemies would put off recruits until they saw the issue of that treaty. Harry

May, the royal messenger, told Montrose that on the very day
Charles wrote to him he had also written to the Commissioners,
appointing a meeting with them at Breda.

There was then no time to be lost. Charles I had hastened his
path to the scaffold by trying to play off his enemies against each
other; now his son was trying to play off his enemies against his
friends.

Montrose saw the danger both to himself and to the King; it
was the latter that he considered most in his reply, warning him
'to have a serious eye, now at last, upon the too open crafts used
against you'—and to be 'just to yourself.' Yet, in spite of the
sternness of that warning, he assured him of his service, howsoever
Charles might hamper it, for 'it is not your fortune in you, but
Your Majesty in whatsomever fortune, that I make sacred to serve.'

To Hurry, that confirmed soldier of fortune, the quiet resolution
of that reply brought a surprised sense of release. His master might
be mad to disclaim fortune, but it saved him a deal of bother; he
had not to reckon up his chances of coming out on the winning
side as Hurry had done so furiously all his life; he had only to go
forward in what he had undertaken, and consider the chances not
for himself but for that undertaking.

Nor were the chances at all bad—if they could be used in time,
before the news of Charles' equivocal dealings spread to spoil them.
Before that could happen, Montrose must summon the clans to
him. They had heard on every side that all Scotland was ready to
rise against the tyranny of the Covenant, and that Montrose was
'gaped after with that expectation that the Jews had for their
Messiah.'

Once again, the cry was 'Oh for one hour of Montrose!' Sir
James Douglas had set sail for Sweden expressly to tell him that he
need not wait for troops or supplies, for once he set foot in Scotland
his own presence would be enough in itself, and 'undoubtedly bring
20,000 men together for the King's service.' Montrose had not
had more than a quarter of that number when he won his greatest

victory at Kilsyth, which had placed him as the acknowledged Governor of Scotland.

And his potential allies had increased since then; his enemies also had diminished. Lord Seaforth, chief of the Mackenzie clan, at present at The Hague, had been against Montrose and was now warmly partisan, according to the Queen of Bohemia, who always referred to him in her letters as 'my Highlander,' as no doubt he was, though that did not entirely convince Montrose that Seaforth was therefore his. Elizabeth, always optimistic, was apt to trust people according to herself. But he had certainly promised the help of his clan, and it was into the Mackenzie country that Montrose was now advancing.

The Covenant's former military leader in Scotland, General Baillie, as busy and efficient a general as his cousin Robert was a minister, had been discredited by Argyll and had lost his command. Hamilton, who had raised his men against Montrose, was now saying all over again that he would be glad 'to trail a pike or ride as a private trooper under him,' though he said this, it is true, at a comfortable distance.

As for old Lord Leven, the official Commander-in-Chief of the Covenant armies, or, as Hurry preferred to call him, "that crooked little bastard, Scrubby Sandy, he is crawling round with one foot in the grave,—I doubt if he could even run for it now as he did from Rupert's troopers at Marston Moor, bawling out for the quickest way back to Tweed. *I* was the best man they had against you, sir, and now I'm with you instead, and that's the best thing we've got against 'em."

But there were some scores on the other side too. The 'Gay Gordons,' those three young brothers, George Gordon and Aboyne and Lewis, and the Gordon Highlanders, had been a fiery though uncertain aid to Montrose. But George Gordon, the only sure and constant one, had been killed in battle by the side of his commander five years ago; and Aboyne had lately died abroad of a broken heart—at King Charles' execution it was said, though re-

morse may have had more to do with it, since he had deserted
Montrose at the very moment when he had most chance to prevent
that 'too rigid fate' of their King's.

And Lewis, the youngest of the three, the wildest and most
erratic, had been so much under the thumb of his uncle Argyll
that Argyll was said to have executed the Earl of Huntly chiefly
that his youngest son should succeed to the title and play into the
Covenanters' hands.   At the moment, however, Lewis was in a
loyal mood and only waiting for his King's command to join with
Montrose; unfortunately he was also waiting for the Garter, and
if he did not get it his loyalty was unlikely to be as strong as his
wounded vanity.   Even as an ally, Lewis had always given more
trouble than help.

'And so did your precious ruffian Alasdair Macdonald, whom
you dubbed "Major-General of His Majesty's Irishes!"' So Hurry
muttered, carefully inaudibly, determined not to recognize that
Montrose's chief cause for regret in this campaign was that he no
longer had that tribal chieftain to fight by his side.   Alasdair had
left Montrose with the bulk of his clan after his final victory at
Kilsyth.   At least he had deserted after victory and not, as Hurry
had done every time, after defeat; but that only increased Hurry's
jealousy, his annoyance that Alasdair's defection should have been
sanctified as it were by the tragic chance of his death.

For that mighty Irish giant who had dealt destruction in battle
with his own hand like the hammer of Thor, whose only sign of
human weakness had been on a day in Belfast when he had been met
walking with his wrist tied up in a string, having a little tired it by
killing fifty Englishmen and forty Scots (Protestants) in one morning,
Alasdair Macdonald, or, to give him his proper name, Alasdair
Mac Cholla-chiotach Mhic Ghiollesbuig Mhic Alasdair Mhic
Eoin Cathanich, had been stabbed in the back in battle, fighting
the Protestants in Ulster.

The MacVurich, his hereditary minstrel, and the MacArthur,
his piper, had escaped from that unhappy and futile fray and had

S

set out to join Montrose in Scotland as soon as they had heard of his project, and were now with that oddly assorted company of large dark flat-faced Orcadians and a sprinkling of Danish and German soldiers. That couple of men from what had been Montrose's main force of Highlanders were the only common soldiers among his force who had shared his ancient glories—and Alasdair's; and naturally it was those of Alasdair that they now sang in their laments for his death.

> 'Alasdair, brave son art thou
> Of Coll the Splendid—o—ho—o!
> 'Twas thy hand that struck the blow,
> Thine the brave deed—o—ho—o!'

Their dirge for their chieftain found its echo in Montrose's heart. Here he was back on the heather again with the wind coming down the hill, and the smell of bog and bracken again in his nostrils, released at last from those many different yet monotonous Courts of Europe where he had served his King as he had promised, 'in passion as in action,' and found how much harder was that passive course. Now it was action for him again, and the old fierce joy of comradeship in arms.

But Alasdair his greatest comrade was dead, the 'Shepherd of the Isles' as his men sang of him, 'whose shape was a fiery blaze overtopping the warriors of Erin.—Stag amongst the deer, salmon amongst the trout, loftiest ship that makes harbour,—

> The gloom of every night is dark
> Since earth was put over Alasdair.'

The wild tune came again and again on the pipes like the cry of the sea-birds through the mist. His name would live for centuries, they cried, in song and in the hearts of his people.

To Montrose that immortality of his friend was here and now, his spirit alive on the hill as in the songs of his men, that fury of life continuing strong and swift in the very course of nature. He believed, as Alasdair had done, in an eternity of courage and high endeavour, believed that the length or shortness of a life counted for nothing, but that the moment where a man strikes into life, and what he does with it, is all.

And now once again he was being given his moment here in his own country where he had so longed to be. He was leading his men there once again. It was better luck than a man could hope for, to be given his chance all over again.

That was how he thought of it.

It was different with Jack Hurry. He had had almost as many campaigns as casks of wine in his belly, but never yet the one he had always hankered after. Now it lay before him, that campaign of gay, miraculous conquest that Montrose had already known.

They talked of it as they walked by the nor'-eastern shore of Scotland and felt the sea-wind come in sharp and biting on their cheeks, that strong easterly frost-bitten wind with the tang of the Northern sea in it, and behind them the clang and clatter of an armed camp that they had both so longed to hear again, the sound of movement and comradeship and action. And now Hurry was beside Montrose instead of against him, and though in his sturdy Aberdeen conceit of himself Hurry tried to present that as the best asset in his Commander's chances, he knew well that it was the best in his own.

"Fine you tricked me at Auldearn," he said, "when I had the chance for once to take a leaf out of Your Lordship's very own book."

"And fine you took it," Montrose answered, "turning on your tracks to attack us in the middle of a forced night march just when I thought we were comfortably chasing you towards Inverness."

"Much good it did me! My 'surprise' found you as ready as on the parade-ground! Was it the devil himself gave you word of it?"

"You'll say it was, when I tell you it was the Macdonald scouts. They'd heard your men firing off the damp powder in their muskets, so I guessed you'd turned to attack us."

"Why, that was five miles from Auldearn and on a night thick with mist and rain. They must have as long ears as the mountain deer."

"That may well be, and I wish to God we had 'em here again."

Hurry did not echo that. Surely to God an officer like himself, trained in the 'civilized warfare' of the Thirty Years' carnage and pillage in Germany, was worth more than the barbaric asset of the long ears of the mountainy men.

"Just when I'd managed to steal the first march on you at last," he grumbled ruminatively, "and with four thousand men and a full quarter of them cavalry. Christ! how did I ever throw away such a chance?"

He knew well enough how it was, for Montrose, even when surprised into a position of defence, the worst possible for his Highlanders, had yet managed to outwit him with a thin screen of musketeers, keeping the Gordon cavalry hidden in reserve and placing the Royal Standard with Alasdair and the Macdonalds so as to draw the first brunt of Hurry's attack Even then that small advantage had been all but thrown away by Alasdair's leaping out from behind the farmyard walls that served for entrenchments, and leading a mad charge out into the open against an enemy that numbered eight to one.

"Will I ever forget the sight of that redhead shooting up like a flaming pole, and the yell of his battle-cry, just when I thought I'd got them all safely tucked up behind the pig-sties!"

Hurry heard the amused admiration as well as exasperation in his General's voice, and it went to his head like new wine. Alasdair had made a fool of himself by throwing away his position at the start, but had fought like a Berserker to recover it. The first to rush out from it, he had been the last to return; Hurry had seen him guarding his men's retreat to it with the scythe-like sweeps of his huge sword, had seen him catch on his wooden targe the points of half a dozen pikes that would have borne any ordinarily strong man to the ground, but round went that sword again and cut them through at one stroke, leaving his shield bristling like a pin-cushion with their pike-heads.

Then that mighty two-handed sword that any other man could

scarcely lift had snapped like a twig, but Alasdair took a claymore
from a friend and struck off an enemy's head with a single blow;
he rushed out again and again from the enclosure that he had swept
clean of their enemies, to bring in any stragglers that had failed to
win through; his battle rage and battle laughter were those of a
giant in a fairy-tale—nor was a fairy-tale the end of it.

No, it was the raw, untried Gordon cavalry that had won the
fight, swung round as they waited shivering in the rain by Montrose's gay shout to them that the Macdonalds were winning the
day, and were there to be no laurels for the house of Huntly? (Of
all God-almighty lies, when the Macdonalds were paying for their
folly at the rate of a Jewish usurer's interest!) But Montrose with
young George Gordon had led the charge home, plumb into the
middle of Hurry's flank guard of cavalry.

"It was the first chance I had to use shock tactics," Montrose
said, "as Rupert had shown cavalry could be used, and now
Cromwell."

"And that finished it," said Hurry, "neater than any mop-
headed, raw-hide-shod, bloody Highland infantry could do."

It finished Hurry's army. He left two thousand dead upon the
field, his ammunition, money, baggage, and the colours of sixteen
regiments in Montrose's hands. All he saved from the rout was
a hundred horse with which he fled headlong through the raining
night. God how it had rained on their grim defeated faces as
they rode! "I'd never have got my ragged leavings of horse
past your scouts if it hadn't been for that thick night—— "

"*And* for your damned impudence, passing 'em off as a force
of Gordon recruits! You had us fairly hoodwinked."

His former victor was laughing at the magnificent audacity
of Hurry's ruse, coming at a moment when most men would
have despaired. It was a manœuvre after Montrose's own heart.
He too was back in the flooding rain after that day of mighty
fighting, heard it thudding on the roof as he saw again the feast
among that camp of heroes for supper (some boiled beef, wasn't

there, and turnips? Mere cattle fodder, but washed down with plenty of good home-brewed ale) in the big raftered room of that farmhouse at Auldearn. He had excused his lie to Gordon and his raw recruits with the question, 'Even you yourself, my lord Gordon, would you have fought singing as I heard you, if you had believed the day lost?'

And young Gordon, leaning across the table towards him, had answered, 'I might indeed, for loss or victory would make little odds as long as I fought with you.' What else had he said, his dark eyes glowing with the fire that shone so rarely in them compared with those of his passionate, headstrong brothers? 'If all your plans should fail, and you had to wander as an outlaw on the mountains, I would be happier to share that with you than any fortune with another.'

That was a friend. And in a few weeks he was lying dead among the young tender green of the uncrumpling fronds of the bracken, the gold and purple patches of broom and wild geranium on the hillside, those glowing eyes shut fast for ever. His friend was dead; his enemy, this time-server, now walked by his side.

But as he glanced at Hurry he saw in his eyes that same look that he had seen in Gordon's, in Alasdair's, in the young King's, in his own son's: that look that he had seen in the eyes of countless men whose names he never even knew, the look of devotion and desire that he should 'lead them in a chain to follow him with cheerfulness in all his enterprises.'

II

DEVOTION is all very well in action, but what the hell is the use of it idle and bone-dry and no chance to show it? And yet it was he, Jack Hurry, despite his name, who had urged his Commander to hang on here instead of striking straight away for the accustomed and beloved hills that Montrose had always used as his base. But now, when so much time had been lost through one infernal delay after another, storms and ice-bound harbours, the broken promises of foreign princes, their companion leaders' deaths, the King's damnable letters, what could a day or two more or less really matter, except in as far as it should almost certainly bring in the Mackenzies to their side?

Seaforth's brother, Pluscardine, who had already headed a Royalist rising, must have had his marching-orders from 'my Highlander' (Hurry could never think of Elizabeth's nickname for him without the snort of 'the war-horse when he sayeth ha ha!'). Unless Seaforth was still waiting for *his* marching-orders from Charles and did not care to show his hand openly until his royal master should do so. It was what they were all doing, doubtless, and why should 'my Highlander' be any different?

Was that then the explanation of this strange lull, as though Fate herself could not draw a breath to decide on which side to cast the die for Montrose?

Was the King's policy stultifying their enterprise before it even began? Had it got abroad that he was considering a treaty with the Covenanters? Was that why the men did not come in? Why didn't the 'magic of Montrose' work as it had done before?

A man might make himself sick asking such questions, and what was the use of it? The magic would work fast enough once it came to a fight. It had always done so in every battle Montrose had fought—all but one, and that had been no battle, but a surprise

of 600 men by 6000. Even those odds of ten to one he had sur-
mounted at other times, but that one time at Philiphaugh the men
had been taken utterly unawares, surrounded in a dense fog and
massacred.

Still, it would not have been lucky to have had no single event
against him, Hurry decided; it might have argued that he still had
a defeat coming to him.

He stepped outside into the sharp air of the spring evening that
he might not see that 'envious sliver' of the new moon through
the green bottle-paned window of the small farmhouse where he
had taken his billet, turned the money in his pocket, bowed his
head three times, and wished for victory   He must propitiate the
goddess of luck, for he was the almighty gambler who put his shirt
on kings and commanders instead of horses. He was backing his
last fancy, for now that he followed Montrose he would change
no more.

But it was a damned dull chilly business standing here, staring
at a thin moon in a cold sky above the black jagged spears of the
pinewood on the hill above, and the little black tarn of Corbiesdale
set in its shelter like a dark mirror that a witch might peer into, to
see what Fate had been writing for them.

He turned and looked downhill at the long valley of the Kyle
of Sutherland where they had turned inland from the sea two
days ago, in order to cross it at its head. They had not marched
on immediately, but dug trenches and breastworks to defend
their front towards the Carron, a brawling frothing little Highland river that dashed through rocks and pools but would make
no serious obstacle in itself to an advancing enemy. This was the
best possible defensive position, with the steep hill of Craigcoinichean,
the Hill of the Scroggy Wood, behind him to guard his rear, the
burn of the Culvain on the one flank, the Kyle of Sutherland on
the other, and their entrenchments towards the Carron. Here
Montrose could wait at any rate for a couple of days and collect
those tardy reinforcements, not only of the Mackenzies but of the

neighbouring clans, the Monroes and Rosses, who, they had sent word, were marching to join forces with him.

'Give them two days,' he and Hurry were agreed, 'and then if nothing happens we'll play for safety and march south for Badenoch.'

It would be essential, for they had only forty horse, gentlemen volunteers whom Montrose had collected up north, under the command of Major Lisle, an English Royalist, and only three or four hundred Danish and German pikemen and musketeers who were trying to instil some idea of soldiering into the raw shepherd and fisher lads recruited in Orkney. The Orcadians were descended from the Northmen, but a long time ago, and mighty little soldiering they had done since; for the last two centuries the kings of Scotland had recruited no levies from them, having found them so simply rustic and unused to war. Since then all raw levies of infantry had become practically useless, for the development of the musket and the pike to guard it required long and hard professional training; nor were even professional musketeers and pikemen any real good, when unsupported, against cavalry.

"A damned schoolroom party of louts and lubbers, that's the stuff we've got to nurse up for this campaign," Hurry grumbled to Robert Monro of Achnes, who had checked his horse at the door of Hurry's billet on his return from a reconnoitre of the countryside. "Even the foreigners are not much good, for what use is infantry in this country?"

"None, if it isn't Highland," answered Monro, leaning forward to stroke and pat his mare's ears as she champed shivering in that raw dusk of the end of April, a little cloud of steam rising from her sweating flanks. "Now I," he went on in his rich assertive voice, "have seen those mountainy men catch up with a horse and tear its rider from the saddle when he was galloping from the field of battle. The Macdonalds did that when Montrose led them against Perth with only three broken-winded hacks for his entire cavalry."

"If you mention the Macdonalds to me again," said Hurry softly, "I'll tear you from the saddle yourself and stick the butt of your pistol in your mouth to gag you. Or will you take a drink to do the job more pleasantly? You've found and heard nothing on your reconnoitre to put us on our guard, I take it?"

"It's sheer waste of time to ride out and look for it."

"You're mighty certain, man. They say Davie Leslie is pushing up north as fast as he can, and Frendraught's precious uncle the Earl of Sutherland with him. If Strachan is Leslie's second-in-command he's a sound fellow as a soldier, though a ranting, canting, *re*canting hypocrite of a Covenant cur. He should be sent on in advance to check us if Leslie's worth his salt."

"Strachan's no further north than Brechin, I know."

"Oo-ay. Ye know a deal."

Monro became more consequential than ever. "Not a thing could happen in these parts without my knowing it. Don't I and my three sons know every inch of the ground and every crofter and shepherd for forty miles round, born and bred here as we are?"

"That is naturally the reason for your being appointed chief scoutmaster," said Hurry, with the faintest hint of sarcasm in the upward twist of that light tufted eyebrow. He had no opinion of gentlemen volunteers, though he had had to admit that it was a great acquisition to have got in a local laird like Robert Monro of Achnes. But he would have thought it a greater acquisition if the local laird had *not* been like Robert Monro—a big loud domineering fellow with his large nose and large soft chin, and bulk that was by no means all muscle, and the slightly uncertain look in his eyes as he blew out some important-sounding nonsense and then looked to see how you were taking it. When had Robert Monro ever seen the Macdonalds tear a man from his saddle? He had lived safe here in Ross-shire all through those campaigns five years ago, and thanked his stars they'd never turned far enough north to catch him and his sons.

Not that that need spoil good fellowship.

"It would be still better news if you could tell me that in forty miles round there was a brothel or a tavern," Hurry said in his dry clipped voice, spitting expertly between the legs of Monro's mare. "The women in these parts are bred out of bits of granite crossed with unbaked dough, and the only drink I've been able to lay my hands on is the raw whisky they brew in the hills that tastes of nothing but peat-smoke and pepper, but at least it can make one drunk."

"What's wrong with the home-brewed whisky here? I've supped it in with my mother's milk. I'll show you how it should be drunk. Hi you, Johnny," Monro shouted to one of the crofter's sons, a dark heavy form that was plodding through the farmyard in the dusk, with a couple of milk-pails slung from his shoulders. "Take my horse and rub her down till you can see your grinning face in her flanks, and then cover her with your thickest blanket, d'ye hear? Set down those pails now and be quick about it."

"The blankets are all commandeered, your honour, for the soldier gentleman's bed," demurred Johnny, setting down his pails nevertheless.

"They'll not be wanted yet," said Hurry pleasantly. "We'll make a night of it, hey, Monro? One must do something while one's hanging about like this" ('even if it's drinking with a fool,' he supplemented to himself). "Come inside."

The two men sat by a fire of smouldering peat that made their eyes smart almost as much as the fiery whisky did their tongues. There was plenty of it, that was all you could say for it, in a big black leather jack. "The Germans say we drink out of our boots," said Hurry, squinting at it as it stood on the rough stone flags of the little kitchen between them, "and by God they're right, for if we'd nothing else left to drink out of, we'd go barefoot and keep our boots for our mouths, wouldn't we, hey, my lads?"

The 'lads' were the crofter and his six sturdy sons who owned this small farmhouse and sat at a respectful distance from their own fireside to listen to the Major-General talking so grandly of the foreign wars, and the laird of Achnes talking still more grandly of their own country.

"All your General has got to do is to walk over it," he trumpeted: "Do you know that his enemies have been crying all this past winter that Montrose is 'a prodigious meteor' hanging over their heads? And no wonder they are quaking in their shoes, for they're turning their own side against them as fast as they can, shoving all the best ministers out of office, saying they're not sound enough on hell-fire and 'Down-with-the-Pope' when they've been preaching nothing else all their lives, even old Andrew Ramsay after fifty-three years in the ministry and the most popular man in it, and yet they've sent him spinning like a horse-boy kicked out for stealing oats. Little Archie Warriston is behind it all, that starved white rat who got his taste of blood preaching fire and slaughter after Philiphaugh. Ever heard him spout on those blessed words of holy Scripture—'Their women with child shall be ripped up'? It was he egged 'em on to do that to the Irishwomen after Philiphaugh."

"Nothing to what I saw at Magdeburg," began Hurry hopefully, but Monro gave him no chance.

"Magdeburg is not Scotland," he said profoundly, "and a Scots minister is not a Papist soldier and oughtn't to behave as such. Warriston has gone drunk with blood *and* with power, and is driving them all the same way. They're so busy cutting their own throats that there'll be precious little left for your General to do, once the country get the chance to come in to him."

"They've got their chance. Why the hell don't they take it? What the devil are your precious cousins the Monroes doing, and the Rosses, and the Mackenzies, and all the rest of those God's own heroes the Highlanders who came flocking to him before when he only had to stroll across the heather by himself without even a horse under him? Answer me *that*," urged Hurry truculently, "why don't the men come in? Are they waiting to see which way the cat jumps?"

"*Which* cat?" enquired Monro portentously. "A cat may look at a king, mayn't it?"

"*Which* king?" reiterated Hurry with equal solemnity.

Monro wielded his pipe like a Field-Marshal's baton, and boomed out, "Aha! Now you've hit it. A king may look like a cat when he's being used as a cat's paw to pull Argyll's chestnuts out of the fire. Doesn't the King write to Montrose with one hand and to Argyll with the other, all on the same day? These things get round."

"Like your belly."

"Hey, what's that?" A large glazed eye swivelled round on the man from Aberdeen. "Yes, I have a belly, thank God, and not a cavity between two haunch-bones. You've grown thin on your name, my friend; hurrying to and fro upon the earth never did anyone any good—even when it's from one side to the other."

It was very nearly the end of a pleasant evening. Fortunately Hurry recollected in time that if he ran this stout piece of bombast through the guts he'd only be hanged himself by his General the next morning.

They drowned their incipient quarrel in more whisky, and Monro good-naturedly remarked that all the best men ratted these days—hadn't their General himself ratted years ago when he first marched against Charles I's army and then afterwards went over to the King?

But that nearly caused another quarrel. Hurry's eyes were like white pebbles as he pointed out that Montrose had fought for the liberty of his country's Church until that Church had denied liberty to all else, including the King. "He went over to the King when the King was the weaker. D'you call that ratting? Rats don't desert *to* a sinking ship."

"Hope not, anyway," muttered Monro, eyeing Sir John dubiously.

They drank in silence after that, Monro dozing a bit and Hurry listening to the crofter and his sons climbing up the ladder to bed in the hayloft.

The woman of the house, whose large pale plain face and scrawny body had inspired his unkind comments on the women of these parts, continued for some time to flump noisily about a hundred mysterious occupations in the background while he eyed her resentfully out of the corner of his eye, wondering why she could not have managed to throw in a plump, tolerably pleasant daughter or two among all these lumps of sons.

Of course it was grand to be in Scotland again, better still when he got the chance to dash south to Aberdeen and visit his little place at Pitfichie and see what was happening to the apple trees he had planted and that breed of small shaggy cattle he had reared in the policies; yes, and to his five brats, all girls worse luck—what *were* all their names?—Margery and Bessie and Annie and Jeannie and Clare—all growing leggy and long-haired by now he'd be bound, with straw-coloured plaits round their funny little heads, for they all had his colouring, he was glad of that; yes, and to Maggie too, though she'd be getting on and was no longer much to look at, nor to dandle on a knee either—too much, in fact, since she'd gone heavy and flaccid and sallow in the way these foreign women did.

Still, he'd be glad even of Maggie this raw comfortless night with the east wind howling in the chimney and searching out that aching spot under his left shoulder-blade where one of Tilly's confounded pikemen had stuck his point into him more than a dozen years ago. A lot of knocks he'd had one way and another, and some fun, but damned little luck considering.

Here he was, Major-General to the finest commander this age could show, and all he had got waiting for him was the same Pitfichie and Maggie that he'd had for more than a dozen years—while his Commander had a lovely princess waiting for him, seeking him out too—would he ever forget the sight of her that night in the doorway of Montrose's room, her white face shining out from her black cloak like the slip of the new moon he had just seen over the black wood of Craigcoinichean? 'You idiot!' she had snapped at himself when his look and tone had insulted her more than his question.

There was a girl worth taming!

Well, he'd had his fun out of his own marriage when he had

carried off a Spanish-Dutch heiress by force from Holland and found
her to be a pretty woman into the bargain, so there was a bit of luck.
They couldn't speak a word of each other's languages then ; it had
made an odd wooing, but there had been no mistaking his intentions!

She had been glad enough to marry him after that, glad too to
escape from the stodgy Dutch burgher, to whom she had been
promised, with a gay adventurer like himself, for there had been
fire and laughter in Maria Magdalena van Jaxheim. But now she
was his plain stout Maggie and all her money spent; and here he
sat drinking this rough stinking fire-and-water that rasped your
throat like iron scrapings, and puffing at a long foul old pipe that
had gone as yellow in the tooth as an old hag, and talking with a
big blowing blustering fellow that gave himself all the airs in the
world as the General's chief scoutmaster, when he had never seen
a campaign in his life.

What had he, Jack Hurry, got out of it, after all he had done?
"You've not done your all yet, nor got your all."

He could have sworn he heard the words in his General's voice
as the door swung open and a gust of keen air awakened the
stuffy room. He looked up to see Montrose standing there,
but he knew that neither himself nor his General had spoken.
The hillside was black beyond him in the open doorway; in his
dark cloak against it his form scarcely showed at all, only his face,
grey in the murk of the peat-smoke, the hair roughened by the
night wind (he was bare-headed), blown across his forehead, and the
rushlight on the floor throwing the black shadows upwards, out-
lining the lean long lines of the jaw-bone and the hooked imperious
nose. In their deep pits of shadow under the fierce peaked brows,
his eyes scanned the two men sitting by the fire with the black-jack
between them.

They sprang to their feet, Hurry trusting he was too old a hand
to show his drink; he could hear his own voice answer the General's
greeting almost too precisely.

Montrose told them he had been taking a stroll round the camp and seen their light. "If all is still clear to-morrow," he said, "we'll strike camp then and cross by the hill road to Alness and get south to the old road I know to the Spey."

"But the rest of my clan, sir," spluttered Monro, "they are on the march to join with you, and the Rosses with them."

"They have had plenty of time to do so," said Montrose dryly, "and are on the march, I know, but have not made their intention so clear as to be worth waiting any longer for them."

"My lord, *I* know their intentions, I've heard 'em a hundred times from their own lips. Now that I and my three sons have shown them the way they'll follow my example, I take my oath on it."

"I hope they will, sir, and they can do so on our march. I shall wish both you and Major Lisle to reconnoitre the ground again to-morrow morning before we start, so you'd best turn in now and get all the sleep you can. Good night."

That was all. He would not, of course, show any displeasure to Hurry in front of a subordinate officer. He went out. There was the thick solid black of the closed wooden door in front of them, instead of that dark figure and the distant hillside. The face that had appeared so suddenly had vanished, yet their confused and guilty imaginations still felt his eyes quick and stern upon them.

"Does he never go to bed?" demanded Monro thickly, flopping back on to the bench.

Hurry eyed unfavourably the sinking figure of the fat man, tugged at a large blue enamelled watch, a pretty bit of loot from the hideous sack of Tirlemont, and discovered it was close on two o'clock. Just his luck to be caught drinking with the scoutmaster.

Was he becoming a Just-his-luck man? 'A bad sign that, Sir John Jonah.' He could imagine the young King's ironic drawl to him. Curse him for that accursed nickname! He must be pretty drunk to be hearing voices in his head like this. No wonder Monro had twisted his tongue round his words a bit.

"A pity you had to talk so much," he remarked unkindly.

"I? I could talk as clear as a whistle after a gallon of this stuff. I've sopped it in through my skin all my life as frogs do water and never turned a hair under it. What does he mean by turning Lisle on to my job as well as me? An Englishman, a damned Southron, what can he know of this country? *I* know it, I tell you, I know it like the back of my hand—*damnation!*"

To illustrate his knowledge Monro had knocked out his pipe on the back of his hand and the red-hot ash made him jump violently, breaking the stem of the clay pipe. There was a strong smell of burnt hair as he ruefully sucked his hand and stared at the broken pieces.

"Ay, you're sober as a frog all right," said Hurry sourly, "and now you'd best take the General's advice, if you can walk to your own billet."

"Walk?" he hiccupped. "Do you think Robert Monro of Achnes can't walk after a drop of whisky?"

He rose with great dignity, tripped over his spur and collapsed on the floor.

Hurry stretched him out by the fire with his cloak over him, loosened his belt and took off his spurs that he might lie comfortably. He'd have slept it off by the morning, and if he hadn't, a can of cold water over his head would set him right. But Hurry was judging by his own head, which long practice in both drink and campaigning had made something tougher than a coconut

It was not so with Robert Monro, who woke late the next morning with a forehead like hot lead, ears like a beehive, and a tongue like an ancient and insanitary blanket.

T

III

THERE was fresh hope of reinforcements the next morning. A scout came in with the report that a body of about four hundred of the Monroes and Rosses, from south of the Dornoch Firth, had forded the Carron and were making a circuit of Strath Carron, no doubt on their way to join them.

That was good news, for without them they would be a very weak little force to encounter the Covenanter garrisons in the Lowlands which had been strongly fortifying their resistance all these past months in dread of that 'prodigious meteor of Montrose.' So it was best to push on in however weak a case and establish the base that had served Montrose so well before in the Badenoch hills.

But here was the morning gone, and still Robert Monro and his scouts had not returned from their reconnaissance, and Hurry had an uneasy feeling at the pit of his stomach as he thought of the night before and wondered how much that might be hampering Monro's quickness of intelligence this morning.

They were striking camp and getting the Orcadians into some sort of formation for the line of march. Utterly raw, undisciplined levies, they went slowly and heavily about their jobs in the manner that showed them to have been farm lads and shepherds for generation upon generation.

"Those slob-faced lubberly bastards will need blooding in two or three engagements before they can smell powder without sneezing," said Hurry to Menzies of Pitfoddels, who was hoisting the grim royal standard with the device of the severed head of Charles I on a black ground.

Hurry disliked that standard. Who wanted to be reminded of a head streaming with gore just before going into battle? He was under the same sentence of execution as Montrose, should he ever be careless enough to fall into the enemy's hands.

The cavalry's standard was black also, but with nothing more grisly than three drawn swords. He liked best Montrose's own banner of white damask, the device, a lion about to leap across a rocky chasm, and the motto, 'Nil Medium.' 'No middle course,' however much the young King might try to steer it; for them that was true now as never before, that they must 'win or lose it all.'

Major Lisle came back with a report from his scouts that a single troop of horse had been seen advancing up the coast, and that this time it was no dubious ally but their undoubted enemy, the Covenanters. It was, however, a small one, and he had neither seen nor heard of any movement of any other of the enemy, and begged leave to go and wipe it out now with his forty 'gentlemen riders' and clear their line of advance.

Young Lord Frendraught, a hot enthusiast for Montrose though his uncle, the powerful Earl of Sutherland, was a leading Covenanter, now eagerly seconded him in this.

"Think of the encouragement to those haverers on the hill, my lord," he urged. "You said yourself that we have only to win the first brush with the enemy and the rest will be easy."

The haverers were the Monroes and Rosses, who could now be seen on the western slopes and seemed to have halted there.

But Montrose would not act till Lisle's report had been confirmed by Monro of Achnes, since the Englishman could know neither the ground nor the peasantry hereabouts as did the local laird.

When at last Monro appeared he confirmed Lisle's report with blustering emphasis.

"There's but one troop of horse in the whole shire, my lord, and you see it away there before you, at your mercy. As for those gentry on the hill yonder, I had word from a cousin of mine that they are but awaiting Your Lordship's movements."

"As we have awaited yours, Mr. Monro," Montrose replied sharply, and the large consequential man seemed to shrink in size, as Hurry noticed unkindly, watching the sagging yellow cheeks that infuriated him the more for his responsibility for the fellow's condition. The first cuckoo he had heard that spring suddenly shouted from a tree near by as Monro subsided; it was a relief to be able to echo it with a wink at Frendraught.

Montrose now gave the order for his whole force to advance down on to the level ground. It would greatly encourage the Orcadians to see Lisle's horsemen clear off that troop, and with that accomplished he would himself go across to the 'gentry on the hill' and see if his personal influence would not do what it had done time and again before, and bring them in to his side.

"Do you remember, sir, the five hundred stout fellows we met on the hill of Buchanty on their way to reinforce the Covenanters at Perth, and after a chat with their leaders they were marching with you instead of against you?"

It was Colonel Sibbald speaking as they started the foot on their line of march; he had been one of the three men who had ridden with Montrose into Scotland up through the armies that their enemies had posted all along the Border to intercept him at the beginning of that Year of Marvels, and the familiar dry grin on his swarthy face brought back to Montrose that summer evening nearly six years ago more vividly than his words. Now he was back on the hill again, starting out on his second great enterprise, the heather springing under his feet, damp with the late April frost that had melted since the morning, the air fresh and biting on his face, and the skirl of the pipes tingling up into the bright cold air.

'Tastes like iced Rhenish,' said Hurry to himself, opening his mouth to draw in great gulps of it and clean away the taste of stale whisky. Here was he following the greatest general of the day into action, and wasn't that enough in itself to make a man drunk?

The level rays of the now slanting sunlight were flooding the whole scene with a pale dazzle. Even the long waters of the Dornoch Firth below, usually so deep a blue between their wide yellow sands, were washed to turquoise, and the strong dark purple currents in them now ran like twisted steel. All the lower ground that sloped towards the Firth was pricked out with bright points from the bursting buds of the whin that would soon be solid masses of heavy gold among the brown reeds, and the thick aromatic scent of it, like ground coconut, was already in the air   There was a shimmer too of fainter, more scattered flecks of yellow from the tall spears of the broom that grew as thick as a low forest all over that land.

The near hillsides, a brownish-pink from dead bracken, were streaked and smeared with that same gold, but further to the west were long white streaks of snow that could still be seen, though the great hills on which they lay were now invisible in the frosty mist of late afternoon, so that it looked as though the sky itself were scarred with those bleak traces of winter.

But here in the wood, from which their troops were moving, it was spring, with flecks of white blossom on the wild cherry trees mingling with the rose-flushed gold of their budding leaves and the feathery-green gold of the young oaks among the white twisted trunks of the birches and the grey crags of rock piercing up like sharp bones through the mossy earth.

The little tarn of black peat-water on the edge of the wood of Craigcoinichean glowed wine-dark beneath the snowy breasts of a pair of mating swans that rose disturbed from their nest by the movement of the troops, rushed across the water and soared upwards with the long strong strokes of their wings creaking as loud as a baggage-wagon.

A throstle was singing shrill and loud close by, and Hurry whistled in answer to it with a few long notes which ended in the tune of a Dutch shanty:

'Skerry merry vip and skerry merry vap
And skerry merry runke ede bunk, ede hoor was drunk a.'

He was in the vanguard, cursing his subordinate officers for the slowness with which the Orkney recruits, shaggy, unwieldy and unmanageable as their own cattle, were lumbering into the line of march, but his curses sounded very cheery, a mere necessary accompaniment to the work in hand.   Thank God they had a sprinkling of German and Danish infantry to put some appearance of shape into this rabble, and some of their sergeants, dispersed among them, were doing their best to tidy up the mess.

Now they were all of them down on the lower ground where they could see nothing of the flats surrounding the Firth nor the high banks of the stream below. Lisle had advanced with his 'gentlemen riders,' flanking the foot, who were still being pushed and shouted into formation, and guarding them from the small troop of enemy horse away down towards the Firth.

But there came a thudding of horses' hoofs along the ground, a thunder from below instead of above, bewildering as an earthquake, and Hurry saw Lisle swinging his men round to meet a large body of cavalry that was charging over the slope out of the low scrub and masses of whin and broom in front of them. At least a hundred horse clashed with Lisle's forty, and the air was rent into shouts and yells, the clash of steel and the long whinnying scream of horses. Lisle's horse looked like being overwhelmed, they were fighting furiously but were being pushed back and back by sheer weight.

'The islanders will never stand this!' and Hurry galloped to summon the Danish and German musketeers together to the support. But as he did so, a second troop plunged out hell for leather from the broom a little further round, and behind them musketeers and pikemen began to appear, while the troop below, that had been so cleverly used as a decoy duck, was fast coming up to the attack. There were now well over a couple of hundred horsemen swinging into Lisle's little force, hurling the struggling remnant of it right in on top of their still unformed mass of raw infantry recruits.

'My God, we've walked straight into an ambush!' Where the hell had they all come from? That strutting cock Monro—had he and his scouts seen nothing?—or was he still sodden?—or a traitor?

Hurry was frantically trying to get the foreign non-commissioned officers together again, no use their being scattered now among those islanders who were breaking already; he had seen in the tail of his eye how their pikes were wavering like reeds in a storm, and some were throwing them down and legging it up the hill.

Montrose galloped into the midst of them, shouting to them to get back to their trenches, but the dazed Orkney lads scarcely understood what he was saying. They had never seen a dragoon before; they now saw a mass of them coming in on top of them, thicker and thicker, overriding them in hideous confusion. They broke and ran in all directions, flinging away their pikes, which trailed and caught in the heather, impeding their flight. Only the Danish and German infantry made some sort of a stand and attempted to carry out a retreat to the trenches above.

Lisle's few remaining horse made a desperate effort to cover this movement, but the whole mass was being driven pell-mell up the hill into the wood and the horsemen were being cut down almost to a man. The great standard of King Charles' head swooped and fluttered to the ground in the dying hand of Menzies of Pitfoddels. He was close to Montrose's side, and so was Major Guthrie, who fell dead at the same moment. Now Lisle fell among the few survivors of his troop, and Douglas, and Ogilvy of Powrie.

The blood was streaming down Montrose's face from a head-wound, but still he rode here, there and everywhere, keeping the men together as best he could, urging them back towards their entrenchments.

But they were driven back over the trenches and into the wood. Hurry's horse plunged forward over the rocky uneven ground, swerved first from one tree-trunk and then another. This should make hard going for Strachan's cavalry.

A queer lull fell for a moment on that nightmare rush and carnage as the still forms of the waiting trees received him into their midst. Some of the little force of Danes and Germans were with him; they at least had kept their heads enough to retreat in the right direction and in something like formation, though that was about all that could be said for them.

"We are not accustomed to receive a cavalry charge entirely unsupported," one of their officers, his face black with gunpowder, panted out in German and a stiff offended tone exactly as though he were lodging a complaint on some score of regimental etiquette.

They had made a brief stand and were firing on their pursuers, but it was a feeble volley, hampered by the trees, and seemed to be having no effect, for here was the enemy pressing their pursuit right into the wood, riders urging their unwilling horses in among the brushwood and the scattered trees, followed by more and more musketeers. They must have got their infantry up in support by now, and these stood far more chance in a wood than the baffled horses that were shying at the trees and stumbling in the sudden pitfalls.

That momentary lull had broken into a confused murderous scramble again, even worse than in the open, since one could not see whether the struggling, scurrying forms that ran or lurked behind the trees were those of friend or foe. The foreigners round Hurry kept breaking apart under the heavy fire of the musketeers; in one moment a band of the enemy foot rushed past him, crashing through the undergrowth like a herd of cattle, and one of them stuck his pike into the belly of Hurry's horse and sent him staggering to the earth, only just missing driving his head into a tree.

He dragged his leg out from under the plunging beast and saw with horror that there was someone standing over him, unnaturally still and passive among all that hurly-burly. Then as he staggered somehow on to his legs, he saw that the man's head had been transfixed by a pike that had pierced clean through the temples and nailed him upright to the tree.

Well he himself was not dead yet, but how soon would he be? Here he was caught in this wood like a rat in a trap—no use to surrender, he'd only be hanged, drawn, and quartered like his General, if those round Montrose were fools enough to let him be caught.

His own fellows were gathering round him again, trying to make a stand against a thick body of infantry that were pushing and panting through the scrub. For an instant Hurry took these for their own islanders, and then realized that they were men of the Monroes and Rosses, who had been waiting on the opposite slopes to see how the tide turned, and now swooped down like carrion crows to share in the victory.

"Sons of dogs, come and get your flesh!" he shouted on a sudden high note of despairing rage as he hacked at one of them who had ventured too far ahead of the rest. Then he turned and ran for it with the foreigners, his breath coming in thick sobs, his heart hammering against his ribs, while his legs seemed to have turned flabby as cotton, his heavy riding-boots dragged along the uneven ground, tripping in the mud and the brambles that stretched their thorny arms to catch his feet, his face, his torn coat, on which a patch of deep blackish-purple was slowly spreading.

This would finish it, there was no chance for him now. What a God-damned fool he'd been to pick the losing side yet once more, or was he indeed Sir John Jonah, did every side become the losing one when he joined it? A curse on him there must be, and he'd never see Pitfichie and the brats again.

They were all being pushed further and further up the heights, and a furious volley from below made them break into a blind run for cover among the brushwood. He jumped into a ditch which felt oddly springy, and found he had jumped on a man's chest, his dead startled eyes staring up past Hurry's shoulder as if still looking in amazement at the man that killed him.

Hurry crouched down beside the body, which he pushed up for shelter from the bullets. One had grazed his arm, another his hand, but he could still use his sword if he got the chance. He got it quicker than he wanted, for a big musketeer came up and attacked him, and Hurry's sword broke on his iron breast-piece as the man leaned over to hack down at him. But he hit him below the belt and sent him on his back, howling, then scrambled up and seized the fellow's sword as three or four more came running up, and swung it round, slashing a man's face and breaking the guard of another man's arm, shouting forgotten foreign oaths as he did so and laughing insanely.

He was making them give before him and had his back to a tree, but another man was coming up round it behind him, he did not know if it were friend or foe, only heard the crack and crash of breaking twigs and the heavy panting breath, and then a sword-thrust got him at the side of his head, and another in front only just missed his eye. He fell headlong, and they grabbed his sword and ran on over his body, thinking him dead, and so did he as the warm blood gushed over his face, blinding him.

But he wasn't dead, for he still wondered what was happening and where was Montrose? If Montrose got away it would be with no loss of troops worth counting; he could get into the hills and start the job again from there, and with better material than the islanders—he couldn't get worse.

'Five hundred Highlanders' went round and round in his head like a squirrel in a cage, throbbed maddeningly in the pulse of the blood that was ebbing from the cut in his head; with his five hundred Highlanders Montrose had got off from a worse fix than this and far worse odds, when Hurry had all but trapped him at Dundee. 'If I'd only been with him then'—even now there was room for that agonizing regret among the pain and deafening confusion buzzing in his head. A just-his-luck man, that was all he'd ever been, and now his death was just his luck, no more and no less.

He heard the crash and tearing rip of branches as horses came plunging through the undergrowth. He'd not lie here to be trampled to death; he grabbed at the wet moss and mopped some of the blood from his face—it smelt fresh and cool and earthy; he struggled up somehow and plunged forward again in short staggering rushes as though he were drunk.

The wood was getting misty, the white birch trunks all bluish— he didn't know if it were the smoke of the muskets, or twilight, or his own dulling vision. The noise of fighting too, the clash and shouts and shots, was streeling away as if going up over the hill—

or perhaps he was going deaf. He saw some of his foreigners making through the wood and joined them, but could not understand a word they called to him though he knew Danish and German quite well.

He had no weapon, but he was too weak to use it if he had one; he was still losing blood fast and his head was singing louder than the noise round him. 'Five hundred Highlanders' it sang; those Highlanders at Dundee, Montrose could have got *them* back into their trenches; but they're all dead now, lying under Slain-Man's-Lea—dead men don't fight any more. He would soon be a dead man himself, he'd shot his bolt and missed as usual—he'd got himself on the wrong side at the wrong moment, and he'd never get another chance to get it right; it was too late now, he'd joined Montrose too late, and even if he lived he was under sentence of death and it would be too late to change again.

The wood was clearer in front of him. There was more noise ahead and sharper. He was coming out into the clearing before the next patch of wood higher up, and his side must be making for it, higher ground, thicker wood, away from the cavalry. His side 'on which side, Sir John Hurry?' 'The same side, the losing side, always the same, it's a damned lie to say I ever change it.' He was laughing again in a silly broken giggle.

He blundered out on to the darkening hillside under a pale sky, and saw close by him a few of his horsemen fighting like mad against some of the Covenant dragoons, flanked by musketeers. His half-shut eyes blinked open furiously, he knew that sword-arm swinging up and down, it was Montrose there in the midst of them, and no sooner had he seen him than he saw his horse rear wildly into the air with a long piercing scream and fall with its rider. So it was done now, Montrose was dead, and it was all over.

No, he was up on his feet, fighting like a tiger with the musketeers. His sword had broken but he tore a musket from one of them, clubbed a man on the head with it, and holding it by the muzzle swung it round, clearing ground as he smashed down first one and then another, his face oddly cool and resolute in the midst of those mouthing, writhing faces.

Hurry's head was suddenly clear for a moment. He got his breath together and gave a hoarse yell to young Frendraught— 'Christ! force him on to your horse and make him ride for it!'

More and more men were plunging out through the wood up over the clearing; they surrounded Hurry's band and called to him to yield. He flung up his hands to do so, and in the same instant crashed heavily forward on his face.

IV

MONTROSE rode off on Frendraught's horse, the one man from whom he could bear to receive it, since Frendraught's uncle would ensure his safety as prisoner.

"I'll yield and live," the young man shouted to him. "Do you live and save the cause."

Major Sinclair seized his bridle-rein and urged him on with them, a little group of them galloping up over the slope into the next belt of wood just as their pursuers, close behind, checked to take prisoners.

Montrose saw Hurry go down in the tail of his eye as he rode off, either dead or taken (which meant death). 'There goes a fine soldier,' he thought, but his regret was for more than that. There were many better men than Jack Hurry, and many loyal friends he had left on that stricken field, but for some odd reason the man who had been his toughest enemy, who had kidnapped his young son and heir James and sent him to prison in Edinburgh, was more in his thoughts than any of them during this headlong flight.

There was no time for any thought at first. With their heads laid low along their horses' necks under the spatter of following bullets, the little group reached those further sheltering trees and then scattered, the better to evade their pursuers.

"Tear off the Garter, my lord!" gasped Major Sinclair. "Your coat too, or they'll see you a mile off."

Montrose whipped it off, flung it into the branches of a tree, then with Sinclair and another of his officers made downhill towards the Oykell, and followed it upstream until they could make an attempt to swim it on their horses. The current was fierce. Montrose's horse was swept away and drowned, but he managed to swim ashore. Any mounted man was a marked man in this valley of death where Strachan's cavalry were riding in all directions to slaughter whatever survivors from the battle could be found.

Their clothes too would give them away to whomsoever saw them.

The other two turned their horses loose. Then the three men ran for it, mostly on hands and knees over the sopping marsh by the river, so as to keep their heads below the reeds as long as it was still light enough for their enemies to see any distance. The Northern spring twilight was long and clear, the budding whin and broom shining through it in points of pale fire. The valley where they groped on all fours ran in a long pit of cavernous shadow between the darkening shapes of the hills, and behind them the great grey crag of Craigcoinichean rose gaunt out of its surrounding woods.

Before it was quite night they stumbled suddenly on five shepherds returning from their lambing on the hillside, and each party drew back startled from the other dim forms in the dusk. But as the peasants began to lumber off in the darkness, Montrose called to them and offered to pay them handsomely to exchange their ragged homespuns for their own fine clothes. No explanation was needed.

"We've had wind of a battle," said one of them; "they said the fighting would reach these parts this time."

They did not dare to take the fugitives back to their homes for any food, and indeed it was likely they might walk straight in on some of Strachan's troopers already searching all the houses near. The shepherds gave what directions they could by the stars, and clothed themselves in as few garments as they could possibly wear. They hid the incriminating finery under a stack of peats, then stared a moment after the three strange gentry they had encountered, wet from the marsh and their swim in the river, and one of them still bleeding from his wounds, who now turned away in the familiar rough clothes they themselves had just been wearing, and struck out north-west over the moor.

Montrose's other companion was also a Sinclair, Sir Edward from Orkney, no relation to Major Sinclair of Brims in Caithness. He was a large fair gentle creature like a rather weak Viking, who took it greatly to heart that his Orcadians should have proved such poor fighters. Montrose had to tell him a dozen times that no infantry, however well trained and used to war, could have stood up against the amount of cavalry they had had to face that day.

"They were led blindfolded into an ambush, and that crime is mine."

"Your scoutmaster's," corrected Major Sinclair, and cursed Robert Monro for a little, but neither of the others cared to echo him, they were too anxious about their direction. The still air of that golden afternoon had broken into gusts and rushes of cold wind, and now a great cloud, palpable in shape as a mountain, was coming up from the west, blotting out the stars as it spread over the sky.

Soon the night was black and void of any guidance, but they struggled on through bogs and water-courses, knowing that at any moment they might sink into a peat-hag, but knowing that their only hope of escape was to put as much ground as fast as possible between themselves and Strachan's troopers, who would be scouring the country for Montrose for days after the battle. Their best chance was to get up to the north-west into the Reay country which was friendly to them, but Sir Edward Sinclair was desperately anxious to get further round on the north coast to Thurso where Montrose had first landed and left a garrison, and so get back to his own beloved Orkney.

"That is our true base," he said; "we'll have no peace, no chance to recruit again until we reach Orkney."

Montrose could well understand his longing for those strangely placid, fertile islands of the north that were his home, but it meant a far longer and more difficult circuit, and Sir Edward was the last of the three who would be likely to make it, for his leg had been grazed by a bullet and the heavy going was very painful to him.

"Wait till we get into the hills," Montrose said, "and then we'll see what we can do." And again and again through that night, "Wait till the morning, then we'll see we're going right."

But the morning came in driving rain and sleet and no hint of sun to show which way they were going, and not one of the three had ever before been in this country. They plunged on through drenched heather and the treacherous bright green of bog moss; they heard running water whispering among the grasses, running fast and low and secret to the sea, and always the light stayed white and obscure over the desolate land, a snow-light reflected from the white heads of the hills, a mist-light with no hint from whence it came in that clouded, hidden sky. They might have been groping their way along the bottom of the sea. And then those low thick clouds darkened down again on them and burst in tempestuous rain.

"A place this to perish the crows," Major Sinclair said.

"And that's why they call it Corbiesdale," Montrose answered.

"The corbies will have fine pickings there now anyway after that ambush," said Sinclair with a laugh like the sharp bark of a fox.

His namesake groaned. "It's my leg," he said quickly in apology, as though he were less ashamed to groan for that than over the fate of his wretched islanders.

They talked desultorily as they tramped, chiefly of the trap that had been so cunningly laid for them. Strachan must have done his job cleverly, got his men across the river and up under its high banks into that scrub of whin and broom. Who had been with him? Major-General Holbourn probably; he was his right-hand man now, just as Strachan was Leslie's.

"They've been too well prepared for us, that's what it was," Major Sinclair said. "All this delay, everyone looking to see what the King will do next, and the King trying to look both ways at once, now to you, my lord, and now to Argyll, who hopes to marry him to his daughter—that ought to cure the young rake, to have that psalming sneaking Campbell for a father-in-law!"

And again he laughed on that harsh note that was far from cheering.

Montrose began to talk instead of foreign captains he had met abroad. The Emperor's brother Leopold, that was a fine man though a damned unlucky leader—he had met him just after Condé had smashed his troops at Lens. "Now there's the greatest genius in the field I'll swear—Condé—though he's as mad as a March hare—or is when he's in a rage. I'd rather have Leopold to deal with as an ally—he's a staunch friend, too, of Prince Rupert's."

"What's happened to the Prince these days? Since he's taken to sailing round the world in those leaky ships he grabbed from the Parliament one hears nothing of him or his brother Maurice. One day we'll hear they're under the waves, or sold as slaves to the Turks, and that'll be the end of them."

And again Major Sinclair laughed, and silence fell like the rain, steady, soaking to their skins, and chill as death itself.

When Montrose could not get them to speak or listen, he sang or whistled marching-tunes until sometimes they would join in. Almost every tune he could remember he sang, going back in music all through his life: the foreign music of late years, German, Swedish and Danish drinking-songs, wild dances from the Tartar steppes that he had heard in Prague, bawdy nonsense set to martial airs that the French troops sang on marches, courtly English love-songs, his own Scots ballads of bold ruffians riding to some Border raid that he had sung at college at St. Andrews or with his sisters in the great hall of Kincardine, now a burnt-out ruin, cradle-songs he had heard his wife Magdalen croon to their babies—'Oh can ye sew cushions?' and

> 'When our gudewife had puddins to mak'
> She boiled them in the pan.'

He even sang the tune he had first marched to in Scotland when he was a 'true blue Covenanter' fighting for Scotland's freedom, only to find that the Covenanters denied freedom to Scotland as to all else. He had given his colours to his soldiers, who had worn his blue ribbons in their bonnets and marched against the English armies to the new song of defiance—

> 'All the Blue Bonnets are bound for the Border.'

U

"A good song, whatever the cause of it," he said, and they joined in:

> "'March, march, why the de'il dinna ye march?
> Stand to your arms, my lads,—fight in good order,'"

until the next night fell on them.

It made but little difference, that deeper, more solid darkness. Cold now as well as danger urged them on. If they lay down in this ice-wet ground in their sodden rags they would surely die. So they struggled blindly on and on. By next morning, said Montrose, they would see they were going right.

But next morning it was snowing.

The snow came stinging their frozen faces, stretching across the vast spaces of the valleys like a cloud walking; it came in the thick folds of a curtain, and then fell on them. Once they were in it there was nothing to be seen but the scurrying stinging air made palpable, a witch's frenzy of small thick flakes hard as hailstones, striking their frozen hands and faces with sharp tiny blows, here, there, there, sharp tiny voices laughing at them, telling them they were caught and lost in a whirlwind of imps.

And when it cleared at last, there was nothing to be seen but the whitened grey flanks of hills like sleeping mammoths, streaked and splashed with snow, their heads lost in the indeterminate grey of the snowy sky.

Montrose stole a glance at his companions and saw how much they had changed since their flight began. Their faces had sharpened till every feature seemed a peak through the stubble on their unshaved skins.

Sir Edward was the worst. His leg had swollen, and every limping step was agony. They were all very weak from lack of food, but Sir Edward with his heavier frame and less practice in campaigning was feeling it the most. There were black shadows in the lines at the side of his big nose that looked as though they had been graven there by the advancing shadow of death.

Montrose himself was so faint with hunger that he began to

chew the leather riding-glove he still wore over his left hand to hide from his friends the amount of blood that had kept seeping down from the cut on his arm.

All the blood in his body seemed to have ebbed away from that sword-cut and the one he had got on his head and a bullet-wound in his side; they could be nothing serious, he assured his companions, or he would not have been able to keep going as he had done. But he had kept going chiefly because of the necessity to keep them going.

To encourage and command obedience in whatever straits was so much a part of himself that he never noticed it, nor did his companions, who knew only that as long as they were with him they had to go on, to the end of the world if need be, even though their only desire in the world had become the blinding, agonizing desire to lie down and die where they lay.

He tried to cheer them on by telling them how he had been lost before on hills as huge and desolate as these, and had found help just as he had given up all hope.

They nibbled young heather shoots when they came on them, but the season was very late after the severe winter and there was little to be found. If only they had carried a little oatmeal in a pouch! It was all he and his Highlanders had been able to take with them on their forced marches over the mountains. A very small quantity, mixed with cold water into a paste on the point of his dirk, would keep a man going for days.

And on that winter march to Inverlochy they had caught a deer and hacked it into collops, which they had been thankful to devour raw and bleeding. The notion of any one of them having the strength to pursue and kill a deer now made him laugh feebly, foolishly, until he saw his comrades looking strangely at him and realized that they were afraid he was losing his senses.

He had quickly to recall some silly story of that campaign to explain his laughter: had either of them heard how they had routed the Campbells at Fyvie, when they had run out of ammunition, with a rain of bullets all melted down from the inordinate number of pewter chamber-pots they had found in Fyvie Castle?

A faint echo of Major Sinclair's barking laugh answered him, but Sir Edward staggered on, plainly hearing nothing. They each took his arm on either side.

"Come on, man. We'll march together, though it's dot-and-go-one to keep step with your game leg!"

Or with this ground, one foot up or down at every step. If only it could be level going for one moment!

Again they sang:

"'March, march, why the de'il dinna ye march?'"

until at last Sir Edward's dragging limp could march no more over that broken, tangled, climbing ground, and he fell between them, dragging them to the wet earth; and this time it was not that he would not, but that he could not rise.

There was no chance for him unless his companions should stumble on some remote shieling in the hills, or a shepherd out after a stray sheep, who could bring him food and help.

Montrose and Major Sinclair decided to part company so as to double the chances. They dragged Sir Edward under an overhanging rock by a stream which would give him some small shelter from the icy wind and also make the best landmark they could find.

Then they went their several ways.

Montrose was alone now, and the silence fell on him like a stone.

For four years he had been in the polite noise, the elaborate careless-seeming chatter of well-bred crowds in one princely Court after another; for the last few weeks he had been in armed camps with the clamour of bugles and pipes and drilling of soldiers all round him, the clank of harness and the firing of musket practice, the sharp words of command, the harsh decisive argument of soldiers; for the last two days and nights, longer than any weeks, than any years, he had been cheering on his two exhausted companions.

Now they were no longer marching with him; he no longer spoke nor sang, no longer heard any sound.

The silence of the hills fell all round him, drowning him; at each staggering footstep he sank into the dripping moss, and only the squelching, sucking whisper of the bog spoke to him. Until in despair he cried aloud into the silence, and the wild birds answered 'Curlew—ew.'

To lie down and never get up again, that was becoming the only thing left to wish for. He had prevented the others from doing it, but now that desire seized on himself, and there was no one for him to command and encourage, to force to do his will, for it had ceased to be his will now it had only to do with himself. His life or death no longer mattered.

'Do you live and save the cause,' young Frendraught had called to him. What cause? The cause of a king who had played him false, had looked both ways 'like Janus' face,' as all men would see when they came to judge between him and Charles. Would they not say of himself :

> 'Alas, he had too just a cause
> Never to love thee more'?

The wild rhythm of his high imperious song of love and war was throbbing now in his spent veins; he had not sung it to his companions, for he could not bear to sing it, too much of his life and strangely mingled loves had gone into it. All his love for his King and country, now wasted and thrown away, had gone into it; and his love for his wife Magdalen whom that other love had finally brought to her death; and now his love for Louey whom that love would leave forsaken, a widow before ever she had been his wife.

With that thought of her he knew that he was finished, which he had not known before, and when next he stumbled he did not try to recover himself, but let himself fall and there lie.

A famished quiet fell over him ; the whole world became empty of regret or of desire, even for warmth and food. It would not take long to die, he thought; but sleep came to tell him he was not dead, for he woke from it to such an anguish of cold and hunger and aching limbs that he could no longer lie still.

He sucked the stiff congealed blood on his hand; it tasted salt and increased his ravenous hunger. A man had been known to eat his own hand before now, but a man was mad when he had come to that. It would be better to chew the glove again; it would be better to move and stumble on somehow, anyhow, even if he could scarcely see where he was going.

And that was not because it was night, but because the drenched heather and dead red shapeless bracken kept shifting and clouding, and his eyes could not focus on them. Still there was no sun, only grey mists now that scudded and wreathed themselves before him— or were they the wraiths of his own mind?

There were eyes watching him through the mist, but as he tried to meet them they vanished into mist. He would not lie here to become a raving beast with pain and hunger, he would stand up to his fate whatever it should be.

'March, march, why the de'il dinna ye march?'

He pulled himself somehow on to his feet, though the wet and cold had frozen him so stiff that every movement put him on the rack.

Now he must take command of himself as of his comrades, and not prove more faithless in obedience than his own men. He would go on, no matter in which direction, and on he went, trying once again to sing as he had done with his two companions.

> " 'The deer runs wild on hill and dale,
>   The birds fly wild from tree to tree,
> But there is neither bread nor kail
>   To fend my men and me.' "

He had not sung that to them either, and yet he had sung it not so very long ago—to two companions. He saw their faces before him, his 'most affectionate friend Elizabeth' and her daughter

Louise. Louise wore a silly peaked cap and her hair was tidy for almost the only time he had ever seen it so, and somehow she had annoyed him, God knows why, and they had quarrelled; they had always been quarrelling then, was it for the pleasure of making it up? It must have been, for they knew what was in each other's minds.

'Wherever you go, whatever you are doing,' she had said, 'I shall know it, I think, long, long before word can come of it.'

Does she know now? Dear God, let her not know.

Passionately as he prayed it, he yet knew that he was praying against something that was in the depths of both of them, that he might as well pray that he and she had never been born. For if it was her agony to be with him, it was also the reason that she cared to be alive.

The rain was now falling heavier and heavier, striking at his face and hands, running in rivulets down his neck, stabbing anew at his already ice-wet skin, and along his bones ran shuddering currents, now cold, now burning hot—they ran before his eyes, dizzying them so that he could not see where to put his next step.

There was nothing beyond this small wet circle of rain and squelching moss and heather through which he stumbled; it spread over the whole world and nothing lay beyond; there was nothing beyond this moment, no change of night nor day, of good or ill fortune, nothing could happen to change it ever again.

He had reached the end of the world, but when you reached the end of the world it went on,—on and on for ever.

He was not alone now. Who was it walking with him? He could not see; thick tempests of cold rain poured between himself and that shadowy wavering figure; there was no sound of any foot-steps but his own, sucking down into the bog, now pausing to gather strength for the next plunge, now staggering, sinking on. He called again and again. A thin cracked voice he heard, so feeble it must come from a great way off—but presently he knew it for his own. There was the tinkle and whisper of little streams running down from the hills through long grasses and moss, the relentless swish of the rain,—these were the only voices beside his own. But he was not alone.

Who walked with him in the rain?

"Louey!" he called. "Louey!"

And now he saw her long hair astream in the thin silver spears of the rain. She turned her head and looked at him, slantwise, as she had so often done when she was laughing; her eyes were of the air, her body of the rain, but they were her eyes, it was herself walking before him; however fast he tried to follow her, she was still always just ahead of him; he could not reach her, for always those long spears of rain were between them, and the trickle of hidden running water whispered and mocked at him instead of her voice.

Then for a moment he saw her quite clearly, outlined against an obscure white light that every moment was getting brighter. The rain swept past him, swept her with it, she had vanished with the rain. Now he saw the hillside beyond, and patches of clear sky above, and across it came the torn dark figures of men fleeing from the lost battle; on dark horses they rode, whose long manes were streeling behind them, his men fleeing and he among them up there in the opening sky.

The rain had piled itself up in black clouds rolling higher and higher up the sides of some of the nearer hills—and he knew them! He knew those rounded humped shapes. He knew that long pale green strip of wood sunk among the dead bracken, purple with rain, the trees huddling low for shelter on the deep banks of a stream. There was a wall of bluish rock that went up in steps like a staircase, spattered with bright moss—he knew that rock on Speyside.

He stood still, trying desperately to pull his wits together. Hope was giving him strength, clearing his mind as the scene began to show itself before his eyes. Louey had vanished, could never have been there. But surely this was real, and these were his own familiar hills where he and Alasdair had held their base through their year of victories? Could he have reached them in this time?

Again and again he tried to count over the times of darkness, for then he would know how many days and nights he had been walking; he must have been going now for three days and nights. If he had missed his direction north as he had intended, but crossed the Oykell at its source and gone south and by luck passed clean through the armies of his enemies, he might well have reached Speyside.

He had marched thirty miles in a single night before now, and on two nights running; he had walked twenty miles over the heather as easily as a stroll round his home of Kincardine, when he had gone to meet Alasdair.

Then he had after all made his goal and could now begin his campaign anew, building up his force among the friendly hills he knew so well. Hope was now racing faster than the fever through his veins. Hurry might have given the slip to his captors, he was quick and cunning as a ferret; Sibbald might have escaped the carnage as he himself had done; young Lewis Gordon he could win to his side as he had done before; the Mackenzies would certainly get their marching-orders from Seaforth and come in to him,—yes, it could all begin again then, starting clean and clear and with the right material this time, instead of those poor wretched men of Orkney and the handful of foreign infantry.

So he stood still, with hope raising his heart and his eyes to the hills from whence would come his help.

The land before him was opening further and further into the distance as the gates of the rain drew back from before it; he saw a long deep blue line of hills with the evening light behind them; and in that light, still further hills of palest unearthly blue, the hills of a further land beyond this world, the Promised Land that his Highlanders believed lay in the west and showed itself but once in a lifetime to mortal eyes.

> 'My soul, there is a country
> Far beyond the stars.'

He had come to his promised land, the haven where he would be.

But now the nearer clouds were rising on either side of him, lit with the colours of flame and blood, and behind them, still wreathed in their stormy colours, there rose vast shapes that seemed higher and more monstrous than those of any mountains he had ever seen in his own land. They mounted guard on either side of the valley down which he had been gazing; in front of them lay a black pit of shadow, the Valley of the Shadow among the flaming mountains of hell.

For these terrible shapes were those of an unknown land.

The wall of bluish rock he thought he knew had receded into the distance as the nearer scene grew clear; he now saw its summit jagging against the sky, and saw that it was a huge mountain all of rock, and the patches of bright moss must be full-grown trees, and the steps like a staircase were steep precipices.

He stood on that bare hillside, looking across the valley at the awful sunset that revealed these strange giants to him. He knew now that he had walked into an unknown and trackless wilderness, knew that he was lost. He had reached the end of his world. There was no more hope for him. 'My God, my God, why hast Thou forsaken me?'

V

SOMETHING was pushing him, tugging him back to life. He tried to resist, but the agony that was consciousness began to creep back into his veins; he heard a groan and knew it to be his own voice; he felt a warm panting breath and something wet, soft, insistent, nuzzling at his face and neck; he opened his eyes and saw the woolly head of a sheep-dog close to his own. A shepherd in a ragged plaid, his hair and beard as shaggy as his dog, was leaning over him and spoke to him, but his voice now boomed in his ears and now faded away to nothing, and Montrose could make out nothing that he said.

The shepherd knelt beside him and began to pull him on to his feet; he got his arm round him under his shoulders so that Montrose's weight was leaning over on to him, and thus, half dragging him, got him over the ground. He did not know how far they went, nor how long.

Behind a huge boulder of rock there crouched a shieling built of shapeless lumps of stones piled together without mortar, roofed with grassy turf, and somewhere in the middle of it was stuck the end of a hollow trunk of tree as chimney.

The door opened on to a blur of shadow and red light from the smouldering peats that lay on the bare floor without any hearth-stone. A woman whose hollow cheek-bones and gaunt skull-shaped head seemed carved out of the darkness, came towards him, stretching thin claw-like hands to help him down on to the creepie-stool by the fire. Little bright faces peeped out at him from behind her shadowy skirts, the faces of children that ran away on their bare feet as lightly as blown feathers as soon as he looked at them. Those thin hands were stretched out to him again, holding a bowl of warm milk.

"Mammie, Mammie, it's our supper you are giving him!" came whispers behind her in the Gaelic which Montrose knew well.

"And would you deny it to the poor gentleman, and he dying famished of cold and hunger?"

"Yon's no gentleman. Look at his ragged plaid."

"Look at himself, and say he's no gentleman!"

He drank the milk, he ate a small piece of oat-cake she gave him; he saw the woman clearly now and her husband beside her. He looked into their faces and said, "I am Montrose and I have lost the fight at Corbiesdale. How far am I from there?"

"Near thirty mile," said the shepherd.

"Where am I then?"

"Near Assynt."

Then he had walked neither north nor south, but, in as far as he had kept any straight direction, due west. But he could not think about it now; the warmth of the fire and the taste of food was bringing back that blinding desire to sleep that had beset him even in the rain and wind. The man asked him about the battle; the news of it had reached here, so indeed had some of Strachan's troopers who were searching out the fugitives in all directions.

But Montrose scarcely heard him, and they stared in concern at the gaunt face that showed grey-white beneath its three-day stubble of beard, and the eyes, bright with fever, sunk in their deep hollows. They laid him down by the fire with some rags under him and an extra plaid over him as soon as his soaked clothes had begun to dry, the steam of the wet wool rising in clouds by the fire.

Before they did so, he had already fallen into a sleep so deep and dead that nothing, it seemed, would ever drag him out of it. He felt them trying to do so, but shook their hands off his shoulders and fell asleep again; he saw the cold light of dawn in the room for an instant and heard their voices hissing into his ears, 'There are troopers on the hill, they are coming to this house,' and his head rolled back on the floor and he was asleep again. They dragged and rolled him to the side of the wall and pulled him into an empty trough and heaped some straw over him, and at once he was asleep again.

But soon there was the jingle of harness outside the hovel, and the tiny room was filled with tramping footsteps and the clank of spurs and loud bullying voices. That woke him at last; he lay in the dead darkness under the straw in the trough and heard a whispering patter of Gaelic from the children, and the shepherd and his wife swearing that they had not seen nor helped any fugitive from the battle.

A soldier thrust his sword down through the straw; it went clean between Montrose's legs and hit against the bottom of the trough, and he drew it out, saying "Nothing there!" Then he asked questions and threatened the shepherd.

"If you lie, we'll pull this house over your ears and leave you both dead beneath it. But if you get a chance to put us on the track of Montrose it will be the best chance you ever got—there's a reward on his head that would make you rich for life."

Now indeed he was awake. Something had woken in him that he had never known before. Those poor half-starved creatures had sheltered and warmed him and given him of their own pitifully scanty food, and were now risking their lives to save his own, when with a word or sign they could buy wealth for themselves and their children for ever.

'Do you live and save the cause!' Frendraught had called to him, and again and again his comrades had told him, just lately and after Philiphaugh, 'What do the lives of a few hundred soldiers matter, as long as you live and can get together more armies for the King?'

But in such a criss-cross of purposes as he had been engaged in all his grown life, it had become too complicated to distinguish any more between them, and who but God Himself could say that his King's life, or his own, was of any more importance than the lives of a man and woman of such simple faith and goodness?

When all was quiet again in the house they came and let him out of his hiding-place, and the woman, whose voice had sounded so dull and unconcerned before the soldiers, was shaking all over, and the tears running down her haggard cheeks. He took their hands and thanked them and told them that never again would he put two fellow-creatures in the danger that they had undergone for him.

"You owe me no loyalty," he said, "and yet you have done as much for me as if I were your chief and your brother. I thank God that you have not come to harm through me."

He insisted on leaving them then and there, though they urged him to stay. But he said he would go to the laird of Assynt, young Neil Macleod, who, as far as he could remember, had served under him for a short time when some of the Northern Highlanders had joined his standard at Inverness just before he had left Scotland four years ago.

He told them, too, of Sir Edward Sinclair, and described the rock under which they had left him by the stream, but it was impossible to say where. Only by chance they might stumble on him.

The shepherd gave him full directions as to the way to Assynt: if he went on down the hillside and along this valley he would see the loch ahead of him, and Macleod's castle of Ardvreck on a long spit of rocky land that thrust out into its waters. He stood in the doorway, pointing out the lie of the land in the misty sunrise, then wished Montrose God-speed, and the woman took his hand and kissed it.

The day brightened as he went down the hill. Sleep and the small amount of food he had eaten had made him stronger. The air was fresh, swept clean of rain, and now the early sun had pierced the mists and was shining on the further slopes where the wet heather and bracken looked as though they had all been spun over with diamonds; a lark's song soared over his head, rising higher and higher into the pale blue.

He had left two unknown friends of a condition as wretched as any animal's, but of a courage and kindness to make glad the hearts of heroes; he was walking to meet a man who had served with him, who had married, he now remembered, into the family of Monro of Lemlair which had been friendly to him. All the freshness of this spring morning shone with his new hope and strength and belief in men.

Nor was he dismayed when he saw two men walking ahead of him. They were none of the soldiery, he could see, and he called to them and said he was seeking Macleod. They were two of his gillies and offered to lead him to Ardvreck. He was still too weak from his wounds to be able to keep pace with them, but they helped him along, and after some time they saw a great stretch of loch below, sparkling in the sunshine. All round it the hills came down as blue and clear as turquoise to that glassy water, and the great mountains behind, that had looked so monstrous in the stormy sunset of the previous evening, were now pale as faint shadows painted on the mist.

In this vast circle of the hills the loch was set like a mirror at the bottom of a cup, a mountain-ridge running in an enormous jagged wall alongside it. A small grass-grown peninsula of lime-stone rock, all the low foreshore whitened at its edges by the water to the unnatural bleached whiteness of bones that have been picked clean by the crows, jutted out into the loch some way down, forming a tiny narrow bay in the shape of a crocodile's long jaws.

On this promontory stood a small, neat, delicately proportioned castle, set in a smooth piece of pasture-land where clumps of blue-green flag leaves made brilliant patches in the rusty turf; the mica on its stones glistened in the sunshine; it looked like a pretty toy dropped by some giant child.

Montrose told his guides they need come no further with him, and made his own way down to the shore. All over that whitened foreshore of low, bleached rock there grew a climbing white rock-rose that he had seen nowhere else, the flowers much larger than the ordinary yellow rock-rose, and dead-white with a golden centre. He picked one as he passed and stared at it, seeing the white starry flowers on the candle-lit table at Rhenen that last night when he had said good-bye to Louey. He had sat beside her mother, answering her gay flicker of talk, and all the time seen Louey's face through the white flowers.

'Shall I see it again?' he asked himself, counting the petals of this strange flower. There were eight of them, so he had better not pluck them for his answer, since it would work out 'No.' And he laughed and threw it away, knowing himself a little light-headed still from his fever, but not minding since he had now so little way to go.

A young man was strolling along the shore towards him, carrying a fishing-rod. He wore a plaid round his shoulders, and his trews showed him to be of the quality, though he had none of the air of it. Montrose realized that this must be Neil Macleod, but was surprised to see how loutish and unformed he looked. He must be about two or three years over twenty, a fair, fresh-coloured lad with a softly rounded jaw inclined to be podgy, a mild blue eye, and an indolent, rather indecisive walk.

Montrose stood still, scanning him as he came towards him. Yes, he knew him. This must have been the raw young cub of seventeen or so who came with his uncle and a hundred men to join his standard at Inverness.

"Who are you?" asked the young laird, and the ragged scarecrow figure answered,

"I am Montrose."

Neil Macleod stared at him, heavily aghast; for an instant it was plain that he thought the man before him must be mad.

But Montrose went straight on: "We were ambushed at Corbiesdale, as I think you must have heard by now. I got away and had these clothes from a shepherd. I have been on the moor since, but there has been no sun till to-day and I have missed my way and come due west. I don't know if you are still of the same mind as when you and your uncle Hugh Macleod served under me before. If you are, will you help me get north to Thurso and so back to Orkney? If you feel that you cannot do so, tell me, and I will go on my way as I am."

"You can't go like that. You're ill—I saw you walking. You must stay here first. Are you wounded, my lord?" There was real concern in his voice, and his smooth face had wrinkled up till it looked like a bull-pup's. "I must tell my wife," he added as though he had said the thing that was of most importance.

"I must warn you," said Montrose, "that it would be to your danger to take me into your house. I've sworn not to bring that danger again on anyone who did not wish to run it for their own reasons. Have you those reasons still? Will you come with me to Orkney and help me start our venture again?"

Macleod had flushed to the roots of his fair hair. "My God, if I only could!" he exclaimed, and then a lugubrious shadow fell over his face and he turned impatiently and said, "But we can't go on talking here. It might not be even safe. You must come back with me, my lord, and at least have your wounds seen to before you go on your way. My wife will wash and bandage that cut. Ardvreck is as secure a place as any in the Highlands. One can see who is coming from miles off—with all that narrow neck of land between us and the shore there's no chance of being taken unawares. I'll have my men out. You'll be safe with me, my lord."

He was talking rapidly, excitedly. He took Montrose's arm to help him along, still talking, with exclamations under his breath: "Back on the hill again—to get away—to see fighting again—to be away from the women—God's blood, if I could do that!"

Montrose paid little attention to these jerks and starts. He was getting pretty well exhausted again, both with his long walk and the mental effort of putting the case fairly and squarely before this oddly boyish creature. He had to tell him also of Sir Edward and try to describe that rock and stream again and give some idea of the lie of the land. Macleod at once promised to send out some of his men to search for him.

They nearly stepped on part of a family of young peewit fledglings walking valiantly along the muddy path that had been

x

worn by generations of feet down the middle of the spit of land towards the peninsula; their mother, who was guarding the rest, piped shrilly from the long grass at the side of the road, but her brood merely flapped their minute and useless wings and strode on right under the monster feet that were descending on them. Neil Macleod stopped to chase them to the side; they rushed back again, he had to pursue them, and their tiny legs marched ridiculously fast, before he could shuffle them along to their mother with his large clumsy hands.

"The dogs would get them," he murmured apologetically as he rejoined Montrose.

They stood beneath the castle; very neat and bright and compact it looked, with the green slope of the little peninsula behind. Macleod pointed out the delicate chisel-dressing on one of the towers—"that's very rare in the Highlands," he said with pride. "It was my ancestor John the Grizzled built this more than a hundred years ago, but our branch of the family have been here far longer. My father died while I was an infant, and I inherited the place on my grandfather's death, long ago, but his second wife kept her own children in possession of it, curse her wicked old soul! It was only last year that we got them turned out of it, and I can tell you it cost a fortune. It was all Christie's—my wife's—doing too," he added dutifully, as though he had said it a good many times before.

Montrose's dazed senses got the impression that his host was really a boy who was only pretending to be a grown married man. He had it still more when as they went into the hall the lad said, "It will be a grand little house to leave to one's children."

"You have children?"

"None yet, my lord." Again there was that lugubrious hang-dog puppy look.

"You are very young yet."

"That is what I tell my wife. There is plenty of time. But we are not lucky. I never had a chance as a child, my parents dead, and my grandfather never gave me any education or care—his second wife saw to that! I was brought up anyhow."

His voice had dropped into the whine of one accustomed to self-pity, but it broke off as a servant came forward, and Montrose heard him calling through the rooms on a high triumphant note, "Christie! Christie, come here! Who do you think I have here?"

The servant, a shabby elderly man with thick red beard, who evidently did most of his work in the stables, stood staring at the strange guest; then, as Montrose swayed forward and put a hand on the wall to steady himself, pushed forward a bench for him to sit on.

He seemed to sit there for hours. Neil Macleod was a long time telling his wife whom he had here. If he did not get some food quickly he would faint before he could speak again. He saw two blurred figures coming down the winding stone stair, he tried to rise, but it was no good—if he did that, he would fall on the floor. The two figures had disappeared and everything went black before his eyes; he held his head down to get the blood back into it, and with a mighty effort kept himself from collapse.

They were round him now, giving him whisky. He whispered, "Bread."

A woman's decisive voice said, "Bread indeed! He shall have my best broth."

He heard her swish off to get it. If only she would bring bread and not wait for the broth!

But at last he got food, and then Macleod helped him upstairs and got him on to a bed, brought him water to wash in, got his damp clothes off him and gave him some of his own to wear. Then Christie Macleod came and washed his wounds and bandaged the cuts with firm plump capable hands. She seemed older than her husband, a fine sturdy young woman with a square jaw and shiny brown eyes like chestnuts, the sort of woman one would expect to have a baby punctually every year, so Montrose thought hazily as she bustled round him, ordering the servants and her husband about on the same high firm note of exasperated efficiency.

Macleod hung behind after the women had left the room, asking a dozen questions as to his guest's requirements, and repeating them: "You are *sure* that you don't want this?—that you wouldn't like that?"

His hospitality was almost pathetically eager, he seemed to be trying to assure himself as well as his guest that everything would be well with him now. "You'll soon be well, my lord. We'll get you off to Thurso. Perhaps I can come too, I don't know. I'd rather go with you than anything in the world, but one can't always do what one wants. There's my wife, you see, and the place is heavily encumbered. We are over our ears in debt. We've not been lucky."

"Neil!" called a high voice, and he hastily went out, leaving his last words echoing in Montrose's ears.

No, they were not lucky; they had a snug, even elegant little castle that had remained intact all through the troubles, while his own homes were either a heap of ruins or in the hands of his enemy Argyll; they were young, comely, in good health, while he was wounded and fevered, an outlaw fleeing for his life.

Yet he would not change places with them; he even had an odd sense of pity for them, at any rate for that kindly, uncertain, apologetic youth; but in another instant he had ceased to think of him, for he had fallen deep into an unfathomable well of sleep.

"If it's money you need for your estate," said Montrose, "you will find it at Thurso. There is plenty there with the garrison I left as my base, and your reward for bringing me back to them will be more than you could get out of several years of your crops and cattle here."

"No, oh no," protested Macleod, flushing hotly, "it's not that, my lord, I want no reward for helping you—if I could go with you, that would be my best reward—it's not a question of money——"

But he had been talking of money and nothing but money for

the last half-hour—"there is no money—if only we had more
money"—while he explained the difficulties in the way of his going
with Montrose. Yet he was genuinely longing to go—that was
quite plain.

They had talked this matter over again and again, and sometimes
Neil swore that he would come with him, and, when he had had
a little whisky, thumped his large purple-knuckled fist (he had had
chilblains all the winter, he said) down on to the table and swore
that nothing should prevent his going with the Marquis of Montrose,
that this was the chance of his life, the only chance he had ever had,
and nothing and nobody, '*nobody*, no damned soft woman's body
either,' should prevent his going with him.

It was plain enough by now wherein he was unlucky. He had
failed to please his wife, Christian Monro of Lemlair, to whom he
had been married since he was well under age; and he could feel
no real confidence in providing her with an heir to this house, of
which she was even more desperately proud than himself.

'Desperately' was the word, for she was a woman to whom
property, whether of the living bodies of husband and children, or
the dead stones of a house, was the thing that mattered more than
anything else in life.

And hadn't she the right to be proud of Assynt when it was she
who had planned, saved, intrigued, and fought, fought, fought all
those early years of their married life to win back the estate that
was rightfully theirs and their children's?

If Neil permitted himself a doubt as to their ever having children,
he never dared show it to Christie, for she would have regarded it
as sacrilege. Her certainty that their line would last in Assynt
had grown into a creed, fierce as creeds are apt to grow in Scotland.
She was a woman who never stopped thinking.

'Remember the Macleods of Assynt,' she would whisper at night
into the ear of her husband, who, married to her since he had been
a nervous, self-conscious hobbledehoy of a youth, found it no
encouragement.

Their uneasy relationship showed itself in their continual irritation with each other; her manner told him he was a fool; and his, that she was a bully; they were at one only in their constant planning for the improvement of the estate and clearing it from debt; then they could both feel that they were people of importance and value, even to each other.

Neil's hope of escape from his galling position was proving an even higher bribe than the money Montrose would certainly be able to pay him once they got to Thurso. There were higher bribes too in further store. The Macleods of Assynt would be remembered to good purpose if Montrose's next venture should succeed, and Neil be made known to his King as the man who had saved the Viceroy of Scotland and through him the country for King Charles. He said this to Christie the night after Montrose arrived.

Outside their curtained bed, outside the thick stone walls, Macleod could hear the wind rising and gusts of sudden rain thrown in handfuls against the shuttered windows; he heard the loch waters lashing up into that regular rhythmic fury that he had heard again and again all through his life. They used to whisper to him in his childhood, 'The Castle of Assynt is yours—yours—yours—those others have no right to it'; and then again that hissing monotony, 'Assynt is yours, yours, yours.'

Now they splashed and shouted, 'Be strong. Be lucky. Get money for Assynt, Assynt, Assynt, that's all that's needed, money for Assynt.'

He heard them saying this yet again as he lay waiting for his wife's reply, and when it came he felt he had known what it would be.

"It is a great risk, all the more now that Montrose's first venture has proved unlucky."

"It was not his first, it was his second, and destroyed before it began. His first venture was lucky over and over again, in six great battles, to say nothing of all his lesser engagements."

But at that she suddenly turned loving and pitiful and sobbed, "How can I let you go? What if you were killed? I should not even have a child to remember you by?"

And though he cursed inwardly, he was proud to find she did still love him, and even if she had been disappointed in him, she at least did not want any other man.

"You do love me then?" he asked; and she clung to him until he felt that he was drowning.

VI

"WHAT is settled then. You cannot go with me, and I will start off now by myself."

"You cannot start yet, my lord. You are wounded, you still have fever, it would not be safe."

"And do you think it safe to stay?"

Again there came that uneasy flush. The young fellow was as sensitive as a girl. Montrose wondered if he had seemed to cast a doubt on his power to protect him. "I know you are in a strong position here," he said, "and that your men are as much to be trusted as yourself. In the Highlands a whole countryside can keep a secret. But I cannot wait. Every hour counts. And it is unfair to your wife."

"My wife! *What* wife?" Macleod exclaimed uncontrollably, and then in haste as if to explain his bitterness, "You need not trouble about Christie. She'll get what she wants, always. She has prevented my going with you—what wife is that for a man?"

Montrose looked keenly at him. He should learn either to be master in his own house, or to put up with the position better. It was not surprising that after such an outburst the young man should avoid his eyes. Perhaps it was from that moment that he seemed to avoid his guest altogether, and certainly talked far less freely to him.

Yet he would not hear of Montrose leaving them just yet while in this condition; if he would but wait a day or two, he said, he should have a guide across the mountains, for a drover of his was going north and Montrose could go with him disguised as a farmer from the south—the drover himself need not know who he was, and would incur no responsibility.

"I had a message from him about his journey only yesterday. You probably heard him riding into the courtyard?"

"I heard a horse's hoofs, yes."

328

"And saw the rider?"

No, Montrose had not seen the messenger, but why should it matter, he asked. But the young man had got into one of his incoherent fits; he talked of his wife's clan to which the messenger belonged, and enlarged on the messenger's history, in which family pride, contempt of his own poverty, and a rather pointless dirty story became so inextricably mixed that Montrose's wearied brain had soon to give up the attempt to follow it.

But again and again he insisted on the certainty of the drover starting north in a day or two, and Montrose, exhausted both in mind and his still painfully wounded body, was glad enough of the delay. Indeed he knew well that he could make no journey now on foot, and that it would be as impossible for him to find the way alone across the mountain wilderness that lay to the north as when he had wandered out of his reckoning up Strath Oykell to these far western mountains.

Canisp, Quinag, Suilven, those were the strange harsh names of some of these giants; they were not really higher than Ben Nevis, which he had seen when he had led his Highlanders across its lower slopes to their victory at Inverlochy, but they seemed so by reason of their sudden and violent enormity, as of mountains belonging not to this world. Even in the calm and sunny spell that had succeeded the mist and rain and that fierce sunset, they looked unnaturally forbidding, mounting guard round this sheltered strip of valley that enclosed the loch, the spit of low green pasture-land and its castle.

That mountain-ridge that ran along the opposite side of the loch fastened itself on his restlessly weary and hectic imagination; wherever he looked he could not avoid the sight of it; even when he turned his back on it he knew it was there behind him, closing in on him, shutting him up in this bottle-neck of land, like a prison wall built when there were giants on the earth.

Yes, this place was like a prison, though he had been treated kindly in it. That wretched boy with his cold red hands shambling past him was a prisoner; and his sensible comely wife, whose ruthless jaw-bone now showed so plainly beneath her fresh rosy skin, was his jailer.

She was always taking her husband's arm and leading him away to talk with her, walking arm-in-arm up and down, up and down beside the long curved jaws of the little bay, their fair heads bent as in earnest contemplation of their feet, Macleod continually checking his loose sprawl to keep an even pace with her short determined steps. No couple could seem more united in equal companionship, and yet—'My wife? *What* wife? I have no wife!' Had the lad really said that, or was it someone long ago in a play? Whichever it was, whatever the reason or no reason, the sight of them walking thus together made Montrose uneasy.

Yet if Neil Macleod seemed less friendly to him than at first, his wife Christian was certainly more so. She talked more at meals and more to her guest, she talked now a great deal in fact, telling him one thing after another about their encumbered estates and their false and wicked relatives who had withheld this their own place from them until this very last year, telling him too of their rapacious neighbours the Mackenzies, and other septs of their own clan the Macleods, all of whom had done them heavy injuries in times past and were now a constant menace.

"And there is no money," she said, "if only we had more money!"

As she talked, her husband sat silent, crumbling his bread into pellets and pushing them this way and that on the table, eating little and drinking a good deal, lowering up at her under his bushy fair brows like a suspicious bullock. Montrose answered her from time to time with some difficulty both in collecting his words and attending to hers, which clanked against his dulled senses like chains. The wavering light of the tallow dips fell on the smooth coils and blobs of heavy fair hair that surrounded her head, making it massive like a helmet, outlined against the great stone hood of the fireplace behind her. He could just make out the crest of their family carved in the stone, the 'Sun in its Splendour,' with its graven lines radiating out from it in a halo behind that powerful feminine head. 'Luceo non uro' ran the motto above the crest.

It was not easy to rest in this house, even when alone. He escaped from it when he could. The little waves in the loch lapped incessantly against the foreshore, reminding him of the sound of the waves on the white shingle below Rossdhu where he had spent his schoolboy holidays,—reminding him of the ruffled water in the canals those windy spring days in Holland a whole year ago now, when he had stood beside Louey and seen the light from that water rippling up from it, clear and sensitive as her laughter, over her tender, brilliant face.

And they had stood beside the river that high summer day when he rode to Rhenen to say good-bye to her, and the sound of the church bells of Saint Kunera echoed up from it as if chiming far below the deep running water.

'You take Saint Kunera's blessing with you then, and Saint Patrick's charm.' That was what she said. Was she praying for him now, on this evening of early May, there at Rhenen, walking by the river in this green dusk, while before him the loch of Assynt turned to a shimmer of grey, and the shadows of the great hills crept across the loch and gathered round the castle? A dream had fallen on him; her face was the only real and living thing in a world of shadows and lapping, whispering water.

He tried to shake it off him, to test his strength by walking along the shore, where those long low ridges of bleached limestone rock now gleamed in the dusk like the whitened bones of beasts long since dead. His legs felt as if they would give under him at every step, and his head as if it were swimming above him at some distance from the rest of his body; no doubt his efforts were increasing his fever, and that was why he had this illusion that he was being followed—just as he had believed that Louey was walking beside him in the rain on the hillside.

But this present imagination was of no friendly familiar, no wraith of his other self; he was being watched, dogged, by some-thing alert and cunning, for its own purposes. He rounded a corner of the shore, then turned sharply back, and saw at some distance the elderly red-bearded servant whom he had first seen on entering the castle. He had hastened his steps as Montrose rounded the rock, and now fell back, disconcerted at being seen. Montrose stood still to wait for him and ask why he was following him, but the servant, after coming a few steps forward, turned round and loafed off towards the castle.

That sharp turn and sudden standstill had made Montrose realize his weakness. Feeling very giddy, he sat down on the rock to rest, and tried to think why the servant had been following him, but he could not, the buzzing in his head was too loud, and now the wavelets against the shore sounded louder still; he could hear voices in them, hushed, half-whispering voices, they came all round him, from behind him as well as from in front on that low white shore.

This must be the fever again; but no, he could hear not only voices now but words, coming nearer and nearer,—"twenty-five thousand pounds Scots," they were saying in a woman's insistent voice, "think—think—*think* what we could do——"

('Think—think—think how little it will mean to you to *die* the richer by a thousand pounds!')

Who had said that? Why, fat Ned Hyde in his miserable lodging at The Hague, telling him with pardonable self-satisfaction how he had thus rebuked some time-serving friend in England. That was a great little man, a pity he had gone to Spain instead of staying with his King this past winter.

Thinking of Ned Hyde and of young King Charles, he had missed the answer to that fierce feminine injunction, but he could not in any case have heard it, for the words that answered her were mumbled and broken on a note of misery. They came as from a much further distance than those brisk tones—and then suddenly they stopped. No woman spoke again. There was no sound now but the soft wordless lap-lapping of the waves.

So harsh and abrupt was that silence that it startled his feverish senses sharper than any sound. He lifted his head and looked quickly round at the grassy slope behind him, and saw Neil Macleod and his wife standing there, staring at him, and in Neil's hand a letter.

For an instant they stood as still as if they had been turned to stone, and then Neil began to stuff the letter into the pocket of his leather coat, but his wife snatched it from him and smoothed it out and came forward to Montrose, striking at it with her other hand, her fair face pushed up into a worried frown.

"The debts on this estate," she said, "are the curse of our lives. You have fairly caught us at our usual game, my lord, discussing how under heaven we can make both ends meet."

He said nothing. He looked at the piece of stiff paper crackling and curving in her hand, a small moving patch of white in the dusk. The silence gathered about them again like a thunder-cloud about to break over their heads.

But it did not break. Christian Macleod saw to that. She began to say what a shock it had given them to see their guest had walked so far; obviously he had tired himself out. She had given Hamish, Neil's body-servant, instructions to keep an eye on him whenever he went out, so as to be at hand in case of need—had Montrose perhaps noticed his following him?

"You must give my Lord Marquis your arm, Neil,—indeed, my lord, you must not try to rise and walk without help."

With a very ill grace Neil shambled forward. Yet Montrose felt that his reluctance to help him showed more kindness of heart than his wife's concern for him. He lifted his head and looked him in the face, but the young laird's eyes fell before his and he stared at the ground as he awkwardly held out his arm.

"Will you tell me," Montrose said, "why you wish me to come back with you to your house? If it is to betray me to my enemies, then I have a last favour to ask you. You have your dirk. If you kill me now, you can tell them that you did it when I was trying to escape, and you will save me a long torture and humiliation. Will you do this for me, Macleod, and I will forgive you my death, for I see that you are helpless."

A low sobbing moan like a hurt animal's broke from the young man; he crumpled up on his knees before Montrose, but in the same instant his wife darted forward and pulled him to his feet, crying shame on him for taking such an insult so tamely,—"but no wonder his heart is broken at your suspicions, my lord, and indeed they come ill from you after all we have done to prove our friendship!"

She was talking now, talking, talking, the air was full of her sharp little cries, of the indignant rustle of her voice, and "Hamish!" she called again and again, the name shrilling high through the dim air, answered by the discordant cries of the startled gulls.

Hamish came running over the dark slope of the land; his mistress spoke rapidly to him in Gaelic, reproaching him for not keeping a better watch on the lord Marquis; he and Neil helped him to his feet and walked him back to the castle, on either side of him and each with a hand on his arm. Now indeed he was a prisoner and could not escape, and why did that woman still try to preserve any contrary fiction, walking beside them, still talking, still fluttering that false white paper in her hand? Or was he indeed delirious and had accused them wrongly?

He said in a low voice to Neil, while she was still talking, "If I have wronged you, I am sorry. I know that you would not willingly betray me."

But no sound came in answer from the young man, and his head was too bent for Montrose to see the face.

The moon, still in her first quarter, had begun to show plainly in the clear sky as they came into the courtyard of Ardvreck, and there they stopped dead.

Montrose felt Macleod's shoulder go rigid against his, and from the horror in the other man's flesh there shot a spasm down his own arm as if a sinew had been twisted. This he felt before he raised his eyes and saw that the courtyard was full of mounted men.

One of them spurred his horse a little forward at the sight of them.

"Is this the prisoner?" he said.

Macleod's hand dropped from Montrose's arm like a stone falling. He swung round and without a word broke into a blundering run, out of the courtyard, away over the moor.

His wife stepped forward.

"You have come very quickly, sir," she said. "Is it Major-General Holbourn himself?"

The burly man on the big horse dismounted.

"Yes, madam. We left on the instant that we got your message, and your husband, I suppose, despatched it as soon as he heard from your brother, Captain Andrew Monro. It was I advised Monro writing to you after Corbiesdale so that your husband might do all in his power to apprehend any fugitives, and particularly James Graham should he come your way."

"Yes, yes, I have my brother's letter here."

She was crackling it backwards and forwards, showing some nervousness now, but Holbourn took no notice of that. In the dim air his round red face glowed fresh from his long ride as he set about his business.

"We've another prisoner here. Have you anywhere we can put them?"

"There are the cellars. Hamish, show the way."

Her voice had won back to something harsher than its usual briskness.

"And my men?" Holbourn was saying instantly. "You have food for them? They can quarter in the barns. And feed for the horses—madam? They've had some hard going."

"Yes, General, *yes*." The harassed female voice came again, anxious to sound eager and obliging, yet with a strained note in it as though at any moment it might break into a scream of rage at all these orders. "And you will dine with us, General—we were not expecting your arrival so soon, but you will find us ready—and glad, very glad to entertain you. My husband—I cannot think where—oh, he has gone to make arrangements for your men, that is why he has left us. This is a small place, and simple, but——"

That voice was still trailing away behind him, getting fainter and fainter above him, up there in the open air of the spring evening, as Montrose was led by two of Holbourn's men down into the cellars, and there turned to see the other prisoner who was being brought down after him.

It was Major Sinclair.

The soldiers went out. The heavy doors swung to on them, and they heard the rusty bolts clanking as they were drawn, and the chill darkness closed all round them, shutting out each other's faces.

VII

" IT is you, isn't it, Sinclair ? Where did they get you ?"

"On the moor, sir."

"Did they find Sir Edward ?"

"No, and if they do, he'll be past them. He hadn't long to last.
So Macleod sold you, my lord."

"For twenty-five thousand pounds Scots."

"You know the figure!"

"I heard them mention that sum. I think I knew then that
it was my price."

Had he known even before then that Macleod would betray
him ? Probably. It was an odd relief to be certain. He was more
free now in this cold darkness with his friend than he had been
with that whispering couple while they were making up their
minds to betray him.

The two men talked a little, but not much. There was no purpose
now to serve by straining their eyes into the future. There was
nothing Montrose could do now any more to persuade Macleod and
try to counterbalance his wife's influence, to test his strength by
seeing how far he could walk, and wonder if he had not better try to
make a dash for it alone, ill as he was, rather than wait here and trust
to those whom he had begun to feel untrustworthy. There was
nothing more to be done but sleep, and he wrapped himself in his
cloak and slept more soundly than he had done since he had come
to Assynt.

He was awakened next morning by hearing the great bolts drawn
back, and the heavy door creaked open. Hamish stood there alone,
there were no guards with him, and both men scrambled to their
feet in the wild hope that Macleod might after all be contriving
their escape. The servant came in, the faint light pouring in
after him through the doorway, and laid a bundle at Montrose's
feet.

In a low, shamefaced gabble of Gaelic he said, "These are Your Honour's clothes, and Herself is asking you to put them on again that you may return those that were lent."

Montrose saw again the torn old dark-reddish plaid and ragged homespuns that he had worn on the moor. Major Sinclair jerked back his head and, for the first time since they had met again, uttered his sharp angry bark of laughter. Hamish's face went redder even than his beard.

"Herself is not of our house," was all he said, as with clumsily deferential movements he helped Montrose to change Macleod's clothes for those miserable rags.

A little later their guards brought them a breakfast of oatmeal and water, and then their journey began.

They saw no sign of Macleod as they left Assynt, but his wife stood on the steps of the castle and said good-bye assiduously to General Holbourn. If her family's credit had been somewhat impaired with those in power by waiting to see the issue of the battle at Corbiesdale before they joined the victors, she at any rate had patched it up with all the 'earnestness' that her brother Andrew Monro had besought of her.

They rode along that spit of land between the little green peninsula and the mainland, and Montrose looked down on those low white rocks and the white starry flowers that grew down to their edge, sparkling now in the quick fleeting sunshine of early May. The clouds were gathering big and white and golden in the blue sky, throwing great coloured reflections that went flying over the ruffled water; the hills were purple shadows round the loch and the narrow strip of low fertile green land along its shores. A smiling and lovely valley it seemed as he looked back on it, with its little castle watching over it from the water, before it disappeared among the enfolding hills.

As they rode past Invershin the clouds that had been piling up heavier and blacker over the mountains broke and fell, and it was raining fast by the evening. They rode along the north side of the Kyle of Sutherland and looked across yet again at the crag of Craigcoinichean and Corbiesdale where they had fought. Holbourn decided to rest his men at the Castle of Skibo for a couple of nights after the continuous forced marches of the last few days, before delivering his charge to his Commander-in-Chief, David Leslie, at Tain on the opposite side of the water.

They came out of the dark rain into Skibo Castle, the glow of firelight and torches and the sound of pipes and fiddles playing up in the little musicians' gallery above the great hall. Robert Gray of Skibo was away from home, but his mother the Dowager came forward to receive General Holbourn, a small wiry old lady with white hair piled high above a wrinkled white face, an enormous beak of a nose, a bright black eye, and a preposterous dress which seemed to be made out of a patchwork quilt, for there was every colour of the rainbow in its composition.

Her manner to Holbourn was full of an exaggerated affectation of courtesy which thinly disguised her annoyance at having to put up these rough soldiers in her house and entertain the officers to dinner. As she spoke to them in her ironic mincing voice, her wide mouth pursed up whenever it did not break into a dangerously gleaming smile, her black eyes under their white lashes glancing here and there among the little awkward group of weary soldiers, she looked like a very old, gay, and probably malicious fairy.

"You will find my fare simple," she said, "mutton, mutton, do we ever get anything else to eat in this country? But at least I have had the prescience"—she shot a glance like an arrow at Holbourn to see how he took that word; he did not take it, and she went on in still more arrogantly courtly tones—"the prescience, I say, of your visit to provide you with music. I hire the pipes and fiddlers whenever I get the chance, for music is the only consolation I can find for mutton."

Suddenly her eyes fell on the prisoners at the back of the group, her mouth widened to an alarming narrow slit across her face, and "*Who* are those men?" she demanded.

"The rebel prisoners, madam, that we took after the battle of Corbiesdale. They can be lodged in your cellars or dungeon."

"You have not said who they are."

"James Graham and Major Sinclair."

"James Gra— my Lord Marquis of Montrose! Mr. Holbourn —or whatever military title this upstart Government may have been pleased to confer upon you—while you are here, His Excellency the Marquis of Montrose lodges in my best guest-room and dines at my table, and so does Major Sinclair."

And, turning, she screamed a command to the gallery to play the battle-march of the Gallant Grahams.

It was a fantastic evening. Montrose could scarcely believe he was not dreaming it as he came up to the long Spanish table set in the hall and spread with fine-spun linen, with Venetian glasses and polished silver sconces to hold the candles of scented wax, while the musicians played the very tunes he used to order whenever he gave a supper-party at St. Andrews or came home for the holidays, and his first thought always was to send for the pipers and fiddlers.

The Dowager appeared as suddenly as at the stroke of a wand, attired in a silver brocade that had been made fifty years ago to spread over a farthingale. Lacking that support, it lay all round her for yards upon the floor and she had to hold it up with both hands as she advanced with the high stepping walk of a peacock towards the table. A high comb studded with rubies burned red in her white hair, and as she seated herself her eyes roved round the table and flashed with an angry fire as red as they.

For General Holbourn had placed himself on her right hand, with Montrose on his other side.

"Do you consider yourself my guest of honour, sir?" she demanded in a voice that rose shrill above the skirling of the pipes.

The unfortunate man began to stammer out that he was only observing the military order of positions that had been carried out on the march.

But he only got out a few words before there was an uprush of swishing gleaming brocade like the soaring wings of an avenging angel. His hostess seized the leg of mutton before her by the knuckle-bone and swung it down on to his head with such force that it knocked him off his seat on to the floor, where she gave him another blow in the chest that covered with grease the fine velvet coat into which he had changed.

His officers sprang to their feet, thinking this was the signal for a surprise attack from her servants to rescue the prisoners, but no one else advanced. The dauntless white figure stood there alone, brandishing the leg of mutton as though it were a battle-axe.

"I would beg you *gentlemen* to remember," she screamed, with such a world of scorn in her stress on that word that it was a worse insult than any term of abuse, "that this is my house and I alone have the right to arrange the order of my table or the conditions of my hospitality. My Lord Marquis, I beg that you will do me the highest honour I have ever received in my long life, and sit at my right hand."

She replaced the mutton in the dish, wiped her hands on a napkin, and swept a deep curtsey to the ragged figure in the wet shepherd's plaid that came slowly forward to take the place of honour beside her. Then she beckoned a servant forward.

"Take away the mutton," she said, "and scrape off the outer portions where they may have made any contact with Mr.— with General Holbourn's hair-oil."

Holbourn clambered to his legs and took his place on the other side of Montrose, squinting ruefully down at his ruined coat. From time to time the Dowager shot a smiling remark at him across Montrose as if to remind herself that she was still his hostess, but he scarcely dared reply, nor did she seem to expect it. She talked all through the dinner and through the music, which was much too loud, to Montrose.

The habit of polite conversation that he had had to endure through the last four years, however anxious and hard-driven, now stood him in good stead. His limbs were aching as though they had been racked, his head was throbbing, his eyeballs burning, his throat so parched that he longed only to drink water, which she would not permit but kept plying him with sweet red wine from Oporto; the shrill music thrummed in his ears, making him at times lose consciousness of where he was and imagine that he was really back at home in Kinnaird or Kincardine and that these last few days had been only the nightmare of a delirium,—and then with a jerk of his mind he would force himself to realize that there was nothing left of Kincardine but a heap of charred stones, that the stout man who sat so still and meek on his right was indeed his jailer, and that this fantastic old lady on his left was not one of the several eccentric and despotic old Scots ladies he had known in his youth, but only a momentary interruption in his journey to Edinburgh where he had been already condemned to be hanged, drawn, and quartered.

Yet he could still talk and appear to listen, answering whenever she gave him time, for she rushed from one thing to another until she fastened on the attractions of young King Charles and the prospects of his marriage. Was it to be his cousin the Princess Sophia? ("but her tocher is no bigger than a dairymaid's"), or his other cousin the French heiress? ("but *she* is a Roman Catholic, that would never do"), or that queer little creature Queen Christina of Sweden? ("but one hears odd stories of her—I don't trust these learned women, they find out too much from the Greek and Latin authors, as I know, having read 'em myself," and a laugh like a screech-owl's pierced her royal gossip).

All the Kirk and Covenant folk here were backing the Calvinist Orange girl of the Dowager Princess Amelia's, "but I'll tell you a newer starter than that, my lord," and her voice hissed into a whisper more harshly audible even than her cries, "and that is that squinting red-haired girl of Argyll's. 'King Campbell' has set his heart on being a King's father-in-law, and if he once gets the poor young fellow into his clutches that's what he'll wish on him, mark my words, and Your Excellency may take my bet on it if you will, at odds of five to one."

"It would scarcely be fair to take you on, madam, since in any case you could not win from me," said Montrose, smiling, and went on quickly, before she should realize she had laid a bet with a man under immediate sentence of death, to answer her previous questions as to the dress of the women in Prague and the atrocities of the Thirty Years' War in Germany.

Yes, he could still talk and appear to listen, he could still rise and escort her to the door and bow his good-night to her and thanks for his delightful entertainment. After which he turned to face Holbourn, who was goggling at their hostess' departure and softly damning his own eyes, the grease on his coat, and all old women.

But for the two days they were at Skibo her effect was such that in her absence, as in her presence, Holbourn and all his officers treated Montrose with as much ceremonial politeness as she had demanded for him.

And he was able to rest, while outside the castle the rain sheeted down.

Sir John Hurry had been sent on with the first draft of prisoners, taken during or just after the battle of Corbiesdale and despatched independently of Leslie's force to Inverness. The Provost of Inverness, Duncan Forbes of Culloden, was a sound man, a grand man, for he had ordered the magistrates to put out tables by the market-cross with refreshments for the troops *and* for the prisoners, and, for the first time since he had been taken, Jack Hurry could drink as much wine as he wanted. With that new long cut on his forehead and cheek opening up the dangerous bullet-wound he had got years ago on the left side of his head, he wanted a good deal.

Amid a group of his comrades in misfortune from Corbiesdale— or Carbisdale, as he had found people calling it—he stood by the fore-stair of one of the big houses looking on to the market-square below the castle, and filled up his pewter mug again and again from the big jug beside them.

Very lean and spare his tall figure looked, its great shoulders squaring out at the top of it as he lounged back with his mug in his hand against the fore-stair, his long legs straddling on either side of the jug like a dog guarding a bone, his belt drawn in to its narrowest hole, his big nose and bristling chin stuck out like promontories, his light grizzled hair cut away at the side of his head where the new jagged scar ran fiery red down to his cheek beside the old dull purplish mark. Yet to look at him he might have been an officer home from the wars, casually taking his ease and his drink as he stared in good humour at the scene before him.

A thin dazzle of bright mist had come up from the sea and spun itself over the sunshine so that the grey stone houses and little gardens, pink and white with blossoming fruit trees, the shining silver fish on the stalls in the market-place, the hilly slopes beyond the town, splashed with deep and pale gold from the whin and broom, the broad glittering river merging into the sea, were all painted in clear flat colours without any shadow.

Some girls had been to fill their buckets with water from the town pump in the middle of the square and stayed there as usual to gossip, with a shrill screech of coy laughter every now and then. They looked across at the prisoners and pretended not to notice two or three self-conscious youths who were gradually edging nearer to them and addressing loud remarks to each other which were really intended for the girls. The girls' white headcloths flapped as they turned and tossed their heads like pigeons coquetting before their possible mates. One of them was a fine buxom lass with breasts swelling up in firm curves under her tight blue bodice; she looked sideways at Hurry and then away as his bold glance swept her from top to toe, then presently looked back again and smiled. No doubt it was a new piece of fun to prink at a man who was condemned to die.

Anyway, it was a good day to be alive, even if you were only going to be alive for a few days longer.

He whistled the chorus to a German drinking-song, and a boy who was squatting by him on an upturned fish-basket to stare at the prisoners took up the tune on a reed whistle, cocking up an eye at that tall tigerish fellow with the raw scar, to see if he were getting it right.

"That's the lad!" said Hurry, throwing him a penny.

A little girl near by hopped up and down in time to the tune, a mongrel dog chased a lean white bitch in and out under the tables by the cross, a blackbird shrilled out a river of clear notes from a tree where the buds were bursting into points of green life.

It was impossible that he, Jack Hurry, should swing out of all this on the end of a rope before the month was over and all the cherry blossom blown from the trees. He had seen the new moon for this month clear in the sky, and not through the cottage window of bottled glass as he might so easily have done—didn't that mean luck? And was it luck to swing at the end of a hangman's rope? It was not. Anything might happen to prevent it. Even if the King were really signing the Treaty of Breda, as was already being rumoured, well, that would only bring him to Scotland the sooner, in time very likely to stop the execution of his most loyal and devoted servants—and *then* those swine the Covenanters would see!

'Rise, Sir John Urré of Pitfichie, knight.' King Charles I had already said that to him, striking him lightly on the shoulder with his sword. Who knew what King Charles II might say? Earl of Inverurie would have a good sound, or the Lord of Dyce would carry a pleasant double meaning.

In any case, it was a very fine day, the first after three days of solid rain, and the Provost of Inverness was a good fellow, and this was excellent wine and plenty of it, enough of it even for him.

The boy with the reed whistle suddenly stopped playing, the little girl hop-hopping on one bare red leg. They were running, everyone was running, calling to each other in shrill excited cries.

There was a thick crowd now, gathering fast and faster about the further end of the market-place where the measured thud of horses' hoofs and a loud formal shouting could be heard.

"What is happening over there?" Hurry demanded, and the answer shuttled down to them from the stragglers about that crowd.

"It is the Marquis! It's Montrose himself."

Hurry sprang to his feet and looked over the heads of the crowd. He saw the Covenant General, David Leslie, riding down one of the streets at the head of his troops, but nobody was paying any attention to him.

They were all flocking towards a figure behind him, the figure of a man wrapped in a ragged dark red plaid with a shepherd's cap of rough wool on his head, mounted on a shaggy little horse with no saddle nor bridle but only a mat of rags and straw on its back, and loops of rope for stirrups, and a tether and bit of halter for a bridle. His feet were tied together with cords under his horse's belly. In front of him marched a herald who proclaimed in that loud formal shout that Hurry had heard:

"Here comes James Graham, a traitor to his country."

"Christ's blood!" exclaimed Hurry. "Why are they doing this?"

A townsman who had mounted the stair beside him answered, "Argyll's orders—that the people should jeer and throw stones at him."

"They don't seem to be doing it."

"Here come two of the ministers, though. I swear they'll ginger 'em up. No one so hot as your men of God."

The procession had stopped at the far end of the market-place. The Provost came forward to greet General David Leslie, the Commander-in-Chief of his Government's armies; he bowed low to him, but lower still to his prisoner, then turned back to David Leslie, and after a short colloquy two of the troopers came forward and untied Montrose's feet from under his horse's belly and helped him to alight.

Hurry saw an old woman come scurrying along like a bat with her black cloak flapping out behind her, hobbling down from the end of the bridge. She shrieked curses at Montrose for the houses on her property which had been burned when he besieged Inverness.

His face did not change under her railing. His majesty made him seem as aloof in those wretched clothes and shameful position as if he were once again at the head of his armies, the conqueror and ruler of Scotland; and so the crowd felt him to be, for in awe rather than pity they drew back from him and pulled the old woman away, hushing her more in fear than anger. It was not canny to curse a man the like of that.

"They can dress him in rags and shackle his feet, they cannot make him alter his countenance," said the Rev. Mr. John Anand to his fellow-minister.

They may have come to reproach but they had stayed to converse. Mr. Anand had met Montrose in the past when that young nobleman had been one of the gilded youth at St. Andrews and he a worthy tutor. Now the undergraduate had become the Commander-in-Chief of the Royalist forces in Scotland, and the tutor a respected minister and servant of the Covenant which had condemned him. But Mr. John Anand's present convictions as to the holiness of the Covenant and the evil of its enemies became strangely insignificant as he looked at the man who was now in its power, but who yet seemed above the power of any man to touch.

The Provost offered him wine, but with that burning thirst still on him Montrose asked for water instead—and for leave to join the little group of his former comrades-in-arms by the forestair.

As he came up to them, Hurry stood as stiffly to attention as if he were on parade, and the others drew away a little from the two of them. The sight of Montrose's wasted face and fever-haunted eyes sunk deep in their sockets, his ragged peasant's clothes, the sound of that horrible voice proclaiming him as traitor still echoing in his mind, had caught Hurry by the throat; all his tough insouciance dropped from him, and he could not speak lest he should howl like a dog with helpless fury.

"Well, Hurry," said Montrose. "So they got you at Corbiesdale. What happened at the end?"

Hurry swallowed so hard he nearly choked, but could get no word out.

"Go on drinking, man—as I'm doing."

"But only water, my lord," said Hurry, as tragically as if it were the worst of his Commander's sufferings. "Won't you let me mix a little of this wine with it?"

Montrose let him, as he felt it so deeply. "Is Frendraught safe?" he asked.

"Yes, my lord, his uncle is seeing to that, though he'll be a prisoner for a bit for the look of the thing."

"And the rest of our men?"

"Strachan's fellows finished it thoroughly, sir—combed the countryside for every man they could find for days after, and cut 'em down as fast as they found 'em."

"Did any of the Orcadians get away up north?"

"Mighty few, sir."

Hurry had taken another long drink and was finding his tongue.

"They were drowned in shoals trying to swim the Oykell, and some of Strachan's troopers were drowned too, pushing off in a boat to shoot at 'em in the water and tipped the boat over doing so—it's the only good laugh I've had since then. They say the tide is bringing the islanders' bodies upstream now as thick as pilchards after a storm, poor devils. Well, for myself I'd as soon drown as hang."

Montrose gave a short laugh. "They told me I was born to be hanged when I swam Tweed in spate three times running one night to make our men cross it."

All Hurry's eternal optimism leaped up again in him. If he could not die, how much more impossible it was that this man should do so!

"They'll never dare do it, sir. There'd be a storm all over Europe."

"So there was when a greater man than I was executed."

"King Charles—that fell like a thunderbolt. But this news is travelling like wildfire, I have just heard of a boat leaving from this very port here at Inverness as much as five days ago with the news of your capture. The King of France, the Emperor, the Dutch States, they'll all raise hell itself to prevent it."

"And therefore they'll hurry it on here before their protests and King Charles arrive."

"If King Charles arrives in Scotland to see his Viceroy's head on a spike, may he take the omen to himself! There's no decent man would follow him after that. If he comes with Lauderdale and that crowd to shake hands with Argyll, may he get what he deserves from Argyll!"

"Well, he may not come. We know nothing. And we don't know what's happening over there even now at this moment, so what's the good of racking our brains? Tell me, were Monro of Achnes and his sons killed or taken?"

"Neither that I could hear, my lord. They may have led us into that death-trap and then joined with those swine their kinsmen against us at the end. Nothing's too bad for a Monro to do, *or* a Macleod,—curse those Northern clans, I'd stamp 'em all out, man, woman and child, if I had my way."

And the man from Aberdeen spat at the names of the man and woman who had brought his Commander to this pass. His fury gave him at last the courage to speak of it. David Leslie had been a decent soldier when he had come across him in the German wars. No doubt he had lost his head a bit in his hysterical relief at the capture of Montrose before he himself had had to tackle him.

"Not unmixed relief," said Montrose with a grim smile; "he is fit to be tied now his subordinate Strachan is getting the credit and already dashing south hot-foot for his reward—he calls him 'that upstart' even to his men."

Hurry could well excuse Leslie for that. But what had happened to him that he could lead his prisoner, the King's Viceroy, in this shameful fashion through Scotland, like a wild beast in a cage?

"Government orders," said Montrose shortly, even indifferently.

'Government' meant Argyll. The agony of fear that he and his colleagues had suffered from Montrose now found its relief in the cruelty of humiliating him to the uttermost. It was also, perhaps mistakenly, a precaution. There must be no sympathy among the people for the soldier who had been so great and terrible a figure and was now broken.

But it had not worked like that in Inverness, except for one old woman.

Nor did his victorious enemies dare take the quickest road south to Edinburgh, lest the Farquharsons, who had fought for him before, should spring down on them as they passed through Mar and rescue him. So the journey would be prolonged all through the eastern counties, and Montrose would be led as a ragged captive behind that accursing herald through the very towns that he had conquered.

"It is a triumph after Argyll's own heart," he said, smiling, as he and Hurry discussed the route.

"If he dared take it!" said Hurry quickly. "He'd not dare accompany you even now, my lord."

After a long pause he added slowly and in some astonishment, "And the triumph is not his."

VIII

ARGYLL'S Government was having to work hard to induce the right point of view among the people. So far from mocking or even shunning him, the gentry in Moray followed Montrose as far as they were allowed to bear him company. Fines and severer punishments had to be used to check his sympathizers.

Men were sent to prison for singing songs in praise of 'James Graham'; a merchant called John Bryson, who had been heard to say that Montrose was as honest a nobleman as any in the kingdom, was sent to Edinburgh and condemned to be imprisoned in the Thieves' Hole for several weeks. Sins of omission, even partial, were punished almost as severely, and a minister who did not preach 'enough' in condemnation of James Graham might find himself deprived of his ministry

Mr. William Kinnanmond, the minister of Keith, took warning by these examples, and when the prisoner James Graham was taken to his church he abused him to his face in his Sunday sermon with such howls of violence that even his Covenanting congregation were revolted. He chose for his text one that was very popular with the Covenant ministers, of the hewing of Agag in pieces by Samuel.

"'As thy sword hath made women childless, so shall thy mother be childless among women.'"

"'Rail on, Rabshekeh,'" Montrose said at last in answer, and turned his back on him.

But the answer he gave himself was even closer to the context. 'Surely the bitterness of death is past,' he said to himself as he lay out that night in his tent on the open moor.

He had asked for that instead of being quartered in a house. He lay on straw, the flap of the tent drawn back to get the air on his head. The legs of the sentry standing just outside the opened flap were as motionless as the stump of a tree. Beyond them, where

351

the moor swept away to the long low rounded hills, he could see the windy, hurrying sky, and one star showing among the clouds, alone and forsaken of its fellows as he had been.

But presently the bitterness of that hideous shouting abuse left him, and since hatred had so little power to hurt him, surely the bitterness of death was past? People made God in their own image, a monster of cruelty or a God of love. Here in the cool stillness of the open moor, though a moment since he had not known it, he knew now that he was neither alone nor forsaken.

As on the hills, starving and wounded in the rain, he knew now that Louey was with him, knew it even though he no longer saw her hair astream in the night wind and her face transparent through the darkened air. He knew it now, not through his disordered brain but through the cool certainty of faith. He could neither see nor hear her, but she talked with him in his mind, and he was able to say all the things he had wished but dared not say while he was with her, for fear of distressing her too much.

'To die for what we love, that should be easy,' he had said when he had asked her to live for it. He had known her thought, that, yes, to die is easy if it is death sought in battle, quick and furious, as she knew he had sought his at Philiphaugh. But how would she bear the death that now lay ahead for him? Could he make her understand that it was but a few hours' agony? Perhaps far less, for the numbed body loses its capacity for pain—in any case far less than in many a death from natural causes where the sick body may lie unrelieved of its torture for days or weeks.

Though there were clouds hurrying over the sky, the air had the peculiar luminous quality of night in a Northern May. And sleep, like the darkness, came to him, not deep nor heavy, but shot through with a shimmer of dream, half sleeping, half waking, and the wind came not in gusts but in a great cool wave of air, bringing him the scents of earth and dew and young bracken, lifting him as a wave of the sea lifts a light boat.

It bore him out of his aching body and the memory of the shouting turmoil of his journey,· the parched thirst and painful riding without saddle or stirrup, the dust from all the horses' hoofs round him, the harsh monotony of the clanking harness and tramping horses of his guards always round him, hemming him in, and of the herald's voice proclaiming him traitor,—and then all the people running and staring, staring, and the raving, frantic preaching of that man to-day, flapping his black sleeves up and down like a carrion crow that only bided his time to fasten his claws and beak in his prey.

All that journeying by day had become a distant nightmare; the wave of wind had borne him away from it to where Louey was leaning from her window at Rhenen, towards the night's loveliness, looking at this one star. Below her the chestnut trees in the garden waved their dark branches—'if you listen on a spring night, you can hear their buds bursting,' she had once told him.

She too had found the night too lovely for sleep. Did she know what had happened? Not yet, but so soon she would, that its advancing shadow already lay deep within her.

All that long bright hot day at Rhenen it had been a shadow, but now at night, when the silence was spread all round her over the sleeping fields, a glimmer of light softer than dawn lay behind the darkness and in her heart. All this day she had not lived at all, but moved and talked and laughed among a show of figures; now she knew that she was not parted from her love, but with him, and giving him the solace that he now gave her.

That day at Rhenen had been crowded with people, and their uneasy, snatching thoughts. There had been bustle since sunrise. Sophie had set sail in a pinnace that afternoon to travel up the Rhine to stay with her brother Carl, the Elector Palatine, at his home in Heidelberg. She had been planning it for months, and now it had come true. To make that long journey in a carriage would have been horribly uncomfortable, but the States of Holland had given her a pinnace. Lord Craven was to take charge of her and the expedition, and Sophie, the Cinderella of the family, started off just

z

six months before her twentieth birthday on a greater adventure than any of her elder sisters had ever had.

All that hot spring day Louey had been helping her pack last-minute treasures that Sophie had kept on discovering simply must not be left behind, for "Who knows when I shall see them again— or any of you, either, for that matter?"

"You will see hills," said Louey, who had also never been out of Holland, "and the great rocks with castles on the top that hang over the Rhine."

"Yes, it will be an amusing journey. I am thankful I have not to go in a carriage, I should have been jolted to death."

"You will see Heidelberg," said her mother. "But from what Carl says, that is not amusing."

"No. It is monstrous we cannot even now sleep in the Castle. But he is repairing it as fast as he can. 'Commissariat House'— to imagine that your daughter, Maman, should have to stay at a citizen's private house with a name like that!"

"Since my son the Elector has to stay in it I can easily imagine it," Elizabeth dryly replied.

She was not pleased by this journey. To her mind it savoured of flight. Sophie had refused to stay and see out the issue of King Charles' hopes in Scotland and this venture there of his greatest servant.

"If it should succeed and Charles should really want me for his Queen, he can still send for me," Sophie had argued with her mother. But she had preferred to go while, as the canny Dutch saying had it, 'the going was good.' She would get clear away to Germany from all English and Scots entanglements lest she should stay to run the danger of being left in the lurch.

For if Montrose failed, Charles' policy, and marriage too, most probably, would be chosen for him by the Covenanters.

And only three days ago news had come from Breda that Charles had signed a treaty with the Covenanters.

"This Treaty of Breda, that settles it," she had said to Louey.

"Charles has not yet taken the Covenant, but that will be only a matter of time, mark my words. Now you see how far-sighted I have been, and how right I am to go."

Yes, Louey saw that. Since it was Sophie, she was right to go. If she had not been Sophie, if she had really loved Charles, might she have influenced him? She might have done so, it might have made all the difference, but, being Sophie, she could not. She was going to Germany and would marry someone quite different, most likely some other German Elector, for she was determined to marry,—and the fate of Montrose, whatever it might be, would be no more to her than the fate of one 'among those who sought their own fortune in my service.'

There was no more here that could be said or done but wait for news of that fate—and help Sophie pack and sort her dresses and trinkets, and promise to give all her messages to her friends and to look after Snowball, her old white dog, over whom Sophie showed more sentiment at parting than for anyone else.

And see Sophie on board the pinnace with little Craven, his face crumpled up into rueful smiles at saying good-bye for so long a time to his beloved Queen, see the white sails unfurl and the graceful boat skim away between the low green shores, and Sophie's yellow scarf waving good-bye on deck, waving, waving till it was no bigger than one of the bright marsh kingcups growing at their feet, and then turn back up the path with her mother's hand in hers.

"When I sailed up this river to Heidelberg," said Elizabeth, "I was four years younger than Sophie is now."

"You have always been younger," said Louey.

"That may be her advantage. She has great spirit and a good mind—more mind that I ever had. She will go far—much farther than Commissariat House," she added with a burst of laughter.

"You will go and stay with them next year, Maman, when more of the Castle is repaired and you can be in your old home again."

"No, I shall never go. Carl has made that quite clear, he doesn't want me for however short a time. And could I bear it, that castle where I went as a bride, now smashed to bits? They can never build it all up again. But one thing is untouched, he tells me—my English garden, the rose-walks, and the stone arch that my husband set up for me in a single night to give me a pleasant surprise when I walked out the next morning. That still stands among the ruins, and his message of love on it to me, his 'Conjugi carissimae.'"

She was crying. "I am an old fool," she said sharply. "As I told Sophie, if my daughters want to leave me, I am sure I do not want anyone to stay with me unwillingly."

But Louey knew that it was not for Sophie that she was crying.

The long day spun itself out in a thicket of chatter, of visitors, of clearing up after the departure.

"Etta will be the one to go next," said Eliza proudly. She had set her heart on Etta's marriage to the young Prince of Transylvania who had fallen headlong in love with her portrait. He had written such charming letters about it that Etta too was in love. If only she were stronger, it would make them less anxious at her having to endure such a much greater journey than Sophie's,—'to go so far for so little,' as Carl had written caustically, since he did not think the match good enough for his prettiest sister. He would do better than that for Sophie, he had already assured her.

That did not trouble Etta. "If only the Prince will love me when he sees me," she confided tremulously to Louey. "That portrait is flattering, I know, and I cannot always wear a pointed cap with a veil billowing out from it."

"It never does billow except in a portrait," said Louey, "it flaps round one's face and gets into one's eyes."

"Is that why you never wear that pretty cap you had in green velvet? Oh, but I think the Lord Montrose did not like it, wasn't that it? Dearest Louey, you will hear soon of him, I know."

Yes, she would hear soon, she knew, as she stood on the terrace playing bowls with the visitors, turning the heavy ebony ball in her hands, and watched the sun setting over the wide earth among huge flame-flushed clouds. On their further edge, high in the sky at the edge of the world, she saw a knight in armour, a dark figure mounted on a horse with wings of flame. A faint breeze played over the terrace but there was no wind, no movement in the further sky; the knight sat unchanged, challenging that final gulf that yawned below him.

'He has reached the end of the world,' she said to herself—but the world went on.

"Your turn to play, Louey," her mother was calling.

When she turned to look again, the knight and his charger had disappeared into flaming space, and only a wraith of grey cloud showed where he had been.

SPACE could make no odds between them; both had proved it now. Should time have more power? Love was free of that, as of all the odd intermingled facts of life. He had loved before, and lived many years with his wife; she had borne him children, and he had now to see them.

The line of march, chosen by Leslie for safety, was through the eastern counties and went past Montrose's birthplace at Old Montrose, and, four miles off it, Kinnaird Castle, the home of David Carnegie, first Earl of Southesk, whose younger daughter Magdalen had been Montrose's wife from the age of sixteen until she had died five years ago.

They came through those familiar flat uplands of grass and water and waving rushes where he had hunted from childhood, up over the path that had been built up through the bog, past that rise in the ground, covered with scrubby bushes and a few firs and thorn trees, twisted into wild shapes by the wind that roves unchecked over the surrounding marsh. 'The Marquis' hill,' the country people had begun to call it when he was last here, for they remembered how in his boyhood when he rode out from Old Montrose with his hawks or hounds, he used there to check his impatient horse and wave a red scarf in signal to any of that enormous family at Kinnaird who might care to ride out and go a-hunting with him.

And once, when he was riding in disguise with only two companions up through the armies of his enemies to begin the enterprise of that Year of Marvels in Scotland, once on a still summer night, white with moonlight, he had met his wife Magdalen in secret upon that hill.

They went through the deer park and the iron gates where he used to throw Lame Tom shillings for holding his horse. The grey jagged shape of the castle rose before him, the massive stone walls of the policies and orchards and the new garden that his father-in-law, Lord Southesk, had banked up out of the bog, the trees he had planted in his confidence in a peaceful and prosperous future for his family that had been so rudely denied.

There were the three young ash trees they used to call Adam and Eve and Samuel, and the fruit trees tossing and blowing in this wind, a thin cloud of their petals whirling upwards against the sky where the great clouds, white and blue-black, were riding like tall galleons. The wind was blowing from the west, carrying a scurry of soft raindrops among the blown petals of cherry blossom. It came from the mountains, from the Grampians that run across Scotland, where Montrose used to ride when he came from his houses in the western hills to his wife's home at Kinnaird. He belonged to the hills and she to the peaceful plains, Magdalen had always told him.

They went into the castle. He stood in that hall again, and saw his father-in-law, now grown very old, coming towards him, saw those eyes, that he remembered as so keen and imperious, now dimmed with age and tears, raised to his.

And Lord Southesk saw this hot-headed young fellow whom he had scolded and tried to guide in accordance with his own canny wisdom; he had always feared he might come to grief, and now in the saddest moment of his long life he was finding himself proved in the right. Young James of Montrose had always been head and shoulders above his fellows, above even Southesk's own four stalwart sons, but—'James,' his bluff friend Lord Rothes had once said, 'you will never rest till you are lifted up above us all in three fathoms of rope.'

And in that grim jest Rothes too would be proved in the right.

Yet this strange, haggard, ragged prisoner could smile as he met his eyes and say, "I would have spared you this if I could. But it was Leslie's command   And I would be glad of a word with my eldest boy."

"Your boy James is abroad—we have sent him there to get him into safety."

"Where is he?"

"At school in Holland."

"I am glad of that. Tell him to go and see the Princess Louise, who has been betrothed to me this last year. She and her mother will be kind to him."

'Her mother'—the Queen of Bohemia, and of the hearts of all true Scots and Englishmen,—the mention of her could take back Lord Southesk's memories further than most people's; it was he who had been appointed by her father, King James VI of Scotland, when he became James I of England, to escort her and her brothers down from Scotland to London—and she the prettiest, liveliest, most troublesome brat of seven years old that Southesk had ever had the bad luck to encounter.

For two generations these two countries had looked to her and her children as their best hope for the English crown; and now one of them was to have married his son-in-law, whom he had seen as the Viceroy of Scotland and now saw condemned to a criminal's death. In all his steadily upward progress since he had been plain David Carnegie the laird of Kinnaird, the first Earl of Southesk had never met with so great advance and retreat of fortune as now when he looked on the son-in-law who had been nearer to him than any of his sons.

Montrose had made his chief home at Kinnaird, for the pair had married so young that he had had to continue his education afterwards; his children had been brought up here; his portrait as a lad of seventeen in his bridegroom suit of brown velvet, the wide sleeves slashed with oyster satin, hung in the great dining-hall. That boy's face, gravely smiling, the wide mouth turning upwards at the corners, the long irregular hooked nose, the frank, considering eyes beneath their peaked brows, eyes so hopeful yet so secure, now looked out of the carved frame at the man that that boy had become.

"If there were anything I could do—" old Southesk began in a low broken voice as soon as they were out of hearing of the guards—

"but I am a disgraced man, my estates under heavy fines for my Royalist sympathies, there is nothing I can do with this Government, nor can any man, I think, for they have lost all sense and reason as well as humanity——" and he glanced round him in terror as he spoke, though it was in all but a whisper.

The sight of his father-in-law's fear in his own house, where he had seemed like a king, showed plainly the tyranny that now beset Scotland.

"If the King were to get here in time," he muttered on, "they could not carry it out then."

"If the King get here with Lauderdale," his son-in-law answered, "he will be Argyll's prisoner as I am, with only this difference, that he is not condemned to death."

His two younger children, Rob and Jean, a tall boy of eleven and a girl of six, were brought in to see their father, both very grave, the girl holding tight to her brother's hand, looking up with large frightened blue eyes. She was small and very slight and had long straight brown hair; he could just remember her mother when she had looked very like that.

He had not seen them since Jean was a baby in the cradle and Rob a sturdy six-year-old. It was bad luck on them to have this moment as their only real memory of their father; he wished they had not been sent for. He asked about their riding—what ponies had they? Dapple and Drake had been the favourites of his two elder sons, Johnnie who had died on that bitter winter campaign of his in the mountains, five years ago, and James, now in Holland.

"James left me his horse Blackamoor when he went to Holland," said Rob, "but I am not quite big enough for him yet."

"Has James grown into a big lad, then? He was small when he was your age, Rob. My friend Alasdair Macdonald, who was a giant, would swing him on to his shoulder and say he was tall enough then. Did James ever tell you that?"

"No, sir, but he has told us that Alasdair was a great friend of his. And he has told us of Sir John Hurry, who took him prisoner when he was buying fishing-tackle in the town and sent him to be shut up in Edinburgh Castle."

"Where he refused to be exchanged for another prisoner, since he was not then quite twelve years old and it was a pity for me to lose 'a more valuable officer than himself.' Did he also tell you that?"

"No, sir, at least not like that. He said prison was the only place where he had time for all he wanted to do."

So James had not changed, however tall he had grown. "Does he still write verses and hide them in his shoes for safety along with his marbles and other treasures? I used to write mine in the margins of my school-books—a very bad habit, I hope you two don't do it."

"They won't let us," said Rob in justifiable indignation, "though Master Forrett is always showing us yours, sir, and says those books you've marked are the most precious of any we have."

"Little Forrett! What, is he here still? Where is he then in God's name?"

There was a second's awkward pause, and then Jean's voice piped up for the first time: "He said he couldn't bear it."

"That's nonsense. I must see the old man—tell him I want it, Jean."

She ran off, and soon Master Forrett, who had been tutor to him and to his two elder sons, came to meet him with the tears running down his puckered cheeks.

"Oh my young lord!" he broke out in a hurried rambling rush of words almost incoherent with grief. "You—I used to take you back to school, and your father's books and silver cups and the red embroidered cushions and golf-clubs and little gilded rapier your father gave you—I have them all, and all the prizes you won, all for sport alas,—I have them all safe and sound—but you, I knew you would never be safe——"

"No man is that, Forrett. And all the account books you kept so carefully—have you got those too? You must show them to these young rascals, not as an example but a warning not to be as extravagant as their father. All those sums I lost at billiards and the Cupar races,—'And golf-balls at three pounds Scots a dozen!' Do you remember scolding me for the new lot I got the day before my wedding?"

"Do I not? And the time of the house-warming at Kincardine when Your Lordship rode all the way to Edinburgh and back without telling anyone why, and all to get presents of necklaces and embroidered gloves for every one of your sisters—all five of 'em no less!"

"Don't forget the rest of the girls in the party, Forrett, since I did not. Silver buttons I got 'em, and Italian boxes and plaited ribbons hung with bells."

"Oh," cried little Jean, smiling at last as he had wanted to see her, "why wasn't I there?"

"Because you were not born, my bairn. Someone else will bring you silver bells.—You don't let 'em play spillikens with your old bones, I hope, Forrett, the way I used to do, riding you over the hills?"

"You went always at the rate of a mountain torrent, my lord."

"There were so many visits to fit in—a couple of days' hunting here and fishing there and dancing every evening. That was a grand night of it when I was Lord of Misrule in the Christmas play at Balcarres!"

"No chance of that now," said Lord Southesk. "The country's too much changed. Even the nobility daren't dance now, and as for acting plays or keeping Christmas, there are State penalties for both these crimes."

"Let's hope it will change again then by the time Jean is grown up—as it should when we have a young and merry monarch on the throne. King Charles will pull down King Campbell in time, you'll see."

Rob's face had flushed furiously at the name of Campbell. "May he die a dog's death!" he muttered under his breath.

"He will do that," said a very old, slow, peasant's voice from the doorway just behind them.

Montrose turned quickly to see Daniel Muschet, who had been gardener at Kinnaird all his life, standing there, straight and tall in spite of his great age, with a tight round knob of sweet herbs and spring flowers in his hand.

"He'd do that howsomever he died," he said, "for it's as a dog he would die. They told me you were come, my young lord, and I made bold to come to you here lest the soldiery prevented me outside—and here's a nosegay to pin in your cloak. It's many a one you've told me to pick for you as you rode out of these gates, and you'll not go out of them now without some of my flowers to keep the smell of your guards off you."

He held his fine old head as high as Lord Southesk's, who might have been his brother, and possibly was, for Daniel had the big Carnegie nose, lean and strong. His keen, screwed-up, triangular blue eyes looked straight at Montrose, who was glad of it, for all the others had been shy of meeting his eyes.

Jean ran to Daniel and caught at his hand.

"What do you see round him, Daniel? You have the second sight. Won't he escape and come back here to us?"

There was a moment's silence.

"Tell us, tell us," the child urged, "won't you tell us what you see?"

"Yes, I'll tell you what I see round him," he said in that slow and ancient voice, "as I told your own mother these fourteen years gone—and that is a great glory and gladness, and stories and songs springing up round him like flowers under his feet. And whatever death he may die, it would be better to be himself than any man in the length and breadth of Scotland."

X

THERE had been an attempt to rescue him at Pitcaple Castle, where the wife of their host for the night, the laird of Pitcaple, told him of a concealed hole in the wall through which he might pass into a subterranean passage and so escape. But Pitcaple was already under suspicion of the Government, having lately refused to subscribe to its last declaration, as his family 'could not take upon them the guiltiness contained therein.' Bad as that was for him, it was even worse that his wife was own cousin to Montrose.

For years past, Argyll had been venting his revenge on Montrose's relatives, even on his young nieces, whom he had had imprisoned at different times. If he should escape from the house of his kinswoman, she would certainly suffer for it, and perhaps all his own family also, even his children. Montrose refused.

Now they came to Grange Castle, not far from Dundee, where old William Durhame was laird, and his wife, Jean Octerlonie, was master. She was a remarkable woman, in late middle age, but with the step and carriage of a young stag, and an aloof, far-seeing look in her wide blue eyes. She was abrupt in speech, her manner casual and unaware of other people; she seemed borne onward by the wind of her own swift resolution, and on this occasion she showed to the full how swift and resolute she could be.

First she settled all the quarters in the castle with David Leslie, going round with him herself and demanding the names of who should be appointed where, so imperiously yet abstractedly, as though it were merely her right to know, and not in any way of interest to her, that it never occurred to the General not to answer her. She then entertained them all royally, both with very old strong ale and very new raw brandy. At supper she herself plied the officers of the main guard again and again, her fair pale face remaining smooth and unflushed as she drank repeated small

365

doses of the heady stuff in compliment and encouragement to them.

Not that they needed much encouragement. The main guard, who were in the hall, were mostly of Lawers' regiment of Campbell Highlanders, notable hard drinkers. But so well and constantly did the butlers at the Grange do their job that before midnight all those practised topers were stark drunk.

It was a little after midnight that Montrose was woken by his door being softly opened. The light of the moon, now just past the full, shone through the small panes of glass in the window, making a check-work pattern on the boards by the door. On those black-lined squares of greenish-white there stood a tall form in a massive black cloak who came in a swift rush to the side of his bed and there dropped the cloak all in one movement, showing the straight grey figure of Jean Durhame.

"This is your moment," she said in a voice more quiet than any whisper; "put on my cloak and go out past them. You'll find all the doors unbarred, and the men will not notice even if you step on them—I've tried one or two to test them."

He was lying on the bed, dressed, for he had no change of clothes; he got up and took the cloak from her hands and looked into the queer pale face that seemed impalpable in the moonlight.

"And you?" he asked. "And your husband? What of you, when they find me gone?"

"My husband has been in bed since before your arrival, and Leslie knows it. They dare not touch me, I have proved that before now. I am not in your cousin's position.—Yes, I know about Pitcaple. You had a reason there not to take your chance. You have none here, only an excuse. If you refuse this time, it would be a coward's way out."

He took the cloak from her and swung it round his shoulders, then knelt and kissed her hands.

She opened the door for him, softly, knowing the way of it. He went out after her into the dark passage, following her round the sentry, who lay in a heap on top of his musket. She stood at the top of the stair, watching while he went very quietly down it in the darkness by the wall. There was still a glow from the heaps of smouldering peat on the hearth, it showed the black huddled lumps of men lying in the hall, the red gleam here and there from the barrel of a musket, the point of a dirk.

They lay like swine on a midden; some had been sick, some were snoring in thick strangled grunts. He stepped through the stench, past the filth and the sunken sprawling bodies. The great outer door was unlocked, and he went through it, out into the cool air and the moonlight.

There was no sentry outside; he must have gone in to share the drink with the others. The old hound lay like one made of stone, his front paws stretched outside his kennel, turned white by the moon; the grass gleamed silver with dew; from the grey stone dove-cot there shone flecks of soft white from the sleeping doves. The few shadows, sharp and black, of trees and walls lay at a distance.

But Montrose had only to reach that dark clump of trees across the field and he would be safe for the moment anyway. The wall of one of the policies ran towards it, and he made for that first of all so as to keep in its shadow as long as he could.

Just as he was reaching it, three or four troopers came out from beside it, towards the castle, singing and laughing together and walking slackly, at ease, but not drunkenly. They were none of the regular guard, and Montrose guessed at once that they must have got wind of the revelry up at the castle and come up from their quarters to see if they could get their bellyful of drink. He had no weapon, he was far too weak to outrun them, and they must have seen him before he saw them in the shadow of the wall, for they were making straight towards him, and now they hailed him.

He walked on resolutely, keeping his head down and his cloak drawn about his face. But now they were running towards him, they had reached him, one seized his cloak and pulled it back, another laid hold of his arm. It was the wounded one, but he scarcely noticed that, except to know that he could at least strike one blow for his freedom, and he swung his good arm round and hit the fellow who was holding him just under the jaw, knocking him out.

But now the others were on top of him, pulling him down. His weakness and the agony of his wounded arm as they dragged at it made him lose consciousness for a moment only, but it seemed some hours of darkness shot through with fiery stabs of pain before he came to and found himself lying on the ground with that tortured arm pinioned to the other behind his back, and above him the white placid face of the moon.

Then other faces swam across it, dark, twisted in jeering triumph. They were saying things to each other and to himself, but he heard none of them. They hauled him up to his feet, he would have fallen but they held him up, and dragged him back to the castle.

Next day Jean Durhame confronted General Leslie and his chief officers together with the members of the Committee of Estates in Edinburgh that had been sent to give greater security to the expedition, since public feeling was showing itself so strong on the side of the prisoner. She met them with the same aloof courage that she had shown the night before, an air too impersonal even for scorn. She merely stated her position, and theirs. She alone had contrived the escape, and regretted only that it had failed. Her husband and servants knew nothing about it; her husband had in fact been in bed when they arrived, sent there by her for his rheumatism ('Get out from under my feet!' was what she had really said).

The old laird looked at her admiringly and without any surprise. It was true he had known nothing of what was happening, but he knew well that this was what she would do.

"Argyll dares not hurt me, and so you will find it," she finished coolly. They knew that, and set her and her household at liberty, only binding her over to appear before the Estates if summoned, but knowing well that she would not be.

Most surprising of all, she even managed to see the prisoner again alone before they went on their way. She would not let Montrose speak his admiration or his gratitude, nor did she give any sign of pity for his disappointment.

"You did all that could be done, and that's all that matters. Death does not; nor how it comes."

But for all that, she offered him her dirk. "If you are too weak to strike quickly home, I will do it for you. I heard from the sergeant who was at Assynt that you had asked that of Macleod. I would not be as niggard in hospitality as he."

"I was spent then," he said. "I am stronger now. I'll take my death when and how it comes, not by an easier way."

Her strange blue eyes looked into his as though they saw them not at all, but saw all that he was; she stood very still; then with a sudden swift movement she leaned forward and kissed him.

"I knew it," she said. "You'll not give Argyll that satisfaction. He cannot make you afraid to meet whatever he can do to you. *What* can he do to you? Nothing. Go now on your way. You are free to meet the end."

She stood for some time on the steps of her house and watched him go on his way, shading her eyes from the bright sunshine as the long line of troops swung into the roadway, their harness glittering and clanking, their horses whinnying to each other, and in their midst the solitary figure of their prisoner.

XI

MONTROSE was led through the Covenanting towns which had lived in such terror of his name five years ago that 'if but a few goats are seen upon the tops of the hills in the twilight,' the country people took them for the scouts of his armies and rushed to give the alarm.

Yet at Dundee, that staunchly Covenanting city that had suffered more than most from his troops, the authorities showed their disapproval of his treatment by insisting on giving him clothes more fitting his rank. But their influence could not prevail on Leslie so far as to mount him properly. The rag-and-straw mat for saddle, the ropes for stirrups that tied his feet together under the horse's belly until they seemed to cut into the bone, were a necessary precaution against escape, said the General, although his troops surrounded the prisoner on every side.

But his journey was drawing to its end. Soon the people in the country towns would flock no more to stare at him as at a raree-show, though in an awe more hushed than ever a monster provoked; soon the ministers would come and howl and intone and flap their ill-omened black sleeves no more; no more clattering of harness and thud, thud, thud of his guards' horses all round him; no more words of sympathy from polite provosts, difficult to answer! 'My lord, I am sorry for your circumstances.'

('So am I, sir'—no, he must not say that.)

There were other things to look on beside all those gaping faces; there were the primroses thick at the side of the roadway; the young shoots of bracken danced as light as feathers over the hillside; the slender white forms of the birches had begun to shimmer with pale green leaf; there were bare-legged children driving their goats or cows, there were larks winging upward high into the blue sky, gypsies roving along, their strange dark faces looking so impassive between their heavy earrings. They came from Bohemia.

'You are so Bohemian,' he had once said to Louey, and so she was, he saw it now, a gypsy princess with her flying hair and her untidy dress, the strange slant-wise shape of her long eyes, and her wild behaviour.

Would he ever have tamed her? He would not have wanted to do so. They were at opposite poles, the ends of the parallel lines which never meet in geometry but do in real life. Life or death? What did it matter? He was a Presbyterian. If he did not live to marry her, she would become a Roman Catholic nun. She had once told him that, and for a little time it had troubled him, but not now.

Now it showed only the infinite freedom of spirit that they shared, yes, and would share after death. She was free of him, as he of her. His death would not break her, as the fear of it had broken Magdalen long, long before it came. For Louey was an artist, and her life was independent of any other human life or chance. Louey would live and work though he was dead. The thought gave him great courage

It could not matter now what that poor driven boy, King Charles II, had to do, or not to do, when he signed the treaty that the Covenanters had set before him. Each man must follow the line that he and his father and fathers had set before him, and Charles II, son of Charles I and Henrietta Maria of France, lover of Lucy Walters, suitor of Sophia of Bohemia, of La Grande Mademoiselle of France, of Agnes of Orange, and possibly of Anne Campbell, daughter of the Earl of Argyll, must follow his.

But he, Montrose, was free of all these, and of all else. He had only to follow the line of his shaggy horse's nose, a nose bristling with rough beard from feeding on the whin of the open moors, the line that was set by his enemies. There was no more choosing for him, no more planning, guiding, leading.

He had gone home to his wife's father and his wife's children and to those who had loved him since he had been a child. Now he was going home indeed, and a line in a play that Elizabeth had quoted to him at The Hague throbbed in his mind in time to the thud of his horse's hoofs:

'All life is but a wand'ring to find home.'

A whole lifetime, his lifetime of thirty-seven and a half years, seemed to have been marched out on this last journey; it had led him through his first memories and stretched out far beyond his own life into that of his children; it had shown him the pitiful baseness of the Macleods, the triumphant gaiety of the old lady of Skibo, the lovely courage of his kinswoman at Pitcaple, and of Jean Durhame, and that moment of deep, warm, astonished feeling in Hurry when they had met at Inverness.

Since that meeting it was odd how they had seemed to march in company, though they had been allowed no further word together. They had passed all through Moray where he and Hurry had played their deadly game of hide-and-seek against each other in just this same merry month of May five years ago, when Hurry, as cavalry leader for the Covenanters, had all but trapped him at Dundee, then cleverly led him in pursuit up towards Inverness, only to turn in the night and make his surprise attack at Auldearn. And now they had passed by Auldearn at just the same moment of the year, in the same tempests of cold rain as had fallen on the battle when they had fought each other, the battle they had so lately enjoyed together as they talked of it walking on the seashore, only a few days before Carbisdale, that last fight for both of them.

As he was helped down from his Highland pony at the end of this day's march (his ankles were so stiff and sore with the continued chafing of the ropes that he could not at first move them) he saw Hurry's hard light eyes staring at him over the heads of his companions, and the two exchanged a slow smile that made their past enmity a curiously close condition of their present friendship.

They were unarmed now; their long march, first against, now

with each other, was all but over. Now they were going home together.

They took boat and landed at Leith harbour on the afternoon of Saturday, May 18th. The Edinburgh magistrates met him there and he was given a cart-horse to ride while the rest of the prisoners walked on foot in front of him, tied together two by two, Hurry one of the couple immediately in front of him, as next in importance.

It was about four o'clock when they reached the Watergate and there saw the guards, the rest of the magistrates, the hangman's cart drawn by four horses, and the hangman in his red bonnet and official livery, into whose hands he was now to be delivered. The magistrates showed him the order for his procession; he was to be mounted on a high seat in the cart with his head uncovered and his arms bound with ropes behind his back, tying him to the seat, and so led through all the town of Edinburgh to the prison of the Tolbooth.

He read the order; he knew well that the reason he was to be bare-headed and tied up with ropes was that he should not be able to defend his head or face from the stones and filth thrown at him.

All he said was that he was sorry that through him his master King Charles, whose commission he carried, should be dishonoured. But without any sign of personal dismay he quickly mounted the cart and allowed the hangman to uncover his head and bind his arms.

The long procession started in the bright chilly sunlight of the late afternoon. The rabble of Edinburgh were all out thronging the streets to see it, encouraged and marshalled by their leaders to hurl their missiles of hate at that sure cock-shy, whom every preacher in the city had assured them for years past was the cause of all their present troubles.

People had been waiting since dawn, were now trampling each other to see the Arch-Enemy go by. From every window in those tall, crooked, crazy houses that seemed to totter over each other's shoulders in their eagerness to see his disgrace, there craned the hungry necks of men who craved to wreak their sense of grievance for all the miseries of their country upon some tangible object, something, moreover, that it would be safe, even commendable, to abuse.

Nor had their Governors trusted only in personal feeling engineered by the ministers. Men and women from all over Scotland that had lost their sons and husbands in those civil wars of five years ago had been searched out and brought to Edinburgh and paid good money in shillings sterling, not Scots, to throw stones at him. A sheer waste of money some had argued, hearing those streets buzzing with fury all day against Montrose's Highlanders. No need to pay these people to take vengeance.

But they did not take it.

He rode through Edinburgh, mounted on the high seat of that cart, his face a sure target for the missiles of that hired rabble that was still being urged on by the ministers, who moved among them even now wherever they could force a passage in their black Geneva gowns, preaching hatred and revenge.

But the people did not notice them; they were staring at that figure mounted high above them, at his white face, unshaved, since his guards still feared he might cheat them of their triumph by cutting his throat with a razor, though he had taken no advantage on the way here of all the opportunities he had had to do so; they stared at the gaunt features, the fever-ridden eyes burning deep within their sockets, they stared and could not hoot nor jeer as they had been instructed, they forgot the duties for which they had been brought here and paid. Their hands with the missiles in them dropped to their sides, powerless, and many fell on their knees and prayed, they knew not for what nor to whom—certainly not to the God of their Covenant, a God delighting in revenge and blood sacrifices, but perhaps to the Unknown God that lives in the deep unspoken humility of all men's hearts when they know that they must worship, and know not whom.

So they fell back in silence from before the hangman's cart, which bore Montrose high above them.

The procession took three hours. He was driven down the steep hill between the tall houses of the Canongate in the clear golden light of the late evening, in a tense silence, broken, not by cries and jeers, but by the tears and sobbing prayers of his enemies.

There had been a grand wedding that day at Moray House, where Cromwell had lodged on his visit to Edinburgh eighteen months ago, and had held long private conversations with Argyll on, it was believed, 'the necessity to take away the life of the King,' Charles I.

Now young Lord Lorne, Argyll's eldest son and heir, sat on the carved stone balcony with his bride, Lady Mary Stewart, to watch his father's enemy go by to the prison from which he would only be released to the scaffold.

His father, that lifelong enemy of Montrose, who had brought him to this pass, was not so bold. He did not dare venture out upon the balcony, but waited behind half-closed shutters with Archibald Johnston of Warriston, the fanatic little clerk whom he had raised from obscurity and penury to so high a seat in the Government of Scotland.

As the cart approached Moray House, the driver pulled up, the horses stood still, and Montrose looked up to see for what reason this horrible procession had been checked. He saw young Lord Lorne in his bridegroom's clothes, his still younger bride beside him; he saw one of the Gay Gordons, Lady Jean, whom he faintly remembered as a spitfire child hurling defiance at her father, Lord Huntly, and demanding seven shillings from him, which he had not got, 'to go to the dwarf's wedding.'

She spat fire now, moved thereto by some twisted, miserable recollection of her splendid, showy, useless father who had met his end on the scaffold by command of her uncle Argyll, stirred to action, too late to be of any help to the royal cause, by his vain emulation of the man below who now rode to the same death. And her eldest brother, George Gordon, the only one of the family that had been worth anything, and she knew it, had adored Montrose, followed him to the wars and been killed by his side in one of his battles; her second brother, Aboyne, had deserted him and died abroad of a guiltily broken heart; the third, Lewis, was busily making his peace with Argyll—and quite right too! All these high notions led only, on a high cart, to the grave.

So she shrilled out an insult at him, and a voice in the crowd cried shame on her, that it were better she sat in the condemned cart herself to do penance for her adulteries.

Then Montrose saw the face of his enemy, Argyll.

Through the half-closed shutters it peered, obliquely, as it had looked, always, at all that life spread before him—an oblique, unhappy, suspicious face, fearful even in victory, knowing that for him there was no victory, no security, no satisfaction even in ordaining and watching the doom of his enemy.

'There is Montrose,' it said, 'whom I have always hated, and now condemned to death. He will die and I will live—but how long, oh Lord, how long, and to what end?'

Did Argyll know in that instant of suspense between two 'naked-thinking souls' that his end would be the same as that which he had ordained for his victim—the same physically, but in spirit very different?

Beside him was the shivering, nervous, blood-shotten spirit of his creature, Warriston.

'Have you not once got your fill of blood?' That was not said to him but to one of his satellites, less bloodthirsty than he. And Archibald Johnston of Warriston had not yet got his fill of it. He gazed down at the pale proud face of the man in the condemned cart, and his hands shook with rage.

"They have cheated us," he whispered to his superior, "all these women—and men too—to whom we have paid good money in shillings sterling, not Scots, to throw stones at the prisoner, and not one has been thrown! His hands are tied behind his back, yet there is no new scar, no fresh blood upon his face."

That strange yellow crooked face of his master looked down on his companion, the squinting eyes, the twisted mouth showed nothing of what he was thinking. But a long hand stretched itself out like a claw from the black sleeve of the man who was the Governor of Scotland, and pushed the shutter to, leaving those two alone together in the mirky half-darkness.

A voice cried out from the crowd below, an alien voice, the voice of an English stranger:

"Small wonder you cowards cannot look upon the face of Montrose! You've never dared do so these seven years past."

Argyll slammed the other shutter to. Now they were shut in together, he and Warriston, whom he loathed, who feared him.

Outside by the Mercat Cross, stark against the pale brilliant light of the May evening, stood the new thirty-foot-high gallows erected for their victim, who had proved victorious.

XII

IT was just on seven o'clock when he reached the Tolbooth where he was to be imprisoned. The City Guard of Edinburgh were drawn up before it, with their Captain, Major Weir, in command. It was he now who would take charge of the prisoner.

Montrose's bonds were cut; he climbed down from the condemned cart and gave the driver a piece of gold.

"There, fellow, is drink-money for driving the cart," he said, and turned towards his new jailer

He saw a tall dark man about fifty years old, in a black cloak, who held in his hand a long staff with a crooked head of thornwood. It was no symbol of office for the Captain of the City Guard, but since his retirement from active military service a year or two ago, Major Weir never went anywhere without it.

He kept his eyes on the ground while General Leslie spoke with him, a practice which Montrose soon observed to be customary with him, but when the General and the troops had departed, he looked at last at his prisoner.

In that instant Montrose saw something he had not seen since as a youth he had looked, uncomprehending, at the bloated, battered face, with its round red cheeks and purposeful joviality, of the Italianate German, Carlippis, servant to Montrose's brother-in-law Sir John Colquhoun, the man who had helped his master seduce and abduct Montrose's younger sister by means of witchcraft.

Major Weir's appearance was as different from that servant's false bonhomie as it was possible to be, for it was commanding, almost majestic, and with so great and formal a gravity that it seemed he must carry that staff to strike upon the ground and give warning whenever he was about to make a pronouncement. And the pronouncement, as Montrose already knew, for Weir's reputation as one of the Covenant's most fervid saints had spread far beyond Edinburgh, was certain to be one of impassioned sanctity.

378

Yet something had left the same mark on him as on that gross sceptic who had helped wreck the home of Montrose's two sisters.

Terrible as his past journey had been, Montrose had been cheered on it by the sight of human beings going about their business, some of them old and patient with the wisdom learned by inevitable experience, some young and glad with the vigorous promise of life These people had been human, even the Macleods, that unhappy weakling and his brutally grasping wife

But now as he stood before Major Weir, at first sight of that ravaged terrible face, the eyes like live coals on either side of the big aggressive nose, he felt that he was to be shut in with a devil. Here was a man to whom life itself, its powers and opportunities, were not enough; who needed to supplement them by unholy means; a man who early in life had sworn himself to the old perverse creed—'Evil, be thou my good.'

He came in out of the clear sunlight, the fresh winds and swiftly falling rain of the open country of these past days, into the tomb-like cold and dark of the prison room in the Tolbooth where the light of day never reached, and by Major Weir's orders only one small tallow candle was allowed to give its guttering yellow light.

He had only just entered the room when there arrived representatives from the Committee of Estates and several ministers, all of whom questioned him and exhorted him to confess and repent his heinous crimes against God and man.

He refused to answer, indeed at that moment he could hardly have done so, whoever had spoken to him. He was worn out physically; he had just looked once again upon his two greatest enemies, and upon the gallows on which in three days' time he was to hang; he had this moment felt in the person of his jailer a stronger will and determination towards evil than could be accounted for by merely human agency.

The power of evil seemed paramount in his country, and indeed in the whole world at this time. Of what use to try to meet it with answers and arguments?

Yet he met it with a smile; for, said he, "You must excuse my talking with you now. The compliments you have put on me this day have proved something tedious."

They went uneasily away. He was left with his guards, and Major Weir.

By Weir's orders the guards who stayed in the room with him night and day smoked continually, for he had discovered how intensely his prisoner disliked the smell of tobacco. It might be only a small annoyance, but nothing was too small for Major Weir's attention if it could give pain of whatever sort. He remained in the room himself nearly all the time, and kept up a current of abuse of Montrose in which 'Dog,' 'Atheist' and 'Excommunicate traitor' were some of the milder epithets.

If, as sometimes happened, the common soldiers with him showed any sign of discomfort at this, if only by getting a convenient fit of coughing when he was most violent, he turned and jeered at them, telling them that it was such half-hearted milksops as they that did God's cause most harm.

"God is not mocked with such feeble service. God has forsaken this heathen dog utterly and spewed him out of His mouth,—lifted him up for a little and given him victory only that he might be the more utterly cast down. And this is the proof of it, that in no one thing will God let him succeed. Look at his attempt to escape, when he had got clear away through all his ordinary guards; but God sent guards extraordinary, as it might be His own angels from heaven, to prevent him."

Mat Caldy, private, under cover of filling his pipe, stole a glance at his Corporal to see how he took this definition of troopers who left their appointed quarters to get a drink, but quickly turned away his eyes as he saw the Corporal did not dare meet them.

It wasn't good to cross Major Weir by even so much as a wink. There were some mighty odd things whispered about him, but none dared do more than whisper; if they did, they got the worst of it. There was a woman just lately who had complained to the minister of New Mills of the Major's conduct in a field near by, and by order of the Magistrates of Lanark had been whipped through the town by the common hangman as 'a slanderer of such an eminent holy man.'

That was the sort of thing that happened to anyone who ventured to cross Weir. So they kept silent while their Major, standing, as if he were addressing one of the 'house-coventicles' of the elect where he had acquired so great a reputation as a preacher, and leaning a little forward on his long staff, fixed those restlessly burning eyes on his prisoner and told him what imbecile hypocrisy and effrontery it was in him to try to pray.

"Look at him, you fellows—there on his knees, pretending to pray to God, who would not let him repent even if he could!"

Montrose raised his head and met those dreadful eyes with a look so piercing that the soldiers remembered it long afterwards, and declared that it made Weir's hand shake so that he nearly dropped his staff.

"You hate me to repent of my sins," Montrose said. "That means that you too, Major Weir, wish to repent, and one day will try to do so."

"Liar!" shrieked the Major, clutching his staff firmly into his grasp again. From the terror in his voice, Montrose might have prophesied the most appalling doom for him, but he quickly recovered and continued to preach, or rather to pray for damnation on his prisoner, with the frantic fluency that had won him an almost miraculous reputation among the 'Bowhead Saints.' The pious women around his lodging in the West Bow by the Grassmarket were wont to speak of him as 'Angelical Thomas.'

The ministers worked their utmost to counteract the impression that Montrose's entry into the city had made on the people. All the next day, being Sunday, the heavy hour-glasses on the pulpits were turned and turned again while the preachers poured forth their fury for three hours, in some cases four, against James Graham, excommunicated by the Kirk, accursed of God; and against the stubborn and craven populace that had refused to throw their stones and filth at him.

And all that day both ministers and members of the Scots Parliament preached at Montrose himself in his prison, abusing him, storming at him, striving to wring from him some confession of his own guilt, or at least a complaint of King Charles' treatment of him.

For that latter purpose they told him that Charles had signed the Treaty of Breda with them on the 1st of this month, 'that their Commissioners and the King's Majesty were agreed, and that his Majesty was coming here to this country with them.'

So that had been done while he was wandering on the desolate moors round Assynt. The news struck him a blow, but he did not show it. He saw what his enemies would be at—to try to ruin Charles through his servant, as they had ruined him through his King.

And the next day, Monday, they were there again by eight o'clock in the morning. He was to be summoned at ten o'clock before the bar of Parliament to hear his sentence. He had not yet had any breakfast, and not one moment of quiet in which to prepare an answer to his judges.

Instead, he had now to summon all his wits to answer these men who were pestering him, in defiance of the fever that throbbed in his brain, so that some of those sturdy citizens present who had slept comfortably in warm feather-beds and breakfasted heartily that morning, considered his manner rather 'airy and volage' for the gravity that they expected from a great nobleman under sentence of death, though at the same time they accused him of being 'aspiring and lofty.'

It did not seem to matter much which he owned to; he admitted that God had made men of different dispositions (how long was this futility to continue?). One of them told him "he was a faggot of hell and he already saw him burning."

There was no answer to make to that, whether 'aspiring and lofty' or 'airy and volage.'

At last came the main charge: that he had taken the Covenant in his youth, then turned against it and broken it. To that he answered quickly that the National Covenant which he had taken, he still owned, a Covenant that had aimed only at keeping the Scots ordinance of religion free from interference.

"But when the King had granted you all your desires, and you were every one sitting under his vine and his fig tree,—that *then* you should have taken the King's enemies in England by the hand, and entered into the Solemn League and Covenant with them against the King, that was a thing I judged it my duty to oppose to the yondmost."

Certainly none of them at this moment could have called his manner 'airy and volage.' It was he who had become the accuser and they the guilty parties. He sternly told them, "that course of yours did not end until it brought about the King's death and overturned the whole Government."

They looked nervously at each other, hesitating in their search for an answer. One said in excuse that it was not they but Cromwell's sectarian party that had "carried things beyond the true and first intention."

"Error is infinite," he answered, and wondered when and where he had said those words before.

He would say no more.

They told him that since he would not submit himself in repentance to them he must die excommunicate, in "the fearful apprehension that what is bound on earth, God will bind in heaven."

They left him to eat a little bread dipped in ale, and then be taken immediately before the bar of Parliament.

He wore a black and scarlet suit of his, laced with silver, which his niece Lilias Napier, then in Edinburgh, had been able to send to him, though neither she nor any of his friends was allowed to visit him. He looked magnificent in spite of his white, gaunt face;

and the very men that showed their agreement of the charges of 'boundless pride and ambition' in this 'the most cruel and inhuman butchery of his country,' admitted in private his 'courage and modesty, unmoved and undaunted.'

He still gave no hint of reproach of King Charles, but maintained that his last campaign was 'by His Majesty's just commands.'

He warned them: "Be not too rash; let me be judged by the laws of God, the laws of nature and nations, and the laws of this land."

And if they would not judge by the laws of men, he bade them remember "the righteous Judge of the world who one day must be your Judge and mine."

But the only answer to that was the command to kneel and hear his sentence. It was read by Archibald Johnston of Warriston, whom Montrose had known and instantly disliked as the sickly, raving clerk who had been used to engineer emotional propaganda in the early days of the troubles. Since then his propaganda had grown into one long howl for blood.

Now surely it should be appeased, as he mouthed the horrible words condemning the prisoner to be hanged to-morrow on a gibbet at the Cross of Edinburgh until he died, and to hang for three hours after in the view of the people; then to be beheaded and quartered, his head to be set on a spike above the Tolbooth in Edinburgh, his legs and arms at the gates of Stirling, Glasgow, Perth, and Aberdeen; the rest of the body, if he died repentant, to be buried in Greyfriars Churchyard, but if he remained obdurate, to be thrown into the unhallowed ground of the Boroughmuir.

That 'evil scraped tongue,' as Warriston had himself lamentably called his own harsh voice, reached the end of the sentence in shrill ecstasy. Montrose, kneeling before him as commanded, lifted up his face and looked the neurotic in the eyes.

Then he was taken back to the Tolbooth, where still the ministers and magistrates thronged in on him in their ceaseless nagging persecution. It lasted till late on this his last evening.

There was one plea for mercy, within narrow limits. The Provost of Edinburgh, an ardent Covenanter, asked: "What need of so much butchery and dismembering? Has not beheading, and publicly affixing the head, been thought sufficient for the most atrocious State crimes hitherto?" He even went so far as to call the sentence 'unmanly.' But his mild protest went unheeded; and those who were in the little dark cell with the prisoner kept on insisting on every hideous detail of the execution.

It made no odds to Montrose.

"Let them bestow on every airt a limb!" he flung at them. It would make no difference what happened to his broken body once his spirit had left it and returned to the God who had created it. So—

'Let them bestow on every airt a limb.'

The words came again in his mind through all the clash of reproach and argument and ceaseless questioning round him; they strung themselves to others in the same rhythm; once again, on this his last night, he was making verses, as Raleigh had done on his last night in the Tower of London.

'Scatter my ashes, strew them in the air,
Lord, since thou know'st where all these atoms are,
I'm hopeful thou'lt recover once my dust
And confident thou'lt raise me with the just.'

He had need of that confidence. One voice after another was insisting, praying, that eternal death and damnation were now the certain fate of his soul. All he wanted now was to be alone with his soul, and he was not allowed it. Their voices clacked and clamoured, unmeaning but disturbing; he was only half conscious of them, but they would not let him think.

The ministers drew back, consulted together, decided that, since their combined efforts had proved fruitless, Mr. Robert Baillie, who had once admired and been on friendly terms with the prisoner, should see what he could do by himself to bring the sinner to repentance. They pushed him forward, Mr. Baillie for once reluctant to make a move. He went forward hesitatingly and

2 B

stepped back as Montrose swung round, his patience suddenly at breaking-point.

"I pray you, gentlemen," he flung out, "let me die in peace."

And he walked away to the furthest corner of his cell, but Mr. Baillie, urged on by his fellows, came after him, and stood there looking up at him, with none of the bold inquisitiveness and confidence in his own sound judgment and upright dealing that he had shown at their last encounter on the terrace of the House in the Wood, but with a puzzled humble expression rather like a spaniel's in his round blue eyes. He faltered out a few words so low and confused that Montrose could only distinguish 'my lord,' but that in itself was surprising, since the Government had decreed his titles forfeit and when he stood before the bar of the Parliament all had been careful to address him only as 'sir.'

"My lord," said Baillie again, with an anxious glance over his shoulder to make sure the rest of his company were not listening, but they had gone through into the outer cell to give him his chance with the culprit, "it may be a sin and vanity in me to address Your Lordship thus, for indeed I do not find in the New Testament that Christ has any lords in His house, which was the reason I gave long ago for refusing a bishopric."

He stopped, having lost his thread.

"Bishops? I care nothing for them," Montrose answered wearily, thinking that the whole subject of the Kirk and the Bishops' War was to be dragged up again.

But that was not Mr. Baillie's intention; he had some difficulty in saying his intention or in knowing it himself. His thoughts were flustering in his head and he did not know which of them to get out nor how to do it, though God knows words had never failed him in his life before whether in speech or writing, they had always come bubbling out of him as fast as a river in spate,—and now, when he most wanted them, they failed him.

He had watched and heard Montrose before his judges that morning and had felt, as he had done at the trial and death of the

great Earl of Strafford, that 'huge things are here in working—
the mighty hand of God be about this great work.' But he could
not feel as sure as he had done that time, when nine years younger,
in what way that 'mighty hand' was moving.

He had come here with his fellow-ministers meaning to pray
and wrestle with the Devil once more for this man's proud and
obdurate soul that he had once called noble and generous. But
all that he had meant to say had gone out of his head as he watched
them swooping and striking their talons into this wounded lion who
would to-morrow be their carrion.

There was nothing now in his head but an unhappy, turgid welter
of emotion that filled his eyes with tears as he stammered out, "My
lord, I too have bairns, a boy called Rob like yours, though now
growing up, and my little Lillie,—and if there were anything that
I could do for yours, you may be sure to trust me in that. I will
consult my Lord Southesk and see what can best be done for them
and for your estates hereafter, for sure the ruin of this present time
cannot endure for ever, and your eldest son and heir will be able to
return when these unhappy quarrels are over, to enjoy his own in
Scotland—as you should have done, my lord—as you should have
done——"

He could say no more, for he was fairly blubbering and it was
high time for him to go.

His companions were peeping in on him; they must not see that
he was weeping while the prisoner, that he should have reduced to
penitence, remained dry-eyed. He wiped his eyes on his sleeve,
giving a prodigious sniff, uttered a word or two of exhortation to
impress the audience by the door, and joined them with a hasty
stumbling tread.

"What did you get from him?" Mr. James Guthrie enquired.

"Did he admit anything of his guilt?" Mr. Robert Traill
demanded.

"The King? Did he still say nothing against the King?"
insisted Mr. Mungo Law.

"We never spoke of him," broke out Robert Baillie in an impetuous burst of anger.

"Never spoke of him?" Mr. Mungo Law's hands swept the air. "Sir, are you clean daft? You spoke with him alone and never got him to admit a word of the grudge he must have against the King? Never tried——?"

"No confession at all?" Mr. Robert Traill's voice was even more strident. "Lord save us, man, what were you about?"

"Of what then *did* you speak together?" came in a deep growl from Mr. James Guthrie.

"Of his private concerns," said Mr. Baillie, and added hastily as he saw those amazed, indignant faces round him, "He spoke to me of his private sins only."

"*What* private sins?" enquired Mr. Mungo Law.

"He means, his being given to women?" Mr. James Guthrie suggested hopefully.

Mr. Baillie answered with what they felt to be quite unnecessary vehemence: "A man's private sins are a matter for private confession, and not to be imparted to any."

They had to make what good they could of that, and Mr. Robert Traill duly noted it in his diary, but without the satisfaction of being able to record to what private sins James Graham had confessed.

But Mr. Robert Baillie, whose impassioned interest in everyone and everything made him write so busily and copiously to everybody, to his wife, his friends, his colleagues, his Government, and himself in his private journals—and of everything, however small, such as what he had to eat and what he had to pay for it and how badly his servant behaved and how lucky he was to get another; or however great, such as my Lord Strafford slipping off in private to the Tower 'lest he be torn in pieces' while 'the King went home in silence,'——Mr. Baillie wrote not one word of his last talk with Montrose.

Like Charles I from Strafford's death-sentence, he 'went home in silence,' to his feather-bed and his good supper, where he broke out not very reasonably about their all being a lot of 'bursten poke-puddings whose care was to dine not wisely but too well'; but Mrs. Baillie, being possessed of much the same sound rock-bottom wisdom as himself, paid no attention to that, but merely followed up the meal by giving him a good large dose of the rhubarb wine she had brewed last summer.

XIII

*T*HE ministers had gone; it was now Major Weir's turn to carry on the cry. As Montrose knelt to pray in the corner of his cell, Weir came in to jeer at him, and urged on his unwilling guards to disturb him by talking both to him and to each other. Leaning forward on his long staff, he puffed his pipe-smoke into the prisoner's face and called to the others to do the same.

"Come on, you fellows, here's a wretch that's too dainty to smell the smoke of tobacco, when he's condemned to burn in the reek of hell fire to all eternity."

The men were uneasy; one of them muttered that a man, however wicked, should be allowed to pray on the last night of his life. The Captain of the Guard swerved round on him, using his staff as a pivot.

"What's that, Dick Brodie? Are you stirring up insubordination with your blasphemies? James Graham has been condemned not merely to die but to burn in hell for ever, and you dare say his prayers are any use to him after that? They are nothing but smoke, the smoke of hell; so let him prepare his soul for it in the only way he can now, with good tobacco-smoke!"

They did not dare go against their commanding officer; they smoked and talked loud, according to his orders

Montrose had been cheered by Baillie's kindliness; now a sick despair fell on him. It had been of no use to plan and work and fight to get his country under a saner, happier rule. Men did not want to be sane or happy, they chose devils for their masters; Argyll, Warriston, even this monstrous creature, the Captain of the City Guard, were proof of it. They delighted in tyranny and cruelty:

'Torture is put upon the rays of the sun.'

If only he could have died fighting—fighting at Philiphaugh or at Carbisdale as he had longed to do, or even fighting these mean

wretches round him—that at least would have given some satisfaction to the end of a life that had now lost all its meaning.

He could not. There was nothing he could do but break out
and revile them,—and that his pride would not let him do. There
was nothing but hate round him, nothing but hate that governed
this world. God Himself was the lie with which men tried to
refute it.

Then, as he despaired, a thin wreath of the tobacco-smoke he
loathed went coiling up against the sickly yellow light of the single
candle, a cloudy spiral of blue mist, and he saw again Louey's face
when he had come on her smoking in the studio, and they had
talked, and he had told her he could not love her, and had done
so. A longing for her presence swept through him, overwhelmed
him; if he could see her, speak to her, touch her, but for an instant,
he could be brave again and know that God and love were real.

But that very torment made him brave, for in thinking of her
he forgot his own misery in the thought of what hers would be
when she knew what had happened to him.

His pity for his love healed the bitterness of his own pain. It
was to comfort her that he now longed to see her before he
died.

At the moment of death, his spirit, released, would wing to her
Knowing this, he saw and heard nothing more of his jailers.
He prayed; and soon they were astonished to find that in spite of
their continued noise and talk together, he was in a deep sleep.

When the next morning, Tuesday the 21st of May, the ministers
and politicians thronged into his cell again, Warriston himself was
with them. They found Montrose combing his hair, a vanity that
struck Warriston as a personal insult.

All the fourteen years since he had first seen Montrose now
rolled away; he was looking again at the young nobleman whose
fire and beauty and easy, unconscious courage had appealed so

swiftly to the people of Edinburgh that they had at once acclaimed him as their leader, even as two days since they had refused their rulers' commands to stone him as their enemy—and why?

Because he had appealed to the pride of the heart and the lust of the eye, where Warriston, shivering and nervous, his voice weak, his eyes red-rimmed and blurred with sleepless nights of prayer, had failed utterly to touch the hearts of the people and incline them to the Lord. Never had he forgot the miserable failure of that first speech of his to the people. He had been up all night preparing it, he had warned Christ how much His own interests were concerned in it, he had told Him, 'Thy credit is now engaged—let me know that Thy Father denies Thee nothing.' Yet God had denied both Christ and him; his speech had failed utterly. But with a careless word or two Montrose had swung the crowd to himself instead; they had surged forward as one man to answer his call, had swept him up on to their shoulders, shouting and cheering, and borne him in triumph round the Mercat Cross—where to-day he was to die.

And that was how God now at last answered His servant, Warriston. At last he was proved the ruler, and he himself had read the sentence of death on this proud nobleman. Of what use to Montrose now were his fine looks and his fine clothes, those carnation silk stockings knitted for him by his adoring nieces, his curling hair, which even now he took care to comb?

Warriston's voice rasped out across the dark cell: "Does James Graham trouble how his head shall look, when in so short a time it will be cut from his body?"

Montrose answered, "My head is still my own. To-night, when it will be yours, treat it as you please."

There was a sound like thunder outside; it was the roll of drums beating to arms. They told him that armed troops were being called out to line all the streets, in case the people were so mad as to try and rescue him.

He flung back his head and laughed. "What, am I still

a terror to them? Let them look to themselves! My ghost will haunt them."

Warriston shivered uncontrollably A sudden sick terror had come upon him like a seizure; he knew in that instant that Montrose's words were true, that he would be haunted all his life by the image of this man, and by the fear that his Highlanders would sweep down into the streets of Edinburgh to avenge his death on himself.

Had the haunting even begun?

'To-night, when it will be yours, treat it as you please.' As Montrose had said the words, his pale gleaming smile had seemed to light that head that he held so high; to Warriston's horrified imagination it appeared to swim in light, already severed from his body, to approach him, offering itself to his hands as if in anticipation of 'to-night, when it will be yours.' Then Warriston could take it between his clutching fingers and look exultantly into those eyes, now bright and unconquered, that would then at last be glazed and ghastly, mere bits of inanimate matter, which Warriston could, if he so pleased, grind beneath his heel.

Would he so please? Would he dare touch that head when it should lie bleeding before him? It was the thing he had longed for, ever since that day fourteen years ago, to deface and trample on this man's destroyed beauty. Now his wish had come true— which is the common idea of heaven, but is more commonly the truth of hell.

So it was to Warriston. For as he fearfully met those eyes that soon would see nothing, their power of vision was so clear that for one blinding instant Warriston saw through them into his own heart, saw it crawling with black and evil thoughts, saw his hideous imaginings as the work, not of God as he had believed, but of the Devil.

He put his hands before his face to shut out those eyes of Montrose.

But they would not be shut out, they would never be shut out, not even when they were glazed and dull; they would still look at him and tell him he was Satan's servant instead of God's.

From that moment uncertainty entered Warriston's frantic mind and drove it on the road to madness, so that when at last he too came to die on the scaffold, his life had for long been so miserable that he would have welcomed death even in this form—but that he had no wits left to know what was happening to him.

XIV

' AND when we cam to the lower prison
      Where Willie o' Kinmont he did lie—
      "Oh sleep ye, wake ye, Kinmont Willie,
      Upon the morn that thou's to die?"

"'Oh I sleep saft and I wake aft,
      It's lang since sleeping was fley'd frae me!
      Gie my service back to my wife and bairns
      And a' gude fellows that speir for me."'

Hurry woke with a start on Tuesday morning the 21st of
May with that snatch of the ballad of Kinmont Willie ringing
in his ears. It was many years since he had heard it as a lad at
Pitfichie while that bold Border thief had been still alive. All
that King James VI of Scotland had done in reparation of that
raid to rescue Kinmont Willie from Carlisle Castle, as the ballad
sang, had been to christen his little daughter Elizabeth as namesake
of his 'loving cousin,' Queen Elizabeth of England, and to ask
that enraged old lioness down in her palace at Westminster to
'stand gossip' to his infant daughter, Princess of Scotland, so soon
to be Princess Royal of England, then to be Queen of Bohemia.

And Hurry had talked with her, had gone and inspected her
stables at The Hague with her in what he had taken to be the
proudest moment of his life. He had never had a chance to tell
his Maggie about it after all; that had gone by like everything
else.

It didn't really matter when you had come to 'the morn that
thou's to die.'

Nobody else thought so, anyway. He had pleaded his 'wife and
bairns' to the Committee of Estates, but they had regarded it as an
insufficient reason for him to go on living. Maggie and all those
long-haired brats of theirs had had to do without him most of the
time all these years at Pitfichie; no doubt she would marry one of

the neighbouring landowners—that respectable widower Dick Tweedie most probably, with his fat foolish face like an underbaked scone—and continue to do without him in much greater comfort. Dick would find tochers for the girls, all five of 'em; he was just the sort of fellow to provide for another man's children—and hadn't he good reason to, if he had only known it, since Hurry had provided him with most of his own?

He'd be one of the 'good fellows that speir for me'—there weren't many left in Aberdeenshire.

The guards gave him a good sup of whisky for his late breakfast. That showed there was going to be no chance of a reprieve; so did their kindly apologetic manner. One of them had brought him a couple of fresh eggs from his own hens, 'laid this morning.' A fellow was no doubt entitled to two eggs for breakfast on the day he was to be executed.

He asked about Montrose. Sleeping had not been 'fley'd frae' him; he had slept as peacefully as a child on the top of hearing that ghastly sentence yesterday.

"Sentence one day, execution the next," said Hurry; "they killed off Rizzio even quicker, and that's all you can say for it. But no one called that an execution—or will call this anything but murder."

"Ay, it's been quick work," said one of the guards, uncomfortably loquacious. "Davie Sands' men were at it all night to get up that giant gallows in time to greet you—and then had to add sixteen wine-puncheons to make the platform big enough for it."

"As to that, I'd as soon die on wine-puncheons as anything."

"Ah, but they're empty, General."

"They'll be full enough of blood by the time your ministers have done."

There was an uneasy laugh. They were good fellows. Like all men, they liked telling him a thing or two against their superior officers, but they evidently had not dared to tell all they would like to against Major Weir. But Hurry's sharp eyes could see as far through a brick wall as most.

As he was led out of prison, his hands bound to his side, Major Weir was standing at the gates of the Tolbooth, waiting for him, his eyes cast on the ground as usual, but he raised them as Hurry approached, and looked into his face with curious delight.

"Your master has gone on before you," he said, "to show you the way to tread the scaffold. You've turned your coat many times, Sir John Joseph, whose coat bears so many colours, but you turned it wrong at the last. Here you are on the wrong side after all at the end, and God and the Devil himself together will laugh you to scorn."

The frosty eyes of his prisoner stared back into those strangely glowing eyes.

"I've been hearing a deal about your City Guard of Edinburgh," said Hurry in a casual conversational tone. "They tell me it's of great antiquity, so old that some of the guards attended the Crucifixion."

"That may well be," said Weir with a touch of simple pride that made him much more human, "since we hold King Solomon's own original portrait which they looted from the Temple at Jerusalem at that time."

"A certain proof of it. And you, Major, have stood at this gate to-day to insult and taunt the Marquis of Montrose as he went to execution—as you've done to every prisoner who's left these gates to his death, and as you'd have done to Christ on the Cross if you'd been there with the City Guards of Edinburgh."

Major Weir knocked his staff down upon the stones with an angry rattle. "You go to your death blaspheming! You have dared compare the dog's death that James Graham is to die with that of our Saviour. You will go to hell with that devil's lie burning your tongue till it withers at the root."

"Ay, you're 'Angelical Thomas' of the Bowhead Saints—but there are one or two things I know now of you, Angelical Thomas, and there's one satisfaction in being condemned to die, and that is, you can't do any worse than is to be done to me to-day, and I can say what more than one man and woman would like to say—your own sister Jean Weir for one—whom you've seduced both to your will and your Master's; and that is, you need a long spoon to sup with the Devil, but even that tall black wand of yours won't be long enough to help you against him when your time comes."

Twice Major Weir had raised his staff in furious signal to the guards to march the prisoner on. But that stalwart fellow, half a head taller than the men on either side of him, held his ground while he rapidly finished his imperturbable speech. Nor were his guards, for all their air of shocked determination, at all sorry to hear to the end of it. They did not dare look at their Major, but stole glances at each other under their helmets as they finally pushed Hurry on.

"No need for that now I've said my say, lads," he told them, squared his shoulders, and fell into the line of march.

All round him he saw troops lining the streets, and behind them the white faces of the crowd, and he heard the amazed murmur of their speech

The day had been heavy and overcast with thunder-clouds, but now the early afternoon sun was piercing them in long white shafts of light. The puddles between the cobblestones gleamed like mirrors, and the windows on one side of the street were a dazzle of pale gold.

In front of him Hurry now saw the square platform of the scaffold and on it the immense new gallows. The guillotine, long nicknamed the Maiden, stood near by for Hurry and the prisoners who would follow him. The executions would be delayed over several weeks, he had been told, so as to give full warning to the people of Edinburgh.

'The Ministers' Altar' they were already calling that scaffold that was to run with blood in the heart of their city.

There was a group of black-robed figures on the scaffold, and among them, as they shifted from him, Hurry saw one in scarlet. Now he saw Montrose again as he had been in his Vice-regal state when Hurry had joined him after Kilsyth, and as the guest of kings abroad who had given him precedence above all the ambassadors. The ministers, who had moved a little away from him to consult together, now came again round him to try to get some word of confession from him. He did not even look at them, but turned from them and looked down the long sunlit street. Now Hurry saw his face, and his heart seemed to stop within him.

Was this the face of a man who in a few minutes would walk up that ladder to be turned off it to hang till he was dead on that enormous engine?

It was the face of a bridegroom.

As he looked on that face for the last time, Hurry saw a glory shining through it that illumined the whole world to him, so that for the first time he saw its splendour, free of results, of success or failure.

All his life he had pursued success as a glittering ball to be chased at all hazards, its capture the one thing that made life worth living, while failure was worse than criminal: it was dismal, depressing, ignoble. But nothing here was dismal or depressing. The suspicion dawned on him that success did not necessarily bring glory, nor failure bring shame; that men would turn in disgust from the memory of Argyll's rule of Scotland or Cromwell's conquest of Ireland, when they would be proud to remember Raleigh's last voyage, or Montrose's death.

Was it then indeed the wrong side on which after all his turnings he now found himself at the latter end? It was by the side of Montrose that he would die; that was as good a death as any man could choose.

The crowd had thronged up to the very edge of the scaffold, but though it was customary for even the worst criminal to be allowed to address them. Montrose was not permitted to do so.

He spoke his last words only to those nearest him, while a young man close by him on the scaffold took them down in shorthand. Hurry missed sentences here and there, but heard the most of it.

". . . In regard of men, they are but instruments. God forgive them and I forgive them. . . . What I did in this kingdom was in obedience to the most just commands of my Sovereign and in his defence, in the day of his distress, against those who rose up against him. I acknowledge nothing, but fear God and honour the King, according to the commandments of God and the just laws of Nature and nations. . . .

"It is spoken of me that I should blame the King. God forbid! . . .

". . . For His Majesty now living, never any people, I believe, might be more happy in a king. His commandments to me were most just and I obeyed them. . . . I pray God he be so dealt withal that he be not betrayed under trust, as his father was.

"I do but follow the light of my conscience—which is seconded by the working of the Spirit of God that is within me. I thank Him I go to heaven with joy the way He paved for me. If He enable me against the fear of death, and furnish me with courage and confidence to embrace it even in its most ugly shape, let God be glorified in my end.

". . . I have no more to say but that I desire your charity and prayers. I shall pray for you all. I leave my soul to God, my service to my Prince, my goodwill to my friends, my love and charity to you all."

Then he turned aside to pray, apart, for the ministers refused in his case to pray, according to their custom, for the criminal's departing soul. He stood there with that strange light of peace, even joy, in his face, then turned to the executioner, who came forward with the tears running down his face and tied Montrose's own Declaration and Wishart's History of the Deeds of Montrose round his neck to share his condemnation. He gave the executioner some pieces of gold and turned with the same simplicity and majesty to go up the ladder. There for the last time he looked down on the people.

"God have mercy on this afflicted land," he said aloud.

An English agent of the Commonwealth, writing of political affairs in an upper window of his lodging looking on to the Mercat Cross, had scribbled:

'What with the early going away of the post, and what with the hubbub we are in—Montrose being now on the scaffold—I must cut short.'

Yet he had found time to describe at some length the remarkable 'composure' of the prisoner, his 'beauty' and 'majesty,' and the general belief that 'he has overcome more men by his death than he could have done if he had lived.'

Then that soberly dressed figure in the upper room, who kept glancing down into the street and whose hand alone was moving busily among all that still host of people, added:

'I should write more largely if I had time; but he is just now turning off from the ladder; but his countenance changes not.'

2 C

EPILOGUE

'BEYOND THE STARS'

EPILOGUE

SHE had reached the end of the world—but the world went on.
It went on and on past that moment when she heard of Montrose's death, and at first it went so slowly that each hour, day, week,
month, was torture; and then it was years that spun past her instead of the infinite minutes ticked out by the clock and hours
struck by those hammers,—'four o'clock now, and so long a time
since it had struck three.' She could never hear those Cupids'
hammers beating their arrows on the anvil without thinking of
rain on the terrace at Rhenen and the busy sound of the French
visitors talking through the open doors, and herself wandering
through the empty rooms, waiting, waiting for Montrose to come
to her.

Time went so slow when one was young, so slow that sometimes
it stopped altogether—as it had done when she heard that Montrose
was dead.

But it had gone on again, days, months, years, spinning a meaningless shadow-show of people who drifted past her, flat and grey, and
when they moved their mouths to speak to her, said nothing—until
that too passed, everything passed, the world went on and was left
behind, and here she was, the elderly Abbess of Maubuisson walking
through the vast grounds of her convent.

Through the orchards heavy with ripening fruit she walked, and
the vegetable-gardens cut as formally as the flower-beds of the
previous century, in huge stars and pentacles of steel-blue cabbages
and artichokes and the broad copper leaves of beetroot, the feathery
pale bronze of carrot leaves, a garden made all of shining metals
like those of the Incas of Peru, and set about it an exotic
guard of tall sunflowers, their negro faces framed in gaudy rays
of gold. She went down through the woods to the oblong
fishpond set in the deep shade, back to the white-hot courtyard
where the big Flemish cart-horses dragged their loads of gleaming

corn and stamped and sneezed in the dust they raised, their harness clanking and glittering in the fierce sunlight while the cooing pigeons swooped and strutted, pecking for fallen grain between the massive tufted hoofs.

Everywhere her nuns bustled through that burning late-August scene, black-and-white figures in their Benedictine robes, their skirts looped up through broad belts to keep them out of the way of their very active work, their round country faces shining with heat and health, some feeding chickens, some stacking corn, some gardening, some fishing, some walking along a narrow plank beside a rapid rushing little stream set deep down below an old wall to the penthouse where the laundry was done, kneeling there and rinsing and floating the fine white linen tablecloths in that turbulent underground water. An act of worship it looked, in an almost hidden chapel dug deep in the cool earth.

And a place of worship was the vast mediaeval barn, its little towers at each end set with hooded windows like nuns' coifs. Louise came out of the blazing sunlight into that cool dark, the stone pillars rising in it majestic as in a minster, soaring to the vaulted roof of wooden beams and the windows high and narrow as in a clerestory. The pillars ran all down the centre, dividing the building into two enormous aisles, and on either hand into side-chapels dedicated to the different products of the harvest, some for roots, some for storing corn, some for threshing it.

Here she felt herself in a place as hallowed as in the chapel, for did not all religion spring from the miracle of the sprouting grain, the resurrection of the green blade of life from the withered dead husk? So she thought as she watched the work of those high priestesses of a faith older still than the Catholic Church.

The nuns worked twice as hard when that cool casual glance of their Mother Superior fell on them as she strolled by, apparently paying but little attention to their activities Yet all this heightening and exciting of their activities was for a very special occasion, much more personal to their Abbess than to themselves, for this afternoon there was to be a visit from the Abbess' youngest sister, Sophia, the Electress of Hanover.

Yes, this afternoon she would see her again, whom she had not seen since Sophie had left them all at Rhenen that fine spring day thirty years ago, had stepped into her pinnace to sail up the Rhine to her eldest brother Carl at Heidelberg.

She wrote back to them of her journey, but not of the castles perched so fantastically on the tops of huge rocks beside the river, nor of the cliffs and hills such as she had never seen before. She told of uncomfortable castles, bad dinners and old-fashioned carriages; in Cologne there was 'nothing to admire but the ramparts,' and 'the heads of 11,000 virgins and three kings had no attraction for her'; she was careful to refuse the Duke of Neubourg's invitation to stay the night after dining with him, since, in spite of her chaperons and his forty years' seniority, it might endanger her reputation, as his wife was away.

At the end of her journey she had met her brother the Elector Palatine and his newly married wife, who would have been very pretty if she had not dyed her eyebrows black in violent contrast to her fair hair; she was already bickering with her husband and making trouble about her coach, which she did not think fine enough. Sophie's first words when apart from the already unhappy couple had been, 'My sister-in-law is very stupid!'

And that journey of Sophie's had begun at the same time as that last journey of Montrose when he had been led down through the length of Scotland to his execution in Edinburgh.

Those two journeys were passing now side by side through Louise's mind; she was living, not in the French convent of Maubuisson on the banks of the Oise where she had been Abbess for nearly twenty years, but in two countries she had never seen; sailing up a broad river through Germany; riding a shaggy pony in a cloud of dust between guards along a rough hill-road.

Among all the 'imaginary portraits' she had ever conceived, the most vivid and constant in her mind was that of Scotland.

Night after night through the long years she had woken to realize slowly, unbelievingly, that she was in a narrow white cell, and not where she had been wandering in her dreams on a wide moor under a storm-driven sky, in union with her lover's spirit, in race-memory of her mother's childhood in her native country, of endless generations of the Stuart clan's campaigning in that wild land and weather.

There had been many Scots as well as English in the convent at Maubuisson ever since the Hundred Years' War between France and England; of late years the Catholic refugees from the Scots Presbyterian Government had been increasing in number, and from them Louise had heard what had been going on in their country.

'Stands Scotland where it did?' Her mother's voice echoed back to her here in this huge barn; she saw again her mother's flashing glance and the grave smile of her visitor as he capped her quotation that bleak wintry afternoon when they were all wearing black for her uncle King Charles I, and she had seen the Marquis of Montrose for the first time.

'Alas, poor country!' he had answered.

Just over a year later his last words on the scaffold had been a prayer for God's mercy on that 'poor country.'

God's judgment had been more evident than His mercy. In that same unending moment when Louise had heard of Montrose's death, King Charles II had set sail with Lauderdale for Scotland, to be greeted with the sight of the severed shrivelled hand of Montrose above the gate of Aberdeen. He was crowned King of Scots by Argyll, who kept him a virtual prisoner, and allowed his armies to be decimated by Warriston's fanatical rejection of all who had shown loyalty to the throne in the past. They were hopelessly defeated by Cromwell, who invaded and conquered Scotland, while Charles returned to the Continent, a beggared fugitive, to be hounded from one country after another, drifting through nine more years of exile before Cromwell's death and the unhappy state of England led at last to his Restoration.

One of his first acts after that Restoration had been the magnificent State funeral, in St. Giles' Cathedral, appointed to the withered remnants of his 'most passionate servant.' The grisly head of Montrose was lifted down from the Tolbooth gate by Graham of Gorthie, who kissed it as he took it between his hands; and in its place was set up the head of Argyll.

There were not many acts of retribution when Charles II came to the throne, but Argyll's execution was one. Montrose's son James, the young second Marquis, whom Louise had grown to know and love in Holland that year after his father's death, different as he was from his father in his cool judicial announcements, had refused to sit on the Tribunal of those who condemned his father's murderer to death. He could not, he said, pretend that he would be an unprejudiced judge. The spirit of greatness, manifesting itself in such different forms, had shot up in the son as in the father, and Louise had been proud to recognize it once again in the son of the man she loved.

Warriston's execution had followed Argyll's, but for him it had been a release rather than a punishment.

Major Weir's turn did not come till ten years later, and then, so unwilling did Fate seem to strike at him, that he had to force it on himself. He rose in the conventicle of the Bowhead Saints, aged, terrible, the evil spirit that had so long informed that frail tenement of clay, burning through his dreadful eyes as he confessed to unimagined crimes of devil-worship.

His hearers could not and would not believe what they heard. Doctors were sent to him with instructions to prove him insane. But they could not do so, and no one could keep him silent. He would not repent, nor evade his punishment. He was burned at the stake, and the tall staff carved with strange symbols, on which he had always leaned for support through his long and hideous career, was burned with him. The doctors had no such difficulty in pronouncing his sister Jean Weir insane, but since she was proved guilty of incest and witchcraft, she too was burned, and that haunted

part of Edinburgh where the horrible pair had lived, known as
Major Weir's land, had been avoided ever since as a dwelling-place,
and would be, it seemed, for ever.

Last of all had come the turn of Neil Macleod, eleventh and last
of Assynt.   For no heirs were ever born to him and Christian
Monro of Lemlair; no money had come to him in reward of his
betrayal of Montrose; he had petitioned for it again and again, and
all that Argyll's Government had ever paid him had been some
sacks of meal, three-quarters of it sour.

'Stripped tree of the false apples,' the Highlanders had sung of
him, and so he proved, for even the few sour apples of his possession
were reft from him.   He was often in prison, and ill.   So desperate
were his straits that he took to piracy and wreckage to try to
redeem them, levied toll on all ships that touched on his coast-lines,
and finally kidnapped a sea-captain and held him for ransom.   He
was put to the horn, declared an outlaw whom any man might kill
with impunity; his powerful neighbours rose against him, stormed
and burned his castle of Ardvreck, leaving only a few ruined walls,
a cornice of elegant chisel-work, rare in the Highlands, and in the
cellars, where Montrose had lain imprisoned, a couple of useless
cannon to rust idle through the centuries.

Argyll, Warriston, Weir, Macleod of Assynt, their toll had been
paid.

Robert Baillie fled to the Isle of Comray the year after Montrose's death 'with my lady Montgomerie, but left all my family
and goods to Cromwell's courtesy.'   A moderate ever, he achieved
a moderate's reward, and was only deprived of his honours as
Principal of Glasgow University at the Restoration, when in any
case he was too old to be able to hold them much longer.   The
letters, journals and documents, public and private, he left were innumerable, but among them all not one word as to that last interview with Montrose in the Tolbooth, which his colleague Robert
Traill so faithfully recorded.

Louise had heard of that; but it was not of men's words to each other that she thought most when she thought of Scotland, as she did now in this dim granary where the life of the harvest was treasured. She was thinking of the hills that had been her lover's help and his destruction, and of the names that they had come to bear in consequence of him. Craigcoinichean, the Hill of the Scroggy Wood, had become the Hill of Lamentation, a word almost identical in the Gaelic, in the speech of the peasants round Carbisdale, that 'place to perish the crows.' There was a ruined cottage there on a hillock they now called the Mount of Tears, where his Major-General Hurry had lodged the night before the battle; for years after the battle a woman had gone on living in that shattered wreck of heaped stones, a woman whose husband and six sons had all gone out to fight for Montrose against Strachan's troopers and had been killed to a man.

The men were killed. The women lived on.

'In the wars of the future,' prayed Louise, 'let it be more equal, dear God, lest the burden be too great for us to bear.'

Yet there was some pride in her burden. Montrose's wife had borne him his children, had borne the agony of lifelong fear for him, borne all indeed that she could bear.

But Louise had a still greater trust reposed in her. She had to bear his death.

An elderly lady, very richly and stiffly dressed, stepped briskly out of a coach in the courtyard of Maubuisson; her step was firm and springy, her complexion fresh, her eye clear and brightly observant, her back as straight as a sergeant-major's. She was followed by her daughter, a plump, Germanically pretty girl whose fair skin had been turned a pale olive-green from the sea-sickening swaying of the coach, but who still held herself rigidly erect under the eye of her mother, Sophia.

A tall thin figure in the robes of a Benedictine Abbess came hurrying across that dazzling dusty courtyard to greet them, scattering the pigeons into a sudden upward rush of fluttering wings all round her. 'And that is my sister Louey!' thought Sophie with a shock of surprise, though she did not know what she had expected instead. Louey had always been the tallest of the sisters, and those long loose robes made her seem taller still, though they did not disguise from Sophie that she was extremely thin. 'A religion that makes one flat as a plank, of what use is that?' she asked herself, unconsciously inflating her own fine bosom. But Louey had always been thin; indeed it was her very likeness to her former self that astonished her sister; Louey came sweeping across the courtyard, dark against the sunlight, not at all like an Abbess nor even like an elderly woman, but like a Northern goddess or warrior maid, so proud and fearless was her swift carriage.

It was just how she used to come down the lawns at Rhenen with her hair flying behind her; her face, too, though thin and worn, did not look old, nor austere; her eyes were shining, she was laughing as she warmly kissed them both, and talking in the old merry inconsequent way.

"Now at last you have come! Sophie, you must make thirty years pass in three days—but oh, this poor child is ready to faint. A coach in this heat—what hardships you've undergone for my sake! Come into the cool of the cloisters and have some very cold light wine, and then you will dine and tell me all the compliments King Louis has paid you, and Monsieur too,—whose do you prefer? How pretty she is, Sophie, though she is not like you—an unsisterly remark! She is like her father—oh yes, I can remember Duke Ernest Augustus' brown eyes and beautiful hands very well; does he still play the guitar? Corbetti's guitar music, do you remember, Sophie, how he kept on sending it to you—that tactful fellow Corbetti to compose so much!"

"My dear, you are just the same, and not nearly as much of an Abbess as Eliza, for all she is a Lutheran one "

"Ah, but we of the old faith have had more practice, so can afford to take it lightly "

So Louey still took things lightly. Had she always taken them lightly, even religion? What a mad schoolboy escapade of hers that had been, when she ran away from home one night, in disguise, quite alone, without money or any possessions, leaving a note on her dressing-table to say she had gone to France to become a Catholic and enter a convent. What a way to become a nun!—she might have been Rupert as a boy running away to join the army. 'My sister has never grown up!' Sophie had exclaimed indignantly to her husband.

It had caused a great deal of scandal; the Hohenzollerns spread it about that Louise had fled because she was about to have a child, though no suggestion was made as to its possible father. Elizabeth had had to make a formal denial of the statements against her daughter, and did not forgive her for a long time.

'Of all the daughters of Elizabeth of Bohemia, Louise is the only true Bohemian.'

Sophie had heard that more than once, and felt self-congratulation that she did not resemble her odd, artistic, disreputable, although so surprisingly pious sister.

They had begun to move towards the cloisters but were checked by a sudden remarkable spectacle: a coach-and-six of magnificent appearance, attended by outriders amounting almost to a bodyguard, drove at a rattling pace into the courtyard, swung smartly round the corner to a flourish of trumpets, and promptly overturned.

Out rushed a fluttering black-and-white host of nuns to the rescue like a flock of chattering magpies, the outriders in blue and scarlet and gold leapt from their saddles and joined the throng, there were cries and exclamations, enquiries, assurances, all at the same moment. Nobody was hurt but everybody was dusty and somebody had a sore elbow, but the upset of a coach was far too frequent for anybody to think much of it.

From the mêlée emerged a little man almost as round as he was tall, with an enormous blond wig somewhat awry at one end of him and a pair of thin scarlet heels six inches high at the other, both of which extremities gave him so top-heavy an appearance that it seemed scarcely possible he should be advancing jauntily towards the Abbess of Maubuisson, wagging that huge unwieldy head archly as he exclaimed:

"Aha! So we have taken you by surprise! Now what have you got for dinner for us? I said to your sister, 'You go to Maubuisson? Then you will dine well.' And then I had an inspiration. I said to my wife, your niece, and to my daughter, 'Why should not we too dine well at Maubuisson?' So here we all are, to prove your Christian charity. Is it equal to the occasion?"

"No, Monsieur. Only my pleasure that you should wish to visit me, and your daughter too, when she has so few hours left in France."

"Ah, don't talk to *her* of that. I tell her she will lose all her eyelashes if she cries any more before she gets to Spain. Holy Virgin, is it such bad fortune to marry the King of the greatest country in Europe?"

"To do that, Monsieur, she must marry your brother King Louis, and that she cannot do, being his niece."

"True, true, France is the greatest country now, but there is an ancient prestige about Spain that appeals to me infinitely, and since Louis will not give her the Dauphin we must put up with what we can get. Come, Marie Louise, stop shaking the dust out of your skirts and for heaven's sake let us get into the cool of the cloisters!"

They went towards the shade, a stiffly moving group, as richly and almost as cumbrously harnessed as their horses: Monsieur, brother to Louis XIV of France; his second wife, the plain, squat, remarkably intelligent daughter of Carl the Elector Palatine, known as Liselotte to her aunts Louise and Sophia. She had succeeded to this high position as Madame of France after the death ten years before, some said by poison, of Monsieur's first wife, Henriette of England, whom her brother King Charles II and all her intimates had called Minette.

The young girl in her teens now walking beside her father, the

Princess Marie Louise, was Minette's eldest daughter, and so like her in her graceful fleeting movements and delicate charm that Louise, who had first met Minette as a shy child in the convent of Chaillot, could scarcely believe that it was Minette's daughter and not herself who came out of that dazzle of light into the cloisters beside her and slipped her hand into hers and whispered, "Oh my darling Mother Louise, how can I live if I must leave home and all who love me?"

Yet, like Minette, she brightened instantly as soon as they were all talking together, and amused the company with her childish extravagance, telling Sophia's rather stodgily good-looking daughter that she wished she were a young man that she could marry her, "and then," she added with a sudden sigh, "I could stay in France."

She had been brought up to believe that she would marry King Louis' eldest son and become Queen of France, but now she was to be sacrificed to Louis' pretended hopes of peace with Spain and to marry the almost imbecile young king of that country, whom she had never met.

Monsieur her father had been enchanted with that former prospect, but was now equally so with this one; wedding ceremonies, presents, the necessity of planning a quantity of new dresses and resetting all their jewels, delighted him in itself. He had chosen and designed Sophia's dresses too, and reset her jewels, although he had never seen her before, but, as he told her with engaging frankness, he did not wish to be ashamed of anyone he was to introduce at Court.

In return she had admired all his clothes, the coat embroidered with diamonds to wear at his daughter's wedding, and even the nightcap tied with flame-coloured ribbons in which she had caught him unawares so that at first he had been put out and turned his head from side to side to avoid her glances, until her tactful bonhomie had put him quite at his ease. She had made a bow for his hat and trimmed it herself, and they had settled down happily to being dress-designers together.

It was all just the same in that ménage, so Sophia found an
opportunity to whisper to Louise while the company were arranging
their toilette before dinner. Monsieur's adored friend, the Chevalier
de Lorraine, who had been banished from France before Minette's
death, was now all-powerful again at Monsieur's Court, and Sophia
herself had had to embrace him on both cheeks as though he were
a Prince of the Blood Royal. Her niece Liselotte went in terror
of her life from him and his associates. The first Madame was
believed to have been done to death by their jealous plotting—
might not the second be also?

Liselotte had seen Minette's ghost in the corridors of their palace
at Saint-Cloud, and once, when strolling in the gardens at evening,
she had noticed a slight figure sitting in what had been Minette's
favourite seat at the foot of the great cascade of gleaming water
that she used to call her 'stairway into heaven'; but as Liselotte
approached, it vanished.

Sophia told this fancied experience of her niece's to Louise,
lightly and mockingly as befitted the pupil of such materialistic
philosophers as Descartes and Leibniz. But her sister, she observed,
had acquired the superstition inseparable from the old faith.

"It is not surprising," Louey said, "that the spirit of Minette
should remain. She belongs to eternity rather than to time. And
her little daughter here, Marie Louise, whom they estranged from
her in her lifetime, must feel it though she does not know it. She is
closer to her mother now than when she was alive."

"My dear, I have no doubt you are speaking good religion, but it
is not good sense. In any case, it is my darling niece Liselotte that
I am concerned for, and not for 'Minette,' as you call her, who
has been in the grave these ten years. Yet you know one must be
philosophic in all things, and if Liselotte were happy in her marriage she would not write me those long delightful letters."

Personally Sophia could not help rather liking Monsieur, he was
so gay and officiously friendly to her; he had been shocked at a
present of some bad diamonds and very poor pearls that King Louis

had sent to her ("indeed it was a bad testimony to King Louis' famous magnificence!" Sophia told her sister with a prodigious sniff) and insisted on his brother substituting some better jewels.

She described Marie Louise's wedding ceremonies with enormous gusto; all King Louis' bastards by Mesdames de la Vallière and de Montespan had attended at them. 'La Grande Mademoiselle' had looked most imposing, but the Prince de Conti positively common, although his cloak was covered with diamonds. King Louis had sworn on the Bible an 'inviolable peace' with Spain, which everybody knew was bound to be broken in a few years. His Queen Marie Thérèse cared only for eating and dressing, and had expected Sophia to kiss the hem of her robe and to sit on a mere stool in her presence instead of an armchair, such as the Empress had offered her, but Sophia had avoided both these indignities. She had seen Molière's players at the Comédie Française, but was far too busy looking at the audience of the Royal Family and Court to pay any attention to the actors.

"Yes, it has all been quite entertaining, but best of all," she ended somewhat surprisingly, "is to be here and free to laugh with you at the folly of the world and all the trouble it takes over such nonsense."

Monsieur had been right. Visitors dined well at Maubuisson. The wine was excellent, the fruit had been picked at exactly the right moment, that stuffed carp was as fresh as if it had been caught this afternoon—which it had, though Louise did not mention it. She herself ate and drank practically nothing, but was so eager both in talking and listening that her abstinence passed unnoticed. There was nothing to suggest the ascetic in her.

The gorgeous company dined apart in the gallery overlooking the great hall of the refectory where all the nuns sat in rows at their long tables,—"Nice simple country girls," Louise called them, "I won't trouble you with their company, it is not amusing, though I like it a deal better than that of the fashionable young women I had to put up with when I was first Abbess here."

Sophia had heard something about that at the French Court.

2 D

Maubuisson had had a bad reputation before Louise had been appointed Abbess; its nearness to Paris had made it a convenient cloak both for lovers' rendezvous and for women who as a result of them found it necessary to retire from the world for a time. But now that was all changed. The Bishop of Condom, Monsieur de Bossuet, who often visited the convent, had declared it to be a centre of genuine and simple piety, rare indeed in this increasingly sophisticated and atheistical age.

Had it not been for this affidavit from so famous a Prince of the Church, Sophia would have been shocked by the worldly tone of her sister's reference to her community, as of her hospitality. The latter proved too much for Sophia's daughter, Charlotte (who accepted far too much of it); she said it was the stuffy coach again and not the stuffed carp. She had to be commanded quite sharply by her mother to come out into the courtyard and wave farewell to the royal visitors as they whirled off again in their coach, this time fortunately with no upset.

Off went that bustle of glory and pettiness and inhumanity,— 'bad diamonds and very poor pearls'—'she will lose all her eyelashes if she cries any more'—'a stool instead of an armchair'— echoes of that rout were ringing in Louise's ears in topsy-turvy travesty of all the values of life, as though its participants were wearing masks and cardboard heads not their own.

She turned to her sister and said, "Shall I show you the woods?"

Charlotte preferred to rest again in the cloisters where she could hear the cool voices of the nuns practising their chants in the chapel, while her mother and aunt walked out into the woods and down towards the river.

The straight paths under that high green shade were like the aisles of some vast cathedral; the level rays of the evening sun, the rich jewelled light of late August, slanted through the tree-trunks as if through windows of stained glass, and dappled the ground at their feet in patches of deep gold.

"Maubuisson used to mean 'the Accursed Wood,'" said Louise;

"there were robbers here and the marshland bred fever, but now all that remains of that are those reeds and bulrushes in the fields and these evening primroses that are just beginning to come out now it is cooler."

They grew everywhere, tall ragged plants whose faded-looking blossoms were opening almost as they watched into cups of pale gold, —"sheer weeds, and very obstinate," said Sophia, who was a great gardener, but she admitted they looked well enough in these woods.

They came to a seat at the edge of the trees; the ground sloped away to the endless convent wall that surrounded all the estate, a wall of rough stones roofed with red brick, grown all over with a pattern of green vines neatly trained on strings—an enormous and admirable labour, as Sophia observed. Below them lay the river, a long grey snake with an oily glitter on its scales from this late sunlight, and a hazy blue line of wooded hills on the far side following its curves. Barges were passing up and down stream with loads of hay and vegetables for Paris. There were fields on the opposite shore, red-gold with uncut corn, parched white where the harvest had been made. From among them the walls and church steeples and towers of the little town of Pontoise rose in sharp grey silhouette on the opposite bank, and over the wooden bridge that crossed the river to it went country carts drawn by oxen, and men on horseback whose harness flashed back the sunlight in sudden sparks.

They sat on the seat, still in the shade; the crickets chirped incessantly; the faint evening breeze stirred the long sun-bleached grasses at their feet with a dry rustling sound, for they were covered with tiny pointed white snails like minute fossilized fir cones which tapped against each other as the stalks waved together, clicking, clicking in an unending dance of elfin castanets.

"You do very well here," Sophia said. "How I wish I could join you! I am far better suited to a convent than a Court. My poor Charlotte and I have been completely worn out by these last days at Fontainebleau—we were abominably lodged, two tiny rooms for us both with our attendants, and who do you think has the best lodging in the Palace? King Louis' Queen, Marie Thérèse? Certainly not, but King Louis' mistress, Madame de Montespan. And the noise, the heat, the crowds crushing one to death, the endless occasions for ceremony lasting from morning till midnight!"

"Did you go to them all?"

"Naturally. I was not going to miss anything that might gratify my curiosity. Besides, I owe it to Charlotte. King Louis took great notice of her, and indeed she is really beautiful don't you think? I had some hopes in bringing her here on this visit that the Dauphin might wish to marry her, but I see very little chance of it, he is the most stupid young man I ever met, can say nothing but 'Yes' or 'No,' if that, and still has his tutor to sleep in the same room with him. To tell the truth, I believe he is half-witted."

"In any case, Charlotte would have to change her religion to marry him, and would you approve of that?"

"Oh, for that, my sons are all staunchly Protestant of course, but for my daughter it would be time enough to decide her religion when one knows whom she is going to marry."

"Dear Sophie, you have not changed either, not one bit."

"You think so really? The German women grow old so quickly, but I am always careful to walk for two hours every day in the gardens, and our English visitors tell me I am as young as ever and completely English still in every way. I wish I could say as much for my son George. He has just returned from a visit to England, but as Germanic as ever, and the visit does not seem to have been a success; Rupert took no trouble over his own nephew, and when George went to visit him at Windsor, Rupert said he was ill and would not see him."

"Rupert ill?"

"So he *said*, but George heard he had shut himself up in his laboratory and was working at his scientific experiments, as he does for days together and even turns out King Charles when he interrupts him. I had hoped he might help in a notion we had of marrying George to the Princess Anne, but nothing has come of it and now his father has decided he had best marry his cousin, Sophia Dorothea of Zelle. After all, Anne's father may be James Duke of York and King Charles' heir, but her mother was only Anne Hyde, daughter to old Ned Hyde the lawyer whom they made Earl of Clarendon. People who have seen it tell me that his History of the Great Rebellion is the most opinionated stuff, and practically no mention in it of Rupert."

"I remember his shouting down his rickety staircase at The Hague to beg Rupert to write him details of the battles he had fought" (A tufted testy face peering over the banisters, and Rupert's impatient shout in answer, and all the doors banging and rattling in the wind,—when had that happened and how was it she had been there? There was only one thing she remembered, it had been the day she had got Wishart's book of the Deeds of Montrose), "and of course Rupert never wrote them, he never writes at all."

"That is because you never write," said Sophia reprovingly. "Now I write to him so often that he sometimes answers, though not more than one in ten."

"And he is happy at Charles' Court? He should be. England was always his home."

"Oh yes, though he is bored with the Court and pays no attention to it, and his temper is more abominable than ever. The other day he took the French Ambassador by the shoulders and just lifted him out of the way because he was annoyed with him."

"Didn't he once lift a mutineer over the side of his ship as though he were a puppy and threaten to drop him into the sea?"

"That was long ago, and I am talking of now, and England. I was saying, though he is no courtier, all the Court try to copy his magnificence when he does appear at it, so Monsieur was telling me, swelling his chest out like a bull-frog and saying, 'Your brother Rupert, I hear he is a leader of fashion, just like me.'"

"*Just* like! With only the difference between five foot and six foot four!"

"The whole country adores Rupert. He has done a deal for

their Navy, as he once did for their Army, and helped in colonization—they have named large parts of Canada after him, and he has founded a company there which they call the Hudson's Bay Company, for trade and exploration, and though he is just on sixty he is still one of the four best tennis-players in England, and you know what that means to them! They would give anything for him to be King Charles' heir instead of his brother James——"

"Who is a Papist."

"Yes indeed that is most unfortunate—for him. The English have set their hearts on a Protestant Succession. Only imagine, there is a strong party who actually wish to put King Charles' eldest bastard, the young Duke of Monmouth, on the throne. He has his father's charm and his mother's beauty——"

"Who was his mother?"

"Lucy Walters, whom they called Mrs. Barlow," Sophia answered slowly "Have you really forgotten her, and all the trouble about her at The Hague that last year?"

Yes, Louey had forgotten. But Lucy Walters, that 'bold brown insipid beauty' and her love-affair with Charles when he was only eighteen, and her baby by him, had not meant as much to her as it had done to her sister. Sophie's 'last year' at The Hague had been, for Louey, the last year of Montrose's life. But it might not have been, had not Lucy Walters and her bastard baby, now Duke of Monmouth, come between Sophie and the young King Charles. In what pitiful tangle of changes and chances were all the threads of life interwoven and held!

"Then life is not enough," said Louey softly, "that is the answer to it."

But it was not the answer to anything said by Sophia, who wondered what had set her sister wool-gathering, just as she used to do in the old days.

"Indeed," she replied briskly, "life is quite enough if it is the life one likes. One cannot live more than once. Why vex one's soul if one can eat, drink and sleep,—sleep, drink and eat? At Hanover we

manage very well, play at ninepins, breed young ducks, amuse ourselves with running at a ring or play backgammon, and talk every
year of paying a visit to Italy."

"Do you ever pay it?"

"Yes, once. I got so sick of hearing my two Dukes talk about
Venice that I had to go once in self-defence, but when I got there,
it was nothing to admire."

"Nothing in Venice?"

"Nothing but water," replied Sophia with finality.

A moment's silence fell between them. The sun had set in a
leaden heat-haze; that faint breeze that had freshened the evening,
rustling the silver backs of the poplar leaves so that they shimmered
with promise of further sunshine or of rain, had entirely dropped.
Even those tiny castanets on the grasses were silent; only the
crickets chirped on. The fields were deepening to grey, the woods
beyond the river dark blue, the river itself nearly black, with only a
hint here and there of steel in its shallows, the little town opposite
was etched in ink. The scene was carved out of a thunder-cloud.

"If Rupert had never done anything else," said Louey, in that
low, absent voice that Sophia now remembered, "he has invented
mezzotints."

"*What* do you say? Oh yes, that odd new method of etching.
They tell me he is a very considerable artist and has done some
pictures that would be thought remarkable if he were not a prince.
And what of your own work? Do you still keep up your painting?"

"Yes. It is a great advantage for me that I have to attend midnight Mass. The loveliness of awe and grave music, the picture
made by the long shadows thrown by the candles in the chapel, the
black robes and white coifs of the nuns, above all the flesh tints of
their faces turned pale and gleaming against the darkness, make an
effect that I never grow tired of studying. My dear Gerard would
have revelled in it, Gerardo della Notte he was nicknamed, you
remember. He was a fine artist though he had the bad luck to be
a Court painter, and they talk more of Rembrandt now."

Again Sophia was conscious of a slight shock. Surely no Abbess should talk so coolly of the artistic advantages of her vocation. Had there possibly been any truth in those scandals of the Hohenzollerns as to Louise's reasons for running away to become a nun?

"Why did you take vows?" she asked on a sudden impulse.

"Because," said Louey, "the story of the God who gave up His Godhead and His human life for the world of humans has always moved me, not with sorrow or pity but with exaltation. Could anything be more glorious than to have so much to give, and give it all?"

Her voice had not changed. It was still soft and absent, as though coming from a great way off in that still evening.

'She has something I do not know of,' thought Sophie. 'What is it I have missed?' And quite inconsequently she remembered her mother's 'English garden' as she had first seen it among the ruins of the Castle at Heidelberg, and the arch that her father had raised there in a single night to express all the joy and hope and fruitfulness of his love for his 'Elizabetae, Conjugi carissimae.' That still remained standing, while on either side of it the walls had fallen and crumbled under the enemy's guns. The fruits of that love had been death and destruction, the horrors of the Thirty Years' War, Sophia had thought; but now she wondered if perhaps Louey would see further than even those results.

Did love last longer than death? If so, Sophia herself had never felt, could never feel such love. It made her feel shrivelled and cold, shut out from immortality like the unbaptized souls of the old faith.

"You are now a Bride of Christ," she said in a strained harsh voice, "does that make up to you for the fact that once, long ago, you were to have been the bride of Montrose?"

Louey did not answer. Sophia, looking at the face beside her, saw only a grey carved shadow against the thunderous evening sky. She went on:

"I will tell you something I have never breathed yet to any living soul. King Charles has no legitimate child. His brother James is a Papist and hated by the English, nor do they want his daughters: Mary is married to a Dutch prince (and would they, after the Dutch wars, stand William of Orange on the throne?), and Anne is stupid and sickly. No, they want one of *us*, as they have always done. But none of all our brothers has a legitimate heir, except Carl's Liselotte, married to Monsieur of France.

"What a strange fatality it is on all our family! Look at us sisters—Eliza, the most beautiful, who never loved anyone unless it were that ugly little dried-up, middle-aged, middle-class philosopher Descartes, and all I could say for him as a potential husband is that certainly his works provide the best antidote for insomnia. She has never married, nor you, and then think of our darling Etta, a mother if ever there was one, dying of a miscarriage within a few months of her blissfully happy marriage.

"Is there something in us not made to last? Etta's death-bringing miscarriage, my odious George, who has nothing of our family in him,—yet it is I and my sons, I, a daughter and the twelfth child, who may come to stand a nearer chance to the English throne than any of us."

"Why do you tell me this, Sophie?"

"Because," Sophie answered, "if you had married the Marquis of Montrose and borne him children, your heirs would have been first in the succession. The Stuarts have been one Scottish family on the English throne, the Grahams might well have been another."

"They might have been. They are not. As you say, the Electors of Hanover are now the nearer."

"You do not speak as though it matters very much," said Sophie bitterly.

And suddenly she wondered what did matter. Different things at different times of her life had seemed to matter with appalling urgency, but they had ceased to do so, and other things had taken their place.

"No," she went on very fast, "the world does not come to an end because one has not been able to marry the man one wanted to marry. I know that as well as anyone, for I went to Germany to find a husband. I spent years at Heidelberg with our brother Carl and his wife, hearing both sides of their endless quarrels and their complaints of the rest of the family, sharing their silly seething intrigues, their confidences, like promises, made to be broken, until I got desperate, for though I was handsome enough I had no fortune and Carl could not afford to give me a dowry. I used Prince Adolf of Sweden with his hideous chin like a shoehorn as runner-up to Duke George William of Hanover until the unfortunate Swede actually imagined he was engaged to me and showed my portrait as that of his betrothed to Duke George. That had its effect. Duke George proposed."

"Duke *George!* But you are married to Ernest Augustus."

"Wait. The effect did not last. Duke George made the surprising suggestion that he should transfer me to his younger brother together with the Duchy of Hanover, as compensation doubtless."

"I never heard of this."

"We were not anxious that many should hear of it," said Sophia dryly.

"But what did you say to it?"

"I? I told Carl to settle the matter as he thought best, for, as I said to him, 'I am not a heroine of romance. All I want is an establishment.' Well, I had it. And within a year or two of my establishment as Electress of Hanover, King Charles was on the throne of England, the most charming and sought-after Prince in Europe, and I might have been Queen of Great Britain."

Again that aching phrase! It struck on Louey's mind like the opening of a wound. And she herself might have been Montrose's bride, might have borne his son to be King of England instead of Sophie's Hanoverian George.

The wound gaped wider. Rupert might have been Montrose's ally, as Montrose had planned, and the two of them worked victory together. But Cromwell's ruinous conquest of Ireland had destroyed Montrose's plan of co-operation with Rupert.

Was the old torture coming back? Would she never, even now after thirty years, stop seeing what might have been? And to what end? Of what use was it to try to unravel the web and weave it again to her heart's desire? Long ago she had seen that happiness must not, could not depend on the event. The Kingdom of Heaven was within one's own heart, or nowhere. Must she learn that all over again, thirty years after Montrose had shown it in his death?

She had to pull her mind back to listen to Sophie, who was speaking in a hurried, urgent voice as though she were indeed trying to cram thirty years into her talk, and so she herself perceived, for "you must excuse me," she was saying, "it is such a relief to talk like this instead of always writing, writing, and then only a very little of what one thinks. I believe I have only come to write so much because one must do something beside embroidery in those long hours sitting on the terrace while my husband dozes with his feet up on the end of my chair so that he shall rest assured even in his sleep that I have not left his side.

"He is jealous, for he can never forget that I was content to be betrothed to his brother Duke George, nor does his brother forget it, and sometimes shows signs of regretting it, and as the two of them continue to be inseparable I have to see almost as much of Duke George as of Ernest Augustus, and you cannot imagine how difficult it is, the scenes they make, Duke George complaining when I do not take his hand, Ernest complaining when I do.

"Two large, heavy, over-fed, slow-moving, slow-speaking men always about one, crushing one, a couple of hot bears! My only real peace is when they go off to their precious Venice together.

"It would have been the other way round if I had married Charles, but more amusing to have had all those gay quick-witted rivals for his love, yes, even that actress from the slums of Drury Lane, than to sit on at Hanover, the half of me inactive, unused, unsharpened, while the slow oxen go trudging past below and the swans drift up and down the lake and my husband snores in the shade, and I thinking that I might have been Queen of England, our mother's country, and the most civilized and modern Court in Europe, instead of wasting myself in a sleepy little German state."

"Do you feel you have wasted yourself with all your fine sons?"

But even as she asked it, Louey thought what brilliant sons Sophie might have had by Charles, while her son George, the inheritor of her chance for the English throne, had no drop of his mother's Stuart blood to show in him.

"Even when he was an infant I looked on him in wonder," Sophie broke out, "so alien he was to us all. Is it some grotesque trick that God has played on me to show how all my care to be wise has only served to spoil my chances? You who are a nun should be able to tell me."

Her voice had shrilled and cracked on a discordant note. She clapped her hands together and exclaimed, "Come, we are talking nonsense and what is worse, blasphemy. I do not mean a word of it, and as for God, I have complete confidence in Him."

But still her sister would not answer for God.

"I blame you for my indiscretion," said Sophia, " for your conversation has always had an untiring charm for me. Tell me more of yourself. Is it true you entertained King Charles here once when he was still in exile?"

"Yes it is true, and I do not wonder at your regrets. Of all living kings he is the only one I have heard of with a sense of humour—but then he learned it in a hard school."

"And never forgave it. 'It was *not* good for me that I was afflicted,' he says. Could *you* forgive him for the part he played towards Montrose?"

"What right had I to forgive or not? The man he injured forgave him, and wished others to do so, that was all I knew."

But in the growing darkness of that still, grey scene with the sulphurous light burning over the river in the far west, Louise began to speak again, slowly, almost unwillingly, the thoughts she had not put into words these thirty years. Then she had hated Charles bitterly. But she loved Montrose. She had found she could not mingle hate with her love for such a man; to do so was to desecrate it. True love cannot lead to hate. Her love had opened her spirit like a flower, but hate had shut it, crippling her like a poison in the blood; it was a small dull-eyed thing; it saw nothing, created nothing.

"Montrose once told me," she said, "that King Charles I was never the same man after he had permitted the death of his servant Strafford. From that moment Charles I knew himself to be doomed—and that showed him to be of a finer nature than his son's. But remorse weakens a man as well as purifies him, and God knows we want no more tragedies. Charles II came here some years after he failed Montrose, a very gallant beggar in a frayed coat, having tried unsuccessfully to borrow even five pounds from his uncle Gaston d'Orléans. The Cardinal Mazarin was turning him out of France, he had been forbidden by the Estates to re-enter Holland, and he did not know how long he would be allowed to stay in Belgium.

"I was glad to be able to feast him royally, glad when his fortune changed so soon after and he could return to be King of England— glad, too, to enjoy the charm of his company while he dined with me.

"'No more tragedies,' I said just now, but perhaps the greatest tragedy of all was there,—that his, one of the finest minds of his age, could not really feel what he had done. His misfortunes and his pleasures had blunted it, rendered it imperceptive in spite of all his wits—and that was perhaps, after all, a safeguard to him. Yes, it was better in the end that he was able to take things more lightly than his father, that his emotions were dispersed and made easy by his 'dissipations' of them, in every sense. For it is only by that light touch, that appearance of ease and security even when his fortunes are at their lowest, that he has been able to control the nervous, touchy, suspicious creature that England had become when he returned to her."

She was silent again, thinking of the tired, battered man whom she had feasted and joked with in the geniality of true religion, recognizing in him the man of the future, disillusioned, good-natured, humorous, taking the world as he found it, making the best of it, showing his own kind of courage, even as Montrose had shown his.

He expected nothing from human nature, least of all his own.

Yet once long ago he had burned to 'stand or fall, to be happy or ruined, with Montrose.'

Never again, since Montrose's death, could Charles have said anything like that. The adventurer had taken the place of the hero. The world had grown tired of tragedies, too tired for heroes. It was no longer the day for remorse, for executions of those who met death proud and glad,—no more black swans ('Oh rare black swan,' —once Montrose had called her that!).

A new air blew across the world like an east wind, it took all the deep colours out of the landscape and the sky and tempered them to a uniform grey.

Sophia's visit brought her the first cold blast of that new rational air of the eighteenth century, that grey blight of certainty that descended on England, cynical, comfortable, and, in strange but necessary corollary, with a higher percentage of suicides than ever before.

Sophia went back to Hanover and left Louise at Maubuisson; both lived to see their rich century fade in a neutral sunset, and the country of England, in which they took more interest than any other, settle itself more and more to suit the interests of its landed gentry and attach less and less importance to its Church and King. They lived to see it depose Charles II's brother James and call in his Dutch nephew, William of Orange, the son of poor pretty Mary Stuart who had so adored her father, Charles I, to rule them instead. They lived to see the rending furies of Cavaliers and Puritans settle down comfortably into the modern politics of Tories and Whigs, lived finally to see the advancing shadow of the English throne fall on George, the squat gross Hanoverian whom his own mother,

Sophia, while working for his English interests with all the passion of her vigorous nature, could not endure.

Was this then the end of it all? If so, then indeed life was not enough. Life itself withered, turned tasteless and foul, if there were nothing beyond to give it sense and form.

Security in itself was nothing to live for; 'only dead things are secure,' Louise had found. She was free of possession and therefore of loss; free of hope and therefore of fear; she had never been Montrose's bride, but she was a bride of Christ. 'My love and charity to you all'—Montrose's words on the scaffold had become the mainspring of her life.

In the hour of his death they had been together; his spirit had winged to her by that 'low road' of the ancient Scottish belief, on which a man's soul, when it leaves his body, travels to its true home. They had met then, in certainty as clear as if she had seen him before her, in that

'country
Far beyond the stars.'

And through all the years since, they had been together, as she walked in her orchards and saw the apple-blossom fall and the fruit ripen, and dynasties fall and new ones come into being, and she lived to be older than any of her family. It was under the apple trees that they found her, a very old woman, who had fallen asleep, it seemed, over her book, 'at her devotions,' the nuns breathed in awe.

But the book was Wishart's later version of his *Deeds of Montrose*. On the page where it lay open on her knee was the passage: 'True love is drowned by no billows of mischance: true love fears no thunderbolts of fate: true love abides immortal, firm, unchangeable. To have loved once is to love for aye.'

Printed in Great Britain
by T. and A. Constable Ltd.
at the University Press
Edinburgh